DEFENDING YOU

THE BODYGUARD AND HIS CRUSH ESCAPE TO SHADOW COVE

THE WRIGHT HEROES OF MAINE
BOOK 7

ROBIN PATCHEN

JDO PUBLISHING

Copyright © 2025 by Robin Patchen

All rights reserved.

No part of this book may be reproduced in any form or by any electronic or mechanical means, including information storage and retrieval systems, without written permission from the author, except for the use of brief quotations in a book review.

Published in Austin, TX.

Cover by Lynette Bonner

Paperback ISBN:

Large Print ISBN:

Hard Cover ISBN:

Library of Congress Control Number:

This is a work of fiction. Unless otherwise indicated, all the names, characters, businesses, places, events, and incidents in this book are either the product of the author's imagination or used in a fictitious manner. Any resemblance to actual persons, living or dead, or actual events is purely coincidental.

CHAPTER ONE

Cici Wright smiled when she stepped into Mr. Delvecchio's Philadelphia jewelry store. Like all the jewelry stores she had seen—and she'd seen her share—the air practically sparkled, reflecting the beautiful jewels displayed in glass cabinets. Classical music played softly from speakers overhead.

Mr. D looked up from wiping down one of the glass cases and smiled. "Ready to find me some treasures?"

"You said you had a new lot for me to appraise?"

"Ah, yes. I've barely had a moment to examine it." He tossed his paper towel in the trash. "I'm afraid it's mostly junk. My niece paid fifteen hundred for the lot, but knowing her, it's worth about fifty." His twinkling eyes told her he didn't really believe that.

Mr. D led Cici through a narrow door into the back room, where he dug into an old filing cabinet and lifted out a black velvet drawstring bag the length of her forearm. "I've been wanting to go through this bag for—" The store's doorbell chimed, and Mr. D flicked his gaze to the front. "And that's why

I never had time to do it. Duty calls." He handed the bag to her. "Let me know if you find Captain Hook's plunder."

"Will do."

As he left, Cici pulled her hair into a bun to keep it out of her face while she worked. She opened the bag on a workbench. Some of the pieces were so gaudy they had to be costume jewelry. There was a pearl ring that might be authentic, and a vintage opal bracelet. A sparkle from the bottom of the bag caught her eye, and she tugged it out.

It was a necklace, looked to be circa 1920s. Cici assumed it was high-quality costume, but her fingers tingled as if they picked up something she'd yet to realize.

She moved the necklace into the light, and her breath caught.

This was no fake. This was...incredible.

Sixty pear-shaped rubies, each at least a carat, separated by marquee-shaped diamonds that were just as large. The piece was set in eighteen-karat gold or better.

The value of the stones alone would be in the tens of thousands. But in this artistic setting? It was stunning.

And familiar.

She pulled out her phone, hands trembling as she searched for an image she was sure she'd saved. There it was, in an article about a ruby necklace stolen during the long-ago murders of the parents of her sister's boyfriend in her hometown of Shadow Cove, Maine. The necklace had been missing for a quarter century.

Cici gazed at the photograph that showed Forbes's mother wearing the distinctive ruby-and-diamond necklace.

The Crimson Duchess. This was it. Charles and Grace Ballentine's stolen necklace. Forbes was its rightful owner.

Not only was it practically priceless, this necklace could

lead Forbes and the authorities to more of the people involved in his parents' murders.

Heart pounding, Cici dialed Brooklynn.

Brooklyn answered. "Hey, sis. You back from—?"

"I need to speak to Forbes." She kept her voice low. "Are you with him?"

"It's nice to talk to you too." Her older sister's voice held a hint of amusement.

"It's an emergency. Is he there?"

"He's at the estate, meeting contractors. I'm at the gallery, but I'll see him—"

"Text me his number, please."

"Are you—?"

"I'm fine. It's fine. I'll tell you everything, or he can. I need to talk to him right now." Because Cici wasn't sure what to do. Should she call the police? Should she tell Mr. D? She had no idea what the procedure was when one found stolen merchandise that might be evidence in a double homicide.

"Texting you now," Brooklynn said. "Be safe."

Cici ended the call. When the text came, from her sister, she dialed.

"Forbes Ballentine." His voice was deep and tinged with curiosity.

Cici assumed Brooklynn had texted him as well, letting him know to expect Cici's call. "You won't believe what I've found."

"Tell me." He must've picked up on her mood because his voice turned serious.

"It's The Crimson Duchess. I'm almost positive."

"Where? How do you...? Are you sure?"

"Hold on." She snapped a photo of it and texted it to him. "You tell me."

The doorbell chimed in the store, cutting through the silence. Mr. D buzzed the customers in.

On the other end of the line, Forbes sucked in a breath. "I don't believe it. How in the world...?"

"Somebody brought it into a jewelry store with a whole bagful of other stuff, like it didn't even matter."

"I have a photograph of it here somewhere. Hold on one minute."

She heard heavy footsteps on hardwood. "Hurry. I need to figure out what to do."

"Good afternoon." From the other room, a man's voice was smooth as a serpent's slink.

She usually treated customers' conversations like background noise, but every sense was on alert right now.

"I wonder," the man continued, "is the charming young saleswoman here? I believe my son did business with her a couple of days ago."

The man must've been asking about Mr. D's niece. As far as Cici knew, he didn't employ anyone else.

"Maria works Tuesdays and Thursdays. What can I do for you?"

"Surely you're not alone here with all these beautiful jewels."

"That's why I keep the door locked and the cameras running. I'm the only one working the counter today."

"Cici." Forbes spoke through the phone. "That's it. That's Mom's necklace. Where are you exactly?"

"I'm at a store in Philadelphia. What do you want me to do? Should I call the police or—?"

"I'll reach out to my contact at the FBI. But you need to make sure that they don't display that necklace or sell it. Would you be able to do that, or should I have the special agent call?"

"Yeah, I think I can..."

"Sir, you're not allowed back here." She'd never heard Mr.

D raise his voice before. "Return to the other side of the counter or I'll be forced to call the police."

"Cici?" Forbes prompted.

"Shh." There was some commotion. She crept to the doorway leading to the store and peeked through.

A man stood behind Mr. D with his arm around his neck. By the way Mr. D jerked, he was struggling.

Another man, heavy-set man with black jeans and a tight-fitting black T-shirt, stood guard. His head was shaved, and he watched the door, blocking the view from outside with his wide body. He'd closed the blinds over the windows.

Aside from the classical music, the room was silent.

And then Mr. Delvecchio collapsed.

Cici couldn't make sense of it.

Had that man just...just committed murder?

She shoved her phone into her jacket pocket, scooped up the drawstring bag, the necklace, and everything that had come with it, and hurried to the rear exit.

"Start looking," the smooth-talking man said. "Find it. Now."

Heart racing, Cici pushed out the door into an alley shaded from the afternoon sun by tall buildings all around. She bolted behind the neighboring store and then down another alley.

"Stop!" a man shouted after her.

She pumped her legs faster, finally reaching the main road and all the shoppers. Except there weren't that many, not nearly enough to give her cover.

She'd parked her rental car on a side street a few blocks away. Rather than run—and draw attention to herself—Cici slowed to a fast walk. She pulled her hair out of the bun, then shrugged out of her black suit jacket, which she draped over the velvet bag of jewels.

She hoped the change would throw off the man following her.

A group of women walked ahead, and Cici jogged until she was right behind, trying to look like she was one of them.

Even though it made no sense, she would swear she could hear the footsteps of that guard catching up.

She couldn't help it.

She turned.

And locked eyes with him. He was maybe thirty feet back and, apparently, not fooled at all by the minor adjustments to her outfit.

She broke into a run, shoving past the women, moving as fast as her too-tall heels would let her. She dodged shoppers and bicycles and anything else in her way.

At the next corner, she crossed against traffic, nearly getting hit by a car. The blaring horn barely registered as she reached the far sidewalk, passed a couple of storefronts, then dashed down a side street, shoving her hand into her jacket pocket to retrieve her keys. She grabbed them and clicked to unlock her car door.

She yanked it open, threw the bag into the passenger seat, and started the engine.

"Cici!" The phone had connected to Bluetooth, and Forbes's voice was a frantic through the speakers. "What's going on? Are you still there?"

She'd forgotten about him.

"Hold on, Forbes!" She checked her rearview.

The man was turning the corner behind her.

She angled the rental out from between two cars and floored the accelerator, lurching forward. She turned onto the next street.

"Cici," Forbes said, his volume one notch below a shout. "Talk to me."

"Mr. Delvecchio. I think he was murdered!" Her pitch was too high, the words coming fast. "Two men just showed up, and one was behind him, and then he fell." She sounded panicked. She *was* panicked. "I have to call the police."

"Are you safe now?"

She checked her rearview again. She'd left the guard behind. "I think so. I'm in my car."

Which the guard had seen. It was a rental, though. Surely, he wouldn't be able to track it to her.

"Call the police," Forbes said. "Then call me back right after you get off the phone with them."

"I will." Cici ended the call, her mind racing as she dialed 911. She didn't know Philly well and had no idea where she was headed, just taking random turns, trying to put as much distance between herself and that guy as she could.

The operator's voice was calm, asking for details, but all Cici could focus on was the road ahead, the memory of Mr. D's body falling, and the fear that she might be next. She gave her name and the store's location. "I think he strangled him."

"Who?"

"Mr. Delvecchio. The owner of the store."

"Someone killed him?" The operator's voice was calm, a stark contrast to the chaos Cici was experiencing. "Or did he kill—"

"Someone killed him. I don't know who! I didn't see his face. I mean I saw...I saw the guard. The thing is..." She thought back to the conversation she'd overheard. "Mr. D's niece is in danger. They were asking about her. You need to protect her."

"Okay, ma'am. I'm going to give you the address of the closest police precinct. Go there and make a report. I'm dispatching emergency vehicles to the jewelry store now."

The traffic was heavy, probably normal for rush hour in downtown Philadelphia. As Cici approached a red light, she checked her rearview mirror again. But of course, she had no idea what kind of car the guard would be driving.

How was she supposed to know if she was safe?

She plugged in the address the dispatcher gave her. Of course she was going the wrong direction, getting farther from her goal with every second.

She managed to turn around and followed the directions to the police station. How had she gone from gazing at the most beautiful piece of jewelry she had ever seen to...this?

The Philadelphia traffic crawled, a sluggish beast of honking horns and exhaust fumes that did nothing to calm Cici's frayed nerves. She gripped the steering wheel, her knuckles white. She'd been in the car for a good forty minutes. She'd swear she sat through every light in the city, some twice.

The precinct was only a few blocks away now—her GPS chirped directions in that infuriatingly calm voice—but every red light felt like a personal attack.

She'd call Forbes from the police station after she was safe. Right now, she needed to focus on getting there and getting inside.

Stopped again and watching traffic inch along the cross street, Cici kept picturing Mr. D's body crumpling to the floor, the way that smooth-talking man's voice had turned cold and commanding. *"Find it. Now."*

The light turned green, and she eased forward. The precinct's address glowed on her GPS screen: two blocks to go. She could do this. She'd tell the police everything—about the necklace, the murder she'd witnessed, and the men chasing her.

They'd handle it. They'd keep her safe.

But she wasn't going to turn over the necklace, not if she

could help it. She would return it to Forbes and let him handle it however he chose. He deserved to get his family's heirloom back, not to have it languishing in some evidence locker.

She didn't hate that she'd be the one to deliver it. Her older sisters had distinguished themselves this year. Alyssa had taken on terrorists, and Brooklynn had helped solve a cold case—nearly getting killed in the process. Cici wouldn't mind doing something noteworthy, even brave. Not that she had anything to prove, necessarily, except...

Well, maybe she did.

A building loomed ahead, much larger than she'd thought the police precinct would be. She was trying to figure out where she was supposed to park and where the front door was when a hulking figure peeked out from behind an SUV, his shaved head gleaming under the sun.

Her stomach dropped.

It was the guard from the store. He'd been behind her, hadn't he? Of course, she'd driven all over the city. Obviously, there'd been a faster way to get here. But how had he known her destination? Had he guessed, or...or had someone told him?

It made no sense.

Her heart thudded against her ribcage.

"Please, don't let him see me."

But before the prayer was out of her mouth, the man's gaze skimmed over her car, and then he stepped back behind the truck.

Hiding, probably hoping she hadn't seen him.

Her heart thumped hard, her hands shaking as she dialed 911 again.

"Nine-one-one, what's your—?"

"He's outside the precinct!" Cici's words tumbled out, high-pitched and frantic. "The man who killed Mr. Delvecchio. He's waiting for me! I can't stop. He'll get me before I can get inside!"

"Ma'am, slow down. Who's outside the precinct?"

"The guy from the jewelry store!" She took a breath. This obviously wasn't the same operator.

She scanned the area, but she had nowhere to go. The traffic was too heavy to turn around. She couldn't do anything but inch forward. "He's big and bald, wearing a black shirt. He saw me. He's coming after me! You have to arrest him!"

The precinct loomed to her left, its brick facade promising safety—if she could just get inside. But she'd never make it from the car to the door before he grabbed her.

"Which precinct, ma'am?"

"The one you sent me to." She fumbled with her phone, pulled up the map, and read the address.

"You're saying there are men outside the precinct, looking for you?"

"I witnessed a murder, and—"

"Dispatching police to your location."

"They just need to run outside!" Cici watched the building, expecting uniformed police to swarm outside toward her.

Nobody came.

She was in the left lane, inching forward. Any second, and she'd reach the truck, the man waiting for her.

She clicked the button to lock the doors, then clicked it again. Just in case.

A half block ahead, there was a right turn, but the cars were stacked like crackers in a sleeve. No way for her to change lanes.

Up ahead, a red light stopped all the traffic.

If she got out and tried to get away on foot, the guard would see her. Her two-inch heels weren't exactly made for running.

But if she stayed in the car, unless the police came, she'd be trapped.

The guard stepped out from behind the pickup. He wore

earbuds and was speaking, probably telling the smooth-talking man exactly where she was.

He stepped into traffic a few cars ahead of hers, one arm swinging naturally by his side, the other tucked into his jeans pocket. He must have a handgun. As soon as he got close enough, he'd kill her. Just like that.

The light turned green, but traffic barely moved. The cars on the cross street blocked the intersection. Horns blared.

"Lord, help me."

"Sit tight," the operator said. "They're coming."

"Not fast enough!"

The guard was getting closer, heading straight for her.

The light ahead turned yellow, but the two cars in front of her snuck through.

Before she could gun it, a sea of pedestrians crossed in front of her.

The guard was ten feet away now, his bulk parting the people like a shark through water.

Cici looked at the building, expecting to see police. Two exited the building, but they were too far away.

She looked to the right.

What she saw turned her blood to ice.

Another man was approaching from the opposite direction. He wore a suit and tie, and though she hadn't seen the face of the man who'd killed Mr. D, she guessed this was him.

They had her flanked.

Her mind screamed at her to move, to do something. The light was red, people were still crossing, but she had no choice.

She mashed her horn and hit the accelerator, sending pedestrians scrambling out of her way. She floored it, the car surging forward, cutting off a delivery truck that blared its horn. She swerved into a right turn, away from the precinct, her tires screeching as she took the corner.

Her eyes flicked between the road and the mirror. No sign of them, but they'd follow.

"Ma'am," the operator said. "Just sit tight—"

"If I'd sat tight, I'd be dead."

"I need you to stay calm. Can you get to the police station? We can—"

"I can't!" she snapped, her voice cracking. "They were too late. I'm driving away. Please, just send someone to get them."

"You need to get to a safe location and file a report. Can you—?"

Cici ended the call. She couldn't stop, couldn't risk it. Her chest heaved as she wove through traffic, her mind spinning. She needed help—actual help.

She grabbed the phone again and dialed Forbes.

"Cici?" His deep voice filled the car, tight with worry. "Did you talk to the police?"

"They were outside the station." She took a breath, working to sound rational. "The men from the store, they were waiting for me. I couldn't stop. They saw me."

"Are you safe? Where are you?"

"I don't know where I am." She checked her mirror again, her pulse pounding in her ears. She had no idea what those men would be driving. "They're going to find me. They saw my car—"

"I understand." Forbes's tone shifted, firm and commanding. "I'll book a room for you under the name Ford Baker. I'll text you the address of the hotel. Get there, use valet parking, and go straight to the desk. Tell them you're picking up a key for my reservation. Don't stop for anyone. Can you do it?"

"If they don't catch up to me."

"Just keep moving. I'll text you an address."

He ended the call, and a moment later, a text came through.

Cici clicked it to open the map. The hotel was on the other

side of town. The farther she could get from those two men, the better. As long as she could reach it before they found her.

Twenty minutes away, thanks to the terrible city traffic. Twenty minutes of praying for safety. She wasn't going to let them take her—or the necklace. She'd get to that hotel, lock herself in, and figure this out.

CHAPTER TWO

The elevator hummed as it descended, a steady drone that matched the low buzz of irritation in Asher Rhodes's bones. He leaned against the back wall, arms crossed, his duffel bag slung over one shoulder. The job—a three-week gig babysitting a paranoid tech exec—had wrapped up rather...abruptly, and he was done. Done with the city, done with the client's ridiculous demands, done with everything but the promise of his own bed back in Boston.

He'd grab a coffee from the shop in the lobby and then get on the road. With luck, he'd be home in six hours, probably closer to seven, considering the Friday night traffic between Philadelphia and home.

The elevator dinged past the tenth floor, and his phone vibrated. He fished it out of his pocket and glanced at the screen. Bartlett, Asher's boss at the agency. He wasn't surprised to hear from him, only that the call had come so soon.

"Yeah?"

"You want to explain what just happened?" Bartlett's gravelly voice crackled.

"He didn't need protection. He's just an arrogant jerk who wants to look important."

"You just described three-quarters of our clients. Those are the clients who pay our bills."

As if Asher didn't know that already. He'd be lucky if he still had a job by the time the elevator reached the lobby. He wished he didn't care, wished it didn't matter.

It did matter, and he did care, but there were lines he wasn't willing to cross.

"From what I heard," Bartlett said, "he was assaulted, and you did nothing to protect him."

"He wasn't the victim. The woman who assaulted him—"

"It was a woman—?"

"—was his assistant. Five four, maybe a hundred fifteen pounds. And she slapped him because he grabbed her. He had it coming."

"Your job was to protect him."

"From a woman he's harassing? Abusing? You really think I'm gonna do that? Would you?"

"You're leaving out some of the story, at least according to the client."

Asher couldn't help a little grin. Not only had the woman slapped him, she'd kneed him in the groin.

The client had ended up doubled over, screaming obscenities as the woman had fled the room.

"Look, I get it." By the irritation in Bartlett's tone, that didn't mean he approved. "But times are tough. We needed that client."

"What would you have had me do?"

"At least make a show of helping. Escort the lady out. My understanding is you didn't move from your spot at the door."

"It took all my energy not to knock the guy's block off. I

wasn't about to pretend he didn't deserve what he got. I signed up for this gig to protect people *from* guys like him."

The elevator stopped and a family stepped on. Dad, mom, two kids. The younger, a curly-haired little boy, looked up at Asher and grinned, showing off some missing teeth.

What would it be like to have a family—and the means to support them? Enough money to stay in a five-star hotel with valets and concierge service?

Asher had never known that kind of security when he was a kid.

The elevator doors closed, and the numbers ticked down—six, five...

"This is my fault," Bartlett said. "I shouldn't have sent you out on your own. It was too soon."

Irritation and worry churned in Asher's stomach. "Respectfully, sir, I don't need a keeper—"

"Apparently, you do. Someone to *keep* you from walking out on a paying client."

Asher hadn't walked out. He'd been ordered from the room when he hadn't *protected* the client from an innocent woman who gave him what he deserved. Had the client really thought Asher would stand there and watch him assault his assistant?

Would Bartlett's *keeper* have expected him to do that?

Asher needed this job. He needed to prove himself and his abilities. With his experience, he shouldn't be an underling but a team leader. He'd been trying to prove his abilities since he'd started working for GBPA a few months before.

Seemed one decision had set him back, maybe permanently.

The elevator doors opened, and more people got on. More people to hear him getting dressed down by his boss.

Through the phone, Bartlett sighed. "I got a new job for you. This one's high priority—someone who is actually in danger."

"Details?"

"Forbes Ballentine, that billionaire up in Maine? You know who I mean?"

"Yes."

"His business could mean a lot of paychecks. He's throwing cash at us for a protection detail, and you just *happen* to be available."

Asher shifted his weight, his mind already running scenarios. Forbes Ballentine. He knew the name, of course. Everyone who grew up in Shadow Cove had heard of Forbes Ballentine. "Recent events make him think he needs protection?"

"Not him. His girlfriend's sister, Cecelia Wright. She's Grant Wright's cousin. You remember him and Summer?"

Asher knew Grant, who'd been one of GBPA's early hires. He didn't work there anymore, but his wife, Summer, was a part-owner. It had never occurred to Asher that Grant Wright might be related to Cecelia Wright.

Cici.

The name was a gut-punch, dragging up memories he'd buried deep—high school, her pretty smile, and the sting of her laughter when he'd dared to ask her to prom. He'd been a scrawny geek then, all braces and glasses and wild optimism.

That humiliation still burned, a quiet ember he'd never let anyone see.

The elevator finally dinged at the lobby, and the doors slid open. Asher followed the other passengers onto the polished marble floor, his footsteps echoing in the gigantic space, all chandeliers and fresh bouquets in crystal vases.

A blur in the corner of his eyes had him turning just as the client's assistant barreled into him, wrapping her arms around his waist. "Thank you so much! I was afraid you were going to stick up for him or something."

Asher didn't move, not quite sure how to handle the woman's misplaced gratitude.

She stepped back and looked at him. "I would never have had the courage to do it if you hadn't been there. I just knew by the look on your face that you were as horrified by his behavior as I was."

"Rhodes? You there?" Bartlett's voice cut through the haze. "Who is that?"

"One sec." He covered the mouthpiece and took a step away from the woman. "No problem."

"Where are you...?" Her eyes widened. "Oh, my gosh, did he *fire* you?"

"He requested a different protection officer, but—"

"I'm so sorry. I didn't mean to get you in any trouble."

"It's fine." At least he hoped it would be. "Just glad you're smart enough not to work for a jerk like that. Good moves, by the way."

She grinned, her head tilting to one side. "If you're not busy, maybe we could grab dinner?"

"Sorry." He indicated the phone. "I've already got another job. Thanks anyway." He hurried past the woman and spoke into the mouthpiece. "What's Cici gotten herself into?"

"You know her?"

Asher forced a steady, professional tone. "We went to high school together. What happened?"

"Ballentine says she found some stolen necklace tied to his parents' murder. A jewelry store got hit today. Owner's dead, and she saw it go down."

The words had Asher's heart rate ticking higher. "She's safe?"

"She got away but thinks the killers are after her. She's holed up at a hotel."

Asher needed a break. What he didn't need was to deal with the prom queen. But it was Cici. If she was in danger...

"She's in Philly," Bartlett said. "Job is to get her back to Shadow Cove alive, preferably with the fancy necklace."

Cici Wright, running from murderers. That polished, perfect little rich girl he'd known had been in the wrong place at the wrong time. Shopping for jewelry.

That figured.

Guarding Cici would mean babysitting the woman who'd humiliated him, who'd probably still look at him like the charity case he'd once been. He didn't need that.

But as much as he didn't want to see her again, he'd hate to think of something bad happening to her. And he needed to redeem himself in Bartlett's eyes.

"This is big, Rhodes. Ballentine's connected. We nail this, we could be looking at steady contracts. I need you on it. Tell me you're in. If not... I guess I could send the new guy."

Asher pictured the company's new recruit, a former SEAL who had all the physical ability required but little in the way of strategic thinking and zero instincts for the job. "I wouldn't trust that kid to guard my Skittles."

Bartlett chuckled. "Everyone else is either assigned or too far away. Fact is, nobody can get there as soon as you can. If Cecilia Wright has any shot of getting out of this alive, we need to get to her now."

Asher stopped near the lobby's revolving doors, the bustle of Philadelphia filtering through the glass. This could be his opportunity to prove his value, his ability to handle a difficult client—and Cici would no doubt be difficult. But her life was in danger.

A lifetime ago, he'd thought he was in love with her. Even if she had humiliated him, he didn't want her harmed. Or killed.

He'd signed up for this gig to protect people, even difficult people he'd hoped he'd never see again.

"Fine. I'm in." He maneuvered through the revolving doors and into the muggy summer air. "I need supplies. Closest store's ten minutes out. Tell Ballentine I'll be at the hotel ASAP."

"Good man. I'll let him know and text you the address."

"Got it." Asher ended the call and shoved the phone into his pocket.

Get the supplies, get to the hotel, get Cici under control. He'd run this op like any other—tight, clean, no room for error. No room for old wounds to crack open, either.

He reached his truck, a battered black pickup that'd seen him through worse days than this, and tossed the duffel onto the passenger seat. As he slid behind the wheel, his phone buzzed again—Bartlett with the hotel details. He gave it a thumbs-up and started the engine.

He'd see this through for his team. And this time, when he came face-to-face with Cici, he'd keep his guard firmly in place.

CHAPTER THREE

Cici paced the hotel room, her bare feet silent against the plush carpet. The muted beige walls and generic artwork closed in around her, the hum of the AC and her own ragged breathing the only sounds.

She'd promised Forbes she'd wait for the bodyguard, but every second in Philadelphia felt like a noose tightening around her neck. Those men—the smooth talker, the hulking guard—were out there, hunting her. She needed to get out of this city and back to Shadow Cove, where she could hand off the necklace and reclaim her life.

Assuming those men didn't know her name. Assuming they wouldn't be able to track her down at her little apartment outside of town.

She'd worry about that later.

Her suitcase sat by the door. She needed the bodyguard to escort her to the airport. She still had time to make her flight. When she was past security, she should be safe.

The TV flickered in the corner, volume low, a local news anchor's voice droning about a fire downtown. Cici paused mid-step, focusing as the screen cut to footage. Flames shot from a familiar storefront, smoke billowing into the evening sky.

That was Mr. D's jewelry store.

Reduced to a skeleton of charred wood and shattered glass.

Those guys had torched it. Had they left Mr. D inside to burn with the building he'd lovingly built and operated for decades?

Probably. What they hadn't left was evidence. That was all going up in smoke. Meaning the only one who could identify them...was her.

And then an even more horrifying image flashed on the screen. It was Cici's photograph, the ugly picture on her driver's license. Cici snatched the remote and turned up the volume.

"...Wright is wanted for questioning."

She was wanted? She was the one who'd called the police in the first place. If they'd arrested those two guys outside the precinct, she'd be safe now.

Instead of protecting her, they'd released her name and photograph to the public.

Her hands trembled with the injustice of it all.

She glanced at the bed, where she'd dropped her purse and the black velvet bag, which had The Crimson Duchess tucked inside. If she hadn't taken it, it would be in the hands of those killers now, and Forbes would never get it back.

The hulking guard hadn't looked much older than her twenty-eight, but the other man looked to be in his sixties, old enough that he could have been involved in the murders of Forbes's parents. Had he come to the store to retrieve the necklace because it was evidence? If so, how had it ended up at the store in the first place?

It didn't make any sense, but Mr. D's murder and the murders twenty-five years before had to be connected.

A sharp knock jolted Cici from her thoughts.

She muted the television and spun to stare at the door, desperate for help but terrified she'd find the opposite on the other side of that door. Had those men found her? She'd been so careful. She yanked her phone from her pocket. Her thumb was hovering over Forbes's number when a voice cut through the door, low and steady.

"Miss Wright. It's Asher Rhodes. I've been sent by GBPA, the Green Beret Protection Agency, who were hired by Forbes Ballentine to make sure you get back to Shadow Cove safely."

Wait. Asher Rhodes?

She knew the name, but it couldn't be the person she remembered, the geeky kid from high school with shabby clothes and ugly eyeglasses.

She crept to the door and looked through the peephole. A tall, broad-shouldered man stood there, a shopping bag hanging from his left hand. No scrawny frame, no ugly glasses.

She unlatched the bolt and swung the door open, blinking up at the stranger.

Except, he wasn't a stranger. He was an old friend. Somehow, that geeky kid from high school had turned into this man.

His dark brown hair, cropped short and neat, framed a face that had sharpened over the years. Strong jaw, high cheekbones, and ice-blue eyes. He towered over her, a few inches taller than six feet, his black T-shirt stretched over a muscled chest.

This wasn't the awkward boy she'd known. This was...well, he was gorgeous.

She searched for an appropriate greeting but couldn't think of anything. Finally, she managed, "What happened to your glasses?" She'd meant the remark as a way to break through the tension, but something hard and guarded flashed in his expression.

He stepped inside without being invited, then closed the door behind him. He engaged the deadbolt, then faced her.

"You need to change clothes." His voice held no hint of kindness or even recognition, though he had to know who she was. Unlike him, she didn't look all that different from how she had a decade before. Just older.

She opened her mouth to say something—charm was her fallback, after all—but he moved past her and upturned the plastic bag onto the bed. A blond wig spilled out, followed by a shapeless gray sweatshirt and black leggings.

She wrinkled her nose. "What are those?"

"Your disguise."

"They're hideous."

He gave her a quick once-over. "That's the point, for you to look different. While you're at it, take off all that jewelry. We don't want them recognizing you." His tone was clipped. "Sun's down. We're slipping out the back. Saw some questionable types in the lobby—don't know if they're the guys after you, but we're not waiting around to find out."

Her stomach twisted. "How could they know where I am? I didn't tell anyone—"

"No idea." He cut her off, those cold eyes finally meeting hers. "Get changed, now."

She bristled at the barked order. Who did he think he was? And what happened to the sweet kid she used to know? She was thankful he was there, but she didn't appreciate his rudeness. "I'm not your underling, Asher. You don't get to snap commands at me."

"If you want to get out of here alive, you'll do what I say."

She was not accustomed to being told what to do, but the news coverage about the fire was still playing on the TV. She swallowed her words.

Asher was right. She needed to get away from those men, and she couldn't do it by herself. She snatched the wig and clothes and stalked to the bathroom.

He'd provided a wig cap and bobby pins. Apparently, he'd done this before.

The blond strands felt cheap and scratchy, and the sweatshirt hung off her like a sack. She had worn her hair all different colors—bright red, dark brown with red streaks, even purple for a while. But she'd never gone platinum, for good reason. The pale color made her look washed out. Unlike her natural strawberry blond, the white-blond wig looked ridiculous with her light skin and freckles.

She felt naked without her jewelry. She always wore at least four rings, not to mention bracelets, earrings, a watch, and a necklace.

Sheesh, Cici. Who cared what she looked like? Someone was trying to kill her.

When she stepped out, Asher was waiting by the door, peering through the peephole. He glanced in her direction but didn't comment on her appearance. His gaze cut to the high heels she'd worn that day, which were lying on the carpet. "Tell me you have sneakers."

"Running shoes." She folded her business suit into her suitcase and pulled on the shoes she wore to exercise. They were the only option she had that would go with her getup.

She zipped the suitcase, then stuck the velvet bag into her purse. She rarely carried it when she was working, usually shoving her phone and keys into her pocket. Her appraiser's equipment was cumbersome enough.

All that equipment must've burned up in the fire. She'd need to replace it, and that wouldn't be cheap. She prayed she lived long enough to deal with that expense.

She faced Asher. "Good enough?"

"Stay close. Follow my lead. We're taking the service elevator."

"Fine." She didn't like this—didn't like him ordering her

around, didn't like needing him. But she'd trust him until she was out of this nightmare.

Then Asher Rhodes could go back to wherever he'd come from, and she could get back to her life.

The service elevator opened to a concrete hallway on the ground floor that was not accessible to the clientele. Cici had no idea how Asher had gotten access to it. She expected him to offer to pull her suitcase for her, but he didn't, so she dragged it along behind her, following him to a steel door.

"Stay with me."

"Sir, yes, sir."

If he picked up on her sarcasm, he didn't let on as he pushed open the metal door and stepped out into the muggy air.

They were behind the hotel in a loading zone. A brick wall hemmed the area in on the far side. It was twilight, a much prettier word than the ugly setting deserved.

Asher looked both directions, then turned left and started walking at a good clip with those long legs of his. Cici wasn't short, but she practically had to jog to keep up.

They reached a road that ran alongside the hotel, crossed it, then entered the alley behind the neighboring building. Traffic sounds were muted. The sharp scent of rotting food mingled with exhaust from a truck idling at the corner. Two blocks down, they turned on a one-way street toward a wider road at the other end of the block. Parked cars lined one side. The thump-thump of music carried out through a door on the right. She glanced through a window and saw a long bar stretched along one side of the room, a few small tables in the rest of the space. It looked like an after-work crowd that had lingered through dinner. They drank from longneck bottles and short glasses, munching from bowls of nuts and plates of food.

At the mouth of the alley in front of them, a police car passed slowly, then parked, its taillights reflecting off the pavement.

Asher grabbed her arm. "Stop."

She did, the slamming of a door setting her nerves on edge. What was happening?

Before she could voice the question, Asher snatched her suitcase and shoved it beneath a car. Then he backed her up to the brick building, wrapped her in his arms, and pulled her close. "Play along."

"With—?"

Her question was cut off when he lowered his head and kissed her.

A thousand reactions hit at the same time. Irritation. How dare he kiss her without her permission?

Fear, because those cops were probably searching for her.

But bigger than both of those—and much more intrusive—was her body's reaction, which had her arms slipping over his shoulders and around his neck, pulling him closer.

Holy cow.

Had she ever been kissed in her entire life? She'd thought so, but she'd never experienced anything like this.

His lips were soft yet commanding. The arms that held her, strong and comforting. She rose to her tiptoes, wanting to get closer, wanting a little bit more. Maybe a lot more.

"Excuse us." The voice came from a woman and held a hint of amusement.

Asher ended the kiss and stepped back, turning toward the cops, who watched from a few feet away.

There were two of them, a man and a woman. The man had his arms crossed over a broad chest. The woman's hand rested on her holstered weapon. Both of them were studying Asher and Cici.

"Oh," Asher said. "Sorry. I mean...not really, but... Uh, can we help you?"

"What are you two doing here?" the woman asked.

Asher chuckled and ran a hand over his hair. "Sorry, we were, uh... Just, you know."

Her eyebrow hiked. "This isn't exactly the most romantic spot for...*you know*."

The male cop smiled, and Asher did too. "Right. You're right. We got a little carried away. My car's parked..." He nodded vaguely in the direction of the alley behind the building.

The woman's eyes narrowed as she focused on Cici. "Do you feel safe, ma'am?"

Asher's arm tightened at her waist, then dropped. He shifted to put space between them.

"Safe?" She squeezed Asher's biceps and giggled. "Who wouldn't feel safe in these arms?"

The cops didn't smile.

They were worried about her, and she understood entirely. If she came across a couple the way they had come across them, she'd probably be just as concerned. "We've known each other for years. Don't worry. I'm in good hands."

The male cop cleared his throat. "We're looking for a woman, reddish-blond hair, twenty-eight years old. She was spotted in the area. Either of you seen someone who looks like that?"

Someone must've noticed her when she'd checked into the hotel. As much as Cici hated the wig, she was thankful for it now.

"Not me." Asher's arm slipped around her waist again.

Cici had an idea. "I saw someone with light red hair sitting at the bar." Cici looked up at Asher. "You didn't notice her?"

"I only have eyes for you, princess."

That last word was probably meant to sound like a term of endearment, but she heard scorn in it.

"Which bar?" the policeman asked.

Cici nodded toward the door they'd just passed. "She was in there a few minutes ago."

The cops thanked them, then headed for the entrance.

As soon as they were out of sight, Asher grabbed her suitcase. "Quick, before they come back."

They ran to the main road, crossed it, and continued down a side street until they reached a black pickup truck. Asher clicked to unlock it and pulled open the passenger door. He shoved her suitcase into the backseat. "Get in."

Cici was climbing—this thing was high off the ground—when he scooped her up and tossed her onto the seat. He slammed the door and ran around to the other side, where he slid in behind the wheel.

He pulled out into traffic, then handed her his cell phone. "Put in directions for New York, just to get us out of town."

"Please."

"Please what?"

"I'm suggesting that you should say please when you ask me to do something."

"*I'm* suggesting that you should do what I tell you when I tell you or I'll drop you at the nearest police station. Except in my case, this is not a suggestion, it's an order."

The nerve of this guy. Was this what she had to put up with, being ordered around by a grouchy guard? Never mind that he was a fabulous kisser, he was short-tempered and rude.

Maybe the police station was her best bet. She hadn't done anything wrong, after all.

But they thought she had. Even if they believed her story, they'd take her statement, then send her on her way. They weren't exactly in the business of protecting people.

And Forbes's necklace would end up in an evidence locker, which was the last thing she wanted.

She hated to admit it, but Asher was her only choice. Rather than argue, she tapped directions into his phone. They displayed on a screen attached to his dash by a suction cup. So fancy.

Not that she was a snob, not ordinarily, anyway. Her snobbery only came out when she was irritated, and at the moment, *irritated* didn't begin to cover it.

CHAPTER FOUR

Asher gripped the steering wheel, eyes flicking between the road ahead and the rearview mirror. Cici sat beside him, her arms crossed tightly over that ugly sweatshirt he'd made her wear.

She'd been griping since they'd peeled out of the alley—something about how he barked orders like she was a dog, not a person. He didn't bother defending himself. Words were a waste when every nerve in his body screamed *focus*. The job was simple: keep her alive, get her and the necklace to Maine.

Emotions didn't factor in. There was certainly no place for the electricity still buzzing through him after that mind-blowing kiss. That reaction was as distracting as all the feelings he'd carried for her since high school. His irrational belief that they belonged together had led to his impetuous invitation to the prom, which led to the most humiliating moment of his life.

Well, one of them. Funny how Cici Wright had twice had a front-row seat to his humiliation.

None of that mattered right now. Normally, he had no problem shoving his personal preferences to the back burner when he was on the job. Cici had his thoughts misfiring, his attention diverted.

"You don't have to act like I'm some grunt in your army," she muttered, her voice sharp enough to cut glass. "I'm not one of your lackeys."

"I don't have lackeys." And if he did, she certainly wouldn't be one of them. "Stop talking."

His gaze darted to the mirror. A black sedan lingered two cars back, pacing them. Could've been nothing, but with their luck so far, he doubted it.

He took a hard left onto a side street, tires spinning against the asphalt.

Beside him, Cici gasped. He did his best to ignore her.

The sedan followed, keeping its distance. Another turn—right this time, cutting through a narrow stretch lined with industrial buildings.

A few more cars separated them from the sedan now, but it was still following.

Beside him, Cici tapped on her phone, the screen's glow lighting up her face—pinched, annoyed, oblivious.

He should've ditched that thing the second they left the hotel. "Give me that," he said, voice low and clipped.

She clutched her phone tighter, shooting him a glare. "You've got your own phone."

He snatched it from her grip with a quick twist.

She yelped, lunging to grab it back, but he held it tightly, lowered his window, and sent the cell phone sailing into the twilight.

"Are you insane?" she shouted, her voice pitched high with shock and fury. "That was my phone! My life—"

"We're being followed." The sedan was still there. "They're tracking you."

She twisted in her seat, looking behind. At the car, or at her lost phone? She turned her glare on him. "How do you know they're not tracking *your* phone, huh? You're not exactly invisible."

"They don't know who I am." He refused to let his irritation loose in his voice. "You're the one they're after."

"My phone has a VPN! There's no way they were tracking me. You just threw out my entire contact list, my photos, everything—for no reason!"

That stuff was probably all stored on the cloud. All she needed to do was plop down another thousand bucks for a new phone. It wasn't like it was out of her price range.

Anyway, a virtual private network might mask her IP address, but it would have no effect on her phone's location services, nor would it keep it from pinging cell phone towers.

"We're being followed," he said again, slower this time, letting the words sink in. "Unless your phone is more valuable than that necklace in your bag—or your life—let it go."

She huffed, muttering something under her breath. He missed most of it, but picked up on the words *arrogant* and *jerk*.

Not that he cared what she thought.

He had bigger worries at the moment, like the fact that killers were on their tail. His truck had become a trap.

"Plug in the address for the train station." He nodded at his phone on the console between them.

She snatched it. "Maybe I should toss this one, too. Even the score."

"Do it"—the threat was implied in his tone—"and you'll find yourself on your butt on the sidewalk about two seconds later." Which would get him fired, no question.

And get her killed.

No matter how annoying she was, she needed his protection.

She jabbed at his cell phone screen with more force than

necessary, still muttering under her breath. The map on his screen changed. They were ten minutes out if the traffic didn't choke them—and their pursuers didn't corner them.

"There," she said, tossing the phone back into the console. "Happy now?"

He took another sharp turn to test the sedan, hoping he'd been wrong.

But a few moments later, it followed.

The train station was their best shot. First, they needed to ditch their tail. Then they would ditch his truck, blend into the crowd, and disappear. Cici could pout all she wanted. He wasn't here to win her approval. He was here to keep her breathing. That was the job. That was all that mattered.

Even if every word out of her mouth made him want to grind his teeth to dust.

A few minutes later, Asher floored the gas, merging onto the highway with a growl from the truck's engine, the Philly skyline shrinking in the rearview.

The black sedan stuck to them like a shadow, four cars back. No doubt they were working a plan to corner him and Cici.

The sign for Thirtieth Street Station loomed ahead, half a mile out. He hated to abandon his truck, but he saw no other choice. He kept his speed steady, then at the last second, yanked the wheel hard, cutting across two lanes to hit the exit ramp.

Tires screeched, horns blared, and Cici gasped, clutching the door handle.

"Warn me next time!" she snapped.

His eyes locked on the mirror.

The sedan swerved, barely making the ramp, its headlights flaring as it closed the gap.

Dang it. They weren't shaking.

He hit the gas, barreling down the off-ramp and through a red light, ignoring the chorus of honks. Cici yelped, but he did his best to ignore her. He spotted a bridge ahead, its underbelly cluttered with construction gear, and made a snap call. He cranked the wheel, pulling an illegal U-turn beneath the overpass, then wedged the truck between a rusted dumpster and a hulking yellow backhoe. He cut the engine.

"Out," he barked, already grabbing his duffel from the back seat. "Now."

Cici fumbled with her seatbelt, her green eyes wide. "What are we doing?" She slid out of the truck.

He snagged her suitcase and shoved it toward her.

His duffel doubled as a backpack, and he shrugged it on, leaving him hands-free and ready if those guys caught up with them. "Let's go."

She kept pace as he bolted under the bridge, boots pounding the cracked pavement. The air stank of oil and concrete, the construction zone a maze of orange cones and bundles of rebar. It was deserted at eight o'clock at night, so there was one small favor.

He weaved past a tractor, his pulse steady but his gut churning. The sedan hadn't reappeared yet. With any luck, it had continued on the surface street.

But he wouldn't bet his life or Cici's on luck.

They crossed the last stretch of gravel, ducked under a flimsy orange temporary fence, and slipped into the glow of the Thirtieth Street Station's grand entrance—old, massive, all stone and arches. Inside, the cavernous main hall swallowed them, its high ceiling echoing with footsteps and muffled announcements. Marble gleamed under warm lights, signs pointing every which way—Amtrak, food court, SEPTA—the local trains. He cataloged the space fast: exits to the left and right, crowds thick enough to blend into, ticket booths straight ahead. He strode toward Amtrak, Cici keeping pace with her suitcase rolling beside her.

At the booth, a bored-looking guy with a scruffy beard glanced up. Asher slid cash across the counter. "Two tickets to Boston. Rear seats against a wall if you've got them."

Cici leaned in, her voice cutting through. "Are there any private compartments?"

The guy shot her a perplexed look, and Asher rolled his eyes and smirked, telling the clerk it was fine to ignore her.

The clerk said, "Sorry, just coach. Next train's in fifteen." He tapped at his screen, then handed Asher the tickets. "Back row's yours."

"Thanks, man." Asher pocketed the tickets and stepped away, turning to Cici, who was glaring at him as if he'd insulted her. Which, okay, maybe he had.

"Couldn't we have gone to the airport?" She shifted her suitcase to her other hand. "We'd get home faster."

"You're lucky we made it this far." He steered her toward the platforms, scanning the crowd—business suits, college kids, a janitor pushing a mop. No thugs, as far as he could tell. "Let's go." The giant space was too big to properly surveil. He needed more cover.

He kept his pace brisk, his mind spinning. That sedan—it shouldn't have found them so quickly. He'd ditched her phone. But if they had been following her cell phone signal, how had they tapped in so fast?

This wasn't some lowlife trying to cover his tracks. These guys had resources. Tracking a phone that quickly... That wasn't average-Joe stuff. It was connected, organized.

How many enemies were out there?

He glanced at Cici, whose jaw was set despite the fear in her eyes. She was stubborn, opinionated, and far too attractive to slip beyond anyone's notice, despite the cheap wig and ugly sweatshirt.

The train was their best shot—public, crowded, a straight ride to Boston, where he could regroup and figure out who these thugs were.

But an itch between his shoulder blades had him scanning the space. Connected and organized... Were enemies here even now, watching?

"Stay close," he muttered, more to himself than Cici.

The platform sign blinked above: Boston. Twelve minutes to go. Surely he could keep her alive until they boarded and got out of this cursed city.

CHAPTER FIVE

The train rumbled beneath Cici's feet, a steady vibration that should've soothed her. She sat pressed against the window, the cool glass a lifeline to the outside world whipping by in streaks of dark and neon, her purse on her lap. The Amtrak coach smelled faintly of stale coffee and body odor.

The train was crowded this Friday night, mostly business travelers, probably headed home after a long work week.

They sat with the wall at their backs like Asher had requested, his broad frame sprawled beside her, one leg stretched into the aisle. His backpack sat between his boots, her suitcase in the compartment over the seat. For the first time since she'd bolted from Mr. D's store, she could breathe—sort of.

She adjusted the itchy blond wig, resisting the urge to rip it off.

Asher scanned the car, his jaw set in that infuriatingly unreadable line. The guy hadn't said more than ten words since they'd boarded, just grunted directions—sit here, stay put—like she was a disobedient puppy. She wasn't used to being ordered around, but he'd gotten them out of Philly alive. She probably shouldn't complain.

She shifted, tucking a leg under her. "Thanks. You know, for getting us this far. I didn't think we'd make it."

"Sorry you have to travel in such shabby accommodations."

His words carried an undertone that she couldn't read. "This is fine."

"No private sleeping quarters." She didn't miss the hint of sarcasm.

"I didn't ask for a private room so I could sleep. I thought it would be safer if we were behind a door. You know, out of sight."

"Oh."

"I can handle riding coach. I do it all the time." Not on trains, but this train was more comfortable than a lot of flights she'd taken. "Anyway, I was just trying to thank you."

He didn't look at her, just dipped his chin once.

That was it? She waited, but he didn't soften. "You're not much for conversation, are you?"

He shrugged, not even sparing her a glance. "Guess you didn't expect your shopping excursion to end like this. What were you doing in Philly anyway?"

She blinked. "Shopping excursion?"

"At the jewelry store."

"I wasn't shopping, Asher. I was working. I'm an appraiser."

He turned just enough to meet her eyes, and she caught a flicker of surprise before it vanished behind that stony mask.

"What, did you figure I just shopped all the time? Flouncing around with Daddy's credit card?"

Another shrug, casual but deliberate. "You're rich. Why work when you've got all that money?"

She bristled, straightening in her seat. "My parents have money. My sisters and I all work very hard. For your information, I own my own business. I have contracts with stores all over the East Coast."

His brows twitched, but otherwise, his face stayed blank. No apology, no backtracking. Just that cool, assessing stare.

She hated how it made her feel, like she had to prove something to him. She rested her elbow on the armrest between them and forced a casual tone. They had to spend time together. They might as well get along. "What about you? Last I heard, you joined the military. What've you been up to since then?"

He shifted, leaning back against the seat, scanning their surroundings again. "Navy. Became a SEAL. Got out after an injury. Now I do this." He nodded vaguely, like *this* was self-explanatory.

He'd been a SEAL?

She hadn't seen that coming. The scrawny kid with the Coke-bottle glasses and thrift-store jeans had turned into a Special Forces warrior? She let her eyes drift over him—his broad shoulders, the quiet strength in his arms, the way he carried himself like he could take on anything.

"That's impressive," she said. "Explains the whole"—she waved toward him—"take-charge thing you've got going on."

He grunted, his standard response.

"So, SEAL to bodyguard. Big shift."

"Not really." His voice stayed flat. "Same game, different field."

"But don't SEALs work as a team? At least *that's* different."

"I work with a team most of the time. Just not this job. I was the only GBPA member in Philly when the call came in."

"GBPA. That's familiar. I think...Did you work with my cousin Grant?"

"His wife is one of the owners."

"I'm guessing Brooklynn recommended your company."

She tilted her head, studying Asher. "You've changed a lot since high school."

"Have I?" His gaze cut to hers, sharp and assessing, and there was something in it—something that made her breath catch. "Maybe you just didn't know me back then."

The words landed like a pebble in still water, rippling through her. She opened her mouth to argue, but wasn't sure what to say.

She hadn't known him well. He'd been short and skinny and geeky. They'd gone to a small school, and Asher had been an acquaintance, not a friend. They were both smart, so they'd been in a lot of the same classes.

Unlike Asher, who'd kept to himself, Cici had known everybody, and everybody had known her. On the outside, people would've called her popular, which she supposed was true. Friends had been easy to come by, still were. But respect, admiration, approval? Those things had always been elusive.

He kept up his vigil as if enemies might drop from the ceiling like they were in some transcontinental version of *Mission: Impossible*, leaving her staring at the side of his face—those high cheekbones, that straight nose.

The train rocked gently. She leaned back, the velvet bag in her purse, a reminder of why they were here. Asher might be right—she hadn't known him, not really. And now, sitting next to this man who'd morphed from a memory into something solid and steady and a little dangerous, she wondered what else she'd missed.

∼

A few hours later, the train jolted to a stop, brakes squealing as it pulled into a station in western Massachusetts. Cici pressed her forehead against the window, the glass cool against her skin, and stared out at the platform.

The darkness was broken by the glow of a few scattered lights. Their conversation had finally helped her calm her racing heart until the steady clack of the tracks had lulled her into a fragile truce with the day's madness. Finally, she'd settled, even drifting off to sleep for a few minutes.

Now, she sat up and stretched. They had to be getting close to Boston. She wished she'd grabbed an itinerary back in Philly so she'd know where they were and how much longer they had to go.

Beside her, Asher reclined, his legs stretched out as if he were completely relaxed. But tension wafted off him. As far as she'd noticed, he hadn't let down his guard for a moment since they'd boarded. Now, he focused on the aisle as a handful of passengers shuffled off, dragging bags and muttering complaints about the late hour.

Her gaze drifted outside, skimming the people milling on the platform.

And then she snagged on a face.

The man was mostly hidden behind a concrete pillar, but she saw enough. Shaved head, blocky shoulders, black T-shirt. It was the guard who'd followed her. Who'd found her at the police station.

Her breath caught. "Asher." She gripped his forearm. "Outside. It's him."

Asher frowned, his eyes narrowing. "Who?"

"The guy from the jewelry store. The one who chased me." She jabbed a finger toward the window, her voice low but urgent. "He's right there."

Asher leaned over her to look out.

The thug was scanning the train windows with a predator's

focus, inching closer to the doors. Any second, he'd board. He'd find them.

She ducked out of the way before he saw her.

"You sure?"

"I'm sure." Her pulse hammered. "That's him."

"Let's go." He yanked his backpack from the floor, her suitcase from the overhead bin. "Go."

She hooked her purse in her elbow and pulled the suitcase behind her, aiming toward the back of the train.

Behind her, Asher slung his duffel over his shoulders. "Into the next car."

She moved fast until she got stuck behind a guy in a rumpled suit who grumbled about personal space. The man was in no hurry.

Asher was a solid wall at her back, following her through the connecting door into the next coach.

The train's warning chime sounded.

"Move!" Asher barked. His voice carried authority, and the guy in front of Cici slid into an empty row.

She hurried forward and was nearly to the exit when the doors started to close.

Asher lunged, wedging his arm between the closing doors, muscles straining as he forced them apart. "Now, Cici! Go."

She squeezed through the gap and stumbled onto the platform, barely keeping her feet, her suitcase bumping her ankle.

Asher jumped out, and the doors slammed shut with a hiss.

Through the window, she glimpsed the bald thug's head whipping toward them, his eyes locking on hers before the train lurched forward, carrying him away.

Her chest heaved with relief. "They're gone. We're—"

"Move!" Asher grabbed her arm and pulled her away from the station's small brick building. She stumbled beside him, confused, until she glanced back.

Two more figures emerged from the building—dark jackets, purposeful strides, closing in fast. The bald guard hadn't been alone. Of course not. That would've been way too easy.

She and Asher reached a fence higher than she was tall—this was not the official exit route. He tossed their bags over, then linked his hands together and held them about knee-high. "You can do this."

Could she? The men were moving their way, leaving her zero choice.

She gripped the vertical rails, stepped into Asher's linked hands, and hoisted herself over, nearly falling on her butt on the far side.

He followed gracefully, looking like Superman to her very clumsy Lois Lane.

He thrust her suitcase at her, slipped his duffel onto his back, and crossed the flower bed they'd dropped into.

She hauled the suitcase onto the parking lot, its wheels rattling over uneven pavement.

A few people wandered through the half-full lot.

Asher scanned quickly, then beelined for an older sedan—a beat-up gray thing that looked like it hadn't moved since the nineties.

"What are we doing?" She'd expected them to run, try to hide from the bad guys, but obviously, Asher had a different plan.

Crouched by the driver's door, he pulled something from his duffel bag—a thin metal tool—and jimmied the lock faster than any AAA roadside assistant could manage. The door popped open, and he slid inside and yanked wires from under the dash.

"Are you kidding me?" Her voice climbed an octave. "We're stealing a car?"

"You have a better idea?" He didn't look up, his hands

moving fast, sparking the wires together. The engine sputtered to life.

She glanced back. Those guys were closing the gap, maybe fifty yards away.

She threw her suitcase in the back and started for the passenger door.

"You're driving." He hopped over the console, giving her the left-hand seat.

"What?" She slid inside, then stared at the stick shift like it was a live snake. "I haven't driven a manual in years! I barely remember—"

"Now, Cici!" His voice was curt, his eyes darting behind them.

In the rearview mirror, she saw the thugs break into a run.

She grabbed the stick and pressed the clutch. "Okay, okay—clutch in, first gear..." She eased the gas. At least the previous driver had backed in, so she didn't have to figure out how to reverse.

The car lurched and stalled. "Dang it!"

He leaned over and hot-wired it to get it running. "Go!" Asher pulled a handgun from beneath his shirt—had he carried that the whole time? He twisted in the seat, watching the men closing in.

She tried again.

The car lurched. Then, the engine coughed and died. "I can't do this!"

Cursing under his breath, Asher slid right into her seat—practically on top of her. "Move your legs."

She squished to the side while steering the coasting vehicle into the lane.

His boots found the pedals. He lifted the clutch and pushed the gas pedal. The engine roared to life.

The car shot forward, Asher aiming toward the exit.

She could barely breathe, a combination of fear and his solid body pressing against hers, but she wasn't about to complain. They were moving, no thanks to her.

"Can you take over?"

"Yes, yes."

"Grab the wheel." She did, and he maneuvered back to the passenger side. She managed to shift into second gear, her hands shaking but functional.

This was insane. They'd just stolen a car! "I'm not going to prison for grand theft auto!"

Asher dove into the backseat and rolled down the window.

She skidded onto a two-lane road. They were in the middle of a business district, the buildings dark, shuttered for the night. "If we get caught, I'm telling them you forced me—held a gun to my head or something. I'm not cut out for jail, Asher! I'd look terrible in orange—"

"U-turn," he snapped.

"What?" She barely registered the order. "I mean, I've got a business to run, and—"

"U-turn! Now!"

She yanked the wheel hard, the car skidding into a sloppy arc. The wheels went off the road. She managed to angle back onto it. A car was coming toward them.

"Floor it!"

She resisted the urge to squeeze her eyes closed, pressed the gas, and shifted into third, then fourth, going way faster than the posted thirty-five-mile-per-hour speed limit. "Is that them?"

In the rearview, she glimpsed Asher as he leaned out the window.

Gunfire cracked in the silence.

The other car swerved and crashed into a light pole.

Cici passed the accident site, slowing to see what'd happened.

"Move!" Asher shouted.

Right. Of course.

She shifted into fifth and hit the gas. The car rumbled down the empty road. They passed the train station again, and then it was shrinking in the rearview.

Asher slid into the passenger seat, watching behind them. Finally, he exhaled and slumped back in the seat.

She couldn't speak. Couldn't think. Her heart was a jackhammer, her mind replaying the last few minutes on a loop.

"Guess I finally figured out what it takes to shut you up," he said, tone dry. "Gunshots."

"Not funny," she croaked, but a shaky giggle bubbled up anyway.

He smirked, a rare crack in his stony facade, and then he chuckled, a low, rumbly sound that felt like a thread of peace in a tapestry of chaos.

They laughed together, the absurdity of it all spilling out, until she remembered… They'd just stolen a car. Nearly gotten caught by bad guys. Nearly gotten *killed*. "What are we going to do?"

"It'll be okay."

"How?" Nothing about this felt funny all of a sudden. Nothing was okay. "They're everywhere. We can't get ahead of them."

"We survived. We'll just take each scenario at a time and figure it out as we go."

Maybe *he* would. She wasn't cut out for this…this running for her life. She'd panicked. All she'd wanted was to return Forbes's jewelry to him, to do something bigger than herself. Maybe even a little…heroic?

Right. She was as far from *heroic* as she'd ever been.

If not for Asher's quick thinking, they'd both be dead.

CHAPTER SIX

Asher steered the stolen sedan along a two-lane state highway, the headlights carving a narrow path through the darkness. The hum of the engine was steady, the only sound breaking the silence since he and Cici had traded places after her panic-and-giggle cocktail back in Springfield.

She was not the cool-under-pressure type, but that was okay. He was, and he could lead her to safety, as long as she trusted him enough to follow his directions.

The giggling, the stress-babbling? They should drive him crazy. And they did, but in all the wrong ways. Like everything else about Cici Wright, the things about her that should be annoying only attracted him more.

Right now, she needed him, and there was no headier drug than being needed by a beautiful woman.

If he didn't put that very inappropriate thought away, it would distract him, which was the last thing either one of them needed.

I-90 would've gotten them to Boston in a couple of hours—sooner at this time of night—but he'd decided they'd do best to avoid the interstate. Too obvious. Too exposed. He'd surely run across at least one cop—a problem if this car had already been reported stolen, though he hoped the driver had parked it for the weekend. More importantly, the guys following them were smart and had resources. This beat-up Ford had an electronic toll pass adhered to the windshield, which would trigger every time they passed beneath a reader on the toll road. Even if he pried it off, toll roads recorded license plates. He couldn't take the chance that their pursuers could access those records.

He and Cici had managed to escape twice. He wasn't sure they'd survive round three.

Where had he messed up? How did those thugs keep finding them?

Their pursuers—he needed to figure out who their enemies were—must've found his pickup near the Thirtieth Street Station and deduced that he and Cici had hopped a train. It took them time to get ahead, though—Springfield was a good haul from Philly. They must've studied the Amtrak schedule, driven like madmen, and waited at the station like vultures. Smart, organized, determined. And the way they'd tracked her cell phone...? That proved they had resources beyond the typical criminal.

If Asher and Cici were picked up in Massachusetts for stealing this car, Cici would be extradited to Pennsylvania to face charges there for arson and murder.

Asher would face charges as an accessory after the fact.

"Are you all right?" Cici had been so quiet that her voice startled him.

"What?" He blinked. "I'm fine."

"You sure? Because you're gripping that steering wheel like you're trying to choke the life out of it. I'm not sure this car can handle that much aggression."

He stretched his hands out. "Just thinking about everything."

"Come to any conclusions?"

None, which was why this whole thing was so frustrating. He needed to ask Cici about what she'd seen and heard in the jewelry store that day. At the same time, he'd needed a few minutes of peace.

"How'd you do that, back at the station. With the gas and the clutch? You got the engine going without hot-wiring it again."

"Just popped the clutch."

"That clears it right up, thanks."

Sarcasm. Nice. "I'm sure you don't remember, but back in high school, I drove a beat-up Nissan." He glanced at her, saw no recognition on her face. Of course she'd never noticed what he drove. She'd barely known he existed.

"Anyway, it stalled a lot, so I learned how to pop the clutch to get it going again. It's just a matter of feeling the sweet spot between the clutch and the gas."

"Wow. Thank God you had that skill."

He'd hated that car. He'd been embarrassed by it, especially considering the other kids in town drove much nicer vehicles. But like so much in his past, God had used it.

He should be thankful.

"I'm sorry," Cici said. "I've been trying to be quiet. I know it annoys you when I talk too much. I'm sorry I wasn't able to drive the car. Thank you for getting us out of that. I'm trying not to be a nuisance. I'm sorry you got sucked into this madness." She laughed. "Sorry. I'm doing it again."

He glanced at her. "What do you mean? Doing what again?"

"Babbling. It doesn't usually take gunshots to make me shut up. I was just...panicking."

Back at the station, yeah. But why was she babbling now?

"Not that you make me nervous. Or...but I guess maybe you do. Or it's just..." Her words faded. A moment later, she added. "Anyway, you didn't seem like you were okay."

"It's not every day I elude killers and steal a car."

"Really?"

Maybe she saw something in his expression, because she added, "For all I know, this is a normal day for you."

She was amusing, even when she wasn't trying to be.

"Not even close. I had more relaxing missions behind enemy lines."

That made her giggle, the sound so lighthearted and unexpected that he couldn't help the smile that tugged his lips.

"That makes me feel better. I mean, most of the time I'm pretty competent. I hate that I lost it like I did back at the station. I was just a little bit freaked out."

"I was a little bit freaked out too."

"Ha. You were amazing. You're a quick thinker and...and you just make decisions and go with them. It's really impressive. I can't imagine being in better hands."

Her words filled him, infused him with a combination of courage and pleasure and determination to prove her right.

Her kindness and gratitude surprised him. But they shouldn't have.

He'd changed in the last ten years. Why was he surprised that she had too?

The gas gauge hovered near a quarter tank, and a glowing sign up ahead promised a station. He pulled in, the sedan's tires crunching gravel, and parked beside a pump. The place was dead except for a bored clerk Asher spied through the glass, sitting behind the counter and scanning his phone.

Cici sat up. "Thank goodness. I wasn't going to ask, but I need a bathroom."

He cut the engine. "I'll walk you inside."

She looked exhausted, still wearing the wig. Somehow, she made it and the oversized sweatshirt look cute.

This woman would look good in a potato sack.

He followed her inside to the back, where a dingy sign pointed to restrooms.

"Lock the door. Stay in there for a few minutes. I'm going to pump some gas, and then I'll be back. I'll knock when I'm here."

"Okay. Thanks."

He normally wouldn't leave a client alone, but aside from the clerk—whom Asher could watch through the window—the place was deserted. And he needed a minute to think.

The night air was cool, the scent of gasoline heavy. He shoved the nozzle into the opening, then stuck in his ear buds and pulled his phone from his pocket. He dialed Bartlett.

"Rhodes," Bartlett answered, voice rough as gravel. "Do you know what time it is?"

"We're alive. That's the headline." Asher had texted his boss after the train left Philly, letting him know the plan. He hadn't had a chance to update him since then. "Train was stopped in Springfield when Cici spotted one of the goons from the jewelry store. We ditched him, but there were more in the station."

A beat of silence. "And?"

"I hot-wired a car. Shot out the thugs' tires when they followed. We're on back roads now, headed to the city."

"You stole a car?" Bartlett's voice spiked, incredulous. "You're not a SEAL anymore, and you're on American soil. You can't just—"

"I understand." If Asher's jaw clenched any tighter, he'd give himself a headache. "They were ten seconds from grabbing her, probably killing both of us. I could've killed them, but if I'm going to prison, I'd prefer it be for auto theft than murder, thank you very much. The client's still breathing, and the necklace is still safe."

Bartlett exhaled hard. "You're supposed to be discreet."

"Discreet went out the window when they murdered an innocent man, torched a jewelry store, and put Cici's face on the news. So maybe cut me some slack."

Bartlett said nothing for a few beats, and Asher figured he'd gone too far. He was justified in his anger, but he didn't want to lose his job.

"You're right." Bartlett's words came with a hint of legitimate regret. "I knew you could handle the paranoid tech guy by yourself, but this isn't that."

"Far from it." Asher gave his boss more details about everything that'd happened. "They must have connections with police or...or cell phone companies at least. I can't figure out how else they could've tracked her phone so fast." Truth was, Asher should request Bartlett send a second man. But for the time being, they were safe, and he needed to prove he could handle the job by himself if he ever wanted to be a team leader.

Asher was good at what he did. Very good. If Bartlett didn't see that, then maybe Asher should find another job.

And he would, except this one paid much better than any of the other security jobs he'd applied for. This one would supply the cash he needed to buy his own place, to start building the life he craved, one with a safety net for himself and his family, including the one he hoped to build someday.

"All our guys are tied up this weekend," Bartlett said. "Do I need to pull someone off another job to help you?"

"I've gotten her this far. We'll make it to Maine."

"Good, good. This is your opportunity to prove your skills."

In other words, don't screw it up.

As usual, Asher was balancing on a thin line. One wrong

move and he'd lose everything. "We need a new ride. It's just a matter of time before this one's reported stolen."

"It won't be tonight. Dawn, at best, if I can get someone out to you. Meanwhile, you need to get off the road. Hold on."

The line went quiet, leaving nothing but the buzz of the lights and the cool breeze whispering through the pines overhead. Asher finished pumping the gas, then jogged into the store. He knocked on the restroom door to let Cici know he was back.

It opened and she stepped out. She'd straightened her wig, not that it would do much good now that the bad guys had seen her in it.

"Should we grab some food?" she asked. "I don't know about you, but I'm starving."

They'd missed dinner, and his stomach was growling. He followed her to a freezer case, where she perused the selection.

Or lack thereof, it turned out.

She grabbed a bag of trail mix and a bottle of water.

He snatched a Coke, then a bag of Cheetos. "Should I get you one?"

She scrunched her nose. "You can't possibly eat those and look like"—she waved toward him—"that."

He looked down, then met her eyes. "Like what?"

Her pale cheeks turned pink, adorably embarrassed.

Causing an entirely unprofessional reaction. *She's a client. Just a client.*

"Never mind." She brushed past him to the counter. "Put your stuff up here too. I'll get it."

Irritation might as well have been a cold shower. "I can buy my own stuff, Cici. I'm not destitute."

She looked up at him, blinking. "I know that." She sounded confused. "I didn't say... I was just...I mean, you're in this because of me. I figured I should at least buy you a snack."

Obviously, he'd read more into her offer than he should have. Swallowing his ridiculous pride, he set his things on the counter and let her pay with cash.

When she was finished, he scooped up the bag with their purchases. "Thanks."

They were nearly to the car when Bartlett came back on the line. "You there?"

"Yup."

Cici gave him a look, and he gestured to his earphones.

Bartlett said, "Secured a house for you. Small place ten miles north of Sturbridge. You can lie low till the car's delivered."

"I'd rather keep moving." After glancing into the backseat to ensure nobody'd climbed in, he opened her door for her.

"I'd rather you not end up in a cell. Hopefully, Forbes can smooth this over—pay off the car's owner so they don't press charges. That is, assuming you get caught."

Asher didn't plan to let that happen. He climbed in on the driver's side and set the food on the console between them.

"A billionaire's got deep pockets," Bartlett added. "Let's hope he's generous."

Asher did not appreciate the suggestion that he'd be relying on the man's charity. He was protecting Cici—Ballentine's girlfriend's sister—and a piece of jewelry probably worth more than Asher would earn in a lifetime. He expected the people he risked his life for to compensate him.

How often had his expectations run counter to people's behavior, though? More times than he wanted to consider.

He rubbed a hand over his face, exhaustion gnawing at him. "Address?"

Bartlett rattled it off, along with a four-digit code to get inside.

Asher tapped the address into his phone and memorized the code.

"Keep her safe, Rhodes. And don't steal anything else."

"Needs must when the devil drives, but I'll do my best." He ended the call and hot-wired the car. He'd done it often enough that it seemed perfectly natural to him now.

"Everything okay?" Cici asked.

"We're stopping for the night."

If she didn't like that idea, she kept her opinion to herself. Maybe, like him, she was simply too tired to argue.

After they returned to the store to grab food for breakfast, they backtracked toward Sturbridge, then turned north on a narrow road, munching their snacks on the way. The sedan rattled over potholes, the backroads twisting through forest.

His mind ran a loop he couldn't break.

Get Cici to Shadow Cove. Deliver her and the necklace to Ballentine. Be done with this job.

It sounded so simple, but it felt like a slow bleed on his career. Stealing a car wasn't a résumé highlight—Bartlett's reaction had made that clear. If he got caught, if Forbes didn't bail him out, he could kiss the agency goodbye. No job, no condo, no stability. Just him, twenty-eight years old, starting from scratch. Again.

And wouldn't that be fitting right now, with Cici Wright a front-row witness to his latest humiliation.

The safe house was a pretty little cabin tucked off the road behind a screen of oaks and birches and maples. One story, weathered clapboard, no neighbors in sight. Perfect for lying low.

He pulled into the gravel drive, killed the engine, and sat there a beat, listening to the night settle. "A new car should be delivered first thing. Once we get into the house, don't come back out. We don't want anyone to know we're here."

"Gotcha. And then what?"

They climbed out of the car, and he spoke to her over the roof. "Then we get you to Shadow Cove." With her suitcase and his duffel, he headed for the door, boots crunching on gravel. "God willing, this ends tomorrow."

He hoped he was right—for both their sakes.

CHAPTER SEVEN

The kitchen smelled of butter and coffee, a warm contrast to the cool morning air seeping through the cabin's old windows. Asher had called it a safe house, but to Cici, it felt more like a cozy vacation spot.

It was a charming little place—two bedrooms, wood-paneled walls, a stone fireplace that probably roared in winter. Last night, she'd barely registered the place, too exhausted to do more than crash. Now, with the first light creeping through the forest outside, she was starving, and she figured Asher had to be too. A bag of Cheetos and a Coke weren't exactly dinner, especially for a guy built like him.

She stood at the counter, flipping eggs in the skillet. She'd found a Keurig tucked in the corner, a small mercy from the cabin's owners, along with a carousel of coffee pods. Her mug steamed on the counter, black and strong, waking her up after too few hours of sleep. Asher had said he'd thought the new car would be here early, so she'd set the old-fashioned clock radio on the nightstand, wanting to get a shower before they hit the road.

Another cup of coffee was brewing in the coffee maker for Asher.

Her hair was still damp, loose and curling at the ends, the blond wig stuffed in her suitcase. Since she'd been seen in the wig at the train station, she figured she didn't need to wear it anymore.

She'd swapped the sweatshirt and leggings for jeans and a T-shirt. She felt human again, or as close as she could get with killers on her tail.

The faint hiss of the shower cut off down the hall. She hadn't seen him yet, but the lights had been on when she'd come out, and she guessed that Asher had been up before her, probably scouting the perimeter or whatever bodyguards did at dawn. She was thankful for the two bathrooms so they hadn't had to tiptoe around each other to get ready.

Footsteps thudded on the hardwood floor, and she turned just as Asher stepped into the kitchen. He paused in the doorway, his broad frame filling the space, and for a split second, his ice-blue eyes locked on her—steady and unreadable, but with a flicker of something that made her breath hitch.

He wore all black, like he had the day before. She doubted it was a fashion choice, but the shirt clung to his chest, and the jeans fit him just right. His dark hair was damp, a little messy, and he carried the faint scent of soap. What had looked like a five o'clock shadow the day before was thicker this morning, more like a closely trimmed beard.

She wasn't sure what he was seeing in her that put that enigmatic look on his face. His pause threw her off.

"Morning," she said, brushing past the awkwardness. "I figured we should eat before we go."

He blinked like he was shaking off whatever had snagged his attention, stepping fully into the room. "Bartlett said someone's on the way." His voice was gruff. "He's dropping off a fresh car and taking the stolen one back to Springfield. Hopefully, he'll get it there before anyone notices it's gone. Apparently, Ballentine's willing to offer the owner a sizable 'rental fee,' if it comes to that, so we should be off the hook for grand theft auto."

"That's a relief." Not that she'd worried much about that since they'd escaped the train station. The murder and arson charges were still hanging over her head—and jewelry theft, but she wasn't sure the authorities had figured that out yet. Even being wanted by the police seemed irrelevant, considering the men tracking them.

He nodded toward the skillet. "Smells good."

She buttered toast, assembled egg sandwiches, and slid them onto plates, which she set on the small table by the window. "It's just grilled egg and cheese. Nothing fancy, but it's better than Cheetos." She grabbed the second coffee mug from the Keurig and placed it beside his plate. "Black?"

"No cream, I guess. Sugar?"

She plopped the bowl of creamers and the sugar dish on the table with a spoon.

He dumped three spoonsful of sugar into the hot brew, then stirred in a couple of single-serving creamers.

"That gonna be enough?"

"I don't drink it for the taste." He sipped, making a face. "Nobody drinks it for the taste."

She tasted her own. It wasn't the freshly ground beans she had at home, but it was still good. "Why drink it if you don't like it?"

He shrugged. "It's always available. Days like today, I need the caffeine."

"My sister Brooklynn doesn't care for coffee, but she loves tea. You should try that."

He made a noncommittal sound and bit into his breakfast, seemed to test the flavor, then set the sandwich down. "That's really good."

"Why do you sound surprised?"

"Just didn't peg you for a cook."

"I have to eat. What, did you think I have a chef on staff?"

He shrugged, biting into his sandwich, his expression neutral but his silence telling. Studying him, she didn't miss the slight flush creeping up his neck.

"Wait," she said. "You did, didn't you?"

"No, not...you."

"My family, then. You thought we had, what? Household staff?"

"Didn't say that," he mumbled around a bite, not meeting her eyes.

She leaned back, half-amused, half-exasperated. "We had money, sure, after Dad started his business. But we didn't live in a mansion with butlers and maids." Mom had employed—still employed, actually—a housekeeper who came once a week, but Cici decided not to mention her. "I learned to cook from my mother."

He swallowed, finally looking up, a flicker of embarrassment in those blue eyes. "Guess I figured wrong."

"Guess you did." She ate a bite of her sandwich. It would be better on an English muffin with a slice of ham, but it was okay. "My parents aren't butler-and-caviar rich."

At least she'd never seen them that way. Dad had amassed a fortune since he'd founded his defense contracting company. And Cici supposed, compared to...well, most everybody, they would be considered rich. But she and her sisters hadn't been spoiled or pampered.

The quiet settled between her and Asher, not tense like the night before but more comfortable, easier. She watched him, this man who'd morphed from the geeky kid she'd barely known into someone who could hot-wire a car and shoot out tires without blinking. He'd surprised her, and she wondered if she'd surprised him too. Probably only in the vastness of her ineptitude.

He polished off his sandwich, and she rose and grabbed him another one—she'd assumed he'd want a second—and slid it onto his plate.

"Thanks." He dove into it, then sat back and sipped his coffee. "For a while, my mom worked at that souvenir shop in town—the one owned by Elvis...whatever her name is. You know her?"

"Elvis Harper. Her shop is next door to my sister's gallery."

"Oh, right. Anyway, my brother and I used to go with Mom on Saturdays because Dad was working and she didn't want to leave us home alone all day."

Cici wasn't sure where this story was going. "Fun place for kids."

"Got boring after a few hours, though. She'd let us walk around town. We were probably...ten and eight? Something like that."

"I bet you were a protective older brother."

He lifted one shoulder and let it drop. "Every Saturday night, I'd look through the windows at Webb's Harborside, and you and your family would be there, eating dinner, looking out over the ocean. The idea that you could go there every week... I didn't assume you had staff, or I didn't think about it. I just figured you ate out all the time. And, frankly, that told me you were rich."

Rich? Because they'd eaten at a local restaurant once a week? "We didn't eat out all the time, just on Saturday nights. Often, Dad wasn't there—he traveled a lot, still does. But Mom felt like Saturday night should be special. It wasn't always Webb's, but that was one of the few places all of us sisters liked."

He tipped back in his chair, studying her through narrowed eyes. "It's funny how kids perceive things, isn't it? To me, it was like you were always there. But if you'd looked out the window and seen me, you might have thought I was always wandering around Shadow Cove."

"True. Kids are weird."

He chuckled. "You're not wrong."

When he smiled, his face transformed. He went from fierce, almost frightening to...she wasn't even sure how to describe him. Handsome didn't cover it. He was...beautiful.

She'd best keep that thought to herself.

His chair hit the floor with a thud, his smile fading. "I need to know what we're dealing with. Tell me exactly what happened at the jewelry store. Everything you saw, everything you know about that necklace."

She took a deep breath, the memory of Mr. D's crumpled body flashing behind her eyes. She'd seen it a hundred times since, in her mind's eye. That moment had yanked her from sleep more than once during the night. "I was appraising a batch of stuff for Tony Delvecchio. He owned the store, one of my regular clients. His niece had bought a bagful of jewelry for fifteen hundred bucks. I've met his niece, and she's a sweet kid, but she doesn't have much experience. I suspect she saw one or two items and made the offer, hoping it was a good deal. I also suspect that, if she saw the ruby necklace, she thought it was a fake."

"It's not? You're sure?"

"This is what I do for a living. Hold on." She hurried to her bedroom and pulled the velvet bag from her purse. She hadn't peeked inside it since she'd escaped the jewelry store.

She carried it back to the small kitchen table and set the necklace in front of Asher. "It's real. I knew it was special the second I saw it. And then I recognized it as The Crimson Duchess. I'd seen it before in an article about Forbes's parents' murder in Shadow Cove. It was stolen the night they were killed. Forbes's mom had been photographed wearing it a few nights before her death. It's been missing ever since. I sent Forbes a picture, and he confirmed it."

Asher nodded to the jewelry but didn't make a move to touch it, as if it might contaminate him or something. "What's it worth?"

"It's hard to say what it would sell for. I need more time to study it, but its value is much higher than that of each individual gem. It's famous, and it's connected to the Ballentine fortune and the murders. Those facts will add to its value. If I had to guess, I think it would auction for over five million, maybe as much as ten."

He sat back. "Ten million dollars?"

She smiled. "Americans do generally trade in dollars."

"That's..." His voice faded as if he couldn't find an appropriate word to finish his sentence.

"Like I said, I'm just guessing. But each one of those stones is...big." She figured he wasn't interested in a lecture on carat, color, and clarity.

He whistled. "That's enough to kill for."

"I think the other motivation is just as big. The owner of this necklace must somehow be connected to the Ballentine murders. And, assuming it's the man from the store the other day, he's also connected to Mr. D's murder, not to mention arson."

"Do you know who it was?"

"No idea. I'm sure Mr. D had records, but if they were paper records—he was an old-school kind of guy—they probably didn't survive the fire."

"Surely there was a receipt or something," Asher said.

"Maybe. Some record of who sold the items to Mr. D's niece."

The thought made Cici wonder...Had the police warned Maria like Cici had asked them to? Was she safe?

Maybe Cici should call and tell the police everything she knew. But they suspected her. Would they take her warning seriously?

She doubted it.

"So you discovered the necklace and called Ballentine. Then what?"

"Two guys showed up. One was in his sixties, I would guess, a smooth talker. He asked about a salesperson, said his son had done business with her. It had to be the niece. As far as I know, she's the only other person who works there. *Worked* there." Considering the store had been reduced to ash, its owner killed. "Mr. D said it was just him working that day."

"You were there."

"But I don't *work* there." Asher acknowledged that with a nod. "I was in the back room, on the phone with Forbes, but something didn't sound right. I peeked through the opening and saw the guard—the bald guy at the train station—standing near the door. And then I saw the older man strangle Mr. D until he collapsed. At that point, I grabbed the bag and ran out the back."

"You call the cops?"

"They directed me to the nearest precinct. But somehow the two men were waiting for me there. That's when I called Forbes again, and he sent you." Recalling the events had her hands trembling. She wrapped them around her mug, the warmth grounding her.

He leaned forward, elbows on the table. "Maybe the man was tied to the original theft."

"The smooth talker," she said. "That's what I assume. But why kill Mr. D? Why burn the store?"

"Loose ends. They didn't expect you to take the necklace

and run. Now they're after you—and it." He tapped his fingers on his mug, thinking.

"Even if I hadn't taken it, they'd be after me, right? Because I was a witness?"

"We need to assume so, yeah. At this point, we need to get you and the necklace to Forbes and let him and the FBI sort it out. Between them and your dad, they'll be able to keep you safe."

She nodded, the weight of it settling deeper. "I just wanted to get it back to him. It's his family's, you know? And after everything Brooklynn and Forbes went through..."

"How did they get together, anyway?"

"That's a long story." Brooklynn had seen something she shouldn't have. If not for Forbes, she'd probably have been killed.

Weird, the similarities to what Cici was going through. If not for Asher, she doubted she'd still be breathing. The difference was obvious, though. In the end, Forbes and Brooklynn had fallen in love.

Whereas Asher couldn't wait to be rid of Cici.

He finished his coffee, setting the mug down with a soft clink. "Good breakfast. Thanks."

His simple compliment heated her more than the coffee had. "Anytime."

A low rumble broke the quiet—tires on gravel. Asher was up in an instant, moving to the window. He peeled back the curtain. "Vehicle's here."

She stood, grabbing their plates. "Guess breakfast is over."

"Yeah." He glanced back at her, that unreadable look flickering again. "Can you be ready in ten?"

"Even faster." She rinsed the dishes and loaded them into the dishwasher before starting it.

After returning the jewelry to the velvet bag, then the bag to her purse, she grabbed her suitcase from the bedroom and met Asher at the front door. He and the driver—a wiry guy in a ball cap—traded a few words. Then the guy handed Asher a key fob and headed for the stolen sedan.

Asher turned to her. "You ready?"

She checked her purse to make sure the jewels were there. "Yup."

Asher took her suitcase and tossed it and his duffel into the new ride, a blue SUV.

She climbed into the passenger seat, The Crimson Duchess still heavy in her purse, and stole a glance at Asher as he started the engine. Maybe he'd misjudged her family, but she'd misjudged him too—once upon a time.

CHAPTER EIGHT

Asher gripped the wheel of the SUV, the engine's low hum blending with the crunch of tires on the back roads north of Sturbridge. The morning sun slanted through the trees, dappling the asphalt in gold and shadow. It was beautiful, but his mind kept circling back to that moment in the kitchen—the air warm with the scent of coffee, Cici flipping eggs and buttering toast. Her strawberry-blond hair was damp and messy, the clean scent of her soap cutting through the grease, and that soft-green T-shirt that hugged her just right. *Beautiful* didn't cover it. She'd looked...vibrant and innocent.

The snapshot had hit him square in the chest.

It was everything he'd ever wanted—a home, a family, that quiet security he'd chased since he was a kid staring through restaurant windows at lives he could never hope to have. And there she was, serving it up in the form of an egg sandwich, all casual competence and grace.

For a second, he'd let himself imagine it—her, him, a life like that.

As if.

Cici Wright was upscale, the product of wealth and security. He was wrong-side-of-the-proverbial-tracks. A guy who, as she'd pointed out, hot-wired cars and shot out tires to survive.

End of story.

His phone rang, the sound loud over the speakers in the silent car. Asher hit the button to answer. "Yeah?"

"It's Ballentine. Cici's with you?"

She leaned closer as if the Bluetooth microphone wouldn't pick up her voice from the passenger seat. "Right here, Forbes."

"Good. Listen, I've got a jet waiting at Hanscom Field. I want you both on it. You'll land in Portland by noon. I'll have someone meet you at the airport."

If Cici was surprised by her destination, she didn't say so.

"I'm headed over to your parents' house to fill them in," Ballentine said. "Brooklynn assures me they'll want you there to keep you safe."

"Yeah, probably." Cici didn't sound excited by the prospect. "Do you know if Delaney's back?"

He blew out a breath. "According to your mom, she's fine, but she's not ready to come home."

"Brooklynn hasn't talked to her?"

"She called but Delaney didn't pick up."

Asher had no idea what was going on with the younger Wright sister. He did know she was a little old to be running away from home.

"Once Cici's safe at the Wright estate, Rhodes, you'll be off the clock."

Done by the end of the day. He could drop Cici and that cursed necklace into Forbes's hands and get back to his life.

But what about Cici?

"How do you plan to keep her safe?" Asher asked. "Those guys aren't going to stop pursuing her just because she crossed into Maine."

"Bartlett's sending a team, and the FBI is involved as well."

Good. A team could keep her safe. The guys Asher worked with were the best.

Would he be assigned? Did he want to be?

Irrelevant, though he wouldn't mind sticking around Shadow Cove for a few days. His parents lived in an apartment in Portland, just a half hour away, no longer in the tumbledown trailer where Asher and his brother had grown up.

"Is it Derrick?" Cici asked.

Was who Derrick? Probably a rich boyfriend. The thought sent ice water to his racing heart.

"He's headed to the airport now," Forbes said. "Where are you guys?"

Asher fielded that. "Just outside of Sturbridge."

"Great. If you take the interstate—"

"We're sticking to back roads."

"We don't have to, though," Cici said. "Nobody knows what we're driving."

Asher shot her a look and repeated, "We're sticking to back roads. I'll send you an ETA."

"That'll work. I'll send you a number. When you get to the airfield, text it, and Derrick will tell you where to meet him."

"Got it." Asher hung up, the tension in his shoulders easing a fraction.

A jet. That was the best solution to get Cici to safety.

But a small, stupid part of him twisted at the thought. Cici wasn't the spoiled princess he'd pegged her for. Her kindness was chipping away at his old image of her. The girl he'd thought of as prom queen for a decade had built her own business. She wasn't just some rich girl coasting on Daddy's dime.

No. She was the type of girl to date guys with private jets.

The thought was acid in his stomach.

She shifted beside him, her purse with that necklace

clutched in her lap. "We should get on the Mass Pike. We'd make better time."

He kept his eyes on the road. "No." He heard the hardness in the word and knew he should temper it. Wasn't her fault he was jealous.

"Why?" Her tone sharpened. "It's faster. These winding roads are taking forever."

"Cameras." He clipped the word, not looking at her. "Toll roads, traffic cams. They'd catch our faces and the license plate. I'm not risking it."

She huffed, crossing her arms. "I figured you'd want to get rid of me as soon as possible. And anyway, it's my life on the line here. Shouldn't my opinion count?"

"I'm in charge."

She twisted in her seat. "Excuse me? I'm the one responsible for the necklace, not you. I decide what happens with it."

"I'm responsible for both you and the necklace. My job is to keep you alive, and I say we stay off the interstate."

She laughed, though the sound held zero humor. "Look, I get that you're better than I am in dangerous situations, but that doesn't make me stupid. My opinion counts. I'm not your soldier or your lackey."

His grip tightened on the wheel, irritation flaring hot. There it was—the rich-girl attitude he'd expected all along, slipping out when she got riled.

"Just because I was poor doesn't mean I'm incompetent," he snapped, the words spilling before he could stop them. "I've gotten us this far, haven't I?" He stopped at a red light, shooting her a look to punctuate his words.

She blinked, recoiling like he'd slapped her. "What are you talking about? What does money have to do with anything?"

"You think you're better than me—always have." He

snatched his phone from the console to get directions to the private airfield north of Boston. "I don't need your ego telling me how to do my job."

"Wow." Her voice dropped, cold and cutting. "You've got some chip on your shoulder. I'm just asking you to consider my opinion. You're the one refusing to trust me—as if I'm some clueless idiot who can't think for herself."

"If this were a jewelry emergency, I'd give you the wheel." He regretted the remark the second it left his mouth.

The light turned green, and he accelerated through the intersection, not taking it back. He wasn't changing his mind, and if that made her unhappy, then so be it.

One minute, she was cooking him breakfast, humble and kind, the next she was throwing her independence in his face like he was some grunt beneath her. He'd proven himself, and still she pushed back. What did she want from him?

The tension in the SUV was an unwelcome change, a far cry from the easy conversation they'd enjoyed over breakfast.

He shouldn't care. This was a job. Cici wasn't his friend, his girl, his anything. Just a client. A paycheck.

She was a means to an end.

But she didn't feel like *just* a client. Not with an ember of the torch he'd carried for her burning into his brain.

The memory of the kiss the night before. How she'd felt in his arms. Her initial shock had softened, as had her lips.

Kissing Cici had felt natural, like waking up in his childhood bedroom on a sunny summer morning.

And it had felt like fireworks and symphonies and a thousand stupid metaphors that still didn't come close.

Which was why he'd been trying very hard not to think about it.

She just stared out her window, arms crossed. The argument hung between them, and he didn't know how to fix it. Maybe it would be better if they kept a barrier between them.

She'd rejected him once, and the humiliation still burned. He didn't need to live through that again, thank you very much.

He kept driving, but the closer they got to the airfield, the more a small, stupid part of him left over from high school wondered what he'd do when she was gone.

CHAPTER NINE

Cici stared out the window to hide her tears.

She felt like a fool for being so upset, but Asher's low opinion of her cut deep. She'd spent her life trying to prove that she wasn't just a frivolous girl.

Growing up the third of five sisters, she'd struggled to stand out. She wasn't the smart one—that was Alyssa. She wasn't the talented one. Brooklynn had earned that title early on with her outstanding photography. She wasn't the kindest one. Even as a little girl, Delaney had claimed that prize. She wasn't the adventurous one. Kenzie had been into extreme sports back in high school and now sailed around the world as the captain of her own sailboat.

Cici had always just been...the other one. The middle one. The one who never stood out.

By finding Forbes's family's long-lost necklace, for the first time in her life, she had the opportunity to do something that mattered, something heroic. Something that might get her father's attention.

Oh, why did she still care what he thought?

If he were here, what would he tell her?

To trust Asher, obviously. Because Asher was trained. And a man. Though Dad had never said so, Cici had always guessed he was disappointed that he hadn't had any sons. She'd even, a few times in her life, wished she were a boy. Maybe then Dad would pay her a little attention.

Stupid. She really needed to get over her daddy issues. She hated being a cliché.

And anyway, Dad would be right. Of course she should trust Asher. He knew how to keep them both safe. She just wanted to contribute...something. To be more than just a useless damsel in distress.

Keeping her face averted from Asher's gaze, Cici wiped her tears with a tissue she found in her purse.

She was tired and nervous and eager to be done with this, even if there was a teeny tiny part of her that regretted not being able to get to know Asher better—and not just because of their kiss.

A kiss he hadn't apologized for or remarked on at all, as if it'd never happened. As if it hadn't meant anything to him.

Obviously, it hadn't.

Any attraction the teenage boy had once had for her had burned off over the years. Or maybe her hurtful rejection to his prom invitation had wrecked it forever.

This version of Asher, all grown up and buff and gorgeous, clearly had no interest in her.

Their kiss had felt so authentic, but he'd been selling a story, nothing more. He probably kissed all his girls exactly like that. He'd been in the Navy. Probably had a girl in every port.

He'd dump Cici in Shadow Cove with barely a see-you-around. He'd forget all about her.

Whatever. She didn't need him or Dad or anyone else. She lived alone. She'd built her business alone.

She spent her life alone, and once she was out of this mess, life would go right back to the way it had been.

And she'd smile and pretend she was happy, just like she'd always done.

She sniffed and wiped away fresh tears.

"Are you...?" Asher's words trailed, but a moment later, he asked, "Are you crying?"

"Allergies."

A plausible enough excuse. Though August wasn't the worst month in New England, there was always something dropping pollen.

"What's wrong, Cici? I didn't mean to..." His words trailed again, as if he had no idea how to handle a woman's tears. He sounded equal parts frustrated and worried.

"I'm fine."

"Is it your sister? What happened to her? Is she in trouble or something?"

"Delaney," Cici said, assuming he'd forgotten her little sister's name, if he'd ever even known it. She was glad to talk about something besides herself. "She was dating a guy this summer. You might remember him—Owen Stratton?"

"Played football, right?"

"He seemed like a nice guy. Really attentive. Delaney's sensitive, always has been, and he was good with her."

"But?"

"You heard about what happened at the Ballentine estate?"

"A little. There was a smuggling ring—connected to the murders?"

"My sister, Brooklyn, got wrapped up in all that. If not for Forbes, she might've been killed."

Asher nodded. "Okay."

"Turns out, Owen was working for the smugglers. He told the police he'd started because he wanted to make enough money to buy Delaney a ring. She was devastated. She's the sort who always thinks the best of everybody. It would never occur to her that anyone she cares about could do anything bad. When she found out what Owen had done, it was like something snapped. She just took off. She's always been a bit of a homebody, the one who checks on the rest of us to make sure we're okay. It's so out of character for her to leave, to worry all of us."

"No idea where she is?"

"None. She checks in with Mom, but she doesn't want us to come after her. We're all trying to give her space."

"You're worried about her." No question in his statement, as if there were no doubt.

"She's not exactly worldly, my little sister. And she has a habit of trusting the wrong people." Though Delaney had sworn she'd never trust anyone, ever again.

"If Owen is bad, then how can I ever believe anyone is good?"

Not that Cici didn't understand her sister's fear. Owen had seemed like the nicest guy. Delaney hadn't been the only one shocked to learn he was involved with smugglers and murderers.

In Owen's defense—not that she'd make it for him—he hadn't known the people he worked for had been guilty of murder. He'd just been paid to offload goods. He hadn't known what was inside the crates, hadn't understood the depths his employers would sink to in order to remain out of jail.

He could claim innocence all he wanted, but he'd been instrumental in helping his *employers* track down Brooklynn and Forbes.

He'd fired a shot that had hit Forbes in the shoulder. After the fact, he claimed he wasn't aiming to kill, but Cici didn't care about his excuses. Owen could've killed Forbes. He could've killed Brooklynn. All in the pursuit of trying to be something he wasn't.

As if Delaney had cared a whit how much money was in his bank account or the size of a ring he might've bought her.

"What's Delaney doing?" Asher asked. "Is she working, or...?" He let the question trail, but she heard what he hadn't said. *Or living off Daddy's money.*

"I don't know. I doubt Mom and Dad are funding her life. I know they've never offered to fund mine. Delaney has worked since college—she worked as a nanny—and she's pretty thrifty. She might have enough to live on. Or maybe she got a job somewhere." Cici hated that Delaney wouldn't just come home and be with the people who loved her. Did she really think they judged her for not seeing Owen's faults? Nobody else had seen them. People as kind and good as Delaney didn't see evil in others. It was one of her best qualities.

Best qualities, like shiny quarters, always had a flip side. Confidence could quickly become arrogance. Kindness could turn into gullibility. Empathy could become charm or even manipulation.

Cici thought of the man sitting next to her. Asher was competent and quick thinking, no doubt. Also, stubborn and controlling.

That was his flip side.

It was so easy to peg others. What would her family say about her? What would Asher say?

"Is that why you were crying?" he asked.

"I told you, I have—"

"Allergies. Yeah. I get them, too, but they don't bring me to tears." She didn't respond, and after a minute, he said, "You don't owe me an explanation. For the record, if I hurt your feelings, I'm sorry."

"For the record, I'm not that fragile."

"Aren't you, though?" The words were muttered under his breath.

Whatever. Who cared what he thought?

She did, more than she should, certainly more than she let on.

She stared through the windshield at the world all around. Rolling hills covered in the deep green foliage of late summer. It seemed calm and beautiful, a stark contrast to how she felt.

"Why did you join the Navy?" she asked, needing to change the subject. "Not that it wasn't a good decision or anything. I'm just curious."

"I thought about college, but I didn't want to end up in debt."

"No scholarships? You were certainly smart enough."

His eyebrows rose as if she'd surprised him, but his intelligence hadn't been a secret. He'd graduated at the top of their class. He'd won academic awards. He'd been valedictorian. "I got a couple, but they weren't full-ride. I figured I could go into the service, then go to college for free. I watched my parents take risks and struggle financially all their lives, and I didn't want that. And, honestly... It sounds corny, but I wanted to serve my country. To do my duty."

"Not corny at all. It's honorable." People their age didn't use the word *duty* that often, at least not without a sneering tone. It felt like a concept lost on her generation, but sometimes, life was about duty. Her father had taught her that, always off saving the world. And her mother had taught her, always managing the family by herself, even when it was hard.

When Asher added nothing else, she asked, "Did you always want to be a SEAL?"

"Made that decision after I joined. I was a scrawny kid, but after high school, I grew a little."

"I noticed."

That had his lip tugging up. "My dad was the same. Said he grew four inches taller after high school graduation. Went back for his reunion, and classmates he'd known all his life had no idea who he was."

"I was this height in eighth grade."

"I remember. You were taller than just about everyone else in our class."

She had been, and for years, none of the boys paid her any attention. And then they grew, and suddenly, she was popular.

"So you were big and strong and decided to become a SEAL?"

"There're a lot of big, strong guys in the Navy. I just wanted to do it. The training was..." He rubbed his lips together. "Not easy."

She didn't know much about the military, but she knew enough to know that was a colossal understatement.

"I wanted to be the kind of guy who could do it."

"Like a personal challenge?"

"Exactly. I loved the Navy, being part of a team. The team mindset is even stronger with the SEALs. We learned to depend on each other for our lives."

"Tell me about some of your missions."

His eyes flicked her way. "I can't talk about most of them. But I did get to be a guard at Camp David for a year. Met the president and his family."

"That's amazing. What did you think?"

"I wasn't in the room with them. That's the Secret Service's job. I just guarded the grounds. But I was there when the helicopter brought them. The president and his wife could've just hurried inside, but they lingered and chatted. The president cracked jokes. He was surprisingly funny and very personable."

"What an honor."

"It was."

"And what about college? Did you do that?"

"Working on it." Before she could ask, he said, "Double

major, political science and criminal justice. I plan to apply for the FBI or Secret Service."

"You'd be good at either one."

He lifted one shoulder and let it drop.

"You should ask my dad for a recommendation when the time comes."

He nodded slowly, a grimace crossing his features as if he didn't like the taste of that idea. Finally, he said, "I'd like to think I can get there on my own merits."

"Don't worry about that. My dad won't recommend you without cause. This—saving my life, keeping me safe—is cause."

He made a sound low in his throat that might have been agreement.

They poked along on the narrow road, passing through a small town. It was a beautiful, sunny Saturday, one of the last days of the summer, and traffic was building as they skirted the north edge of the Boston metro.

"How about you?" Asher asked. "Why jewelry?"

"I wish I could say something...corny. You know, like I wanted to provide gemstones to the needy."

He chuckled, and the sound buoyed her spirits. She liked that she could make him laugh.

She couldn't help but be a little self-conscious about her life choices. Here she was with a man who used the word *duty* in everyday language while she spent her time assessing baubles.

"You built a business and fulfill a need." Asher glanced her way. "As long as your work is honest, your work is valuable."

"That's a good way to look at it."

Silence reigned until he prompted again. "So...why jewelry?"

"We went to a festival when I was seven or eight, and there was a jewelry store where you could watch the jewelers work through the windows. I was mesmerized. I remember thinking how lucky those people were to get to work with such beautiful stones."

"But you don't design jewelry, right? Or do you?"

"I did, back in high school, but I couldn't afford real gemstones, and working with crystals and colored glass didn't do it for me. I realized my real passion lay with the stones themselves. I find it fascinating the way they're formed deep in the earth. Think of it. These bits of minerals and chemicals surrounded by dirt and rock. But because there's just the right amount of pressure, just the right amount of those minerals and chemicals, little bits of seemingly random things turn into rubies or sapphires or emeralds. I mean, it's amazing."

He flicked his gaze toward her hand, and she figured he was looking at all the jewelry she'd put back on that morning.

She was always scouring estate sales and pre-owned cases at the stores she visited, looking for deals. And she often found them. Her ability to appraise gemstones made it easy for her to skim past the trash and home in on the treasures.

"It's good you do something you love." His tone held no irony or scorn. He seemed genuine, which she appreciated.

"It's not important like what you do."

"It's important. That ruby necklace in your purse is important to the Ballentine family. An heirloom. I bet there are people who appreciate being able to put a value to what they own, maybe even raise money to pay their bills."

"My mother always told us to follow our passion, that God gave us passions for a reason. I think she was paraphrasing someone else, but she once said, 'Maybe your dreams aren't dreams at all. Maybe they're God's to-do list.'" Cici shrugged, feeling self-conscious. "No idea why God cares about jewelry, but I guess He cares about what we care about. Anyway, I took Mom's advice. I mean, you have to spend forty hours a week or more at work. You might as well enjoy it."

"And you do."

"I love it."

"Forty hours?"

She laughed. "More than that most of the time, and of course there are aspects to my job that I don't like. Writing reports isn't fun. But what job is a hundred percent enjoyable?"

"None that I've found."

"You like being a bodyguard?"

"Most of the time. For me, the hard parts are usually related to the people I'm guarding."

"Oh, no. I hope you don't consider me one of the hard parts."

"You're not on that list." He chuckled, his smile transforming his face. "Yet."

"Thanks for the 'yet.'"

Her remark earned another chuckle.

"I bet you have some stories."

All that got was a slow nod.

"Care to share?"

Before he could answer, the navigation system interrupted, and he turned left at the next intersection.

His eyes flicked to the rearview, then narrowed.

"Everything okay?"

Again, he checked the rearview. "I think so."

She didn't love the hesitation that came before his answer. "What is it?"

"Probably nothing."

She twisted to look behind them. A beige sedan followed, maybe fifty yards back. She faced forward again. "Something suspicious?"

"It's been back there a while."

They were on a four-lane road. He sped past a car on the

right, then continued going what she guessed was at least twenty miles over the speed limit.

"They can't possibly have found us," she said.

"Mmm-hmm."

The man clammed up when he was worried. Good to know.

"Hang on." He ran a yellow light, then banged a last-second left that had her bracing her hand on the ceiling as the tires screeched on the asphalt. They were on a narrower road now, only two lanes, flanked by homes set a good fifty yards back on each side. This was an upscale neighborhood with perfectly landscaped lawns and expensive cars in the driveways.

She looked back again.

The sedan was still there.

Asher uttered a low curse word, then an apology only louder by a degree.

"How could they have found us?"

"No idea."

"But you think that's them?"

"Who else would follow us?"

She was shifting in her seat to watch the trailing car when Asher slammed on the brakes, jostling her and everything else in the car.

He narrowly avoided crashing into a green pickup that pulled out in front of them and turned left.

Behind them, the pickup did a quick U-turn, joining the sedan.

"What's going on, Asher?"

"They knew we were coming."

"How?"

He didn't answer. Obviously, if he knew how they'd been found, it wouldn't have happened.

What mattered now was getting away from the men in the

two vehicles that were closing in. She had no idea how they were going to escape this time.

CHAPTER TEN

Asher's gaze flicked from the road to the rearview mirror. The truck and sedan were both back there. He pressed the accelerator, tearing down the narrow road.

The sun was high, the trees arching over the road casting shadows that moved them from light to darkness like a strobe.

Hanscom Field was close, but their pursuers were closer. The way the truck had U-turned, the way the sedan had blown through the red light... Their skill and precision set Asher's teeth on edge. These weren't amateurs. They were organized, relentless, and somehow always one step ahead.

"Cici, check the map." His voice was taut, his hands so tight on the wheel that his knuckles were white. "Find me a turn—something sharp, something they won't expect."

She fumbled with his phone, her fingers trembling but quick. "Okay, um...there's a left in about a quarter mile. Looks like it loops around a pond, then reconnects with this road further up."

"Good enough." He downshifted to slow without hitting his brakes, the engine growling. The turn came up fast—a dirt track veering left, barely visible beneath overgrown brush. Asher yanked the wheel, fishtailing the SUV as it hit loose gravel, praying the driver of the sedan didn't see where they went.

Cici braced herself, sucking in a gasping breath.

Asher floored it, the vehicle bouncing over ruts, branches scraping the sides.

If this didn't work...

"Do you see them?" he asked. "Did they follow?"

She twisted in her seat. "The sedan... It's still back there!" Her pitch rose in panic. "And the truck's right behind."

"Dang it." His mind raced, cataloging options. He'd trained for this—evasion, improvisation, survival. SEALs didn't quit when the odds stacked up. They adapted.

The pond loomed ahead, a glassy shimmer through the trees. He spotted a faint trail branching off to the right, barely more than a deer path that disappeared into dense woods.

Their SUV was high off the ground. The truck was, too, but it was behind the sedan. Maybe....

"Hold on." He cut the wheel hard.

The SUV lurched onto the trail, tires sinking into soft earth, the undercarriage groaning as it scraped roots and rocks.

Cici yelped, gripping the strap over her door.

He wrestled the steering wheel as they bounced on the uneven ground. "Are they following?"

She watched behind. "I don't see them."

With any luck, the sedan had gotten stuck. It would have to be moved to let the truck pass.

He pushed deeper into the woods, the canopy swallowing the sunlight, until the trail widened into a clearing. An old barn sagged at the far end, its red paint peeling, its doors hanging ajar. The trail led straight to it.

He scanned the clearing for another road, but there was nowhere else wide enough for the SUV.

Asher jerked the wheel into the clearing and stopped in front of the barn doors. He hopped out and opened them, the old wood and rusted hinges groaning in complaint. Back in the vehicle, he drove to the center of the dilapidated structure and hit the brakes. "Out, now."

Cici didn't argue, just hitched her purse over her shoulder and climbed out.

He did the same, then hurried to close the doors.

He grabbed his duffel and slung it on his back.

He stopped and took a breath, needing to think.

It was quiet now, but those men were coming.

The air carried the musty scents of dust and hay. Sunlight streamed through gaps in the walls, illuminating stacks of old crates and rusted tools. Asher peeked into a horse stall, then stepped inside. "In here."

Cici followed, and they both dropped to a crouch behind the weathered planks. "Stay low."

Her breathing was ragged, but she nodded, eyes wide. "How do they keep finding us?"

"No idea. Sit tight." He left her hiding there and looked through a crack in the barn wall, waiting for the truck to come, praying it would pass right by the narrow path.

But if his plan worked and the sedan was stuck on the trail, then the truck would have no way to get past it.

Those men shouldn't have found them. Not after the train, not after swapping cars. Something was off—way off.

He bolted to the far end of the barn, where another set of doors was closed, these secured with a rusty bolt.

Not exactly helpful, considering the broken windows on either side. He spied an old ranch house—almost as small as the trailer where Asher had grown up. Past that, a narrow path wove into the woods in the direction of the pond. The trees were overgrown, the grass surrounding the house knee-high.

Asher turned and searched the barn, looking for anything that might help him create a diversion.

A sound had his stomach souring. He ran back to the front as the truck rolled into view on the trail.

Back up. Nothing to see here.

It was moving slowly and deliberately. Just when Asher started to think it would do as he prayed, the pickup aimed for the barn and parked a dozen yards away.

Four men spilled out.

The bald guard from Springfield, his bulk unmistakable, a handgun glinting in his grip. Another guy—older and wearing a suit—barked orders, pointing at the barn. Was this the slick-talker Cici had told him about?

The other two men weren't familiar. One was tall and built. His hair was cropped military style, and he had a bushy beard. The other was shorter, leaner, and probably faster on his feet. His face was clean-shaven, and he had longish brown hair with just enough curl that Asher imagined him adding product to make it look just so.

A linebacker and a pretty boy.

Those two headed for opposite sides of the property, weapons drawn, scanning the woods.

"They're coming." Panic carried on Cici's whisper.

"Quiet." He unsnapped his holster and pulled out the Glock. He had his training and the advantage of cover. He could shoot through the gaps in the walls, then move before they retaliated.

He could kill all four without breaking a sweat.

But, as Bartlett had reminded him, this wasn't a war zone. He was in rural Massachusetts, where it wasn't okay to shoot people because they'd followed you.

He'd prefer not to end up in prison. And he'd prefer not to have to live with more bodies on his conscience.

He needed something to slow his enemies down, to distract and confuse them. His eyes landed on a rusted gas can in the corner, half-hidden under a tarp. A long shot, but it might work.

He crept over, keeping low, and shook the can. A faint slosh. It would be enough. He grabbed a splintered board, wedged it into a gap in the barn wall, and doused it with the gas, letting it drip down the dry wood. He doused more gas on the wood from there to the front of the structure, then found an old rag.

He moved back to Cici. "Start moving." He pointed at the broken windows. "When I light this, you go out and head west—toward the pond. There's a path, but stay off it. Don't stop."

"Where will you—?"

"I'll be right behind you."

He hoped, anyway. He found a crowbar and then silently opened the SUV's door.

She started creeping toward the windows. When she was almost there, Asher started the engine and wedged the crowbar against the gas pedal.

He yanked the gear shift into reverse and dove out.

The SUV barreled backward.

Asher pulled a lighter from his pocket and lit the cloth, which he tossed at the gasoline-soaked wood just as the vehicle splintered the doors.

Shouts outside told him he'd gotten the men's attention.

The flame caught the gas-soaked wood. It flared fast, flames licking up the wall toward the front doors.

Cici scrambled out the window, and he followed, the fire crackling behind them.

More shouts erupted as the flames spread, smoke pouring through the gaps. The barn wouldn't burn long—he hoped. The last thing he wanted was to cause a forest fire. But the ground was damp, the clearing sparse.

They bolted into the trees. The pond glinted ahead, and he

veered left, getting in front of her, pulling her along a muddy bank.

She glanced behind, but he propelled her forward, toward the forest on the far side of the water.

The men behind them had gone quiet, which told Asher they hadn't been distracted for long. Unless they'd seen where Asher and Cici had gone into the woods—and Asher didn't think they had—they'd fan out.

Now that they were in the forest, the going was slow, the underbrush challenging to navigate. He paused and turned a circle, scanning the landscape.

"What are you doing?" Cici hissed. "We need to move."

There. A boulder rose from the ground, maybe forty feet away. He aimed toward it.

She followed silently.

When he reached it, he circled to a huge bush growing against one side. He dropped his bag. "Duck down right here and don't move."

"Where are you—?"

"Please, Cici." He met her eyes, trying to infuse his look with kindness and confidence. "Just do as I say."

She blinked, seemed to take that in. "Okay."

He left her there, kept low, and sneaked back toward the barn. When he heard the telltale snap of someone moving, he crouched between two bushes and behind a log.

Ahead, the linebacker crept through the forest. Unlike Asher, he was terrible at stealth.

Or it was a trap.

Asher watched him for a long time, until the man's gaze moved to his right.

Asher flicked his focus that way.

Sure enough, pretty boy was inching forward, silently.

The linebacker was a decoy to get Asher to show himself.

He moved slowly, carefully, circling pretty boy.

Without a sound, he came up behind him, caught the man's neck with his arm, and squeezed.

Pretty Boy fought. Asher had been right, the man was strong.

But Asher was stronger.

It took about ninety seconds for Pretty Boy to go limp. Not dead, just down for the count.

Asher was tempted to slice his Achilles but reminded himself, again, that this was America. That he couldn't just take people out, especially unconscious people.

He searched the guy, pocketed his cell phone, his handgun, and a sheathed knife, and left him in the bracken before scanning the surroundings again. Aside from the linebacker, who was still moving forward, Asher didn't see any more enemies. The guy must not have seen Asher take his buddy out.

The thug was getting too close to Cici.

Asher got low and eased toward him, picking his way around bushes and over fallen limbs and tree trunks.

He was about ten feet away when the man turned toward where Pretty Boy should be. He froze. Then scanned his surroundings.

Their eyes met.

The man's mouth opened to yell.

Asher sprinted forward and barreled into him.

They both went down.

They wrestled for the upper hand, but this guy was huge. And strong, and trained.

Asher aimed for his eyes, but the guy jerked away and kidney-punched him.

Pain momentarily blinded him, but he couldn't give in to it. He fought hard, punching and kicking, but the guy was made of iron.

Nothing fazed him.

In seconds, Asher was on his back, the linebacker's meaty fist poised to put Asher's lights out.

There was a *thwack*, and the man's eyes widened. He slid off Asher and landed in the dirt.

Behind him, Cici held a tree limb like a baseball bat. "You okay?"

"Uh, yeah." Because of her. Holy cow, that could've been... fatal for both of them.

He shoved the heavy man off and stood.

The guy was out cold.

"Good hit." Who knew the prom queen had such a powerful swing?

"Now what?" she asked.

After ridding the thug of his cell phone, ammunition, and guns—he'd carried two—Asher looked around again but didn't see any more enemies. Either Baldie and the boss were waiting back at the burning barn, or they'd searched in the other direction.

He returned to the boulder for his duffel, then handed Cici one of the handguns. "You know how to use that?"

She checked the magazine for bullets, popped it back into place, and engaged the safety like a pro.

That was a yes.

"Let's move." They continued to the south side of the pond, where he tossed both thugs' cell phones into the marshy water before they continued into the woods.

He prayed they would reach people and cars—houses, a town, a strip mall—and soon. "Don't slow down, and don't look back."

Cici kept pace, barely breathing hard, even though he moved fast. She was in good shape, not just slender but strong. He liked that.

"How are we going to get to the airfield?"

"We aren't." They'd been so close to safety, to the end of this mess. "I don't know how, but they knew where we were going."

"If we could just—"

"What?" He stopped to face her, not bothering to hide his frustration. "Please, if you have an idea, I'd love to hear it."

"It's just, if we made it to the plane..." She blinked up at him.

He didn't say the obvious, that the problem lay in that small word. *If.*

If they hadn't been tracked, they wouldn't be in this situation, but they *had* been tracked. And like at the train station the night before, Asher doubted these four were the only ones looking for them.

Likely, more enemies were on the road, ready to ambush them if they got anywhere near Hanscom.

Cici and Asher were moving again when distant sirens told him somebody had reported the fire. He hoped it wouldn't be hard to put out, that it hadn't done too much damage.

Why not add arson to the growing list of charges against him?

At least a mile from the burning barn, he slowed to a more comfortable pace. No sense in either one of them falling and getting injured. "We have to get another car."

Her green eyes glistened with frustration. "We're driving?" Though she didn't cry, emotion overflowed in her words.

"I'm doing my best," he snapped, then felt immediately guilty. Danger wasn't her life, her world. He felt alive in these situations. Competent and strong.

She was clearly terrified, and for good reason.

"Sorry," he muttered. "I wish we could hitch a luxury ride with your boyfriend, but that's off the table now."

"What are you talking about, my boyfriend?"

"Derrick? The guy who owns the jet? Is that not...?" He realized he'd jumped to conclusions. Again. "It belongs to somebody you know, right?"

"Derrick is my cousin. He's a pilot, owns a charter business."

"Oh." Asher's stupid heart did an equally stupid little jig, as if that were the best news it'd heard all year. "Well, anyway. I wish we could take his plane, I really do." But they'd been found, again. Obviously, their enemies had known their destination.

Which made no sense, unless...

The answer seemed obvious.

There had to be a leak in Forbes's operation. That was the only option.

Someone working for Forbes was also working for the bad guys.

It ticked Asher off that he had no idea who the enemies were, a fact he needed to remedy ASAP.

He scanned between the trees for buildings or the glint of a vehicle. "We'll locate another car."

"Steal, you mean." She didn't bother to hide the censure in her voice.

"Open to suggestions, Cici. So far, all you've offered is criticism."

"I didn't mean... I'm just saying..."

He gave her a few moments to finish her thought, but apparently, she had no decent defense.

Though her purse had a strap, which she'd slung over her shoulder, she clutched the bag in front of her as if afraid it might blow away. "You're right. You know what you're doing. Whatever you think."

That was a nice change. "Just keep up."

Asher moved on. He needed to unravel this mystery, but

first, he had to get them out of this alive. One skill at a time, one mile at a time, until they were free of this mess.

∼

Asher's boots sank into the squishy earth, the dense canopy overhead blotting out most of the midday sun. The ground was marshy, the air thick with the sounds of birds and insects and frogs, the scents of sweet wildflowers and bitter water.

They'd entered a nature reserve south of a ritzy neighborhood. He'd vetoed cutting through those manicured streets—too many Ring cameras, too many security systems itching to catch a glimpse of a guy in tactical black and a woman toting a purse stuffed with a million-dollar necklace.

Best stay off everybody's radar until he figured it out.

Cici had been quiet since she'd caught sight of a luxury home and suggested they knock on the back door and ask to use a phone. "We can just tell them we were in an accident, and our phones were broken or something. We can call for an Uber to take us to Hanscom."

"No." He'd added a quick, "Sorry, but we can't go to the airfield, even in a clean car. They'll find us."

"You don't know that."

"You don't know they won't. Are you really willing to risk both our lives?"

That had silenced her.

He didn't trust anybody right now, certainly not strangers in big fancy homes. And besides, where would they wait until help arrived? In the fancy house? How could they trust the fancy-house people not to call the cops, and then what would happen?

An hour passed before she spoke again.

"Asher, we can't just wander through the woods forever.

Unless you're planning to hike all the way to Maine, we need a plan. When we find another neighborhood, we should knock—"

"We can't." He didn't break stride. "No doors. No people. You're wanted, Cici, for arson and murder, and I'm on the hook as your accessory. Let's not forget grand theft auto. And the barn we just burned down—another arson charge. One call to the cops and we're both in cuffs."

"Whatever." A few beats passed. "My feet are soaked."

God forbid the prom queen got wet feet.

That wasn't fair. Wet socks scraped against tender skin, and her skin wouldn't have toughened up the way his had, thanks to all his training, then all his missions. "We'll get you some dry shoes and socks."

"How?"

He didn't know, but it wasn't an unsolvable problem. A solution would present itself, eventually.

They walked a few yards more before she said, "Let's rent a car. There's got to be a place nearby. I'll pay—"

"No credit cards. They'll trace you in a heartbeat."

"You can use yours. They don't know who you are." Her tone was sharp, challenging, like she'd caught him in a logic trap.

He ducked under a low branch and held it up for her. "I'm not so sure." He muttered the words, mostly to himself.

"What?" Her voice pitched up. "How would they?"

They moved away from the swampy land onto firmer ground, now back in a forest thick with underbrush. "They found us on the train in Springfield, tracked the stolen sedan, and then the SUV. How? It all happened too fast. It was too... precise. Even with serious tech, they can't be tracking you. We ditched your cell in Philadelphia. So maybe..."

He'd powered his cell phone off, but with the right kind of equipment, that wouldn't make a difference.

Could be that the bad guys were waiting at the next road.

He hated to do it, but he had no choice. He pulled his own cell from his pocket, turned, and threw it back toward the swamp. He was rewarded with a faint splash.

"What are you doing?" Cici stared at the place where the cell phone had disappeared. "How are we going to—?"

"They could be tracking me."

"How?"

"I don't know!" He hadn't meant the exasperated tone and felt a twinge of guilt when she winced and stepped back. "Just... let me think, please."

"Think faster, because I'm freaking out here." She dodged a root, her purse thumping against her hip. "Maybe there's a bus station? There's got to be one somewhere. Of course, we can't find it because you just tossed your phone. We're totally...lost."

"I'm not lost." He wasn't. He knew basically where they were and what direction they were walking. They'd hit civilization soon. When she said nothing, he glanced back and caught her swiping a finger beneath her eye. Was she *crying*?

"We're in the middle of nowhere." Her words were squeaky and barely audible.

They were a couple of miles from town. More importantly, when he'd been in the military, none of his teammates had cried.

None of his teammates had looked like Cici, either. At the moment, that wasn't a point in her favor. He needed fewer distractions, and everything about her distracted him. It was why he walked in front of her, not beside her or, even worse, behind her where he could watch her move.

He needed to jiggle those thoughts loose, then stomp them into the bracken.

"I just thought we could catch a bus to Boston, or a flight to Portland." Her voice was pitched high and getting higher. Soon, only dogs would be able to hear her.

The snarky side of him thought, *good*.

But that guy was a jerk.

"Won't work," he said.

"Of course not. Of course nothing will work." She sighed. "Could we steal a horse? Find a hot-air balloon? Hitchhike with a serial killer? I'm sure there's a tandem bicycle rental somewhere."

Turning, he watched as she made a show of looking around, though they were surrounded by nothing but trees on every side.

He snorted despite himself. "You're making it really hard to concentrate, you know that?"

"Maybe you'll actually listen to one of my ideas instead of grunting like a caveman."

He stopped short and faced her, and she nearly collided with him. Her green eyes blazed, cheeks flushed from the trek and her agitation.

"Sheesh, Cici." He felt a grin breaking through and tried to temper it. "I'm having flashbacks to high school. Trying to think when you're around is impossible."

Her annoyance seemed to fade away as her head tilted, confusion flicking across her face. "What do you mean?"

What was he thinking, reminding her of the loser he used to be? His neck heated, and he shook his head, trying to wave his remark off. "Nothing. Just... You had to know, right? You were like"—he gestured vaguely toward her, grasping for something safe—"the prettiest girl in school." *Sexiest.* That was the word that had popped into his head, though thank heavens he hadn't said it aloud. "All the guys tripped over themselves watching you."

Her lips parted, surprise softening her features. "Pretty?" she said, almost to herself, like she was turning the word over.

He started walking again, silently cursing himself.

And then one of his eyes stung, sharp and sudden. Not tears

—don't even think it. He was a Navy SEAL, and SEALs didn't cry.

No. A speck of grit had lodged itself under a contact lens. He blinked hard, then rubbed it, but the pain only got worse. "Hold up." He slid his pack off his back and fished for the small case he always carried. No choice now. He popped out the right contact, and the pain was gone instantly, though his vision blurred. He held it up to the dim light filtering through the trees and closed the bad eye. Whatever had gotten in his eye had torn the contact lens. It was useless now.

With a sigh, he flicked it away. He had fresh lenses, still in their sealed packages, but to use them, he'd need to wash his hands. Not like there was a sink and soap nearby. He removed the left contact, and his vision blurred even more. He found his glasses—chunky black frames he only wore when nobody was looking—and slid them on.

The world snapped back into focus.

A small smile played at Cici's lips. "They look good on you."

He knew that was a lie. He had a mirror, after all. He was the geeky kid all over again. "Whatever."

She was being nice—much nicer than she'd ever been in school—and it was messing with him. She was a shallow prom queen who'd burned his confidence to ash.

He had to keep reminding himself to focus on the mission.

Even if this Cici wasn't playing her part, she was kind, quick-witted, and despite her tears, holding it together better than most would with killers on their tail. If he wasn't careful, she'd suck him in again.

He couldn't afford that—not now, not ever.

He started walking, faster now, as if he could outrun his thoughts.

She fell into step beside him. "We need a real idea." Her

voice was lighter. Was she trying to encourage him? Did she read his embarrassment?

How...embarrassing.

"I was kidding about the tandem-bike thing, but seriously, what if we found a bike shop? We could borrow a couple of mountain bikes and pedal our way out of here. If they need a credit card, I could get one of my parents to provide one. No cameras, no cards, just...us and the forest until we reach a safe place."

He grunted. It wasn't a terrible idea, except that, as confident as he'd sounded when he'd told her he knew where they were, finding trails suitable for biking was a whole different matter. And off trails, they wouldn't move any faster on bikes than they were moving on foot.

"Or," she went on, "we could find a river, build a raft like Huck Finn. Float all the way to Maine. I mean, I'm no Tom Sawyer, but I can tie a decent knot."

He shook his head, fighting another grin. "You're ridiculous."

"Ridiculous is my middle name."

Rose was her middle name, and ridiculous was the fact that he remembered that. Ridiculous was the fact that he'd ever known it.

Proof of his...yeah, the word still worked. *Ridiculous* crush.

"Come on, Asher, throw me a bone. I'm doing my best here."

He glanced at her, her strawberry-blond hair catching a stray beam of sunlight, her eyes bright despite the fear she was clearly wrestling. She was trying to help, which threw him off. He wanted to stay mad, to keep her at arm's length, but her kindness made it impossible.

They reached a shallow creek, the water gurgling over smooth stones, and he paused to check their bearings. The forest stretched on, but he could hear faint traffic in the distance—a road, maybe a mile off. They needed a ride, but stealing another car felt like tempting fate. He fished his water bottle from his bag and handed it to her.

She took a long sip, then he finished the bottle and refilled it in the stream, using his small filter, then added iodine to kill bacteria.

"Why do you have that?"

He wasn't sure what to say, so he said nothing.

"You just walk around prepared to survive in the wilderness?"

He shrugged.

"Seriously"—she nodded to the filter still sticking out from the top of his pack—"how do you have those things?"

"For such a time as this?"

She cracked a smile. "Does this happen to you a lot, getting stranded in the forest with helpless damsels?"

"You're not helpless." He splashed his face to clear his head, then stood, water dripping from his chin. "I always travel with essentials."

"Me, too. Lipstick and hand cream. Not"—she waved at his filtration system—"that."

He'd been taught to be prepared when he was a Boy Scout. He'd learned how to do it—and everything to be prepared *for*—as a SEAL.

"What about a library?" Her voice was thoughtful now. "They've got free internet. We could use a public computer, contact Forbes without a phone. He could arrange a pickup, somewhere discreet. No cards, no trace."

Libraries were low-key and anonymous, and nobody would bat an eye at two people using a computer. He nodded slowly, letting the idea sink in. "Actually, that might work."

She crossed her arms, smirking. "Wow. The 'actually' was a nice touch."

His mouth twitched, caught off guard. "I didn't mean... You're not a pro." He hadn't meant to insult her and wasn't sure how to dig himself out. "It's a good idea."

"High praise." She laughed, the sound carrying no malice. "I'm like a stopped clock, right twice a day."

She'd thrown out a thousand ideas. One was bound to stick.

That wasn't fair. She was doing better than he'd ever have predicted, better than he was in the idea generation department. And that was a problem, because every time she surprised him, every time she flashed that smile or tossed out a quip, it chipped away at the wall he'd built around her memory.

"Let's move. Stay sharp."

She nodded, falling in beside him, and he caught the faintest whiff of her shampoo—something fruity and out of place in the wild. He shook off the scent and his attraction so they couldn't distract him.

Cici Wright was his job, nothing more. But as they moved toward the hum of civilization, he couldn't shake the feeling that she was becoming a heck of a lot more than that. And he wasn't sure he could stop it.

Or wanted to.

CHAPTER ELEVEN

Cici's legs burned, her soaked sneakers squishing with every step through the woods. She longed for her suitcase, probably burned to a crisp back in the barn. Not that she would have been able to haul it through the woods, but she could sure use a pair of dry socks.

Her purse slid off her shoulder, and for ten-thousandth time, she hiked it back up. Eyeing the pack slung on Asher's back, she considered asking him to shove her purse in there with his things. But the necklace and all the jewelry she'd stolen were her responsibility. Besides, Asher's duffel was already bulging at the zipper.

Exhausted as she was, she couldn't help but feel a tiny spark of pride in her chest. Asher had agreed to her library idea. She'd contributed something that might help get them out of this nightmare.

And there'd been that moment in the woods near the burning barn, when she'd hit that thug with a branch. She'd heard the ruckus and known she'd needed to help. But how? The guy had been huge.

She'd searched frantically until she'd found the limb, then

swung it like a baseball bat. Not that she'd ever been much of a ball player, but they used to play at family gatherings, Wright brothers and Wright sisters combining to create two teams. Her swing might not have hit the ball into the orchard at Uncle Roger and Aunt Peggy's house—an automatic home run—but it had been good enough to knock the guy over.

The shock on Asher's face, his blue eyes wide, his mouth open, had been worth the sting in her palms.

If not for her, he might not have survived that moment. Cici wasn't just a liability. She could contribute.

Even he'd admitted she wasn't helpless, and she'd never confess to a soul how much those words meant to her.

The forest hummed with life—birds chirping, leaves rustling—but the distant roar of traffic cut through. They'd trudged in underbrush for hours, sticks snapping underfoot, when a two-lane highway came into view through the trees, a busy stretch of asphalt alive with cars.

"Civilization," she said. "Thank God."

"Stay low," Asher muttered, his voice all business. He didn't head for the road but walked parallel to it, out of sight of passersby.

She was too tired to argue. Her morning runs and yoga had not prepared her for this.

They'd been paralleling the road for about twenty minutes when a sign appeared ahead. It was a convenience store, the kind that carried a good selection of groceries. Its parking lot was a patchwork of sedans, SUVs, and a lone motorcycle. None of the vehicles looked familiar. No beige sedan or green pickup. Surely they'd be safe there.

It felt like gasoline-scented salvation.

She was about to ask—maybe beg—that they go to the store when Asher stopped and gazed across the street. He watched the lot and door for what felt like hours. The man was vigilant, she'd give him that. Finally, he muttered, "Keep your head down," and led the way to the edge of the highway and, at a break in traffic, to the other side.

Cici kept her gaze on the ground to keep her face from being picked up by strangers or security cameras.

When they stepped inside, the bell above the door jingled. The cool air and scents of coffee and baked goods were sweet relief.

Even more so, the *Western Union* sign above the clerk.

Asher moved into the aisles quickly. He grabbed a handful of burner phones, a baseball cap, a couple of protein bars, and two bottles of water.

Cici's eyes landed on an end cap—Crocs, flimsy but dry, and packages of socks.

She raised a thank-You to her Provider, who'd obviously known exactly what she'd need.

The only pair in her size was pink. They didn't exactly coordinate with her outfit, but she snatched them up, along with a cozy pair of white socks.

Asher paid in cash while Cici kept her gaze on the scuffed linoleum, her pulse thudding. What if those men—the bald guard, the smooth talker—parked outside? Somehow, their pursuers had managed to locate them over and over. And they wouldn't have gone far from that burning barn, knowing Cici and Asher had escaped on foot. They were probably patrolling the narrow highway, looking for them.

What if they stopped here for a snack? What if they walked in?

But the bell didn't jingle once before the clerk handed over a plastic bag.

Asher led the way to the door, which he held open for her. They slipped out and ducked into the woods behind the store.

Beneath a canopy of pines far enough from the road that the

traffic was barely background noise, Asher plopped down and tore into the burner phone's packaging. "No library needed now." He didn't look at her. "This'll do."

Cici peeled off her soggy sneakers, wincing when the damp socks clung to her blisters. She let her feet dry in the warm air before covering them with Band-Aids Asher had found in his pack and then gingerly pulling on the new socks and shoes. Godsends both, even if the Crocs looked like bubblegum had thrown up on her feet.

"Why don't I reach out to my dad?" She stuffed her wet items in the plastic bag, then tried to get the bag in her bulging purse, voicing a question that had been humming in the back of her mind since she'd seen that sign in the store. "He could wire us money."

Asher took her plastic bags and somehow made room for her wet shoes and socks in his bag. "Your dad's phone could be tracked."

"Please." She didn't temper the exasperation in her voice. "Do you know who my dad is? Former CIA, runs a defense contracting empire, security clearance right up there with that of the Joint Chiefs? His phone's so secure that even he can barely get into it."

Asher's ice-blue eyes narrowed behind his glasses. The black rims did nothing to temper the man's attractiveness. If anything, they added to it, making him look studious *and* buff, like a sexy professor.

Stop that.

She braced for an argument, but he exhaled. "Okay. But no texts—calls only. Texts are too easy to intercept."

Not that she wanted to talk to her father, but at this point, she'd take his raised voice and disappointment if it meant not having to walk a hundred soggy miles from Massachusetts to Maine.

Asher handed over the cell phone, which he'd plugged into his portable charger and activated, and she dialed her father's number, her stomach knotting as it rang.

When he answered, she said, "Dad, it's Ci—"

"Cecelia!" His voice was whip-crack sharp. "Where in God's name are you? Why didn't you call me?"

"I'm fine, Dad." Not that he'd asked. His tone made her feel like a kid caught sneaking in after curfew. "I've been...dealing with some stuff."

"Some *stuff?*" His voice rose, and she could picture him pacing his home office, his hands balled into fists. "The police called looking for you. You're wanted in connection with a murder."

"I know, it's just—"

"Your mother is losing her mind. She deserves better than this. And so do I."

"Dad, just let me explain."

"No need." He took a breath but continued before she could get a word in. "I talked to Forbes and Brooklynn. I know about the necklace. The point is, you should have called me right away. Surely you don't think you can handle this on your own?"

The words stung. Of course he didn't believe her to be competent. He never had. "I'm with a bodyguard. We're okay, but we need help."

"I want to know exactly what happened, from the beginning."

She spilled the story—Mr. D's murder, the necklace, the men chasing them. The train, the stolen car, the safe house. And then today, their attempt to get to the airfield, eluding enemies yet again, the barn fire, and the long trek through the woods.

No wonder he didn't trust her to take care of herself. The more she talked, the more she realized what a huge mess she was in.

She couldn't help the tears that fell and averted her gaze from Asher, who was too close not to have noticed. At least she managed to keep emotion from seeping into her voice. Tears would not endear her father to her. He'd been immune to his girls' tears as long as she could remember.

Dad listened, his silence heavy.

She finished the story with her reason for calling. "We're low on cash, and we can't use our credit cards. I'm hoping you can wire me some money." She gave him the information for the Western Union. "I'll pay you back."

"You think I care about that? I'm sending someone to get you?"

Asher bumped her shoulder, and she quickly swiped her tears and looked at him. Though she hadn't put the call on speaker, Dad's voice was loud enough that Asher had probably heard his every word. "Tell him we'll call back with a location once we have the money. We need to move."

He was agreeing to have Dad send a car? There was a surprise.

"That was him?" Dad asked. "The bodyguard? What's his name?"

"Asher Rhodes. He works for the same company Grant worked for. I don't know if you remember Asher's family, but he grew up in Shadow Cove."

Asher's jaw clenched as if she'd said something wrong. He looked away.

"Rhodes?" Dad said. "Yeah, I remember them. Military, right?"

She looked toward Asher, but he was staring through the trees toward the highway. "He was a SEAL."

"Good, good. Tell me where to wire the money. You stick with Rhodes, you hear me? Rhodes, if you can hear me, you keep my daughter safe or you'll answer to me."

Asher held out his hand for the phone.

"He wants to talk to you, Dad. Hold on." She gave it to Asher.

"I'll do my best, sir," Asher said. "Meanwhile, you need to do something for me."

Cici cringed. Dad wasn't accustomed to taking orders from anybody. But Asher didn't seem to care.

"Tell Ballentine—in person—that I believe he has a mole in his operation."

"How do you know that?" Dad's voice was easy to make out.

"They were waiting for us near the airfield," Asher said. "There's no way they could've guessed that."

A beat of silence, then Dad said, "I'll tell him. Keep her safe."

Cici expected Dad to ask to speak to her again, but he didn't, just hung up.

She shouldn't have been surprised.

Asher powered down the phone. "Let's eat. We'll give your dad a few minutes to wire the money. No sense lingering where we can be seen."

They munched protein bars and sipped water in silence. It wasn't enough food, but once they got to Shadow Cove, they'd have a proper dinner.

After ten minutes, Asher stood and held out his hand for her.

She slid hers in it, and a spark of awareness zinged through her. She ignored the strange response, one she hadn't had to any man, ever. Except when Asher had kissed her, which felt like years ago but was actually less than twenty-four hours before.

Crazy.

He pulled her to her feet, and they headed back to the store.

Her father's money was waiting. They pocketed the cash.

"Let's go." Asher scanned the lot through the store windows. "No sense taking chances."

"Agreed."

His eyebrows rose. "No arguments?" Amusement sparkled in his eyes. "No 'better' ideas?"

She felt the air quotes in his attitude. "Shut up and lead the way." Sheesh, she wasn't *that* difficult.

He nearly smiled as they slipped out of the store and back into the woods, the new burner's map app glowing on Asher's screen.

"What's next?" she asked. "We just keep wandering around like lost hobbits?"

Her Crocs slipped on a root, and she flailed, aiming for— and missing—a skinny branch.

Asher gripped her arm, and thanks to his help, she managed to stay upright.

"You all right?"

"Sure." She tried to sound casual and confident despite the fresh adrenaline pumping in her veins. "I'm loving these new shoes."

When she was steady, he said, "We need to get far enough away to hide out." He studied the map. "Somewhere safe."

She chewed her lip, then said, "The library? It's still a good place to hide. Dad can send a car there."

He didn't look up from the phone screen, and she braced for a dismissal. But after a moment, he nodded. "Concord's got one. It's not far. Not even two miles as the crow flies...which is how we'll get there."

Two miles might as well have been twenty. The trek was brutal, especially in slippery rubber shoes. The tangled underbrush and uneven ground were bad enough, not to mention the flies and mosquitoes and spider webs.

Her legs ached, her patience frayed, and the necklace felt like a brick in her purse.

They reached pretty streets lined with manicured lawns and elegant homes. She was glad to be out of the woods, literally if not figuratively, but tension hovered over Asher like heat over an asphalt road. He swiveled his head in every direction, scanning for threats.

It was late in the afternoon by the time the Concord Free Public Library loomed ahead—a stately brick building with white columns, its grounds whispering of minutemen and 1775. Cici's high school history lessons nagged at her: the shot heard 'round the world, Paul Revere and all that. This place probably had a wing stuffed with Revolutionary War relics.

They slipped inside, the cool air a balm after the muggy woods. The space was serene, its polished floors and tall shelves a stark contrast to the chaos dogging them. They'd made it, thank heavens. Though she wouldn't relax until she was safely back in Shadow Cove.

∼

Cici followed Asher to a computer room, empty this late on a summer afternoon. She settled on an upholstered chair by the window, and Asher plopped down in front of a computer.

"We made it." She couldn't help the tone of surprise, but very little else had gone right that day. It was nice to see a plan coming together.

His smile was slight as he set a cell phone on the desk. "Go ahead and call your dad."

She inhaled a deep breath, finding a sense of peace in the quiet space, and dialed.

"Cecelia?"

"We're at the public library in Concord."

"Copy," Dad said. "Car will be there in thirty. Stay with Rhodes and don't do anything stupid."

Thanks for the vote of confidence.

She wished she had the nerve to say that out loud.

She ended the call and went to the restroom to freshen up. Not that there was much she could do to improve her appearance. Her cheeks were blotchy, her eyes rimmed in red from crying and fatigue. Her hair was a frizzy mess after an afternoon in the moist summer air. She finger-combed it, then searched for a hair band, feeling triumphant when she found one. She pulled her mop of hair into a ponytail, then rubbed lipstick on her lips.

Didn't help.

She gave up and returned to the computer room, where she peeked over Asher's shoulder. He was scanning a website. She picked up enough to see he was studying Philadelphia crime.

"What are you looking for?"

"Trying to figure out who's after you. The murderer is obviously connected, and he has wicked resources. I thought maybe he's organized crime, but I can't find..." He huffed a breath and powered up one of the phones—he insisted on carrying them all, the control freak. He said nothing else to Cici, but a moment later, he spoke into the phone. "It's Rhodes. I need a contact, preferably a Fed who can tell me about organized crime in Philadelphia. Better yet, if you can get a list..."

He listened for a minute, then said, "Yeah, email it." More listening, then, "I'll fill you in later. Suffice it to say, these guys are resourceful." Asher ended the call, powered off the phone, and stood. "You ready to move?"

She checked her watch. "We have twenty minutes before the car will be here."

He crossed to where she'd been sitting earlier and looked outside. He said nothing for a long beat, but she could tell by the intense look on his face that he was cooking up something.

"What?"

His gaze flicked to hers but didn't hold. "We're not taking your father's car."

"Why? I just called him. He'll kill me. He already thinks—"

"I should've told you, but I didn't want him to suspect."

"What are you talking about? You don't trust my father now?"

"Him, I trust. But anybody listening... Look." His voice lowered to a conciliatory tone. "We need to throw those thugs off our tail." He reached out as if to touch her, but she backed away.

"I know. That's why—"

His arm dropped. "If they're watching, if they're anywhere in town, they might see your dad's hired car. It's not worth it."

"That's absurd. It's just a car. How would they—?"

"How did they find us at the train station?" He no longer sounded placating but irritated. "How did they find us outside the airfield? How do they keep finding us?"

"Not because my dad told them!" Her voice was too loud, especially for a library.

"I don't distrust him. He's probably got a bunker under his office."

A safe room big enough for the whole family, complete with iron walls and its own ventilation system.

"If your dad were coming with a team," Asher continued, "then maybe I'd wait. But he didn't say that, right? Just that he'd send a car? Maybe it'll be driven by a pro, but we both know your enemies always come with a lot of firepower."

A few months before, Cici might have argued. Dad's drivers were always hulking guards, trained and ready. But the one Dad had trusted most had been killed back in the spring when their car was ambushed. Mom and Brooklynn had been terrorized. A child had been kidnapped.

And Shadow Cove and Dad's security detail were far from here, so who knew who he'd tasked with picking her and Asher up.

"I know it stinks," Asher said. "Believe me, I'd love to ride back to Maine on leather seats in an air-conditioned car, but it's possible those thugs picked up on your phone call. They have a lot of equipment and a lot of manpower. If they heard our plan, they'll be looking for us to leave here in twenty minutes. Since I don't know how they keep finding us, I have to assume no communication is safe. Which means we have to be gone before then."

"On foot? Or—?"

"We'll go out the back door."

Not an answer, she noticed. "And then what?"

"We'll probably have to steal—"

"We're finally safe, and you want to play Grand Theft Auto again?"

"We need to do something they don't expect." A muscle ticked in his cheek. He was losing patience with her, that was obvious enough. "That means *not* doing what we said we'd do."

"You should have told me. I'm in this, too, you know. My life's on the line too."

"I'm very aware of that, Cici." His eyes darkened, his brows lowering. "It's why I'm here, to keep you alive. And I don't plan to gamble in the hope that your father's driver can get us to safety."

She crossed her arms. "Instead, you're adding one more felony to my future rap sheet."

"Better a rap sheet than a toe tag." He slung his duffel over his shoulder. "Let's go, and try to keep your voice down."

She wanted to argue. She wanted to stay right there in that safe and air-conditioned library until her daddy rescued her from all this craziness. She was hungry and irritated and... scared.

She snatched her purse. "You're insufferable, all 'Ooh, I'm a SEAL, trust my gut.' Your gut's gonna land us in prison."

"And your mouth's gonna get us caught." His eyes dipped to her lips and held there a beat too long.

Her body warmed under his regard. He was mad at her, and she wasn't feeling all fuzzy and warm toward him, either. But that didn't lessen the zing of attraction between them—a zing he must've felt, too, the way his cheeks reddened.

He headed for the door, not looking back. "Move."

She followed, cursing bossy ex-SEALs and their felonious fetishes.

The library's quiet halls felt too serene for the chaos in her chest. They slipped out a side exit—no alarms, fortunately—and cut across a side street, the late afternoon sun casting long shadows.

Asher led her down a residential road as if he had a plan.

She was too tired to argue anymore. Frankly, she was just tired. She wanted to rest. She wanted to eat a nice meal and go to sleep. Was that too much to ask? Meanwhile, her bodyguard looked and acted like he could go another three days without closing his eyes. The man was strong and competent and had more energy than four Cici's plus a Brooklynn.

So she trudged behind him silently, praying he knew what he was doing.

He finally slowed down the street from a giant brick house complete with wings and...a sign out front, which told her it wasn't a house at all. It was a museum.

"Probably not the best place to steal a car." She tried to add levity to the remark.

"I'm trying to find a way *not* to steal a car."

"That would be better."

He looked at her, one corner of his mouth tipping up. "I'm afraid you're not going to think that if I manage this."

Without explaining his cryptic remark, he dropped his pack in a narrow spot between two giant bushes. "Sit there, please. I'll be right back."

"Where are you going?" But before she finished the question, he was gone, walking along the sidewalk as if he belonged. She settled on top of his duffel bag, losing sight of him.

As frustrating as she found him sometimes, it was disconcerting being alone. What if those guys tracked her here? She still had the handgun Asher'd given her, tucked away in her bag. She pulled it out, ensured the safety was engaged, and then stuck it in her waistband at the small of her back. It was cold and hard and didn't make her feel any safer at all.

Worry morphed to fear, and panic was right on its heels by the time Asher returned, his footsteps sounding seconds before he peeked between the bushes. "Come on."

"To?"

"Just trust me, Cici. We don't have time to argue about this."

She hadn't planned to kick up her heels. She just wanted to know his plan. Apparently, that was too much to ask. She stood, hiking her purse over her shoulder. He grabbed his pack and led the way down the street, then across toward a pickup parallel parked on a side street near the museum. It had New Hampshire plates.

"I'm thinking they're here to see the museum," Asher explained, "and then they'll go home."

"What if they're here for the weekend?"

"Then we'll find another ride. But at least we'll have lost your thugs."

They weren't *her* thugs, but she knew what he meant.

They reached the back of the truck. The bed had a cover to

protect what was beneath. After a furtive look around, Asher opened the tailgate.

No luggage inside, but there were tools, lumber, and other construction supplies.

Asher set to work moving them to one side of the bed. When he'd made sufficient space, he motioned her in. "I'll get something soft for us to rest on, but we need to shut that tailgate."

This was crazy.

They were going to...to stow away? On that hard metal for who knew how long?

She could already feel the bruises on her hips. But she was the one who'd argued against stealing another car. She couldn't exactly go back on that now.

She climbed up and crawled past Asher—there was barely enough room for him, much less both of them.

He closed the tailgate, plunging them into darkness and cutting off the only source of fresh air.

The space was hot as a sauna.

"This is crazy."

"Shh." His whisper was barely audible. "They could return at any time."

"Or not at all."

He sighed, the sound loud in the silence.

She was being difficult. She hated being difficult, but she was even less fond of torture, and at the moment, this felt like torture.

The sound of a zipper opening was followed by the whoosh of cloth, she guessed, rubbing against the hard floor.

Then something soft landed in her lap.

"Spread that out." His voice was barely audible. "We'll lie on top of it."

"Okay." She tried to match his volume. Spreading a blanket

beneath where she was sitting was no easy task, especially with the low ceiling. Finally, she got it done.

Asher handed her a couple more things, also soft. Sweatshirts, she guessed. "For our heads."

She folded them and placed them near the cab.

"Come on." He stretched out beside her. "Let's get comfortable."

Right. Seemed impossible, but why not try? She was tired enough to rest anywhere at this point.

She settled on the blanket—how did he have a blanket?—and bunched the sweatshirt beneath her head.

Asher lay beside her. His shoulders were so wide that she had to scoot down to find room.

"Sorry about that," he whispered, like he could control his own size.

"You should be, space hog."

That earned a low chuckle.

They were quiet for a few minutes. Cici was trying to get comfortable on the hard truck bed, and so, she assumed, was Asher. The blanket helped, but not much. They both kept shifting, moving this way and that. Bumping each other. Every touch brought a fresh jolt of awareness. It was almost too hot in the space to enjoy Asher's closeness. Almost.

Flat on his back, he stilled, exhaling as if he'd given up. "I'm guessing your cousin's plane is a little more comfortable than this." His voice was a low rumble beside her, though his sarcasm was evident.

"Only by a few degrees."

Another chuckle, one she felt as much as heard.

"I'll admit," she said, "a stolen car would have been less…"

"Agonizing?" he supplied.

"But I'm not complaining," she was quick to say. "We're off our feet, and we're…safe?" Against her will, her voice pitched up at the end like a question, revealing fear she hadn't wanted him to hear.

"We are, Cici. We're safe. Worst case scenario, the owner finds us and kicks us out." He shifted again. "Do you mind if I...?" His arm stretched across the truck bed above her head. "I just need to—"

"It's fine." It gave her a little more space, a little air between them. The air was refreshing, but a tiny part of her missed the contact with him.

A voice outside had them both stilling. It was a man, answered by a woman.

The truck beeped, and then doors opened.

She felt Asher's tension rising. He was preparing for a fight.

The truck jostled as people climbed in. New voices, too. Kids, maybe?

Doors slammed, the truck roared to life, and then they started moving. Heading...somewhere, hopefully north, toward Maine. But wherever they landed, they'd have escaped their pursuers.

Though the thought brought relief, her fear was still there. Somehow, the men following them kept finding them. And they had no idea how.

CHAPTER TWELVE

Asher shifted in the cramped bed of the pickup truck, the metal floor beneath him digging into his back. The cover overhead trapped the heat, but a small gap let in a trickle of cool air, easing the stifling warmth that had roasted them before they'd started moving.

He didn't know where they were and wasn't about to fire up his cell phone to find out. They were going fast, so he guessed they'd started on I-95, which ran just south of Concord. Whether they were still on that interstate or had merged onto I-93, he had no idea.

Cici had fallen asleep a few minutes after the truck started moving. She was curled up on the blanket, her back spooned against his ribs, her strawberry-blond hair fanning over his arm. It felt a little too good, having her tucked there, trusting him so completely.

He'd tried, at first, to strategize. Where would they end up, how would they get somewhere safe, how would they contact Forbes without leaving a trail, what should they do next? He'd tried to work out how the thugs kept finding them. Problem was, he didn't have enough information. After a while, exhaustion had dulled his mind. He'd given up, closed his eyes, and let himself rest and savor Cici's nearness.

He'd never been so affected by a woman. Even back in high school when he'd felt drawn to Cici, his attraction hadn't been this powerful. The feeling that should be long gone had grown stronger. This wasn't just attraction—he'd met his share of gorgeous women—but an overwhelming need to protect. Not because he was being paid to, but because she was precious.

Soon enough, she'd wake up, and he'd need to climb back into his armor and guard himself. His attraction to Cici was unique, which meant she had a unique ability to wound him.

The wound she'd inflicted a decade before still smarted.

They'd been driving for more than an hour when the truck slowed and made a sharp turn, surprising him. He slid and bumped against the plywood, nearly toppling the pile.

He lifted his free arm to keep it from clattering on top of them, breathing through a sudden burst of adrenaline.

Somehow, Cici still slept.

When he was sure the pile was secure, he settled again.

Beneath him, the tires bounced over asphalt. The way grew rougher, twisting through bends, jostling them with every bump. Asher needed to be ready for whatever happened next. But for all he knew, they had an hour of driving ahead. Maybe more.

He hated to wake Cici, and they were still moving at a good clip. If they slowed to residential-area speed, he'd wake her up. That would be his clue.

After another twenty minutes, the truck slowed, turned suddenly, and rolled to a stop.

So much for Asher's plan.

Doors opened, bringing the low murmur of voices, too low to make out until one cut through.

"Call the pizzas in," a man said, "and I'll pick them up. Be right back."

Asher waited until the truck started moving again, then propped up on one elbow and gently shook Cici's shoulder. "Cici, wake up." He bent to whisper into her ear, prepared to drop his hand over her mouth to keep her quiet. Hopefully, that wouldn't be necessary.

Though it was too dark to see, he knew when she came awake by the tension in her shoulders.

"Oh, I'm sorry, I didn't—"

"Shh." His voice was low, and she silenced. "Scooch up closer to the cab. Be ready."

"For what?"

"Anything."

He imagined her making a face at him or rolling her eyes, but it was too dark to see her reaction. After she moved, he pulled his Glock from its holster, the weight of it grounding him, then sat up, hunched over, and faced the tailgate, putting himself between Cici and danger.

She tugged on the blanket they'd used as a bed, and he shifted to let her slide it out from beneath him.

"Give me the sweatshirts," she whispered.

He handed the items they'd used as pillows back to her, and she shoved them into his pack.

He settled the gun on his lap and waited.

They drove ten minutes over bumpy ground that only got bumpier, which felt wrong. What restaurant would be at the end of a road like this?

Asher's pulse ticked up, every sound amplified—the rumble of the truck, the whir of the tires on asphalt, which shifted to something else. By the high pitched, irregular pings off the bottom of the pickup, he guessed they were on a gravel or dirt road. They inched forward, and the engine cut off.

A door opened and slammed, the sound sharp in the stillness.

Then, silence. No traffic, no voices, just an eerie void that pressed against his ears. His body coiled, his Glock aimed at the tailgate.

Behind him, Cici's breath was shallow. She could feel it, too.

Something was wrong.

A loud click, and the tailgate suddenly dropped, but nobody stood there. Fresh, cool air filled the stifling space.

"I'm not going to hurt you." The man's voice was calm and steady.

Asher wasn't sure about that, but he tucked his weapon beneath his T-shirt, the barrel cool against his skin. If necessary, he could fire through the material.

He prayed it wouldn't come to that.

A man peeked, barely in sight long enough for Asher to get a read on him. Tall, short brown hair, forties. He was out of sight again when he said, "You two comfortable back there?"

"Cozy as a coffin," Asher said. "Though we need a candle for ambiance."

The man chuckled. "I've got backup on speed dial." He didn't sound amused now. "I'm not going to hurt you. Can you promise the same?"

"Yes, sir." The *sir* felt right. By the way the guy spoke, he was accustomed to being in charge.

"It wasn't so much a shift when we turned off the highway, but the lack thereof. I didn't secure the lumber well enough, and it moved around a lot on our way to Mass. Knew something wasn't right." The owner of the truck must've pressed a button because the cover whirred above, moving back slowly.

Asher sat up straight and inhaled the cool air, reveling in the breeze against his sweat-dampened skin. They were in a forest, surrounded by tall pines rising to the blue sky.

Behind him, Cici said, "That's much better. Thank you."

The man stood to the side. Though Asher couldn't see a weapon from his vantage point, he assumed one was there.

Asher noted the way he held himself—shoulders back, weight balanced. Like a cop. This guy's instincts were sharp, dangerously so.

"You two running from the law?" His question was casual, as if it didn't matter to him one way or another. Asher doubted that.

"Not...exactly." Asher hated lying, but he didn't know this guy. Still, something about him felt... trustworthy. "We've been on the run." He recited the short version of events, leaving out the stolen car and burning barn. "People are trying to kill us. We just needed a way out."

The man's expression didn't change. "I'm not one of those people out to hurt you, so you can holster that gun."

Asher's pulse skipped. He hadn't shown the Glock, but this guy knew it was there. "You first."

The man moved in front of the tailgate and held his arm out to his side, a gun dangled from it, proving Asher's instincts correct.

Asher stowed his, moving carefully.

The man tucked his own away, his eyes flicking past him to Cici. "You okay back there?"

"Yes, sir." Cici's voice was steady despite the tension in the air. "Asher's my bodyguard."

"That story he just told... All that true?"

"Unfortunately."

Asher met his gaze. "I'm Asher Rhodes. I'm with GBPA out of Boston. I'm going to get my credentials." With slow and deliberate movement, he managed to shove his hand in his back pocket and pull out his wallet. From there, he extracted a business card. "Call them. Check me out."

The man took the card. "Wait there." He pocketed the card, then tapped on his cell. A moment later, he lifted it to his ear.

He hadn't trusted Asher's business card, had instead looked up GBPA's number online. He was savvy, this guy.

The man said, "I'd like to speak to..."

"Bartlett," Asher supplied.

"A man regarding the employment of Asher Rhodes," the stranger said.

He hadn't asked for Bartlett—still not trusting Asher—but Bartlett would be the one to answer the call.

In the silence, Cici started to say something, but Asher shook his head. He wanted to hear every word.

"Afternoon. Name's Brady Thomas, chief of police in Nutfield, New Hampshire."

Brady Thomas. Interesting name for a guy from New England. Asher figured he'd gotten a lot of ribbing over the years about that. No matter how good he was at football, he'd never be as good as the quarterback who flipped his name.

He was a cop, of course. And why not? Nothing else had gone right for him and Cici.

That wasn't true, though. They were in New Hampshire, so that bet had paid off. And they'd shaken the killers, for now.

"I've got a guy here who claims to work for you," Chief Thomas said. "Name's Asher Rhodes. He's with a woman called..." He listened, then looked at Cici. "Name?"

"Cecelia Wright."

Thomas focused on the call again. "Yup, that's her. They stowed away in the back of my pickup. I was in... Right. Took the kids to the historical sites down there." The man took a few steps back, nodding at something Bartlett must've said. He motioned for Asher and Cici to get out of the truck.

Thank God. Asher's legs were cramping. He scooted out

first, then helped Cici down. She stretched like a cat, and he tried not to enjoy the sight. He failed.

They were on a narrow dirt road barely wide enough for the pickup, dwarfed by towering trees. Asher did a slow circle. Nothing but forest in every direction. The sun was low in the sky. They couldn't be more than an hour from sunset.

"Don't need a reward." Thomas was talking to Bartlett, pacing a few feet away. "Just wanted to make sure..." More listening, then, "As long as I get it back or get... I see. Okay, I can do that."

Hopefully, Bartlett was arranging for transportation, though at the moment, what Asher wanted more than anything else was dinner.

"Sure," Thomas said. "I'll take care of it."

Asher took a few steps toward him. "Chief."

The cop turned, spying Asher's outstretched arm.

"Mind if I talk to him?"

He handed over the phone, and Asher said, "It's me."

"You two safe?" Bartlett sounded calm, which was a nice surprise.

"For now." He gave his boss a quick update on everything that had happened since they'd last spoken. "We needed to shake the tail."

"You remember what I told you?" Bartlett asked. "We need this client. We need to do this job well with minimal screw-ups. Which is the opposite of what you've done so far."

As if Asher should worry about the fate of the company. He walked away, lowering his voice. "She's still alive. The necklace is still with us. You tell me what I should have done differently."

That brought a beat of silence. "I wasn't there."

"That's right, you weren't, so you're going to have to trust me." Asher didn't appreciate being second-guessed. He might not have worked for GBPA for long, but he'd always gotten the job done and done well. He was good at what he did. The fact that they were still alive proved that.

"I'll trust you when you quit dillydallying and get her home," Bartlett said.

Dillydallying? He sounded like Asher's late grandmother.

"What's your plan?" Bartlett demanded.

"Still making our way there. I think the client has a mole, told Cici's father to tell him in person, which he said he'd do."

"That would explain how they keep finding you."

"Gavin Wright sent a car for us in Concord, which we didn't wait for. Call and tell him we're safe, and tell Forbes the same, but nothing else."

"Done. You got a clean phone?"

"Yup. A few of them."

"Good. Be safe out there." Bartlett ended the call, and Asher handed the cell back to the police chief. "Thank you."

"I can get you wheels," Thomas said, "but probably not for a few hours. I'd have one of my guys drive you somewhere, but we're short-staffed as it is. Can't spare anyone tonight."

"A car would be great. We've been on the road—"

"And on the run," Cici added. She'd been unusually quiet since they'd stopped.

"That too." Asher glanced in her direction. She looked okay, a little pale, maybe. "What we really need is a place to rest," he said. "A cabin, somewhere remote. Somewhere we can regroup. Rustic is fine, as long as there's Wi-Fi. Any suggestions?"

"I can get you that. And a hot meal."

"You read my mind."

"More like heard your stomach growling." The man smiled, setting Asher at ease. "Stretch, move around. I'm gonna make another call." Thomas walked away, and Asher turned to Cici.

"You okay?"

"A little groggy. Sorry if I..." Her cheeks pinked, and she dipped her chin. "I managed to get some sleep."

"I noticed. You were drooling."

"Was not." She grinned. "Anyway, sorry if I got too comfortable."

She'd curled up beside him like a kitten, and he hadn't minded one bit, though it seemed safer not to say that. "Glad you got some rest."

"Did you?"

"If the chief comes through with a place, I'll sleep tonight."

They walked deeper into the woods along the narrow path, chatting about nothing important—mostly food, proving she was as hungry as he was—then returned to the truck to find Thomas seated on the tailgate. The three of them waited in strangely comfortable silence until a second man arrived driving a Camry —tall, fifties, with the same cop-like bearing.

"This is a friend of mine," Chief Thomas said, "Garrison."

The man sized them up, then regarded the chief. "You into human smuggling now?"

"Something like that." But he was smiling. "I'll explain later."

"Gotcha." Garrison motioned to the sedan. "Climb in."

Asher shook the chief's hand. "Thanks. We appreciate this."

Cici thanked him, too, while Asher stowed his duffel bag in the trunk. He opened the passenger door for her.

After she settled, her purse in her lap, Asher sat in the back beside a brown paper bag that filled the car with delectable scents. Something fried, and maybe a hamburger?

He hoped the food was for them.

Garrison drove about fifteen minutes before turning off the narrow country road and parking in front of a log cabin deep in the woods.

He shut the car off. "My wife owns this place, so be careful with it."

"We will." Asher opened the door and climbed out.

Cici stood, too, and gazed around. The world was awash in greens and browns, all pines and oaks with the occasional white birch to brighten it up. There were no other cabins in sight. "Thank you so much for letting us use it. For everything. You have no idea what this means to us."

The man smiled at her. "Happy to help."

Garrison gave them the food, along with a couple of grocery sacks he'd stowed in the trunk. He handed Asher a folded piece of paper. "If you need help."

Asher angled the phone number toward Cici, who said, "We're trying not to use our phones."

"There's Wi-Fi. Call over the internet, or even text. All the info is in a binder on the kitchen counter. Someone will be back tomorrow. Not sure if they'll drive you somewhere or bring you a car or what. Brady's working on it."

Asher dropped his duffel so he could shake Garrison's hand. "We're grateful for you and your friend. You might've saved our lives."

The man grinned, nodding to Cici. "No trouble at all. Have a good night." He jogged back to his sedan and drove away.

Asher pushed open the door and followed Cici into a cozy little haven—bare log walls, a stone fireplace, and a beige couch and love seat facing a round coffee table. The living room bled into the kitchen, a small, efficient space with a big table off to one side. Through the windows on the back wall, he spied a patio and, beyond that, a small pond.

It was idyllic.

Asher set the bag of food on the counter, his shoulders loosening. They'd survived another day. They were safe, for now.

∽

The sun dipped low, casting a golden glow over the small pond beyond the screened-in patio where Asher and Cici sat, the cool evening air a relief after the truck's stifling heat. The forest added a melody of croaking frogs and buzzing insects batting against the mesh between them and the night. Fireflies flickered around bushes on the edge of the property, growing brighter as twilight deepened.

Garrison and Chief Thomas had supplied a feast—a burger, a chicken sandwich, onion rings, french fries, a container of rich clam chowder, and a couple of oversized cookies.

Cici claimed the chicken sandwich, Asher took the burger, and they poured the soup into two bowls, sharing the fries and rings. They sipped lemonade they'd found in one of the grocery sacks, not talking much beyond remarking on the meal. This place reminded him of where he'd grown up. Not the cabin itself, which might be small but was much nicer than the trailer he and his family had called home. The land, though. The forest, the sounds, the smells. All of it brought back memories of Asher's childhood, climbing trees with his brother, or catching lightning bugs and trying to keep them in a jar. They'd poke holes in the metal top and enjoy them for a few hours. Amazingly, the little bugs always managed to escape by morning.

In retrospect, he'd realized Mom had let the poor creatures go after Asher and Drew went to bed.

When the last cookie had been reduced to crumbs, he pulled a laptop from his duffel bag.

"What else do you have in there?" Cici eyed his bag. "A rocket launcher? A three-course meal? A parachute?"

"If I'd had food, I'd have scarfed it down hours ago."

"Hmm. I noticed you didn't deny the rocket launcher and parachute."

Chuckling, he set up the laptop and connected to the cabin's Wi-Fi.

"Should you do that?" Her joking tone was gone as she straightened. "They can track your IP address."

"I've got a VPN. A virtual private—"

"I know what it is. You sure it's secure?"

He gave her a look intended to convey *This isn't my first rodeo.*

When she said nothing else, he opened his email and found a message from Bartlett that contained a link to an online folder. It was packed with lists, mugshots, and articles about people involved in or suspected of being involved in Philly's organized crime.

"Whatcha got?" Cici asked.

"Bartlett came through." He angled the screen so she could see, and she scooted closer to study the information.

Asher clicked through each file quickly. When nothing jumped out, he slowed down, studying each mug shot.

None looked familiar to him.

Cici shook her head. "Maybe the guys following us aren't organized crime?"

"Maybe." He gazed at the photos on the screen. "They're definitely organized, and definitely criminals, so this seemed like the place to start." He clicked on one of the lists, then began the painstaking task of pasting each name into Google and searching for a photo.

There were hundreds of names.

They'd gone through about ten when he stifled a yawn.

"I feel the same way." Cici sat back, frustration etching her face. "We're never going to find him like this. Can you cross-reference the names with Maine?"

Asher raised an eyebrow. "Why Maine?"

"That's where Forbes's parents lived, where the necklace

was stolen. It just makes sense that the thief is from there, or somewhere in Northern New England. New Hampshire, Vermont?"

"You're assuming the man tracking you stole the necklace. What if he bought it from the thief?"

"No." She spoke the word as if there were no doubt. "The necklace never hit the black market. If the thief sold it, then he had to have known the buyer personally, and the buyer would have to have been willing to spend money on a piece of jewelry he could never showcase, a collector who didn't care about showing off his collection. Those people exist, but they're rare. Usually, when something as famous as The Crimson Duchess is stolen, the thief already has a buyer lined up, but this was a crime of convenience. I'd bet money the thief has held onto it all these years."

Asher started to argue, but she lifted her hand to put him off. "Plus, the guy murdered the store owner when he could've just asked to buy the piece back. No, I'm convinced it was one of the smugglers, an accomplice in the Ballentine murders. He wanted his necklace back, but mostly, he didn't want to be linked to a double homicide. He needed to destroy all of Mr. D's records. Would someone guilty of buying stolen property cover up that minor crime—relatively speaking—by committing murder and arson? I don't think so."

"Then why sell it in the first place?"

She rubbed her lips together. "He didn't sell it. He said that his son had worked with the other clerk—Mr. D's niece. I'm guessing the son stole the items from his dad and sold them to the jewelry store."

"Let's go back, though." Not that Asher didn't agree with Cici, but he wanted to look at this from every angle. "You're assuming the theft of the necklace was...what did you call it? A crime of convenience. But what if the Ballentine murders were related to the necklace? What if the necklace was the reason for the murders?"

"We know why the Ballentines were targeted, and it had nothing to do with jewelry."

Asher let his raised eyebrows ask the obvious question. The crime had happened in his hometown, so he'd read about the recent developments in the old murder case. But if the authorities knew the murderers' motives, that information hadn't been released to the press.

"Forbes's father was a confidential informant," Cici explained. "He was gathering intel on a smuggling ring that operated through an inlet—you remember the Haunted Inlet?"

Asher nodded. Like everyone else in town, he'd heard the stories.

"Charles Ballentine was being coerced into letting the smugglers operate on his property. He agreed, but then he passed intel along to an FBI agent."

"They're holding that information close to the vest."

"Still trying to gather up everyone who was involved at the time."

"But you know it because...?"

"Because Brooklynn is dating Forbes. It's a long story, but they've discovered two of the people involved in his parents' deaths. One is dead and the other is in critical condition."

"Meaning he's not talking."

"She. But yes, she's not talking. They're still trying to round up everyone else. They're keeping what they know quiet because they don't want those people to go to ground."

Asher considered that. "So you're saying the Ballentines were killed because the smugglers found out he betrayed them? The father?"

"Right. The killers and their accomplices searched the

house after the murders. The necklace must have been found during that search."

"Was it just...lying around?"

Her head tilted to the side, her eyes scrunching. "If memory serves, Charles and Grace Ballentine had gone to some kind of charity function where she'd worn it. My guess is they hadn't returned it to the safe yet."

"So the smugglers...murderers were looking for something else—"

"Evidence Charles Ballentine had collected—"

" and stumbled upon the necklace."

"Exactly." Cici dipped her head to punctuate the point. "A crime of convenience. I'm guessing the thief pocketed the things and never told the rest of the crew or...whatever you call a band of smugglers. I think he figured he'd take all the profit, but then he realized what he had and got spooked. He was afraid to sell it, so he just hid it."

"You think it's been...what? Shoved in the back of a drawer?"

"That's exactly what I think. Hold on. I'll show you." She went inside and returned with the velvet pouch. She pulled out The Crimson Duchess. "See how unused it is?"

She held it out to him, so Asher took it, surprised by its weight. All those diamonds and rubies. He'd never touched an item so valuable. He tried to see it like Cici did, but he had no idea what she was talking about. It looked like any other necklace to him. It didn't help that the sun had set. Aside from the light from the computer screen, they were sitting in the dark.

He found a light switch near the door, which illuminated the low-wattage bulbs in the ceiling fixture. He stood beneath it to study the necklace. "Can you show me what you mean?"

She picked out something from the velvet pouch and joined him, raising the item to the light. "This is silver."

It was a heart-shaped locket. He was pretty sure silver wasn't generally the color of a flat black chalkboard. "Are you sure you're a professional?"

She laughed, the sound so lighthearted that he couldn't help but smile. "You know how you keep jewelry from tarnishing? By wearing it. I'd guess this hasn't been worn in years, which is why it's so dark. If we had polish, we could make it shine." She set the locket back on the table and lifted the necklace from his hand. "It's not as obvious with this because the metal is gold. The purer the gold, the less it tarnishes. And of course the gold is outshined by the gemstones. But you see how brassy it looks? It's not as yellow as gold should be. And look here." She shifted it so the clasp was on top.

He tried to see what she meant, really he did. Maybe there was a little spot of something there, but he wouldn't testify to it. "I'm not sure."

"I can get out my jeweler's loupe—"

"I'll take your word for it. What's your point?"

"The tarnish tells me this hasn't been worn—or cared for," she continued. "Which tells me the owner knew it was stolen, knew it was recognizable, and didn't dare let anyone see it." She reached for the laptop. "Can I check something?"

"Have at it."

"I know other things were taken from Forbes's parents, but I don't remember..." Her voice trailed as she searched the internet. "Here we go." The screen displayed a few items. "A Cartier watch, a pair of ruby-and-diamond earrings, and a matching tennis bracelet. She probably wore them all to the charity event." Cici spread all the items from the velvet bag onto the table. Most of the pieces looked like junk, at least compared to The Crimson Duchess.

Cici plucked earrings, then a watch and a bracelet, which he assumed had also been stolen from the Ballentines' property.

"Those things aren't nearly as valuable," Asher guessed.

"Maybe not, but the earrings are distinctive."

"How so?"

She held them out for him to see. "The diamonds are around two carats apiece. Usually, with a design like this—a big centerpiece gem, then smaller gems surrounding it—the more affordable stone is the centerpiece. This is flipped, with diamonds in the center. In fact, if this piece was made in the eighties or after, then these diamonds could be laser-etched."

"Meaning?"

"They'd have ID numbers etched into them, small enough that they're only visible with a magnifying glass."

He hadn't known jewelers could do that.

"The point is, the thief was smart to hold onto them. If he'd sold them, he might have gotten caught." Cici returned the Ballentines' possessions and the rest to the velvet bag.

"What else is in there?" He nodded to the jewelry stash. "Anything good?"

"I've only glanced inside, but I saw nothing else that stood out. Nothing like The Crimson Duchess. What do you think?" She rubbed her bare arms in the cool air. "Is there a way to check the list your boss sent to see if anyone's from Maine?"

Right. Back to business, Asher pulled the laptop closer. "And has a son."

"Good point." She stood. "If we can't do it, I can ask Alyssa."

"I can do it." He certainly didn't need Cici's sister's help.

While Cici stepped inside, he pulled up the list Bartlett had sent and logged in to a secure database used by his company, which allowed him to cross-reference the names.

Not many had lived in Maine. Asher narrowed the search parameters to include only men between forty-five and sixty-five.

That narrowed the list even more.

He plugged the remaining names into Google, one at a time, searching for images, and found one that looked familiar. He hadn't gotten a good look at all the men outside the barn earlier that day. This could be the one who'd been issuing the orders.

The photograph looked professional, plastered to the *About the Team* page of a business that sold some kind of tech.

His name was Wendall Gagnon, sixty-three, and according to the attached dossier, he was the president and major shareholder in a company that developed software for retailers. He was clean-shaven with white hair, wide-set hazel eyes, and perfectly straight teeth.

He looked every bit the entrepreneur. No mention of a wife or family, but that didn't mean they didn't exist.

Apparently, the authorities had picked him up once, though for what, the file didn't say. Which was odd.

More odd was the fact that Gagnon had never been charged with a crime, and he seemed not to be linked to any of the other criminals on the list Bartlett had sent. It was almost as if his name had been included by accident.

The sliding door behind him opened and closed. "I got us some more…" Cici's words ended on a gasp. "You found him!"

He shifted to give her a better view of the screen. "You agree? That looks like him?"

"I can't believe you found him."

Thanks to Cici's suggestion. "Do you know the names of the suspects in the Ballentine murders?" Maybe that would help him figure out how this guy had been involved.

"Leonard Taggart. He was a cop at the time, the chief of police when he was killed last month. The other one, Lois Stratton, is still in the hospital after a gunshot wound."

"Okay, let me cross-reference those names…" Sure enough,

Gagnon had once been arrested by Taggart in Shadow Cove. "I'm betting that's how they met."

"Maybe Taggart pegged him as someone who could help." Cici shifted to face Asher. "I heard he used his position with the police to recruit, so that tracks. Now that we've found Gagnon, what do we do with this information?"

Asher saved it all, then started an email. "I'll send it to Bartlett tonight and have him get a contact in Philly for us. We can call them tomorrow." The last word came out on a yawn. "Of course, that puts you back on their radar, but I doubt you've been off. Are you okay with that?"

"Sure. I've done nothing wrong."

He finished the email and hit Send. It was a solid lead, the first step in turning the tables on Wendall Gagnon.

Soon enough, God willing, this cat-and-mouse game would be over.

Asher was tired of being hunted. It was time to become the hunter.

CHAPTER THIRTEEN

The laptop closed with a muffled thump, blending into the chorus of frogs and crickets outside the cabin's screened-in patio.

They'd both taken quick showers. Now, Cici sipped her lemonade, enjoying the sweet tang.

Beside her, Asher's face was lit by the faint glow from the overhead light. The air was cool now, a relief after the stifling heat of the truck. Her skin prickled with goose bumps, and maybe a little fear, which came from seeing the face of the man who'd murdered Mr. D, a reminder of the danger they were in.

"We need to figure out how Gagnon and his goons keep finding us." Asher's voice was low and steady.

"I thought you were convinced it was someone in Forbes's operation." Though Cici wasn't sure she agreed.

"I am. The question is, who is it? How can we smoke them out?"

"I'm not disagreeing with you, but if a mole is behind this, then how did they find us at the barn? How did they know we got on a train? Forbes didn't know those things."

Asher leaned back, thinking it through. "The Philly train

station was near where I ditched the truck. They know who you are and where you're from, so they must've assumed we'd head north and east. The train to Boston was a solid theory. And who knows that they didn't send men to intercept other trains that left last night?"

How could it have only been the night before?

"Do you think he has that many men at his disposal?"

"No way of knowing."

"But Gagnon himself was at the barn, meaning he'd been reasonably confident he would find us near the airfield."

"Which is why I suspect a mole. Someone told them we were going to Hanscom. They were watching for us. There weren't that many hiding places on that road, so the barn was a logical spot to check after we tried to lose them."

That made sense. She swallowed hard, the memory of those men closing in sending a shiver down her spine. "We need to figure out who the rest of those guys are. Maybe there's some connection to...somebody. Maybe organized crime. We need to know what we're dealing with."

"You saw the same photos as I did. Did any of them look familiar?"

They hadn't, which seemed odd to her. Where had Gagnon hired all those men? "I need to call my sister and see if she can identify the men who've been following us."

Asher smirked. "How in the world could she do that?"

Cici wasn't sure, but now that it had occurred to her, she realized that if anybody could track them down, Alyssa could. She reached for the cell phone Asher had left sitting on the table.

He cupped his hand over hers, the connection sending awareness through her body. "Wait. Seriously, how could she possibly—"

"Traffic cams? She has resources."

"But..." Asher didn't move his hand. She could practically hear his gears spinning, looking for a reason why her idea was bad.

"We can trust my sister."

"I'm not saying... It's just, Gagnon knows who you are. He might be tracking her."

"Alyssa used to work for the NSA. She knows how to keep her activity hidden."

Another moment passed before he slid his hand off hers. "Okay. Go ahead."

She dialed her sister's number and, when Alyssa answered, explained what she was looking for.

"Best option is CCTV outside the police station." Alyssa didn't waste any time with niceties, worries, advice, or silly *How you holding up?* questions. She got right to work, the sound of typing carrying through the phone. "Can you give me the address?"

"I don't remember. It was a huge building, though, not far from downtown."

"Here's one on Broad Street," Alyssa said.

"That sounds right."

"What time Friday?"

"Late afternoon...around four, I think. And then they found us again yesterday. Hold on a sec." She focused on Asher. "Where were we yesterday when they caught up with us?"

He navigated to a map on his laptop and read off the name of the street and the cross streets.

"Got it," Alyssa said. "Doubt there are cameras there, but they had to get there somehow. Any chance you got a license plate number?"

Asher shook his head.

"No. It was a green Ford pickup truck," she said. "Four

doors, newer model, and a beige Honda Accord. I'd guess eight to ten years old."

Asher's eyebrows hiked, like he was impressed she'd observed so much.

"Would have been between eleven thirty and noon," Cici added.

"All right," Alyssa said. "If they went through any major intersections, I'll find them. I can call you back at this number?"

Asher shook his head.

"I'll call you tomorrow from a fresh burner."

"Call in the evening. That'll give me time to find what we're looking for."

"Will do. Thanks, sis." Cici ended the call, thankful she'd done something to help, even if that was only reaching out to someone smarter than she was.

"You really think she can ID them?" Asher asked.

"If there are cameras that picked up those guys' faces, Alyssa will find them. Even if she just gets license plate numbers, that'll help, right?"

He shrugged. "Can't hurt."

"I've been thinking." She gazed at the burner on the table. "We were talking about how those guys found us. What if they were tracking your phone? That would explain how they didn't catch up to us in Concord after you'd dumped it in the swamp."

"Right." He nodded slowly. "But that still circles back to Forbes. He's the only one who had my name and number. No one else knew who I was."

"True, but..." She straightened, a new thought hitting her. Scaring her. "What about GBPA? Could someone there have—?"

"Not a chance." Asher waved the idea away like it was ridiculous.

"Okay..." She didn't want to argue, but Asher wasn't perfect.

And neither were the people at his company, no matter how much he respected them. "Forbes is a billionaire. It's possible he has enemies he's not even aware of. People like him—and maybe some of his rivals—have deep pockets. Pockets deep enough to turn even the most loyal—"

"We protect people like Forbes all the time." He shifted, leaning back. "I trust my team, Cici. I trust Bartlett with my life."

"Okay, but maybe someone else—"

"There's no reason for anyone at GBPA to turn." The words were hard and confident.

"Money is always a good reason."

Asher took a breath and blew it out. She sensed his frustration, and maybe he was right. His judgment had kept them alive so far.

On the other hand, they needed to consider all the possibilities.

"The leaks are coming from Forbes or his people." He spoke the words slowly, as if she were too dull to understand. "I'm not taking you to him until we know who it is."

"Forbes is independent. I can't imagine he's sharing details about what we're doing with anybody."

Asher rolled his eyes, one side of his mouth tugging up. "Come on, Cici. He's a billionaire. You think he's booking charter flights and hiring security all by himself?"

"Billionaires are capable of making phone calls." Even as she said the words, she remembered... "Brooklynn did say something about an assistant."

"Just one? He probably has a butler and a valet and who knows how many staff."

"He doesn't. He lives in a hotel because his house is being rebuilt. He's a nice, normal guy."

"Mmm-hmm."

"Anyway." She was careful to keep her tone even. No sense arguing tonight. "We should email Forbes so he's warned."

"Won't work. If the assistant sees it, he'll know we're onto him. I had your father warn him. For now, we need to go dark."

She blinked, caught off guard by how quickly he'd shut her idea down. Then his expression shifted, a shadow of doubt crossing his face. "Unless...what if the leak is Forbes himself? Maybe he doesn't want the necklace back. Maybe he's hiding something."

"And trying to have me killed? No way." She couldn't help the defensiveness that seeped into her tone. Forbes was practically part of her family now, soon to be her brother-in-law, if his relationship with Brooklynn progressed the way everyone guessed it would. "Forbes risked his life to get justice for his parents' murders. He's not playing some kind of game here. He wants that necklace back, and he wants the person who stole it to face justice."

Her irritation must've seeped into her tone because Asher raised his hands. "All right, fair enough. Just brainstorming. You never know with rich people."

What? What was he talking about?

She'd been trying not to argue with him, but that remark had her irritation flaring. "Money doesn't make a person trustworthy or untrustworthy. Generous or greedy. Kind or cruel. My mom comes from old money, and she's the kindest, most trustworthy, most generous person I know. I've met plenty of selfish rich people, but I've met a lot more selfish middle-class and poor people." Though, to be fair, those were much larger groups. "You can't judge someone's character by their bank account."

His gaze hardened, something bitter flickering in his eyes. "Maybe not, but it builds walls. You of all people should know that."

"What's that supposed to mean?"

Asher's voice dropped to a near whisper. "We were 'friends.'" The word dripped with scorn, his finger pointing from her to him and back. "But only up to a point. You knew who I was, where I came from, and that knowledge separated us."

"What are you talking about?"

"Oh, don't pretend you don't remember. You and your sisters and your mom on your little charity run, bringing Christmas gifts to my family. You saw where I lived, the rusty trailer."

Her heart stuttered, shock washing over her.

The Wrights had always sponsored a local family at Christmastime. Mom would get a wish list from the church, and Cici and her sisters would have a blast shopping, crossing off every item on that list.

And then, every year, they'd deliver the wrapped presents. It was her favorite Christmas tradition.

She remembered the year they'd ventured into that rundown trailer park. She remembered dingy siding and a dilapidated front porch. She'd been sitting in the back seat of the SUV as Mom and Alyssa carried the gifts to the front porch. Cici and her sisters had wanted to go, too, but Mom insisted they wait in the car.

She hadn't understood at the time, but she did now. What for them was an act of love and generosity was, for the recipients, a moment of shame.

Not that it should have been. Not everybody was blessed with financial resources. And people went through hard times. Her parents had drilled that lesson into Cici and her sisters, reminding them often that money didn't make them who they were.

"You knew where I came from," Asher continued. "So our

friendship was always just you feeling...sorry for me. I never measured up."

Cici visualized the situation from a different perspective. From inside the trailer, behind the windows. "I didn't know... You lived there?"

"Oh, come on, Cici." His eyes rolled. "Don't lie. You knew."

"I wouldn't lie." She pushed back her chair and stood. "And I didn't know."

"You saw me in the window."

"I didn't. If I saw someone and I don't remember that I did—I had no idea it was you. And I don't appreciate your assumptions. Even if I had known, it wouldn't have changed anything. You were my friend."

He scoffed. "Right. Friends don't laugh when *friends* ask them to prom." He clamped his lips shut, and she had the distinct feeling he hadn't meant to say that.

The memory hit her like a slap, and her cheeks burned.

She dropped back into the chair, afraid to look up and meet his gaze. She'd buried that moment, tried to forget how cruel she'd been. "I..." Her voice caught. "That was the worst thing I've ever done to another human being. I thought...I hoped you'd forgotten."

"Forget?" His laugh was humorless. "I still have nightmares about it."

Tears welled, and she pressed a hand to her mouth. "I'm so sorry, Asher. I was young and selfish. I didn't mean to hurt you. I've replayed that moment in my head a thousand times. It's my penance. My...punishment for being so self-absorbed. Can you...?" She forced herself to meet his eyes. "Can you forgive me?"

His expression went from hard to worried in about half a second. "Oh, uh... I didn't mean to... Look, I wasn't trying to make you cry. I'm just—"

"I deserve it." She hid her face. "You're right."

"I didn't say that." He scooted closer and slipped his hands around her wrists, tugging them downward.

She didn't fight him, just lowered her hands to her lap, letting him see her tears. Her shame.

"Cici, it's okay."

"It's not okay. That night... Prom night. It was awful. It was...exactly what I deserved."

His brows lowered. "What do you mean?"

"It was only that, when you asked, Tucker Benson was listening. He was behind you, and I wanted to go to the prom with him."

"Which you did, if memory serves."

She nodded. She had gone with Tucker, the boy she'd crushed on her entire senior year. Captain of the football team, pitcher of the baseball team, and best-looking guy at Shadow Cove High.

He'd been the proverbial Big Man on Campus, compared to skinny, nerdy Asher.

What an idiot she'd been.

"What happened, Cici?"

"It doesn't matter."

"It does matter. Tell me."

She didn't want to, didn't plan to.

Until he added, "I deserve to know, don't I?"

He did. He deserved to hear the whole awful story.

"I was all dressed up and thought... Well, I thought I looked good."

"You looked beautiful." Of course he'd seen her. He'd gone to the prom with another girl.

Now, his words weren't meant as a compliment so much as agreement, an encouragement for her to hurry and spill it. His patience seemed to be hanging from a very fragile thread.

"It was fine," she said. "Not great, but, you know. Just a dance, only with fancier outfits. After, Tucker and I were supposed to go to a party, but he decided to take us...somewhere else."

He'd told her he had a surprise for her. She was excited until he pulled into the parking lot of a cheap motel. He'd rented a room.

She'd tried to be nice, always wanting everyone to like her. That was her problem. One of her problems. She had replayed what happened next a million times.

Tucker walked around to open her door, so she got out, but she didn't move. "What are we doing here?"

"What do you think?" He wagged his eyebrows.

"I think...I want to go to the party."

"Come on, baby." He tugged her hand. "We'll go after."

After. As if it was a foregone conclusion what would happen between then and *after*.

She told him no.

Somehow, he misunderstood the word or thought he could change her mind. He kissed her, he got handsy. He tried to drag her to the motel room.

She told him to stop. She tried to fight him off.

If not for the couple who pulled up in the parking lot, she didn't want to think about what would have happened.

"Cici." Asher's voice pulled her back. "What did he do?"

"Nothing. I mean, he tried, but..." She swallowed, cheeks on fire. She'd been cruel to Asher, and Tucker had been her reward.

"He tried what?" Asher's eyes flashed with fury. "I'll find him. I'll—"

"Dad took care of it."

Cici probably wouldn't have told her father, but the couple who ran Tucker off insisted on calling her parents.

She wasn't sure exactly what Dad had said to Tucker when he caught up with him, but for the rest of the school year, he'd kept his distance, and nobody had ever heard about what happened.

Dad had done that for her.

Of course, he'd also spent an hour lecturing her on all the things she could have—and apparently, should have—done differently. By the time he was done, she was pretty sure the whole thing had been her fault.

Asher took her hands. "Unless Tucker's been walking with a limp for the last ten years, your dad didn't punish him enough."

She attempted a laugh, but it was thin. "You're much kinder to me than I deserve."

"Everybody deserves kindness."

"You're right. That's exactly right. And what I did to you was cruel. It was awful, and I'm so, so sorry."

Asher stilled. A moment passed before he nodded, then leaned closer and met her eyes. "I forgive you, Cici."

No lectures? No driving the point home? No reminding her, in case she'd forgotten, what a terrible person she was? Just... forgiveness?

Apparently, because he didn't move, just held there, a few inches from her.

The air between them thickened, charged with attraction and history. He was so different from the boy she'd known. She'd always thought of him as a really smart, nerdy kid. This man, though still smart, was strong and powerful and so incredibly kind.

She'd never felt anything but friendship toward Asher when they were in school together.

What she was feeling right now was far, far from friendship.

"Thank you," she whispered.

He swallowed, then dropped her hands, pushed back, and stood. "It's late. We should sleep."

"Right." She nodded, her voice soft. "Yeah." Even if sleep was suddenly the last thing on her mind.

Asher grabbed the laptop and opened the door, waiting for her to step inside. She wanted to sit a few minutes longer on the patio, process everything they'd learned, everything that'd happened, but Asher wouldn't let her stay outside by herself.

She passed him, the heat from his body warming her skin. Despite his forgiveness, her heart was heavy with regret and something else—something that felt like longing.

Asher had forgiven her, but the past still lingered, a barrier between them.

She realized that she desperately wanted to break through.

∼

Cici woke to the soft light of dawn filtering through the cabin's gauzy curtains. The room was cozy, with log walls and a quilted bedspread that smelled faintly of pine. She stretched, feeling Asher's oversized T-shirt slide against her skin. It was longer than some dresses she owned, hanging to her knees. He'd been kind enough to share it, along with a pair of boxer shorts, which were so big she'd needed to roll them about five times to keep them from sliding down.

The clothes she'd packed for this work trip—her business slacks, her blouses, her favorite shoes—had all been in her suitcase, which they'd left at the barn. She figured everything had burned in the fire.

Clothes could be replaced, but the jewelry had been precious to her. The delicate gold necklace her grandmother had given her for her eighteenth birthday, the vintage onyx bracelet she'd bought from a jeweler in Tampa, the silver ring, one of the five she'd designed for herself and her sisters, each of their birthstones mounted along one side of the infinity symbol.

All gone, melted or stolen or charred.

But she and Asher were still breathing, and as much as she loved jewelry, what really mattered had survived.

So far, anyway.

Quietly, she slipped out of bed and tiptoed to the laundry room off the kitchen. She'd thrown her clothes into the wash the night before but had fallen asleep before moving them to the dryer.

She did that now and started it, then headed for the kitchen.

The shower was running in the other room, so she figured Asher would be out soon. She might as well get breakfast going while she waited for her clothes to dry.

The sun was still low on the horizon, painting the pond outside with golden hues. She started a pot of coffee, thankful when the rich aroma filled the air, then opened the fridge to survey their supplies: eggs, a pound of sausage, English muffins, a couple of firm apples that smelled exactly like fresh apples should, and a pint of blueberries in a cardboard container, the berries so big and fragrant that she guessed they'd come straight from a farm.

She plucked one, rinsed it, and popped it in her mouth. Sweet and tangy. She closed her eyes to savor the flavor.

By the time she was finished slicing the apples and rinsing the berries, the shower had turned off. When the coffee finished brewing, she poured a cup for herself and another for Asher, adding a generous splash of cream and three spoonsful of sugar to his, just as he'd taken it the morning before.

She was cracking eggs into a bowl when Asher walked in.

She looked up and smiled. "Good morning."

He stopped dead, his gaze sweeping over her.

"What?"

"Nothing." He swiveled and headed back to his room.

"I poured your coffee," she called after him.

He returned, grabbed the cup, and reached for the fridge. He paused when he must've noticed she'd already doctored it. He took a sip, swallowed, and muttered a grudging "Thanks" before retreating again.

What was his problem? Here she was, cooking them breakfast. What had she done to deserve his rudeness?

The answer was a splash of cold water on her irritation.

Their conversation last night must have dredged up bitter memories. It was one thing to forgive. It was an entirely different thing to forget, or to ever trust after that. Asher didn't want to be around her, and she couldn't blame him.

As she fried the sausage into patties, she drifted back to that moment years ago. She'd been obsessed with Tucker Benson, barely registering Asher's quiet presence. When Asher asked her to prom, Tucker and the other kids watched to see what she'd say. She hadn't meant to laugh at Asher. It'd just bubbled out on a wave of nerves. She'd felt no malice toward Asher, just flustered, caught off guard.

She could still see the hurt in his eyes before he walked away. Regret had stabbed her then, a self-inflicted wound that had never fully healed.

She toasted the English muffins and whisked the eggs, then cooked them as thin omelets, which she folded onto the bread. When it was finished, she went down the hall and knocked on Asher's door. "Breakfast is ready."

"Coming."

She returned to the kitchen to set all the food on the table, adding a glass of ice water for both of them.

Asher came in and stood beside his chair. He wore another rendition of what she was coming to think of as his uniform—

black T, black jeans. He must've had a spare pair of contact lenses because the glasses were gone.

She'd liked them. They'd reminded her of the geeky kid she'd known in high school—except without the geek. Nothing about that buff body said *geek*.

"Thanks for breakfast." He waited until she sat before he did, his good manners a stark contrast to the anger he'd shown earlier.

She helped herself to some fruit. "Sleep okay?"

"Like a criminal on the lam," he said, a dry edge to his voice. "You?"

"It took some time to fall asleep, but once I did—"

"Uncomfortable?"

Not even close. The bed had been soft and welcoming, and she'd been a little *too* comfortable in Asher's things. Maybe she'd imagined it, but she'd gone to bed inhaling the scent of him, sandalwood and strength.

Though his tone was cordial, she still sensed an undercurrent of anger. "Have I done something to annoy you this morning?"

He took a giant bite and chewed slowly.

She sipped her water, watching him, waiting for him to explain.

"I'm fine," he said after he swallowed, then added, "not annoyed."

"Because you're acting like I injured you, or...I stole your favorite shirt."

"Maybe you did." His tone was distant, his eyes on his plate.

Silence settled in, heavy and tense.

They finished eating, and Cici started the dishes while Asher cleared the table.

She couldn't stand the tension. "You might have forgiven

me, but that doesn't change anything, does it?" She turned off the water to face him. "We'll never be friends again."

He dropped their napkins in the trash. "What are you talking about?"

"You're distant. There's a wall between us. It feels like...like you'll never get over what happened in high school."

He scoffed. "It has nothing to do with that."

She raised her eyebrows. "Is that so? But there is an *it*? What? What's the problem?"

He gestured at her, frustration flashing in his eyes. "It's that. It's you, dressed like...that. In my clothes."

"I don't understand. You said I could borrow—"

"I know."

She was confused. "My clothes are in the dryer, but I can wear them damp. You want me to change right now?"

His mouth clamped closed.

"What?"

If anything, he looked angrier. Maybe he didn't have much to spare. Maybe she'd taken his generosity too lightly. "I appreciate the loan," she said softly. "I promise I'll get them back to you. Washed and folded."

"It's not that."

"Fine, then." She threw up her hands. "What's your problem? Because I'm doing everything I can to make it up to you. I'm trying, and all I'm getting from you—"

He crossed the room in two strides. His hands braced against the refrigerator, trapping her between his arms. "Tell me to stop."

"What? I don't..."

"Tell me to stop, Cici."

Oh. *Oh*. She should. Of course she should.

She just didn't want to.

Before she could fully process what was happening, he kissed her—hard, urgent, his lips firm against hers.

Her surprise turned to heat, melting her inside out. She gripped his shoulders, and he deepened the kiss, electric and alive.

She could do *this* for the rest of her life.

In fact, if this was payback for annoying him, she'd come up with new, fresh annoyances every day of her life.

She rose to her tiptoes, anything to get closer to this old friend she'd obviously never known at all.

But he pulled back, eyes wide. And stepped away. "I shouldn't have done that."

"Why?" she breathed, still dazed. "It was—"

"You're a client. I'm here to protect you."

Protect her?

For a moment, she'd felt protected, cherished even. But the cold look in his eyes changed that.

Now, she didn't feel protected—she felt exposed.

She finally understood the problem. It wasn't that he didn't like her in his clothes, it was that he did. Apparently, very much.

The realization sent fresh warmth through her body and shame to her cheeks. This wasn't affection. It was base desire, nothing more.

Now, he was looking at her like she was the worst mistake he'd ever made.

"What?" Her single word came out like a demand.

"You shouldn't have—"

"Me?" Her volume rose. "What did I do? You started it."

"You started it! You, in that..." He waved at his giant T-shirt as if she wore a corset and fishnet stockings. "Wearing my T-shirt like a dress. You shouldn't have... You should've...stopped me."

"Could you let me read the script in advance next time so I can rehearse my lines?"

"I'm just saying..." But apparently he didn't know what he was saying because his voice trailed. After a moment, he blew out a breath. "You're right. My fault."

She wasn't blaming him. They said it took two to tango, and she'd certainly been swaying to the music.

He took another step back, then retreated all the way to the doorway. As if she were a virus and he didn't want to be exposed. "It was a mistake. It was just stress and...physical. Nothing else."

"Great." Her word sounded exactly as authentic as it felt.

"You could..." He raked his hand over his hair, causing it to stand on end and stick out adorably. "I'd rather you didn't because I would definitely lose my job, and that would keep me from ever getting another one, at least... The point is, you can call Bartlett and tell him what happened. I'd understand."

"I'm not going to get you fired, Asher." Did he really think she'd do that?

"Okay." The tension in his shoulders didn't lessen at all. "Then... Okay." He swiveled and marched down the hallway. A moment later, his door slammed.

Cici stood there, heart hammering, body still thrumming after that kiss.

It hadn't been like the one in the alley, the one she'd known was all for show. She'd enjoyed that one. She had a feeling she'd enjoy every Asher-kiss available.

This one had been real, passionate. And it had meant something. At least it had to her.

She touched her lips, still warm from his, and wondered what in the world she was supposed to do now.

CHAPTER FOURTEEN

Asher leaned against the bedroom door, his breath ragged.
He'd kissed her. He'd given in to his desire, he'd let himself be carried away. He'd *kissed* her.

It was worse than that, though.

That one kiss had shattered every wall he'd built. It was life-altering, the kind of kiss that made him wonder if losing his job might be worth it if he could just kiss her one more time.

His pulse hammered. She'd tasted of apples and blueberries and something uniquely her. And he was sure, no matter how much time passed, he'd never forget that flavor.

What am I doing?

He raked a hand through his hair, tugging hard as if the pain could pull him back to reality.

He needed to move. He needed the gym, his punching bag—a way to release this tension.

Push-ups. That would help. On the floor at the end of his bed, he started. Up and down. Focus on the carpet. Focus on the burn.

Anything to replace the memory of her.

He couldn't return to his fantasies about Cici, that she was his, that she loved him. She'd shown her true colors way back in high school. Even if she'd changed, even if that kiss hinted at something more, did he really want to reignite a flame he'd spent years smothering? He'd been a stupid kid with a crush, dreaming of her, only to have those dreams squashed under her careless laughter.

He wasn't going back there.

And he wasn't about to destroy his future for her.

That moment back in high school, that moment when she'd laughed at him, had changed his life.

Despite his parents' financial troubles, Asher had come to believe he could achieve all his dreams. He knew he'd be valedictorian, since he was at the top of their class. He'd been offered scholarships. When his parents had warned him about the risk of college—how he might not be able to handle it, how he might flunk out or lose his scholarship—he'd assured them he could handle it.

Like most people his age, he'd been young and cocky. And like most people his age, he'd gotten knocked down a few pegs.

In his case, Cici had done the knocking.

After that day, he'd changed his plans. He hadn't wanted to stay in Maine, where all his scholarship offers had come from. He hadn't wanted anything to do with Shadow Cove or the kids he went to high school with. He'd wanted to leave it all behind.

Mostly, he'd wanted to leave his humiliation behind.

Not that he regretted the decision. The Navy had been good to him. The Teams had been good to him. But he did sometimes wonder what life would've been like if he'd gone on to the University of Maine and majored in economics like he'd planned. Or finance. Back then, he'd dreamed of political office. His fallback plan had been to become a financial planner or a stockbroker.

Those dreams had crumbled, along with his self-respect, the day Cici had laughed at him.

She'd changed the trajectory of his life. And yeah, he'd let her. He should've gotten over it. He could've faced the humiliation and gone to college.

He wasn't blaming her. He had to own his fears, fears he could kick himself for now.

At the same time, he wasn't going to let her screw up his life again.

When he delivered her safely home and got paid, he'd have the down payment for his condo. He'd buy it, then leverage it to buy a real piece of property—land and a single-family home, a place that was his alone. A place nobody could take away from him.

He was going to build a foundation, the kind of stability he'd never had growing up. Someday, God willing, he'd have a family, and when he did, they'd never wonder where their next meal was coming from.

Never.

He was going to have the kind of stability Cici'd had all her life—with zero effort on her part.

Not that he was bitter. He knew who he was and what he wanted. He'd envisioned a future, and Cici wasn't in the picture.

She was attractive, sure, with those intelligent eyes and her quick humor, but she was shallow. Even now, where he'd built a life that revolved around protecting people, she'd built a life that revolved around jewelry.

See? Shallow.

Except, was she?

He flipped to his back for sit-ups, wishing he were at the gym where he could get a real workout.

Her family mattered to her. Forbes, who wasn't even a part

of her family yet, mattered enough to her that she guarded his necklace like Asher guarded her, as if it were precious. And not because of its value but because it was an heirloom.

Justice mattered to her. She wanted the people who'd been party to the Ballentine murders to pay for their crimes.

Maybe she wasn't totally shallow. Maybe she had a few values he could respect.

And she wasn't bitter or cold. She wasn't the self-absorbed snob he'd painted her to be. She was kind—too kind, refusing to report him even when he'd crossed every professional line.

Ugh.

Those thoughts weren't helping at all.

Asher needed security, something solid he could build for himself.

Cici was nothing but a distraction.

By the time he finished his *punish myself* workout routine, he needed another shower. Which was probably a good idea, anyway. A nice cold shower should shock the woman out of his head.

Clean, in fresh clothes, and eager to get moving, he messaged Garrison—the guy who'd delivered them to this house the night before—who responded with a message that he was on his way with wheels. Asher prayed for something discreet, not that he'd bet on it, not with their luck.

A few minutes later, an engine rumbled outside.

Asher grabbed his pack and opened the bedroom door, finding his T-shirt and boxers folded neatly on the floor in the hallway.

Nothing sexy about that, except he'd never get the image of Cici wearing them out of his mind.

Cursing the woman, he shoved the clothes into his pack and strode to the living room.

Cici stood by the back door, gazing at the lake. Her hair was brushed, her clothes from the day before hanging off her. She was beautiful, as always, but certainly not at ease. Her arms were crossed, her shoulders tense.

"Time to go." He was careful to keep his voice even.

She turned, her expression icy. "I'll sit in the backseat, since we're not friends. Isn't that what a client would do?"

"Don't be ridiculous." He moved to the window. Maybe she *should* sit in the backseat. The more space between them, the better.

He expected to see two cars, one for them, one to transport whoever dropped it off. Maybe a car and a truck. A truck and an SUV.

Any combination would have worked.

But what rolled into view was Chief Thomas's pickup with a motorcycle in the bed.

Unless Garrison and Thomas, who'd climbed out and were moving to roll it down a plank to the ground, planned to ride the bike home—and he highly doubted the chief was about to hand over his sixty-thousand-dollar truck—the bike was for them. Which meant Cici wouldn't be in the backseat. She'd be right behind him, arms around his waist, body pressed against his for miles and hours.

Exactly the last thing he needed. He needed distance—professional distance, not to mention actual, physical distance. He did not need her warmth seeping into him all the way to Shadow Cove.

"Seriously?" Cici's voice cut through his thoughts as she joined him at the window. "A dirt bike?"

"Not...technically." It had lights and a license plate, but it was hardly larger than a dirt bike, and the mud caked on the sides told him it could handle off-roading. "You'll have to hold on tight."

Her eyes narrowed. Then, one eyebrow ticked up. He could swear he heard her thoughts.

I can handle it if you can.

She grabbed her purse and marched outside.

Asher followed, her coldness hitting hard. He hated that he'd hurt her. He really hated that she thought he still wasn't over what she did to him in high school.

Fine. Maybe he wasn't. But this wasn't about that. This was about the job, about keeping his life on track. Still, her frostiness felt like a wall he didn't know how to scale.

He wanted a wall between them, though. It was safer this way, even if it hurt.

"Good morning," she called as if all were right with the world.

They reached the bike, and Asher got a better look. It looked…old. Wide wheels told him it was probably mostly used for off-roading. But it was a Kawasaki. He suspected it could go fast enough.

Helmets hung from each handlebar.

Garrison handed him the keys. "Stick to back roads or trails if you want to avoid civilization."

"Thanks." Asher shook the older man's hand. "I'll get this back to you."

"Not a problem. It's my son's, but he hardly ever uses it." Garrison flicked some dirt off the back. "Or cleans it, obviously."

Beside him, Chief Thomas said, "We'll worry about getting it back when you two are safe. I'll let Bartlett know you're on the road." His gaze rose to the sky, where puffy clouds rolled overhead.

"That'd be great. Thanks." Asher shook the chief's hand as well.

Cici thanked them both and put on the smaller of the helmets.

After he shoved her purse under the seat and fastened his pack to the back, he swung a leg over the seat and strapped on the second helmet.

She climbed on behind him.

"Try not to fall off," he snapped.

Her arms circled his waist, but her grip was loose, barely there—like she couldn't stand touching him. It was a stark contrast to the heat of their kiss. He didn't like it, at all. Even if it was better this way.

He fired up the engine, the roar drowning out his thoughts.

Get her to Shadow Cove, he told himself. *Then walk away.*

But deep down, he knew that kiss had shifted something, and there was no outrunning it.

∽

The motorcycle's engine growled beneath Asher as he guided it along the winding backroads of New Hampshire, hugging the Maine state line.

They'd ridden in silence, the roar of the bike and the whipping wind making conversation impossible. The morning sunshine had faded, replaced by a heavy blanket of gray clouds.

Then came a drizzle that turned to a deluge, pelting his helmet visor and blurring the world into a watery haze. When he could barely see the road, he started praying for a bridge. Finally, he spotted one ahead and slowed to a stop beneath it.

He killed the engine, the abrupt cutoff as jarring as the storm's assault. Beyond the narrow overpass, rain slanted to the ground, a steady roar.

He could hear Bartlett's voice in his head. Would the man consider trying not to die in a motorcycle wreck *dillydallying*?

Cici loosened her hold on his waist and shifted behind him. "Well, that was fun." Her sarcasm was thick.

"We can't ride in this."

She climbed off the bike, took off her helmet, and stretched, then stared out at the storm, brushing damp strawberry-blond hair back from her face. "'I'd keep playing,'" she deadpanned. "'I don't think the heavy stuff's gonna come down for quite a while.'"

He couldn't help it. He laughed. "Did you just quote 'Caddyshack'?" He climbed off the bike and removed his own helmet.

Her smile seemed hesitant, maybe a little embarrassed. "My sisters and I watched that movie one night when our parents were out. We got in so much trouble, but"—she lifted one shoulder and let it drop—"it was worth it."

"It was one of my dad's favorites." A wind gust blew through the tunnel beneath the bridge, and he shivered. "Dad was always quoting lines from it. 'We have a pool and a pond—'"

"'Pond would be good for you.'" Cici finished the quote, grinning.

"'You'll have nothing and like it!'"

She pulled her soaking-wet sweatshirt away from her skin. "That sounds about right today."

The way her clothes hugged her body... Suddenly, he didn't feel so chilly. "Anyway..." He gazed beyond her, needing something to focus on besides the beautiful and altogether too alluring woman he was stranded with. "We might as well be swimming."

"We passed a sporting goods store a few miles back. We could grab ponchos."

He hadn't seen it, but then he hadn't dared shift his focus from the road.

He chin-nodded to the rain. "You want to go back out in that?"

"It doesn't look like a passing shower. If we want to get home today, we're going to have to get wet."

She wasn't wrong. Why hadn't he thought to check the weather before they took off? Not that they'd had any choice.

Asher considered all the options. "Yeah, let's go back."

They were both shivering by the time they stepped inside the small store tucked in a strip mall between a restaurant and a bank.

"Go grab some dry clothes." The last thing Asher wanted... Well, the last thing he *needed* was to see her in his clothes again. "Just take the tags off before you change so we can buy them."

"On it." She headed for the women's section.

While she was gone, he grabbed ponchos, a couple more burner phones, and some snacks, his mind spinning through contingencies.

She returned a few minutes later, wearing form-fitting yoga pants and a slim T-shirt that hugged her trim waist, a hoodie draped over her arm.

She couldn't have found something less attractive? Thick sweats would've been nice. He figured she'd look good in anything she wore. She had on a new pair of tennis shoes to replace the bright pink Crocs.

By the time he'd paid for their purchases—with her dad's cash—his stomach was growling. It hadn't been that long since breakfast, but apparently kissing your old crush and riding for your life through a rainstorm burned a few calories.

Oh, and there'd been the *punish myself* workout that morning.

He and Cici stood beneath the overhang in front of the store, staring at the soaking-wet motorcycle.

If the look on her face was any indication, she was no more eager to climb back on than he was.

"Let's grab some lunch." He nodded to the restaurant next door.

Her shoulders relaxed. "Good idea."

Inside, the scents of pancakes and bacon and frying burgers had his mouth watering.

Apart from the server on the opposite side of the room, the place was deserted. She called, "Sit anywhere you like."

Asher chose a booth in the back corner, farthest from the door and nearest the kitchen, where they could make a quick getaway if necessary. He faced the windows that overlooked the parking lot, studying each car that splashed past.

Very few people ventured out into today's weather.

The server delivered menus and two glasses of water. They perused, and as soon as they set the menus aside, she was back.

They ordered their meals, and then he went to the bathroom to change into dry clothes he'd pulled from his bag.

Felt like a new man.

By the time he got back, their food had been delivered. Cici was munching on her french fries but hadn't touched her burger.

His fish and chips looked delicious.

He was about to take a bite when Cici said, "Would it be all right...?" She faltered, started again. "Would you mind if I pray for us? I know it's weird, but all things considered—"

"Sure. Go ahead."

She bowed her head and closed her eyes, and he did the same.

"Father, thank You for bringing us this far. Thank You for all the help You've given us along the way. Thank You for keeping us safe in the rain, and for delivering us safely to Shadow Cove, which we pray You'll do today. Protect us between now and then. Give us wisdom and knowledge to face everything coming our way. Thank You for Asher for all he's already done. Bless him in a thousand ways. And bless our food. In Jesus's name..."

"Amen." He smiled at her across the table. "Thank you for that."

"Sure. Seems like we should thank God. I mean, I don't know where we'd be without Him. And if not for you, I'd be dead, so..." She said it so matter-of-factly, then lifted her burger and took a bite as if there were nothing else to say.

She might be dead, and the thought of it twisted inside of him. It was one thing to protect a teammate or a stranger. Protecting Cici had become something altogether different.

And here she was just talking to him as if everything was fine. All the tension between them had somehow washed away in the rain. "You're very...gracious."

She looked up from her meal. "What do you mean?"

"You should be furious with me."

"Oh, that. Well..." She waved off his words. "It's fine." She took another bite.

He watched her, this woman he'd judged so unfairly. "I shouldn't have kissed you, and I shouldn't have acted like it was your fault. I shouldn't have been rude about the whole thing. I actually do have some self-control, and I just wasn't employing it this morning. I'm sorry."

She set down her burger and studied him across the table.

When she said nothing, he prompted her with, "I hope you can forgive me."

"Are you apologizing for kissing me, or for being rude, or for accusing me of starting it?"

"Uh...yes?"

"You're forgiven for the rudeness and the accusations. I won't forgive you for kissing me because I'm not sorry you did. I don't know about you, but it's not every day I get kissed like that." Though she'd held her eye contact, it slipped then. "I refuse to regret it."

Her tone turned almost defensive at the end, as if she thought he'd judge her for her words.

"I don't go around kissing women without their permission." He lifted a piece of fried fish, then put it back down. "I owe you an apology for that."

"I thought it was nice."

"Inappropriate."

She considered that, her head tilting to the side. "Okay. It was both."

Both nice and inappropriate? Was that a thing?

Well, it had been. She was right.

"Maybe it wasn't so nice for you." Her eyebrows hiked like the surprising thought had just occurred to her.

"Cici." He wasn't sure what she saw on his face, but her lips twitched. "Obviously, it was nice for me. It was so nice that..." He didn't finish the sentence. Didn't tell her about his workout or his cold shower or the fact that, if there weren't a table between them, if they weren't in a public place, she'd be pressed between the wall and his body right now, his lips on hers.

Did it matter that they were in public? The place was empty. Who cared what the server saw?

Oy.

Stop.

How did she do that to him?

"So." Cici's tone was bright. Maybe she needed a subject change as much as he did. He didn't hate that thought. "What was your favorite thing about being a SEAL?"

He forced his mind to focus on her question. "I loved so much about it. I loved proving that I could do it, you know? Pushing limits that should have been limits but weren't because

I refused to acknowledge them. I loved becoming more than anyone ever expected me to be."

Now, she wiped her fingers on her napkin, head tilting to the side. "People had high expectations for you. I'm sure your parents did. How could they not? You were the smartest kid in town."

Maybe, and the fact that she thought so meant something. But the rest of what she'd said registered. "My parents weren't the most encouraging people in the world."

She leaned toward him. "I'm sorry to hear that."

"It's...whatever." He bit into his fish—flaky and salty and delicious. "Dad was always taking risks—and usually losing. Sometimes big. Mom had her own dreams, but she spent her life scraping just to survive. They weren't disappointed when I skipped college and went straight to the military. To them, it was the safer bet. A guaranteed paycheck, a place to live, three squares a day. And when I told them I applied to the Teams, they were...not discouraging, but certainly less than enthusiastic."

"They didn't think you could do it?" She seemed shocked, but that was only because she already knew he had. Going into it, there'd been no guarantees. A lot of strong, smart guys washed out.

"They didn't want me to be disappointed. I think...I think they feel like their fate is in someone else's hands, and maybe that someone else is..." He groped for a word.

"Cruel?"

"Kind of. Or, more like a trickster. You know, like life was Lucy, and they were Charlie Brown, always believing that *this* time, the football would be there when they kicked. They always landed on their...pride, so to speak."

"They must have been thrilled when you made it."

Had they been? If so, they hadn't shown it. "They quit worrying that I'd wash out and started worrying I'd be killed."

"They sound..." Her words trailed.

"They're really good people. They just think differently than I do. They see themselves as victims, and I never did.

"You liked being a SEAL."

"I loved it, the camaraderie. There's nothing like knowing people are depending on you—and knowing you're capable and can come through. And they came through for me. You figure out who you are, what you can do, and what your limits are real quick when the bullets are flying."

"And you learned you're amazing."

He grinned. "If you say so."

"And then you were injured, right?"

He rubbed it, not that it hurt at the moment. It rarely did, only if he pushed it too hard. "Wasn't a big deal, but I had to leave the SEALs. I didn't want to do anything else in the Navy, so I got out."

"You like being a bodyguard?"

"I don't...hate it." That wasn't an easy question to answer. "Most of the time, I stand on the edge of the room and observe other people living their lives." He thought of his previous client, the way he'd practically attacked his assistant while Asher stood by and watched. The guy probably thought having Asher in the corner made him invincible.

He could still picture the agony on the guy's face after his assistant kneed him in the groin. Until this assignment, that had been the most exciting thing he'd witnessed on the job. "Most of the time, it's pretty boring."

She made a show of looking around. "Yeah, I can see that."

"As usual, you make everything more exciting."

Her eyebrows hiked.

Whoops. "Not that...I mean, it's only..." His bonehead remark had no backpedals.

She laughed. "You're hilarious when you get flustered."

"Shut up." But as he ate another bite of fish, he wasn't annoyed with Cici. He was having fun.

They ate for a few minutes in comfortable silence, something he'd never have guessed possible after the morning's awkwardness.

Thunder cracked overhead, and Cici practically jumped out of her skin.

She was obviously on edge. Though he remained vigilant, he was nearly certain they were safe.

"Tell me about you," he said, wanting to distract her from her worries. "Do you like what you do?"

Her shoulders relaxed. "I love it. I'm doing exactly what I always wanted."

There was a hint of something in her voice that told him she wasn't telling the whole story. "But?" He prompted.

"I've always had this...this silly dream. Sort of a secret dream."

He leaned toward her, wanting to know what it was.

"I'd like to open my own jewelry store in downtown Shadow Cove."

"Why don't you?"

"It costs a pretty penny to start a jewelry store."

"But your family—"

"My parents are wealthy. I'm not."

"They wouldn't loan you money?"

"They probably would, if I asked."

But she wouldn't ask. Interesting.

"Right now, I'm enjoying appraising, and I love the travel. When I tire of it, I'll look at opening a store. How about you? What's your secret dream?"

"Oh, well... It's not that ambitious, actually. I just want..."

To not tell her his secret dream. She'd think it was stupid and small.

She worked on her burger—she'd hardly eaten any of it—and watched him.

"It's not really a dream so much as just...what's next." He chewed a fry and swallowed it. "I've got my eye on this condo just outside of Boston. I can't afford a house there. It's a nice place. Not one of those new, fancy high-rises. It's one side of a duplex with a little yard in the back."

"Sounds lovely."

"It's small and old." Why was he downplaying it? Because for someone who grew up in a mansion, it would seem dingy. "The plan is to hang onto it for two years, then, if the market cooperates, sell it and buy a house on some land."

"You'll stay in the Boston area?"

"That's where the job is."

"You like the job enough to stay there? Because I'm sure there are security companies in Maine or wherever you want to live."

He ate the rest of his fish, thinking about that. This job was secure, and as much as he liked to think of himself as a risk-taker, the truth was, risk was scary.

Risk meant landlords tacking eviction notices on doors.

Risk meant no food in the fridge.

Risk meant danger.

He'd take on terrorists and crazy murderers bent on silencing witnesses. No problem.

But risking financial ruin? That was something he didn't dare flirt with, not after watching his parents all his life.

Cici was watching him like she was trying to read his mind.

"I like Boston." Aside from all the people and cars, anyway.

"That surprises me. I see you as more of a—"

"Country bumpkin?"

That brought a laugh. "Hardly. I guess just because I know you're from Maine, I can see you there, not in a condo but in a nice house with lots of land, lots of trees. Maybe a garage where you could tinker on...whatever it is men tinker on."

The picture she painted was exactly what he wanted. How did she know?

She was much more insightful than he'd have guessed.

"I wouldn't hate that. It's just that the job is in Boston."

"There are other jobs."

"Well, for now, it's where I am. I guess it's like what you do. As long as I'm still enjoying it, I'll keep doing it. When I tire of it, I'll look for something else." He peered through the glass outside, then back at her. "How do you do that?"

"Do what?"

"Get me to talk about myself. I never talk about myself. You should've been a detective or a trial lawyer. Prying is your superpower."

"Uh, thank you?"

"That wasn't a compliment. It's the most annoying superpower I've come across."

That brought a grin his mouth wanted to answer. He forced his gaze outside again. "I think the rain's tapered off. We should go."

She finished her drink and then went to the restroom, giving him a minute to regroup.

Not only did Cici remind him of the crush he'd apparently never gotten over, she represented everything he wanted in life. She was free and hopeful and comfortable in her own skin.

She had the kind of security he'd only ever dreamed of. And the way she talked to him, questioned him, as if she really wanted to know him, to know everything about him...

She made him long for things he'd given up on.
Being around Cici was downright dangerous.

CHAPTER FIFTEEN

It was drizzling when Cici found Asher outside, shoving their shopping bags under the seat. She handed him her purse, which barely fit.

When they had been at the sporting goods store, she'd bought a thin travel pouch, the kind designed to hide a passport and cash. She'd transferred The Crimson Duchess and the rest of Grace Ballentine's jewels to it, then strapped the pouch around her waist. She liked knowing the jewels were hidden on her body. Even if she got separated from her things, as had happened with her suitcase, she'd be able to protect Forbes's property.

It was probably overkill, but it made her feel better. It made her believe she was doing something besides just...not getting murdered. The jewelry was her responsibility, and she would do her best to protect it.

She'd explained all of that to Asher before they'd left the restaurant. She'd expected him to ask—demand—that she hand over the pouch for him to carry, but he didn't.

"Good idea." He must've seen her surprise, because he'd

added, "If I do my job and keep you safe, then the necklace will be safe too. If I fail, then who cares about the necklace?"

She cared, but she didn't hate that he placed her value above that of a priceless treasure.

Asher handed her a poncho. "As long as I can see, we'll press on. God willing, we'll make it to Shadow Cove in the next few hours."

She slid on the yellow plastic covering and secured her helmet over the hood, then climbed onto the motorcycle behind him. He'd wiped the seat, though with everything glistening with rainwater, she figured getting wet was inevitable.

It was late afternoon by the time they hit the road again. Cici stayed mostly dry, thanks to the poncho—and the fact that she was blocked from the worst of the weather by Asher's body. But her feet got soaked, as did the lower part of her jeans. She was cold and damp and miserable. She couldn't imagine how much worse it was for Asher. This glorified dirt bike didn't even have a windshield.

She watched the world pass by, a blur of green and brown. As they passed into Maine, it seemed like they left civilization behind. The narrow two-lane road was hardly interrupted by towns or stop lights or stores.

They were in the middle of nowhere when lightning cracked overhead.

Cici felt more than heard Asher's frustrated exclamation. He slowed and pulled off the road, down a rain gully and into the forest, where he cut the engine.

"What are we doing?" She had to shout to be heard over the rain.

"Trying not to die. Hop off."

She did, then removed her helmet. At least the foliage overhead blocked some of the rain, though it was coming down harder than she'd realized, plopping against her poncho, soaking the motorcycle seat.

Asher followed suit, yanking his own helmet off. He was mostly hidden behind the yellow plastic poncho, only his face and the lower parts of his legs showing.

Somehow, he made even that look good.

"I guess this is hard to drive in." Sort of a lame observation on her part.

"You *guess*?"

She decided to ignore his sarcasm. "What do we do? Wait it out?"

Sighing, he pulled out one of the burners and powered it up. It reminded her...

"We need to call Alyssa."

"And Bartlett, but let's wait until we're somewhere a little less drenched." He returned his focus to his phone, checking the weather app.

Since she didn't think he'd appreciate her looking over his shoulder, she watched his expression. His annoyance didn't fade. If anything, the little furrow between his eyebrows grew deeper.

"I take it the news isn't good?"

"Thunderstorms and heavy rain for a couple more hours. In fact, according to the radar, what you said earlier is true. The heavy stuff hasn't even started."

She hated the thought of riding in this terrible weather all the way to Shadow Cove, but they were so close.

She'd be safe when they got to her parents' house. She could turn over The Crimson Duchess, knowing she'd done something heroic and admirable, something her family could be proud of.

And Asher could drop her off and be on his way.

As eager as she was to be finished with this adventure, the thought of never seeing him again brought a twinge of sadness.

Maybe more than a *twinge*.

He was looking at something on his phone, but he'd shifted so she couldn't tell what.

Finally, he settled his helmet back on his head. "Let's go."

"We're riding through it?"

As if to offer its opinion, thunder rumbled.

Asher looked toward the sound, then shook his head. "I can hardly see. The point is to keep you safe, not get us both killed."

"So where are we going?"

His lips twitched at the corners. "Camping."

Camping? Cici liked the outdoors as much as the next girl—as long as the next girl hated camping.

But Asher always had a reason for the things he did. He'd gotten them this far, anyway.

∽

The rain intensified until it felt like a living enemy, a relentless beast, clawing at Cici's poncho as Asher guided the motorcycle down a muddy road. She directed, using the map he'd pulled up on the burner phone, attempting to protect it from moisture with her body. Even though the screen showed her they were going the right direction, she couldn't imagine anything at the end of this lonely dirt path.

The storm swallowed the last of the late afternoon light, dark until lightning split the sky. Thunder rumbled so close it vibrated through her chest.

"The campground is two hundred feet ahead on the right," she shouted.

Asher's head bobbed, and he slowed long before the turnoff,

then veered left, off the path, steering between trees through the woods, aiming for who knew what.

She didn't bother to ask. He wouldn't explain anyway, certainly not loudly enough for her to hear above the cacophony.

A lone cabin materialized ahead, its wooden frame drenched. It looked deserted—no cars in the driveway, no lights shining through the windows.

He got close and cut the engine, and she dismounted.

After he did, he grabbed his duffel bag, scanning the campground.

The outlines of a few cabins were barely visible through the trees, but she saw no lights, no indication anybody was staying here, certainly not close by.

"Come on." His voice was low, the words sneaking in beneath the storm.

She followed him to the squat, weathered structure, thankful for the porch roof that protected them from the rain.

He dropped his backpack on a bench and looked through it, coming out with something too small for her to see.

"What's the plan here?"

She didn't know why she bothered to ask. Asher's plan was obvious when he crouched by the door and worked tiny metal tools into the lock. A moment later, the door creaked open. He stood and stepped aside. "After you."

"Breaking and entering?"

His eyebrows quirked. "Better than grand theft auto."

He wasn't wrong about that. She took off her helmet and the poncho, then left them on the bench just outside the door so she wouldn't drip all over the floor. After toeing off her shoes, she stepped into the tiny room. Tiny, but mercifully dry.

She stood in the dark space, watching the door until, a few minutes later, Asher joined her, having shed his helmet, poncho, and shoes. He dropped her purse and his backpack on the floor just inside the door.

The cabin smelled of damp wood and mildew, a faint mustiness that clung to the air. It was barely bigger than a walk-in closet. The bed took up most of the space. An old bureau stood against one wall, and a single wooden chair rested beside it.

No heat, no lights, but a small gas fireplace was tucked into the corner.

She nodded to it. "You mind if I fire that up?"

"Go for it." He was digging through his bag again. "If anything, the bike will be the thing that gives us away, though I did hide it in the woods."

She twisted the valve, and a flame sputtered to life, casting a golden glow across the room. It wasn't much, but it pushed back the chill. She held her hands toward the fireplace to warm them.

"Any reason why we couldn't have paid for this cabin?" she asked.

He pulled his laptop from his duffel bag. "This seemed simpler. They probably don't take cash, and I didn't want to give a credit card. This way, we stay off the grid."

"Makes sense." But somebody owned this cabin, and they had a right to be paid for its use. On the other hand, Asher's caution was the reason they were still alive. "We'll leave some cash on the bed."

She checked the travel pouch strapped around her waist, the weight of Grace Ballentine's jewels a quiet reassurance.

Asher tapped on a burner phone. "We need to call that Philly detective."

They'd planned to do that this morning. The memory of their kiss flooded back—his lips on hers, urgent and eager, the way his passion had turned to anger in a heartbeat. They'd been too rattled to think straight after that, and that distraction had cost them hours.

"Is there cell service," Cici asked.

"Yup." He wiggled the phone, urging her to take it. "Let's start with the detective and get that over with."

"Me?" Her stomach twisted. "Why me? They think I'm a murderer. Maybe you—"

"That's why you should make the call. You need to show them that you have nothing to hide."

Reluctantly, she took the phone, seeing that Asher had already tapped in the number. "What should I say?"

"Tell them everything that happened and what we've learned, including Wendall Gagnon's name."

"But not where we are."

"Right. But do tell them that you're returning Forbes's necklace to him, and you plan to turn over everything else as soon as you're in Shadow Cove."

Cici sank to the edge of the bed, breathing a silent prayer for help, then dialed and put the phone on speaker.

"Detective Harris." The woman's voice was sharp and professional.

"My name is Cecilia Wright. I called Friday afternoon to report—"

"I know who you are, Ms. Wright. Thank you for reaching out."

"I've been on the run since then."

She made a noncommittal *hmm*. "You and a friend?" By the way she asked, she knew about Asher.

"He's a bodyguard who's getting me safely back to Maine, where I live. You're on speaker, and he's listening."

"His name?"

Seated in the hard-back chair, Asher gave her a go-ahead nod, so she said, "Asher Rhodes. He works for GBPA out of Boston."

"You always travel with bodyguards?"

"No. I just said he was hired—"

"Why did you think you needed a bodyguard?"

"Because I witnessed a murder." Cici kept her voice level, though her blood pressure shot higher than the cabin's low ceiling.

Asher leaned forward, eyebrows hiked.

She guessed he wanted to say something. "Go ahead," she said.

"Detective Harris, I was hired Friday afternoon by Forbes Ballentine to protect Cici and get her back to Maine. Do you want to know what we've learned or not?"

"Learned about what?"

"The men who killed Mr. Delvecchio and burned down his store."

"Okay, shoot." She sounded skeptical, but at least she was willing to listen.

Asher nodded to Cici.

She took a breath and began. "There were two men in the store Friday afternoon. We haven't ID'd one, but the man who I think was in charge is named Wendall Gagnon. He's a majority shareholder in a tech company in Philadelphia." She shared how they'd gotten the information and what they knew about him, including his connection to Leo Taggart, one of the people who murdered Forbes's parents.

"You're saying what happened Friday night is related to the Ballentine murders?" Harris sounded as if she found their investigation amusing.

Cici stifled irritation and explained about the necklace. "I was in the back room when Gagnon came in. He wanted to know if the other clerk was there—Mr. D's niece. He said his son had dealt with her earlier in the week. Mr. D had already told me that the bag of stuff he wanted me to appraise—

including the necklace—had been purchased by his niece. I can only assume she bought it from Gagnon's son."

"Which is why you wanted us to protect the niece," Harris said.

"I explained all of this to the 911 operator."

"Sometimes they don't take great notes. I can listen to the call."

Seemed she should already have done that, but what did Cici know about detective work?

"Did you?" Cici asked. "Protect his niece?"

"She was pretty distraught about her uncle. We recommended she get out of town. Far as I know, she did."

"You need to make sure! She's in danger."

"So you said, Ms. Wright. We're not a protection agency. All we can do is warn people. We can't force them to do anything against their will."

The police could've protected her. They could've put her in a safe house or something. Assuming they had safe houses.

"Tell me about this necklace," Harris said.

Cici gave her the short version. "I took it and the whole bag of stuff the niece had bought."

"You stole it?"

"If not, he'd have it, so you're welcome. I'm giving the necklace and the rest of Grace Ballentine's things to Forbes. Everything else, I'll send back to you. I'm not a thief."

The remark earned a long silence.

"What do you know about Wendall Gagnon?" Asher asked.

"Uh..." After a pause, she said, "Far as I can tell, he runs a legitimate business."

"Not sure everyone in your department would agree with that. His name was forwarded to me when I asked for people in Philly with ties to organized crime."

"I'll look into it. And we'll keep our eyes out for him."

"He was in Massachusetts yesterday, tracking us," Cici said. "Only by the grace of God did we escape."

"Oh. Well…" Papers shuffled in the background. "I'll do some digging. I can reach you at this number?"

"No," Cici said. "If you need to reach us, contact my father, Gavin Wright. We should be at his house—"

"*The* Gavin Wright." Harris sounded almost awed.

As if Dad were some sort of celebrity. "I guess." She gave the detective her dad's number. "We'll be in touch."

"Okay. Stay safe." The detective ended the call.

"She's not exactly a fount of knowledge," Cici said.

"At least now she can focus on the actual killers and quit looking for you."

"One less hound on our heels."

He smiled, the expression transforming his face. He was gorgeous when he smiled.

"I need to check in with Alyssa."

"Just change burners." He handed her another one, then opened his laptop. "I'm going to connect to the hotspot and see if Bartlett has any more intel for us."

Cici's hands trembled, though the little gas fireplace had warmed the room considerably. The cold didn't have her shaking so much as the weight of it all, the realization that they weren't close to the end of this, no matter how near they seemed to Shadow Cove. Gagnon wasn't going to quit searching for her until he was behind bars or dead.

She dialed Alyssa, again putting the phone on speaker. "Hey, sis. You're on with Asher, too."

"You two okay?"

"We're fine. Just hiding from bad guys and bad storms."

"I can't wait to hear the whole story."

"Did you learn anything?"

"You doubt me?" Her voice held a hint of humor. "You

already ID'd Gagnon. The bald guy he was with outside the police station is Gustavo Souza, a low-level criminal out of New York City. He's tied to a gang there."

"Is there a connection between that gang and Gagnon?"

"I see no link between them."

"Obviously, there is one, or between them personally."

"Whatever it is, it's not detailed on the internet, at least nowhere I've been able to find."

"What's the name of the gang?"

"They're called the Fourth Hood. I guess they're an offshoot of the Bloods."

The Bloods? That was a real thing? The name alone was enough to give Cici the chills.

"There's a guy running the Fourth Hood, Maxwell Pierce," Alyssa continued. "According to a report, he's a community activist, but the NYPD believes he's dirty. No proof, though."

Sounded a lot like Wendall Gagnon. "Can you dig into that leader? See if he's connected to Gagnon?"

"Already on it," Alyssa said. "Nothing yet, but I'll keep looking."

"You learn anything about Gagnon?"

"Yeah, lemme just..." Her voice faded. "Here we go. He grew up in Waterville, Maine, one of seven kids. Single mom. I guess the kids had a few different dads. She was on welfare, food stamps. Gagnon dropped out of school at sixteen and started working construction. Here's something interesting. He applied for a software patent when he was nineteen, some kind of cybersecurity." She made a little *hmph* sound. "Ahead of his time, it seems. He was denied, but obviously, he was tinkering with programming. Then he got arrested... Oh, in Shadow Cove."

"We know about that. Check out the arresting officer."

A pause, then, "Ah, I see. Our own Leonard Taggart, back before he was chief."

"Before the murders," Cici explained. "We think it's how they got connected."

"Gotcha. Okay, so after that... let's see. He moves to Philly and starts a tech company at the tail end of the bubble. Suddenly, he's a successful, wealthy businessman."

"Seems his cut of the smuggling operation was enough," Cici guessed.

"I don't know." Asher'd been quiet, but he'd lifted his gaze from the laptop to her. "Why get out of the business if it was so profitable?"

"Maybe he got spooked by the murders," Alyssa suggested.

"Maybe he thought the necklace was his ticket to riches." Cici was sure the necklace was related, somehow.

"Guys like that... Would he have been investing his take? My guess is he was a grunt, being paid a pittance compared to the value of what they were moving. And we already know he didn't sell the necklace, so... What happened? What changed?"

Cici had no idea and guessed by Alyssa's silence that she was just as stymied.

All the questions only led to threads in a huge web she couldn't follow. "Anyway, this is great info, sis. We'll keep digging."

"I'll do the same and let you know if I learn anything."

Cici ended the call. "It's all so convoluted."

"True stories usually are." Asher leaned back in his chair, the front legs tipping off the floor, his gaze distant. "How's a guy like that go from dirt poor to filthy rich?"

"Maybe he took out a loan against the necklace?"

"Maybe." By Asher's doubtful tone, he didn't think so.

"He must've leveraged it somehow, either—"

"That's it." Asher's chair legs hit the floor with a thud. "He leveraged the necklace. Not with a bank, but with Taggart and Stratton. The necklace was proof he was involved with the smugglers, proof that he knew who the murderers were."

"Well, yeah, but if he'd turned them in—"

"He would've implicated himself, sure." Asher stood, dropped the laptop on the end of the bed, and paced the tiny path between his chair and the far wall. "But he could've made a deal, the names of the murderers and everyone else involved in the smuggling ring for immunity. He might've gotten off scot-free. Meanwhile, Taggart and Stratton would've gone to prison for murder. The whole thing would have been solved a quarter century ago."

"So he blackmailed them?"

"Why not?" Asher froze a few feet from her. "Think of it. Here's this poor kid from the wrong side of the tracks making peanuts compared to what the big bosses were making. Maybe even working for them because Taggart offered him a deal—maybe the kind of deal he felt he couldn't say no to. He was arrested, but no charges were brought. Maybe the deal was that Taggart would "lose" any evidence he'd collected in exchange for Gagnon's labor. So Gagnon does what he's told, gets paid next to nothing. Then gets lucky. The night of the murders, he finds the jewelry and pockets it, his ticket out. Maybe he was friends with Taggart, maybe not, but what's friendship when there's money involved? So he starts blackmailing them."

"The seed money for his business."

"Maybe. Maybe the business is just a front, a money-laundering operation." Asher paced again. "And maybe he got a taste of easy money and started blackmailing more people."

"How? You have to have solid information to pull something like that off." But even as Cici asked the question, an answer came to her. "What if...what if the tech thing is the answer. Alyssa said he was into programming. And cybersecurity. He must've been good to apply for a patent." She met Asher's eyes. "What if he's a hacker?"

Asher froze and met her eyes. "Call Alyssa. See if she can—"

"On it." Cici dialed her sister and relayed the question.

"Interesting theory. I saw nothing that backs it up, but then hackers are good at covering their tracks. On the other hand, hackers talk, so if Gagnon's one of us...them, I mean." She chuckled. "Old habits. Anyway, if he's a hacker, someone's heard of him. This'll take longer, so be patient. I'll see what I can learn."

Cici ended the call and tossed the phone on the bed, allowing a seed of hope to take root. And she'd come up with the idea. She'd helped. "I think we're on to—"

"Your sister's something else."

Cici's self-satisfaction deflated like a popped balloon. "Yeah, she is."

"This is a great lead, Cici." Maybe Asher read her disappointment. Probably, which was why he tried to encourage her. "If we can expose him as a blackmailer, then maybe we can send him on the run, not just from the authorities but from everyone he's been blackmailing."

"Maybe." But reality took the rest of the air out of her balloon. "Except, assuming they know who he is, whatever he's got has kept him safe all these years."

"He's careful." Asher's tone turned pensive. "He thinks he's untouchable. But the necklace could be his downfall, especially now that the Ballentines' killers have been exposed. He has no leverage. If it's proved the necklace was in his possession, then he's an accessory to murder. He goes to prison."

The soft hiss of the gas fire mingled with the rain's steady drum on the roof. Cici rested against the pillows propped in front of the headboard, wishing she could close her eyes for just a moment. "You can kind of understand it. The guy grew up with nothing. He got an opportunity to make some money, and he took it."

Asher's jaw clenched, his gaze fixed on the flames. "I get being broke, but selling your soul for cash? That's a line I'd never cross." His voice carried a raw edge.

Of course he wouldn't. The firelight carved shadows across his face, highlighting the tension in his jaw. "You sound like you know that fight." Her words were soft, probing gently.

His fingers twitched as if he wanted to reach for something, or maybe just a way out of the conversation. Then he sat on the chair again. "Growing up, we had nothing." His voice was low, almost swallowed by the rain. "We lived in trailer parks, in rented trailers, and even those weren't secure. We faced evictions... Seemed we were always one step away from losing it all. But my parents were determined to stay in Shadow Cove. Said they had the best schools in the region. Which meant we were always surrounded by rich kids and mansions—people who'd look at us like we were trash."

"I hope you know I never thought that. My family never thought that."

He shrugged. "It's possible I read into people's looks and comments. I thought everyone knew how poor we were, but maybe..."

"I didn't know."

Asher acknowledged that with a nod. "My dad... He's a good man in so many ways, but he took risks, stupid ones, always chasing the quick buck. He gambled, he borrowed. He lost just about every penny he got his hands on. Thank God Mom was a hard worker, but she had no education and two kids to raise. She could only do so much."

Cici leaned forward, her hands clasped in her lap to keep from reaching for him. "That must've been so hard."

His eyes flicked to hers, then away. "Knowing one mistake could unravel everything. And maybe I knew too much—much more than my little brother, who just took everything in stride. Not me. I wanted to help. I wanted to fix it. But I was a kid. What could I do?"

Her heart clenched with pity for the little boy Asher had been, pity he would scorn if she voiced it.

"I'd see those big houses on the coast, the kids with their new sneakers, and I just felt...invisible."

"You weren't invisible, Asher. Not to me. Not to the school. You were valedictorian."

His smile held no humor. "Even as small as our class was, I bet half the kids didn't know who I was until I stood on that podium at graduation and gave my speech."

She'd argue, but was he right? How many people had known him? She had because they'd been in classes together. She'd always liked Asher. But he'd been quiet and kept to himself. He hadn't played sports or been involved in clubs. She'd never thought to wonder why not.

Now, she guessed his family couldn't afford the fees and couldn't promise rides after meetings and events. Maybe they'd lived so close to the edge financially that even student council was beyond their means.

She swallowed, her throat tight. "What about now? Where are your parents?"

"They've got an apartment in Portland."

"They're doing okay?"

"They're not going to lose it, if that's what you mean."

"You'll make sure of that."

He shrugged, telling her she'd guessed right.

"How about your brother?"

"Drew's...still trying to figure out his life, but he supports himself."

"I get it, why it's so important to you to buy your own place, to own something of value."

He didn't meet her eyes. "It probably seems stupid to you. Stupid and small and...irrelevant, but it's all I want. Just to be able to take care of myself and...and them, if they need me to. I just need to be...enough."

He was so much more than *enough*. He was brave, loyal, fiercely protective, fully competent. Yet he settled for so little, tethered to a past that kept him from soaring. "You could aim higher, you know." She kept her voice barely above a whisper. "You're...amazing, Asher. You're far more than just 'enough,' and you deserve a condo, a house, and so much more."

His eyes locked on hers, raw and unguarded, and the air felt as charged as the storm outside. For a moment, she thought he might move closer, might bridge the gap between them. But then he looked away, clearing his throat. "I need to check the weather." He shoved his feet into his shoes, then dug in his duffel bag and pulled out a sweatshirt.

Cici swallowed the words she wanted to say, that she admired the way he'd risen above his childhood. That she admired the way he took responsibility for his parents and his little brother. That he could've gone the way of Wendall Gagnon, stealing to get ahead, but instead he'd become a great man.

But his walls were back up. So she kept her lips clamped tightly closed.

"Grab something warm to wear, if you're cold." He toed his bag. "Take whatever you want. We'll be on the road again soon." With that, he stepped outside onto the porch. To watch the weather, and to get away from her.

Outside, the rain still pounded, a relentless curtain hiding the world. But the storm would pass, and they'd continue their journey to Shadow Cove, and after that...

After that, he'd go back to his life and leave her in the past.

CHAPTER SIXTEEN

Asher guided the motorcycle through the darkness, its headlight cutting a narrow path through the wet night. The roads gleamed like mirrors, reflecting what little light existed, making it nearly impossible to distinguish between asphalt and standing water. He kept their speed painfully slow, every muscle tense as he navigated the treacherous conditions.

Behind him, Cici's arms tightened around his waist each time they hit a patch of standing water or when the bike's tires struggled for purchase on the slick pavement. The rain had finally stopped, but its aftermath made the ride almost as dangerous.

Though less dangerous than being holed up in a cabin with Cici. He always said too much when he was with her, always revealed too much about himself. She made it easy to talk, and unlike the cruel prom queen who still lived in his head, today's Cici was kind and generous, never judgmental and always looking at him with that...that fully invested expression, as if every word he spoke mattered to her.

She was not who he'd built her up in his mind to be. She wasn't cruel, and sure, she'd been prom queen, but that was it was because she'd been admired by so many people. Because she'd been kind, even back then, except for that one ugly moment.

And he was falling for her all over again. He'd call himself a fool, except who *wouldn't* fall for her? She was exactly the kind of woman he dreamed of building a life with someday.

When he completed his assignment, he'd deliver her to Ballentine and her family, and then...and then he'd figure it out. Because Cici had become the spectacular woman he'd known, instinctively, back in high school, that she would be. And if she'd consider someone like him, then he'd be a fool not to pursue her.

They were almost there. By his calculations, they were an hour from Portland, maybe an hour and a half from Shadow Cove. So close. But his stomach cramped with hunger, and his shoulders ached.

As they rounded a sharp curve, the bike's headlight illuminated a small, weathered sign that read "Millerville." The faded lettering promised gas and food, exactly what they needed.

"There's a town ahead," he called over his shoulder. "We should stop."

He expected an argument—she always seemed to have an opinion—but her only response was "Okay."

As Asher guided the motorcycle down the winding road toward the distant glow of civilization, he felt a rush of relief.

Millerville turned out to be little more than a crossroads with a few buildings clustered around it. They passed a fast-food restaurant. Right beyond that, the gas station's fluorescent lights cast an eerie blue-white glow over the wet pavement and deserted gas pumps. Asher pulled in and cut the engine.

"Thank God," Cici murmured as she dismounted. She peeled off her helmet and shook out her hair, a wavy mass of strawberry blond that, even after hours matted to her head, still managed to look good.

Asher surveyed the gas station with its dim interior lights. "Let's fill up and use the restroom."

"I need to stretch anyway." She did, raising her hands and arching like a kitten.

He looked away. He needed to keep his focus on the task, not on the too-distracting woman who had no idea how she affected him.

While Asher filled the tank, Cici headed inside. He watched her through the window as she spoke to a clerk, who pointed toward the back of the store. When she disappeared from view, Asher scanned their surroundings, the habit so ingrained he hardly realized he was doing it. The road remained empty, only puddles reflecting the station's harsh lights.

Once the tank was full, he pushed the bike to a parking spot and followed her inside.

When he emerged from the bathroom, Cici was waiting by the door.

"There's food next door," he said as they stepped outside in the cool evening. The thought of fried chicken and mashed potatoes and gravy had his stomach growling. "We should grab something."

Cici glanced at her watch. "We're so close. We had lunch—"

"Hours ago."

Her lips pursed. "Couldn't we just push through?"

Maybe *she* could, but he was the one behind the wheel. "I can't drive safely if I'm running on empty. And I can't exactly munch a snack while we're on the road."

She looked between him and the restaurant, then sighed. "Twenty minutes won't make much difference at this point."

They dashed across the parking lot, hunched against the drizzle that had started up again. Though cars snaked around the restaurant for the drive-through line, the dining room was nearly empty—just an older couple in one booth. The fluorescent lighting made Cici's skin look pale, the shadows under her eyes more pronounced. She needed rest. They both did.

They ordered quickly—fried chicken and all the fixings for him, a grilled chicken sandwich for her. They filled their cups with ice and soda.

"Smells like heaven in a cardboard box." Asher slid into a booth in the corner, where he could keep an eye on the door. They unwrapped their food, and he took a bite that had him moaning with satisfaction. What was it about fast-food fried chicken that tasted so good?

Lard, probably, but he wasn't going to worry about that.

Cici removed pickles with the very tips of her fingers, as if just touching them turned her stomach, then nibbled the edge of her sandwich. "Should we check in with Alyssa? See what she's learned?"

"Good idea." He pulled out a burner phone and handed it over.

Cici dialed her sister and put the call on speaker before setting the phone between them.

"Glad you called," Alyssa answered. "I was starting to worry."

"We're getting close," Cici said. "Did you learn anything new?"

Asher was happy to let Cici direct the conversation, eating his dinner as quickly as possible so they could get back on the road.

"Actually, yes." Keys clicked rapidly in the background. "I managed to identify two of the other men who tracked you down near the airfield. I found traffic cam footage from when they passed through town."

"Were there more?"

"There's a guy in the backseat of the sedan. Looks like a big guy, bearded, but I can't get enough of his face to ID."

Cici met Asher's eyes. "Could be the guy you fought with."

"The linebacker you took out."

"Wait," Alyssa said. "Cici took him out?"

"The guy's head was a fast ball over the plate, and your sister hit it like Big Papi in the ninth."

Cici shook her head. "Not exactly."

"Nice," Alyssa said.

"Anyway..." Asher wiped his greasy fingers. "Names?"

"Mendez. Like Souza, he's connected to the Fourth Hood in New York. Sending a photo."

The phone dinged. Cici looked, then showed it to him. It was Pretty Boy, the one Asher had put in a sleeper hold.

"The third guy, though, that's where it gets interesting. His name is Dominic Falcone, and he runs with a completely different crew out of Boston. They call themselves the Northside Kings."

He looked at the photo. This one had a couple of face tattoos that didn't hide the acne scars.

"I've heard of them," Asher said. "They focus on illegal drugs, right? How are they connected to the Fourth Hood? Aren't they into human trafficking and prostitution?"

"According to law enforcement," Alyssa said, "not only are they not connected, they're rivals." Asher didn't know Alyssa at all. Even so, it was easy to tell by the tone of her voice that she was saving the juiciest news. "On paper, there's no connection between them."

"Gagnon." Cici spoke the obvious—and the most important piece of the puzzle. "He's the connection. Somehow."

"Exactly," Alyssa said. "I'm sending you a photo of Maxwell Pierce, the Fourth Hood's suspected ringleader."

The phone vibrated with an incoming text, and Cici navigated to look at it, then angled it for Asher to see the guy. Clean-cut, perfect smile, expensive suit. Nothing about him screamed "gang leader" or "human trafficker." Rich guy with rich-guy resources, exactly the kind of person Asher didn't trust.

Cici's remarks earlier about pegging all rich people—or poor people—had him amending his first thought. He tended not to trust rich people, but that was his problem, not theirs.

Alyssa continued. "He presents himself as this champion of urban renewal while running one of the most vicious trafficking operations on the East Coast."

Asher angled toward the phone. "I'm guessing you've figured out how he's connected to Gagnon?"

"Pierce has been paying him like clockwork. A hundred thousand every quarter since 2020. The payments go through shell companies and end up in an offshore account that belongs to Gagnon. It's pretty impressive the way he's covered his tracks."

Asher did the math. "That's two million dollars."

"And counting," Alyssa said.

Cici pushed her sandwich away. "I'm guessing Gagnon found proof of Pierce's involvement in the human trafficking ring that law enforcement couldn't find, and rather than turn the guy in, he's using it for profit."

Asher fought to control his facial expression, though his smirk wanted out. "The guy's a murderer, Cici. Don't tell me you're surprised."

"You'd think selling little girls into prostitution might be a line even someone like Gagnon wouldn't cross."

The problem was, once people started operating on the wrong side of the law—and the moral good—that line became harder and harder to see. Asher had gone up against terrorists who adored their own families but didn't hesitate to kill innocent children in order to further their own political—or financial

—ends. Gagnon was no different from the worst of the worst—and Asher had met his share.

"So he's blackmailing Pierce." Asher directed his words to the phone. "He must be doing the same thing with the Boston guy—Falcone's boss."

"Haven't proved it yet, but that's my theory."

"It explains why men from rival gangs are working together to find us." Cici's face lost what was left of its color. "Depending on how many gang leaders he's blackmailing... He could have a nearly unlimited number of people at his disposal."

"Yeah." By Alyssa's tone of voice, Cici's remark had sobered her. She sounded more serious as she continued. "I'm looking for similar payment patterns from the Northside Kings' ringleader. Haven't found anything yet, but given what we know, it's a reasonable assumption. Gagnon created a network of criminals who have no choice but to help him."

Cici's hand trembled as she reached for her cup. "That's a dangerous game he's playing. What keeps the people he's blackmailing from taking him out?"

Asher fielded that. "He must have a contingency plan, some kind of dead-man's switch. Something that automatically releases all his blackmail material if he doesn't check in regularly."

Cici's eyes widened. "So every single person he's got dirt on—politicians, crime bosses, whoever—they all have a vested interest in keeping him breathing. It's not just that they can't kill him. They actually need to protect him."

"That's how I'd do it," Alyssa said.

She was a unique soul, this sister of Cici's. Asher got the feeling she'd ridden that line between good and evil a few times in her life, unlike Cici, who was innocent and still seemed to feel the pang of disappointment when she learned of another person's evil.

Maybe Asher was too jaded, but he couldn't help the cold satisfaction that filled him. "Maybe his enemies have a reason to keep him alive, but what's that to us?" He glanced around to make sure nobody in the restaurant was close enough to overhear. "Way I see it, we eliminate Gagnon, we're doing the world a favor, taking out a whole pile of...excrement in one shot."

"Asher." Cici's voice went sharp. "You're talking about murder."

"Not murder." Despite his words, he touched the gun tucked into its holster beneath his T-shirt, a reminder it was close. A reminder that he could do what needed to be done. "I'm just saying I won't lose sleep if this guy and his army of thugs don't make it home." Cici's eyes were wide with shock, though what did she expect? These people were trying to kill her. "In my defense, Gagnon started it. I plan to finish it."

Cici's jaw tightened. "After what happened to Mr. D... I see what you mean."

"You two go ahead and plot homicide." Alyssa's voice cut through his dark contemplation. "Meanwhile, I'll see if I can find the connection between Gagnon and whoever's running the Northside Kings. And Callan is encouraging me to notify the FBI."

Asher straightened. "Who's Callan? I thought it was understood—"

"He's my fiancé." Alyssa adopted a *relax, I've got this* cadence. "He's former CIA."

Cici reached across the table and took Asher's hand. "He's a good guy, Asher. You'd like him."

Since he hadn't been consulted about reading this Callan guy in, he figured he didn't have a choice in trusting him.

"I know Forbes has some guy at the FBI on speed dial," Alyssa said. "Is it okay with you if I forward this information to him?"

"Yeah, that's a good idea."

Cici took the phone and started scrolling. "Sis, we've got a contact in Philly." She read off Detective Harris's number. "Let her know what you've learned. We might as well all work together."

"Good plan," Alyssa said. "Maybe we can take this guy down without killing him. Novel concept, I know."

Asher supposed that would be ideal. But at this point, after everything they'd been through—and knowing this guy wouldn't stop until Cici was dead—Asher couldn't make himself reject the idea of taking Gagnon out permanently. Whatever it took to protect her.

"Look," Alyssa continued, "this guy's network is…huge. You shouldn't be out there alone. You should bring in—"

"We're almost there," Asher said, his voice clipped. "By the time anyone can get to us, we'll be in Shadow Cove."

Cici's head tipped to one side, and he could see an argument forming on the tip of her tongue.

He'd gotten them this far, hadn't he? Through every ambush, every close call. He could finish this job. He *would* finish it.

Alyssa said, "I'm just saying—"

"I understand." He leaned toward the phone as if she could see him. "We're less than two hours out, and nobody knows where we are."

"It's okay," Cici said. "Asher knows what he's doing."

Her words surprised him, fortified him. He'd earned her trust, and he wasn't going to let her down.

"All right, then," Alyssa said. "I'll keep digging. You two stay safe."

"Will do." Cici lifted the phone. "Thanks, sis. Love you."

"Back atcha. By the way, we're at Brooklynn's. When you're close, we'll go to Mom and Dad's to meet you."

"You're in Shadow Cove?"

"Of course. We're all praying you two make it here without incident."

Cici's eyes filled. "That means...so much." She and her sister traded a few more words, then Cici ended the call and handed the phone to him.

He pocketed it. "Thank you for...that. For believing in me."

"Are you kidding? If not for you, I never would've made it out of Philly. Now, thanks to Alyssa, we know what we're doing. I should just be quiet and let you two handle everything."

Asher caught something off in her tone—a brittleness that didn't match her words. "What do you mean, be quiet? You've been plenty helpful."

She picked at her sandwich, not meeting his eyes.

"You were the one who suggested Gagnon had leverage. You're the one who suggested we call Alyssa for intel. And don't think I've forgotten how you saved my life. If you hadn't whacked that guy in the woods, I'd be dead."

"Rather be lucky than good, I guess." She let out a sharp laugh, but there was no humor in it. "You don't have to try to make me feel better, Asher. Alyssa's crazy smart. You're a Navy SEAL, for crying out loud. I'm..." She gestured vaguely at herself. "I'm here too."

"Why are you downplaying your role? I don't understand."

"It doesn't matter."

"It does matter. It matters to me."

She looked past him, and he watched indecision play across her face. When she finally spoke, her voice was barely above a whisper. "I was in that school play, back in fifth grade. You remember?"

He had no idea what she was talking about. "I wasn't into drama."

"Well, I was, a little. I got a good role. I was so excited about it, about my whole family coming to see me. It's stupid, I know, but...I guess I always felt overshadowed by them."

He couldn't imagine how someone as beautiful and kind and talented as Cici could feel overshadowed by anyone.

"The night before the play," she said, "I overheard my mother reminding my dad about it. He scoffed, said he had to work. He said, 'If she ever does something important, I'll be there.'"

Ouch. "I'm sure he didn't mean—"

"He didn't mean for me to hear it, you're right. But he meant it. He didn't come to the play. He's never shown up for..." She shook her head, still not meeting his eyes. "He didn't even make it to my high school graduation. I guess that didn't rise to his level of importance."

"Not defending him, but he had a pretty stressful job, right? At the CIA?"

"He was also a father." She leaned forward, warming to the conversation. "Once, one of my jewelry designs was nominated for a prize. It was no big deal—"

"It was a big deal," he said. "Go on."

Gratitude flashed in her eyes as if he'd done her a favor by stating the obvious. "There was an event at the little art gallery where I took classes. Dad showed up." She sighed. "He spent the whole evening talking to my cousin Daniel, who'd just graduated from medical school, telling him how amazing he was, how proud of him... He's never once said that to me. I waited all night for him to actually look at the pendant I'd designed. He never did."

Dad had his issues, but Asher had never doubted his love. He realized Cici's seemingly perfect family wasn't so perfect after all. "Sounds like your dad wasn't so great at the whole fatherhood thing."

She crumpled the sandwich wrapper into a tight ball. "That's the understatement of the century."

"It also sounds like you've let your father's deficiencies define how you think about yourself." It felt weird, talking about this. He believed in God, but he didn't go around sermonizing. But Cici needed to hear the truth, so he'd speak it, even if it felt uncomfortable. "Your dad wasn't great at loving you, so you don't think you're lovable. What would God say about that, hmm?"

Her eyes narrowed. She lifted one shoulder and let it drop.

"You do know what He'd say. That you're the person He created you to be, and He adores you. So…not that it's easy or anything, but I guess my point is, who cares what Gavin Wright thinks when you have the King of the whole universe pleased with you?"

That brought a hint of a smile. "When you put it that way…"

"It's the only way to look at it." He loved this window into Cici's heart, but time was ticking, and they needed to get back on the road. Reaching for her trash, he asked, "You're finished?"

"Yeah."

He dumped the trash, and they headed for the door.

In an hour and a half, they'd be in Shadow Cove. At that point…at that point, he'd have to figure out what to do next, because the last thing he wanted was to walk away from Cici again.

CHAPTER SEVENTEEN

The warmth spreading through Cici's chest had nothing to do with the restaurant's temperature and everything to do with Asher's words.

"Thank you."

He held the door open, and she stepped back into the cool night air.

"For what you said in there about how God sees me," she clarified. "I needed the reminder."

He stepped into the shadow of the building and gazed down at her, his eyes serious. "I meant every word."

Of course he did. He wasn't the kind of man to say what he didn't believe. That was why it had affected her so. "I need to stop letting my father's opinion define my worth. Maybe I'm just the middle child who never quite measured up in the Wright family, but God thinks I'm special."

"He's not the only one who does." The intensity in his voice made her breath catch. He stepped closer, holding her eye contact. "Cici, if I had every Wright sister to choose from—heck, if I had every woman in the world to choose from—I'd still choose you."

She inhaled sharply. His words were a shock...and a balm. "Asher..."

"I know. It's crazy and...probably feels sudden to you, but it isn't, not for me." He shifted his hands to her waist, his voice dropping to that low rumble that made her pulse quicken. "I knew back in high school that you were special. I've been trying to get you out of my head for a decade, but when I saw you in that hotel room the other day..." He shook his head, a rueful smile playing at his lips. "All those years of telling myself I'd imagined how incredible you were, and then there you were, beautiful and...a little flustered to see me." His lips tipped up in a small smile. "No matter what I've been telling myself, I knew I was in trouble all over again."

"I've thought about you, too," she whispered. "I used to wonder what would have happened if I'd been smart enough to accept your invitation to the prom."

His whole life might've been different. They could have found each other years earlier. "Maybe it was better this way. If I'd had you, I wouldn't have gone into the Navy, and..." He shrugged. "It was good for me, getting away from Maine, becoming someone I never imagined I could be."

Though he wouldn't say it to her, as a SEAL, he had made a difference. He'd saved lives. He was a different man now, a better man.

His thumbs traced gentle circles on her waist. "But now I'm back, and while so many things have changed, how I feel about you... You matter to me, Cici. More now than you did back then, because now I know who you really are. Your courage, your heart, the way you see the best in people."

She reached up, her fingers grazing his jaw. "I care about you too. More than makes sense, considering we've only been together a few days."

"Feels like longer."

"In the best way." She tipped toward him, but reality crashed back in. "What happens when we get back to Shadow Cove? You live in Boston, and my work takes me all over the East Coast."

"We'll figure it out." He leaned his forehead against hers. "I'm not giving up on this. On you. Not again."

The certainty in his voice made her chest tighten with hope and fear. "Promise?"

"Promise."

She stood on her toes and kissed him, soft and quick, tasting the future in that brief contact. When she pulled back, his eyes were dark with emotion.

"We should go," he said reluctantly.

"We should." But she didn't want to. She wanted to stay in this moment, in this bubble where they were just Asher and Cici, where the world held promise instead of danger.

But the sound of an engine turning over in the distance reminded her that they weren't safe yet. They returned to the motorcycle, donned their ponchos and helmets, and climbed on. She wrapped her arms around his waist, holding him a little tighter than necessary.

The road stretched dark ahead of them as they pulled away from Millerville's glowing lights. Asher kept their speed steady, navigating the winding curves with ease.

Cici pressed her cheek against his back, feeling the steady rhythm of his breathing. Less than two hours to Shadow Cove. Less than two hours until this nightmare was over and they could figure out what came next.

∼

Peace, Cici realized, was a luxury they couldn't afford.

The twenty-minute pitstop had stretched into an hour, but

now the motorcycle's engine hummed beneath them as they wound through the Maine countryside. The headlight carved a narrow tunnel through the darkness ahead, illuminating rain-slicked asphalt that gleamed like obsidian.

Cici pressed closer against Asher, the conversation at the restaurant replaying in her mind. For the first time in years, maybe ever, she felt truly seen. Not as the overlooked middle child or the Wright sister who never quite measured up, but as herself. Special. Chosen.

The thought filled her with warmth, but fear twisted in her stomach. They'd been stationary too long. Every minute they'd spent talking had been another minute for their enemies to close the distance. Asher was certain they were safe, that nobody knew where they were. But Gagnon and his goons had caught up with them before when they'd thought they were invisible.

She'd already had so much to lose. Now there was this new hope for her future, maybe even a future with this amazing man. The thought that she might not get to see where their feelings took them raised fresh terror inside her.

The road stretched ahead, flanked by dense forest that no longer felt safe but pressed in like walls. No streetlights, no other vehicles, just the two of them racing through a void toward Shadow Cove and safety.

"How much farther, do you think?" she called over the engine noise.

"An hour, maybe less." Asher's voice was steady, calming her worries.

He knew what he was doing. He'd proved that over and over. She needn't worry.

She settled in for the final stretch, deciding to enjoy the closeness. The miles passed in a hypnotic blur of darkness and engine vibration. Cici let herself imagine what it would be like to see her family again, to sleep in her childhood bed without fear. To wake up tomorrow and plan a future with Asher instead of just trying to survive.

The daydream shattered when twin beams shone in the rearview mirror. Probably nothing. There were towns around here, homes and farms. Surely that was just a local.

It caught up fast and then hovered a dozen yards behind them.

Even as she told herself she was fine, worry churned in her stomach. "Asher."

"I see them. Hang on."

She tightened her grip as the motorcycle shot forward.

She expected the car to shrink behind them, but it didn't. It kept pace. No matter how fast Asher drove—too fast for the wet roads—it stayed on their tail.

Cici's stomach dropped as they accelerated into a sharp curve, the bike leaning at an angle that made her squeeze her eyes shut.

Their pursuers didn't drop back at all.

"We're going to have to lose them," Asher shouted. "Look at the map, find us a narrow road, better yet, a trail."

She fumbled for the phone she'd shoved in her pocket, gripping Asher's shirt in her other hand. When the app was open, she searched for someplace where this glorified dirt bike could be an advantage over the sedan behind them.

Terror had her hands shaking so hard she feared she'd drop the phone. If she didn't find a trail, they were sunk.

Somehow, impossibly, they'd been tracked down again.

"There's a narrow road up ahead. Not a trail, but maybe—"

"Warn me when we're close." As frightened as she was, Asher sounded calm and in control, as if he dealt with this kind of thing every single day. She thanked God for his skills. If anybody could get them out of this, Asher could.

The car behind them suddenly accelerated, its engine roaring as it pulled alongside them on the narrow road.

Cici's heart hammered against her ribs as the passenger window rolled down, something gleaming in the darkness.

"Gun!" she screamed.

Asher swerved hard to the right, the motorcycle's tires bouncing off the edge of the pavement. The crack of gunfire split the night air. The bullet missed, but she could swear she'd felt the heat of it whizzing past her face.

The bike wobbled dangerously as Asher fought to maintain control, getting it back onto the pavement. There was a deep gully separating the highway from the forest, filled with water. Impossible to tell how deep.

There was no exit until they made it to the turnoff.

"Two hundred feet!" She could barely force the words out over her terror, watching the map.

Another shot rang out, this one shattering the motorcycle's side mirror. Fragments battered her helmet.

She dipped to the side, looking for the road. "It's just ahead!"

Asher had just downshifted when she caught the glint of something, right where the side road should be.

They were nearly there when that something materialized—a truck.

It lurched onto the road in front of them, blocking their way.

Asher swerved to avoid it, the bike's tires skidding on the wet pavement.

The world seemed to slow as the bike skidded, veering toward the far edge. It hit the lip and careened into the forest.

Beyond the layer of trees ahead, there was nothing but blackness. A cliff?

The bike crashed into a clump of bushes and small trees.

She lost her grip on him and flew, then landed in the bracken a dozen feet away.

She lay there, shocked, on the soft ground. Everything hurt, but she could move. She wasn't badly injured.

She crawled to a nearby tree and pulled herself up. "Asher!" She stumbled toward him.

He lay half covered by the dirt bike. He wasn't moving.

Lights shone behind her. The men were coming.

They were running out of time.

Moving toward him, she yanked off her helmet. When she reached where Asher had fallen, she lifted the heavy, ruined bike off him, pushed it out of the way, and knelt at his side. "Asher, please!" She shook his shoulder.

Her hand came away sticky. He was injured. Shot?

"Run." His word came out on a rattling breath. "Run, Cici."

What? No, she couldn't leave him here. She needed him to be all right. "Come on. We have to—"

Someone gripped her arms and pulled her away.

She screamed and twisted, her elbow connecting with something solid. A grunt of pain, then rough hands dragged her backward through the underbrush. Branches tore at her poncho as she fought against her captor's grip.

"I'll take care of her." The man's voice was gravelly. "Check the bodyguard."

A couple more men closed in, surrounding Asher and the bike.

"He's done," one of them said.

"Get rid of him," the one holding her said.

"No!" Cici thrashed, panic flooding her system. "He needs help!"

A flashlight beam swept across Asher's still form, and her heart clenched at the sight. His face was deathly pale.

"Please," she begged, her voice breaking. "I'll come with you, just let me—"

"You're coming either way, sweetheart." The man's hands were vises on her skin. Even so, she fought to escape, eyes fixed on Asher. *Please, be okay. Please!*

Asher wasn't fighting as another man checked his pulse. He was unconscious. Or...she couldn't even let herself think the other possibility.

One thug yanked Asher's bag off the back of the bike, then rolled the bike deeper into the woods, toward the void. He disappeared in the darkness.

A moment later, the sickening sound of metal crashing against rocks. He must've rolled the bike off a cliff.

"Toss the bodyguard over with it," one of the men said. "Maybe it'll look like an accident."

"No!" She screamed. "Please, just leave him!"

But they gripped Asher's arms and dragged him away.

A moment later, they came back without him.

He was gone. Asher was gone, and she was all alone.

∽

The warehouse smelled like rotten eggs and despair.

Cici's captors manhandled her through a maze of dusty machinery and empty crates, her wet sneakers squeaking against the concrete floor.

They'd only driven ten minutes, maybe fifteen, from the accident site, but they might as well have been a thousand miles away. Nobody knew where she was. Her only hope for help was...gone.

The men hauled her up a flight of stairs and into an office. A large metal desk and a couple of cheap rolling chairs were arranged haphazardly. The lights overhead buzzed and flickered, giving everything a sickly yellow glow. Dark fabric had been nailed over what she assumed must be exterior windows.

The other end of the room was filled with filing and storage cabinets, one of which had been shoved in front of a door that must lead outside. Only the top of the jamb was visible.

The men stepped in behind her, then released her in the center of the space.

Leaning against the desk was the man whose face had filled her nightmares.

Wendall Gagnon smiled when he saw her—a slow, satisfied curve of lips that held no warmth, only predatory pleasure. His straight teeth gleamed, and those wide-set eyes assessed her like a butcher examining prime cuts.

"The bodyguard?" Gagnon spoke to the men who hovered nearby.

One stepped forward, slender and well-dressed. He'd been in the forest. Now, she recognized him as one of the guys who'd followed them from the barn the day before. "He's dead."

The words, spoken so casually, hit hard. She sucked in air, panic and grief working their way up her throat.

"Good." Gagnon turned his attention to her. "Miss Wright." His voice was cultured, almost pleasant, as if they were meeting at a cocktail party. The same tone he'd employed moments before he'd murdered Mr. D at the jewelry store. "Do you have any idea how much trouble you've caused me?"

Cici's legs threatened to give out. The image of Asher's still form being dragged away played on repeat in her mind, and she couldn't stop the sob that escaped her throat. She pressed her hand to her mouth, trying to hold back the tears that had been threatening.

"I asked you a question." Gagnon's tone sharpened, cutting through her jumbled emotions like a blade.

She forced herself to look at him, this monster who had destroyed everything. "He's dead because of you." The words came out raw, broken. "He's dead because of your greed."

"Your friend chose to interfere in my business." Gagnon smoothed his suit jacket with manicured hands. "Actions have consequences, Miss Wright. Surely your father taught you that."

His reference to her father didn't surprise her. Obviously, he'd done his homework. It was the casual dismissal of Asher's life that hit her like a physical blow. She wanted to scream, to launch herself at Gagnon and claw that smug expression off his face. But she forced herself to stay still, to think. Asher had died trying to protect her. She wouldn't let his sacrifice be meaningless.

"What do you want?" Her voice was steadier, though her hands still trembled.

"Straight to the point. I appreciate that." Gagnon gestured to one of his men—the bald one who'd been with him in Philadelphia. The one who'd grabbed her in the forest. "Search the bag."

This was Souza, she remembered. He upended Asher's duffel onto one of the metal desks. Contents spilled across the surface clothes, toiletries, the burner phones. First-aid supplies, Asher's laptop, a tightly folded blanket.

The man's sausage-like fingers pawed through everything.

The search went on for several minutes, Souza growing increasingly agitated as he found nothing of value. He shook out every piece of clothing, checked every pocket, even unscrewed the cap on Asher's shampoo bottle to peer inside.

Cici held her breath, the necklace burning against her ribs where she'd hidden it in the zipper pouch. As soon as they found it, she'd be dead. Simple as that.

Souza straightened, his expression grim. "Nothing."

Gagnon's smile faltered, replaced by something much more dangerous. His cold gaze fixed on Cici. "Where are my things, Miss Wright?"

"What do you mean?" Her voice was high-pitched with fear, her question not at all convincing.

He pushed away from the desk and approached her with measured steps. "Search her."

Terror spiked through her chest. "Wait—"

"Too late for that." To the men, he said, "Do it now."

Rough hands grabbed her arms, pawed at her body. She twisted, but there were too many of them.

She'd tell him if she could make her voice cooperate. Anything to get these disgusting goons away from her. Finally, she managed, "I have it. I have it." The words came out just as one of the men gripped the buckle holding the pouch around her waist.

"Got something, boss."

In an instant, the buckle came undone, and the man took the pouch to Gagnon, presenting it as if it were a prized treasure.

The other men stepped away, though she felt Souza's presence right behind her.

"It's just jewelry," she snapped. "Gold and stones. Why is it so important to you?"

Gagnon took the pouch, his eyes glittering with something that might have been amusement. "Just jewelry?" He laughed, a sound devoid of humor. He unzipped the pouch and upended the contents onto the desk. The Crimson Duchess spilled out, along with the rest of Grace Ballentine's things.

Gagnon poked through them, lifting them, studying them, then setting them back down. The necklace, the Cartier watch, the earrings, the bracelet. All valuable. None as valuable as Asher's life.

He set the items down and lifted his gaze back to her. "Where's the rest of it?"

The question surprised her. "There was nothing else in the bag as valuable as those pieces."

"My dear girl, you truly have no idea what you stumbled onto." He picked up the Cartier watch, turning it over in his hands. "This? This is pocket change compared to what I'm really after." His fingers moved to the necklace, stroking the rubies with reverence that made her skin crawl. "Beautiful, certainly. Worth a fortune. But it's not what's going to keep me out of prison."

What was he talking about? What else could there be? She'd seen everything that had been in Grace Ballentine's jewelry case.

"Where is the bag?" He stepped toward her. "Where are the items that were inside it?"

Tucked in her purse, hidden beneath the motorcycle's seat. She wouldn't tell him anything. The sooner he found it, the sooner he'd order her killed. Not that anybody was coming to her rescue, but even so... Even so, she'd do everything in her power to put off the inevitable.

"There was a locket." He watched her expression, and she tried to hide her reaction, but she remembered the locket. She'd shown it to Asher the night before, so unloved that the silver was tarnished black.

"Ah, you know it." His voice was silk over steel. "Hardly worth anything, the cheap old thing. It belonged to my mother, a gift from her parents for her high school graduation. I stole it from her jewelry box many years ago, a reminder to aim higher than she ever did. A silly little trinket, but to me?" He leaned closer, close enough that she picked up the scent of his cologne, which on him somehow smelled like decay. "To me, it's worth more than all these baubles combined."

Her pulse hammered in her throat. She had no illusion that the locket held sentimental value for this man. What could possibly be so important about it?

"I don't know where it is." The words felt clumsy on her tongue.

Gagnon studied her for a long moment, those pale eyes dissecting every micro-expression. "You're a terrible liar, Miss Wright." He straightened, brushing imaginary lint from his sleeve. "But that's quite all right. If you don't have it on you, it must be with your deceased bodyguard."

He nodded toward two of his men—the well-dressed one from the barn and a hulking brute with cold eyes and face tattoos, one of the men Alyssa had ID'd. "Go back to where you found her. Search the motorcycle and the body."

The men exchanged a glance, and she caught the hesitation in their eyes, the way they looked anywhere but at Gagnon's face.

"Is there a problem?" His voice dropped to that scary whisper again.

"No problem, boss," the well-dressed one said quickly. "We're looking for a locket?"

"It should be in a velvet bag. Please, retrieve the bag and all its contents."

"On it," the slighter one said.

"And gentlemen?" Gagnon's smile was razor-sharp. "You don't want to know what happens if you fail."

As the two men hurried out, Cici felt a flicker of something that might have been hope. The men were afraid to tell him they'd thrown Asher and the motorcycle over a cliff. Now, they'd have to climb down that cliff and search what was left of the bike. She figured the remains of it were scattered all over the bottom.

It might buy her precious time.

Time for what, she didn't know. No one was coming for her. But every minute she stayed alive was another minute to figure out an escape, another minute to pray, and another minute to honor Asher's sacrifice by surviving.

CHAPTER EIGHTEEN

Pain throbbed in Asher's skull, dragging him back to consciousness.

He lay face-down in wet earth and scattered leaves, the metallic taste of blood and failure coating his tongue. For a moment, the world spun in sickening circles, memories crashing back in jagged fragments—the motorcycle skidding, gunfire splitting the night, Cici's scream echoing through the darkness.

Cici.

He pushed himself up on his elbows, ignoring the fire that shot through his shoulder. It took him a few tries to unclasp his helmet, his hands trembling, but finally he managed it, yanking the thing off.

Exhausted, he flopped onto his back and gazed above, where steep walls of rock and dirt rose on either side. He was in a deep ravine. He must've rolled down here—and now that he thought of it, flashes of memories peppered him. He hadn't rolled. He'd been tossed. The slope was maybe thirty feet. He'd have bounced off rocks and roots until the undergrowth had finally stopped his fall.

A rough trip, but he was still breathing.

The silence pressed against his eardrums, broken only by the trickle of water in a stream nearby. No voices. No footsteps. No Cici.

He pushed up and looked around, half-expecting to see her broken body, but she wasn't there. If they'd killed her, they'd have dumped her body too. But they hadn't.

The faint memory of her screaming.

They'd taken her.

Please. Let her be alive.

The world swam around him, and he fell back, staring up at the slice of cloudy sky visible between the canyon walls and tall trees. How long had he been unconscious? Minutes? Hours? Every second that passed was another second Cici was in Gagnon's hands, another second closer to—

Don't go there.

He'd failed. After everything—all his training, all his promises to keep her safe—he'd let them take her. The woman he'd just confessed his feelings to, the woman whose kiss had felt like his future, was now in the hands of killers.

Asher forced himself to his feet, swaying as vertigo threatened to drop him again. His old knee injury ached. His left shoulder screamed, and when he pressed his hand against it, his fingers came away sticky. He tried to move his arm, but the jolt of pain was sharp and deep.

The blood needed to be dealt with, but this he'd experienced before. The fall had dislocated his shoulder.

He looked around, gaze landing on a nearby oak. He hobbled toward it and leaned his back against it. This was going to hurt.

Relax, he told himself. *Relax.*

He took deep breaths, praying for success, and slowly lifted the wrist on his injured arm with his other hand, holding it straight out in front of him.

It was torture, and he sucked in through his teeth, clamping down on the scream he refused to release.

And then, just like that, his shoulder shifted back into joint.

He was out of breath, but the worst of the pain was gone. Now, to deal with the blood.

He explored the wound with careful fingers. A bullet had grazed him where his neck met his shoulder—not deep, but it'd been close. Another inch and it could've hit his spine, or an artery.

Thank You, Lord.

The wound was mostly clotted now, telling him he'd been unconscious for too long.

Every minute he spent patching himself up was another minute Cici spent with monsters.

He patted his holster, expecting to find his gun gone. It wasn't, though. Somehow, those men had not thought to search for it.

He searched the area, hope flickering when he spotted debris from the motorcycle scattered among the rocks. The bike itself lay twisted against a boulder on the far side of the gorge, its frame bent beyond recognition. He hobbled that direction, ignoring the pain in his body that came from tumbling down a thirty-foot slope, and hopped the narrow stream.

His duffel bag was nowhere to be found. They must've taken it, which meant the burner phones were gone, along with any chance of calling for backup.

He picked through the wreckage, tossing aside chunks of twisted metal and plastic. There—a flash of leather wedged beneath a fallen branch. He yanked Cici's purse free, his hands shaking as he unzipped it. She'd had a burner phone, hadn't she? It had to be here.

He dug through her bag. The bag of jewelry was there, along with her wallet, lip gloss, tissues. He grabbed the tissues, dipped them in the stream's clear water, and dabbed at his wound. He needed something to patch it up, but unlike him, Cici didn't travel with first-aid supplies.

No phone, either.

Nothing in her bag would help. He shrugged out of his sweatshirt, careful of his injury, then took off his T-shirt and tore it into strips. He folded a small scrap and placed it over the wound. The rest he used to hold the makeshift bandage in place, covering the bandage and then wrapping the strip of fabric around his body, hooking it under the opposite arm. He tied it off.

It was the best he could do.

After pulling his sweatshirt back on, careful not to jostle the bandage, he hooked Cici's purse on his arm and jumped back over the stream.

He needed to figure out where they'd taken her, but climbing out of this ravine would be a challenge with just one good arm. He studied the steep walls, looking for handholds among the exposed roots and rocky outcroppings. He found a spot that looked manageable, with a series of natural ledges carved by years of erosion.

With Cici's purse slung across his good shoulder, he began the ascent. Every movement sent fresh waves of pain through his injured shoulder, but he gritted his teeth and pressed on. Dirt cascaded down as his boots scraped on loose stones. Halfway up, his grip slipped, and he slid back several feet before catching himself on a jutting root.

He stopped, realization hammering worse than the throbbing wound.

This was his fault. If he hadn't been so stubborn, so determined to prove to Bartlett that he was capable of handling this job alone, he'd have asked for backup. Not that Cici's sister wasn't good, but all her information about who Gagnon was and what he was doing hadn't prepared Asher for this ambush.

He needed a real team of trained pros on his side. He never should have tried to get Cici back to Shadow Cove on his own. Now...now if he didn't find her, find help, she'd pay the price for his arrogance.

By the time he hauled himself over the lip of the ravine, his vision was swimming again. He lay gasping on the forest floor, sweat stinging his eyes. But he'd done it.

Now he needed to find their trail.

The accident site wasn't hard to locate. He studied every twig, every rock, half-expecting to see Cici's body somewhere.

Tire tracks scarred the wet earth, and broken branches marked where the motorcycle had careened off the road. He found boot prints in the soft ground, multiple sets converging where they must have grabbed Cici. The thought of rough hands on her made his jaw clench, his head pound.

He saw where they'd pushed the bike. Saw where they'd dragged him. He followed the marks and stared over the cliff, seeing the distance he'd fallen in a new light.

He was lucky to be alive. He'd be finished if they'd thought to take off his helmet before throwing him down. Thank God for small favors—and big boneheads.

Maybe they'd believed him dead. If not, they must've thought the fall would kill him.

He turned and followed the tracks back to the road, where tire impressions showed that at least two vehicles had parked. Looked like they'd headed back toward Millerville.

Asher stood in the middle of the road and replayed what had happened. The sedan had been behind them. The truck had been waiting for them, parked in the intersection of the narrow road Cici'd found...

Wait.

Cici had been looking at a map. On a phone.

He turned a slow circle. She must've dropped it… somewhere.

Slowly, he retraced his steps, gaze scanning the forest floor. He remembered how she'd gripped his shirt, her arm tight around his left side. Meaning, she'd had the phone in her right hand.

He focused his search to the right of the bike's tire tracks. It must've flown out of her hand. It *must* be here.

Please, God, let it be here.

Because if he couldn't find that phone, then…then he had no idea what he'd do next.

CHAPTER NINETEEN

The silence in the warehouse office was suffocating, broken only by the incessant buzz of fluorescent lights that cast harsh shadows, making everything look like a crime scene. Which, Cici supposed, it *would* be soon enough.

She sat on the floor with her back pressed against a filing cabinet, trying to make herself as small as possible. Souza had zip-tied her wrists together and bound them to the handle of a file cabinet, his fingers *accidentally* skimming her body. The chill she'd felt had nothing to do with the cold concrete floor.

Now he stood near the door. Gagnon still leaned against the desk. They weren't talking, hadn't spoken since the other two men left to search for the velvet bag. The tension between them crackled like a live wire, dangerous and unpredictable. Whatever relationship they had, it wasn't built on trust or friendship. More like mutual necessity. One dangerous man using the other until he proved more useful dead than alive.

Every time she lifted her eyes from the floor, she caught Souza watching her. Not with disdain or clinical assessment. This was darker, hungrier. The way his gaze traveled over her body made her want to crawl under the nearest desk. There was hatred there, yes, but also something that turned her blood to ice. The look of a predator stalking its prey.

She forced herself to focus on something else. Anything else.

Letting her mind drift back to the jewelry store, she saw the situation more clearly. She should have run the moment she saw Mr. D collapse. Should have dropped the velvet bag and fled empty-handed out the back door. But no. She'd clutched those jewels like they were her ticket to glory. Until now, she'd never realized how desperately she wanted to be seen as more than just the irrelevant, unimportant Wright sister.

The irony wasn't lost on her. She'd wanted to be a hero, like Brooklynn, who'd helped solve a decades-old cold case. Like Alyssa, who'd saved a child's life—and played a part in taking down a terrorist. Cici had wanted to prove to her father that she could do something important, earn more from him than disdain and anger.

Instead, she'd gotten Asher killed.

The realization stole her breath.

If she'd just left the jewelry behind, maybe Gagnon wouldn't have bothered tracking her at all. Maybe he would've figured out who she was and tried to buy her silence. That was more his style. She wouldn't have taken his money, of course, but he might have tried negotiation before murder. Even if he *had* tracked her down, at least Asher wouldn't have been involved.

But no. Cici had to be the hero. She'd taken the bag, made herself a target because she'd been desperate to return Forbes's jewelry to him, to do something that mattered.

She pressed her face against her knees, giving in to her tears. She'd pretended she wasn't lonely as each of her cousins married and started families, and now two of her sisters were in long-term relationships. All the while, she'd been alone.

Now she understood why. She was no hero, and she was a fool to ever have believed she could do something important.

"Where are they?" Gagnon's words shocked her back to the moment. "How long does it take to find a bag?"

"Is the thing live?"

Gagnon tapped on his phone, then shook his head. "Those idiots went the wrong way."

What were they talking about? Was he tracking his own men?

Souza shifted his weight, his jaw tightening.

"The accident site is ten minutes from here." Gagnon's tone carried a sharp edge of impatience. "They've been gone almost an hour. What are they doing?"

"How'm I supposed to know? I'm stuck here with you."

"They're your men."

"One of them, and he's not *my man*. He was ordered to work with you, just like I was. Besides, the bike crashed, so they're probably having to search the whole area." Souza's defensive response only seemed to irritate Gagnon further.

And Cici could see why. A crashed bike didn't break into a thousand pieces. His answer made no sense. Obviously, he didn't want to tell Gagnon the truth—that they'd pushed the bike over a cliff.

He shot her a look, and though it came with no words, she got the message. Keep her mouth shut about what'd happened.

Her mind raced. How could she use what she knew against Souza? Would doing so help her or hurt her?

"Or maybe they decided my property was worth more than their loyalty." Gagnon's voice carried a dangerous edge. "If they're running, they'd better not stop, because I will catch up with them."

"They're not running," Souza said. "Least not Mendez.

Can't speak for Falcone. I wouldn't trust that guy to clean the john."

"You'd better hope neither of them betrayed me. Whether it's Mendez or Falcone, your boss will be the one to pay the price. And he won't lose sleep if you don't get back to New York. He doesn't suffer incompetents any more than I do."

When Gagnon turned his back—an arrogant display of power—Souza stared at him with pure, undiluted hatred.

Cici watched the exchange through her lashes, recognizing the dangerous shift in the room's dynamic.

She didn't miss when Souza's hand skimmed the bulge at his hip. He'd come armed—and prepared to kill. It seemed likely that one of these men wasn't walking out of here alive.

She prayed that, when bullets started flying, she wouldn't get caught in the crossfire.

CHAPTER TWENTY

An approaching engine rumbled like a storm gathering strength.

Asher had been combing the underbrush for nearly twenty minutes, searching for the phone Cici'd had in her hand when that truck came out of nowhere. The truck that had known exactly where they would be.

He had no idea how they'd been found—again. And no bandwidth right now to figure it out.

Especially now that someone was coming. Asher moved toward the road, preparing to step out in front of the car and request the use of a cell phone.

Or demand, if that proved necessary. He didn't want to threaten anyone, but he didn't have time to play nice.

But the car was slowing down, which told him maybe this wasn't a random passerby.

He crouched behind an old oak, coiled tight. The sound grew louder, gravel crunching under tires, as a vehicle parked on the shoulder.

Maybe it was law enforcement. Maybe someone had seen

the parked cars after the accident or heard the crash. Maybe someone had called 911.

Hope flickered like candlelight in a breeze.

But the voices that reached him were sharp and argumentative, and their words extinguished his hope.

"—your fault we've been driving in circles," one man snarled.

"You're the one who insisted we turn left. I shoulda known you don't know your left from your right."

Asher's blood turned to ice. The hunters were back. But why?

He didn't move, forcing his breathing to slow as the men walked within ten feet of him, continuing their heated exchange. Once they were past, Asher angled to get a look. Though he couldn't see faces, he recognized Pretty Boy, the one he'd put in a sleeper hold back near the barn in Litchfield, and his stockier companion. Since he wasn't the bald guy, Asher assumed this was Falcone.

They picked their way along the crash site, gazes skimming the ground, heading toward the gorge where the motorcycle lay twisted among the rocks.

"Gagnon's gonna put us both down if we don't find that bag." Falcone's voice carried a tremor of genuine fear.

They were looking for the velvet bag Cici had taken. Thank God Asher had found it first.

"You remember what he did to Arnold," Falcone added.

"Don't act like you give a crap." Pretty Boy—Mendez, Asher remembered—sneered the words. "He was my friend."

"He was supposed to be too strong to get taken out by a blow to the head. And anyway, you're the one we found unconscious. Ask me, it oughta be your head with the bullet hole."

Asher remembered the linebacker who'd nearly killed him.

If not for Cici, he'd have done it. Cici had whacked him in the head, and then Gagnon had killed him.

Asher wouldn't be shedding any tears. The guy was vicious. Even so, the thought had his stomach dropping. If Gagnon did that to a guy on his side, what would he do to Cici?

The men squared off, and then Falcone lifted his hands. "Look, I'm sorry about your buddy. If we don't find that thing, Gagnon's gonna kill us both. So let's just..." He gestured deeper into the woods.

That *thing*?

Who would refer to a priceless ruby necklace as a *thing*?

They continued their slow search, inching toward the gorge.

Asher moved silently through the woods, keeping his distance but wanting to hear what they said. They must not have searched Cici or else they'd have found The Crimson Duchess. What else could they be looking for?

The men reached the gorge, and Asher ducked behind a bush to watch.

"Jeez," Falcone muttered, peering down the cliffside. "Look at that mess."

"The bike's completely trashed."

"What if the bag got thrown somewhere?" Desperation laced Falcone's words. "Could be anywhere in these woods."

"We keep looking until we find it." Mendez pulled out a flashlight, its beam cutting through the gathering dusk. "We gotta find a place we can climb down." He kicked a loose stone over the edge. It clattered on the rocky slope. "This spot's as good as any."

"You first."

"It was your brilliant idea to throw the bike over a cliff instead of searching it properly."

"My idea?" Seemed Falcone's Boston accent deepened

when he was angry, so the word came out as *idear.* "You're the one who said we needed ta make it look like an accident."

Their bickering faded as first Mendez, then Falcone, lowered themselves over the edge.

Asher listened, half-hoping he'd hear them tumble to the bottom—turnabout and all that—but they both made it.

It didn't make sense that they hadn't found the rubies. It wasn't as if Cici's money pouch was that well concealed. A quick pat-down and they'd have had it.

Maybe there was some other valuable piece of jewelry in the velvet bag.

He moved deeper into the woods, away from the thugs and the crash site, careful to leave no trail. When he was so far away that he could no longer hear their voices, he found a boulder and tucked Cici's purse, velvet bag and all, between it and a cluster of ferns.

That should be far enough away and well enough hidden that Gagnon's merry band of morons would never find it.

He was making his way back toward the crash site and the pickup when he heard a muffled curse from the gorge. He stalked in that direction.

"What?" Falcone's tone implied more irritation than curiosity.

"I just realized... Where's the bodyguard? Where's the body?"

Asher peeked over, barely making out the men in the darkness. They both stood still, looking around.

He ducked just as Falcone lifted his gaze to the rocky hillside where they'd tossed Asher over.

"He was dead," Mendez said. "I mean, maybe not completely."

As if *partially* dead were a thing.

"But he couldn't have survived." Pretty Boy's tone was panicked. "Right?"

"If he's not dead," Falcone said, "then you are."

"No, no. Even if he survived, he can't have gone far." He looked at the water running through the deep ravine. "Maybe his body was carried downstream."

Falcone followed its meandering flow. "Don't know much about the wilderness, but I don't think that's strong enough to carry a full-grown man."

Mendez must've realized that because his searching became frantic. He pulled out a gun, started peeking behind bushes and boulders, occasionally saying, "Gotcha" and "Freeze."

As much fun as this was to watch, Asher needed to move.

His window of opportunity was narrow. They'd search the wreckage, realize the bag wasn't there, and climb back up. He had maybe ten minutes before they returned to their pickup, furious and empty-handed.

He resumed his search for the burner Cici had held. His knee ached thanks to that old injury, and his shoulder throbbed, the makeshift bandage damp with fresh blood. He ignored the pain. Cici's life depended on him finding that device.

A reflection caught his eye in the middle of a clump of bushes. He crouched there and reached, his good hand closing around smooth metal and glass. The phone's screen was cracked but functional, the battery showing thirty percent.

Thank You, Lord.

He unlocked the phone and tapped in Bartlett's phone number.

The call rang, then went to voicemail.

Great. The man who always answered his phone was too busy tonight.

He waited for the automated voice mail greeting, then said, "Check your texts." He ended the call, then opened a text, adding Bartlett and Alyssa. She was the only person they'd dialed with that particular burner, and he was grateful her number was there.

He dropped a pin at his current location, then typed a message.

> Cici's been taken. I'm at the pin. Sending this phone in the bad guys' truck. Follow it back to Cici.

He sent the message, then stared at the screen, waiting for someone to reply.

Neither Alyssa nor Bartlett did.

He'd add Gavin Wright to the text, but he didn't know the man's number. He'd committed to memory other bodyguards' phone numbers, but the thugs were coming, their voices sharp with anger as they headed to the truck, bickering about what to do next.

It was possible, since they were empty-handed, that they would run from Gagnon. Should he attack? He could incapacitate Falcone and force Pretty Boy to take him to where Cici was being held. And then...then figure it out.

He could do it.

Except that was what he'd thought about getting Cici home. And where'd that landed him?

He was injured, there were two of them, and they were both armed. Armed and powerful. And who knew how many men were guarding Cici?

He'd made the mistake of thinking he could do this by himself. He needed his team.

His other option was to toss the cell phone in the pickup and hope like crazy these guys went back to where Cici was hidden. If they didn't, then Bartlett would send people to intercept them.

The team could do it if they got the message.

The thugs' voices were growing louder. Asher had an instant to make up his mind.

Lord, what do I do?

He heard no divine voice, but the answer was clear nonetheless. He needed to trust his team, not try to do this all by himself.

He opened the pickup door, shoved the phone beneath the driver's side seat, then closed it as quietly as possible and bolted across the road. He hid in the woods just as the men climbed in the truck and drove away.

Either they'd lead Bartlett, Alyssa, and the whole team back to Cici, or Asher's split-second decision had been wrong, and… and maybe Cici would be lost forever.

CHAPTER TWENTY-ONE

The tension in the warehouse office grew until it felt like a living, breathing presence.

Cici didn't dare move, fearing any activity might ignite the men who silently squared off against each other.

"Time's up." Gagnon slapped his hand on the desk, sending a zing of fear down Cici's spine. "Track down those idiots." He glared at Souza. "They should've been back an hour ago."

Souza shifted his weight. "Maybe they ran into trouble."

"Or maybe they decided my property was worth more than their lives. Go find them and bring them back, along with my property."

"I'm sure they're still looking—"

"I'm not sure of anything." He lifted his cell phone, turning it over in his manicured hands. "And don't even think about double-crossing me."

Cici's gaze bounced from Gagnon to Souza, whose jaw tightened. "I've done everything you've asked."

"Men like you always think they're smarter than they are." Gagnon set down the phone and leaned back against the desk. "Tell me, how is your little brother doing? Alfonzo, isn't it?"

Every line in Souza's body went rigid. "What did you say?" The words were whispered, carrying a threat.

"Doing time, isn't he? Went in as a juvenile at sixteen. Should get out in another year if he keeps his nose clean." Gagnon's tone was conversational, as if discussing the weather. "You've visited him every single week since he went in. Rain or shine, there you are, playing the devoted big brother."

Gagnon wielded information like a weapon, cutting straight to what mattered most.

Souza's hands curled into fists. "You leave my brother out of this."

"A touching display of family loyalty." Gagnon's smile held no warmth. "It would be such a shame if something happened to young Alfonzo. Prison can be a dangerous place, especially for someone so young and vulnerable."

"You son of a—"

"Careful." The word was smooth as butter. "I have contacts inside that facility who could be persuaded to arrange an accident. A slip in the shower, perhaps. Or maybe a disagreement with another inmate that turns fatal."

Souza took a step forward, his face contorting with rage. "Or I could just kill you right now."

If evil had a voice, it would sound like Gagnon's laugh. "And then my dead-man's switch activates, and your boss goes down. You might have a couple of days, a week at most. Maybe you could run. Of course, poor Alfonzo's trapped. When your boss learns you screwed up—and trust me, he'll know who to blame—he'll take you out, and probably your baby brother, too." Gagnon's lips rose with malicious amusement. "I guess your choices aren't very good. A better option—you could just do as I say and not screw it up."

Cici held her breath, watching Souza's internal war play out across his features—fury battling with fear, loyalty warring with self-preservation.

Finally, he turned toward the door. "I'll find them."

"And my property." Gagnon's voice followed him. "And keep me informed."

Souza's head dipped and rose, and then he disappeared out the door, his footsteps clanking on the metal staircase.

A moment later, a heavy door slammed far away, the sound echoing through the warehouse, leaving her trapped with a monster.

He tapped on his cell phone, then lifted it to speak. "It's me. Are you close?"

Who was he talking to? She couldn't hear the answer coming from the other end of his call.

"Good, good. I doubt I'll need you, but better safe... Yes, outside and in. Don't disappoint me." He tossed the phone on the desk.

He'd called in reinforcements? Why? Clearly, he didn't trust Souza and the other two to complete the job, but who did he fear? Or...or maybe the new thugs would take out the old ones. But who'd take out the new ones? Did Gagnon intend to kill everybody he used?

"Ah, the beauty of leverage." Gagnon smiled, smoothing his suit jacket with practiced ease. "That's why it's better not to have anyone you care about, Miss Wright. Love is a liability."

The casual cruelty in his voice made her sick. She pressed her back harder against the filing cabinet, wishing she could disappear into the cold metal. "You're horrible."

"I'm practical." He paced, hands clasped behind his back. "Sentiment makes people weak. Predictable. Souza will do whatever I ask because he cares about his brother."

"Is that what you tell yourself? What did you do when you discovered your son had betrayed you?"

The question escaped before she could stop it, hanging in the stale air between them.

Gagnon went perfectly still. When he turned, his pale eyes were arctic. "What did you say?"

She should have been terrified into silence, but something reckless had taken hold. Maybe it was grief over Asher's death, or maybe it was the knowledge that she was going to die no matter what she did. "He's the one who sold that bag of jewelry, isn't he? Your own son?"

He said nothing, just glared at her, daring her to keep talking.

"Unless you lied to Mr. D—which, maybe you did." By the look on his face—pure hatred—Cici guessed he hadn't lied. "Then I know your son's decision to sell that bag of jewels is the reason we're here. If love is a liability, then I can only assume you aren't affected by such problematic emotions."

Gagnon's face turned a dangerous shade of red, but she didn't care if she made him angry. What did she have to lose now?

Asher had told her she was good at prying information out of people. She might as well employ that skill. Maybe she'd learn something useful.

"Actually," she said, "I guess you probably sent one of the many people you keep dangling from your puppet strings to take care of him. That'd be easier, offer a little distance." She forced a casual tone, as if the thought of murdering one's own child didn't turn her stomach. She held Gagnon's eye contact when every instinct screamed at her to look away. "You might as well tell me. I'm going to die as soon as you find that locket."

Or maybe not. Maybe he'd keep her alive, and she'd be his leverage against anyone looking for her. Her father, her cousins... They wouldn't stop until Gagnon paid for her murder, but if she were still alive, if they had hope she could be rescued

—and fear she'd be tortured or killed—then Gagnon could keep on breathing.

She had no idea what his plans were, but she figured this wasn't going to end with a bubble bath and a good night's sleep. So she wanted to know. She needed to know all the ugly details that had gotten her into this terrible mess. And gotten Asher killed.

Gagnon's breathing was controlled, measured, but she could see the rage simmering beneath his polished exterior as he stalked toward her. "You want the truth?" He crouched in front of her, his voice dropping to that terrifying whisper. "Since you're so eager to understand the depths of my cruelty."

He leaned so close she could smell his breath, minty with an undertone of decay.

She pressed against the cabinet, trying to put distance between them. What was she doing, goading a psychopath? She should've kept her mouth shut. Either way, she was going to die, but she feared now there'd be a lot more pain involved.

"Do not speak of my son."

She nodded. She'd agree to just about anything at this point.

He stood and moved to the desk, giving her fresh air to breathe. "He got himself addicted to drugs. And gambling. I've paid his debts. I've tried to help him. I've tried to protect him. He doesn't know what I do, only that I'm a very wealthy man."

Gagnon spoke about his son in the present tense. There was hope in that.

He lifted The Crimson Duchess. "I assume you know where this came from?"

She nodded.

"Since your sister and Forbes Ballentine are an item…"

How did he know that? It wasn't exactly public information that they were dating.

He must've seen her surprise because he smiled that evil little smile. "You'd be surprised at the things I know about you."

She worked to hide the fear his words raised in her. It was one thing for her to be in danger, another thing entirely for her to suck her entire family into peril with her.

"I know all about Brooklynn," Gagnon said. "I know about all your sisters, and your mother and father. It's my job to know everything about everybody." He sighed, shaking his head. "Haven't found anything to use as leverage against you yet, except of course their lives, but your father has them all wrapped up tight, all but the missing one."

Delaney. Did he know where she was? If so, then he'd be able to get to her, considering nobody knew where Delaney had gone. If Gagnon held that card, he didn't show it.

"I assume," Gagnon continued, "you're aware that Leo Taggart and Lois Stratton were the ones who shot Charles and Grace Ballentine that day. Taggart was the shooter, of course, but the woman wasn't exactly against the idea, not from what I saw. I was a small cog in the operation. I'd be surprised if either one of them even knew my name, back then."

"You were there, though. You searched the house. You stole that necklace."

He caressed the jewels like a better man might caress a beloved child. "This is the piece that started my business, my life." He lifted his gaze to her. "It was foolish of me to keep it, but I never could bring myself to dispose of it."

People he could dispose of, no problem. But jewelry proved difficult?

"When I heard about what happened in Shadow Cove this summer, about Taggart and Stratton—Whitmore, as you know her." He shook his head, a look of disgust on his face. "Idiots, both of them, to start the operation again, and in the same place. They were arrogant. They deserved what they got. If they were both dead, I'd be safe. But if Whitmore survives, mine will be the first name she drops."

"Because you've been blackmailing her all these years."

He waved that off with a flick of his wrist. "She had the money. It didn't bankrupt her to share it."

There was the chink in his armor. Once one of his victims' crimes was exposed, they had no reason to keep paying him. Or to keep from pointing a finger at him.

"I haven't been able to get to her," Gagnon said, "though I've been working the problem. But on the off chance I can't silence her permanently, I needed to dispose of the items I stole from Grace Ballentine that night. I was trying to decide what to do with them. I'd taken a box out of the safe to separate her jewels from the rest of my valuables. I was still ruminating on the problem when William came in. He'd been staying with me for a few weeks. His mother needed a break."

"You're divorced."

"Never married her. Never wanted to get bogged down with all that."

Right. Family could be such a drag.

"The kid wasn't my idea, and if I'd known about him before he was born..." He shook his head. "Anyway, I didn't realize he'd seen the jewels. He was involved in some great teenage drama." Gagnon smirked. "I was trying to be a good dad, trying to help. Later that night, I put the box back in the safe. I didn't look inside it, never dreaming my own kid would steal from me. When I took it out a few days later, I discovered the velvet bag and its contents were gone."

"Including the locket you're so keen on getting back. You said it was your mother's. Is that why it's so important to you, or—"

"Please." He waved off the suggestion. "Don't accuse me of sentimentality."

She should drop it, but she was about to die because of that stupid thing. She wanted to know why. Before she asked, he spoke again.

"Inside that cheap, tarnished locket is an SD card that contains all the information I've uncovered about all my...shall we say, clients. My lawyers have access to a drive with the same information, which they'll share with authorities in the event of my untimely death. But I like having a copy with me, just in case."

Oh. Wow. She'd stolen the key to taking Gagnon down.

"You didn't know what you had, but it was only a matter of time before someone opened that locket and found it."

She was sorry she'd taken it, sorry Asher'd paid for that decision with his life. But if this situation ended in Gagnon's defeat, she certainly wouldn't grieve that.

"Can I ask another question?"

"Why not?" He swept his arm around the dingy room. "It's not as if there's anything else to do."

"How did you keep finding us?"

"Oh, that's easy. The SD card is programmed with a locator."

A locator? All this time, they'd been traveling with a *locator*?

"It piggy-backs off phone signals," he explained. "We started tracking it immediately, guessed you were headed to the police station. We got there ahead of you, just barely. We lost you—the card has to be close to a phone—then picked you up again at a hotel. We were waiting in the lobby, and then you were on the move again. Your bodyguard was quick, getting you out the back and to that train. It took us a while to get ahead of you."

She was reeling.

All that time, they'd been carrying a *locator*?

It was a miracle they hadn't been caught. How *hadn't* they been caught?

"We'd get an inkling where you were, then lose you," Gagnon said. "You kept turning off your phones. It was maddening."

Oh. That explained it. They'd been careful to keep their phones off when they weren't using them.

"It triggered in that dinky little town last night—Nutfield, but the signal was never strong enough for us to find you. Then it triggered again a few times during your drive today. We finally caught up with you while you rested a few miles back. Gave us the chance to get in front of you and find this place."

If only she hadn't stolen that bag. If only she'd looked through it, maybe opened the locket. If only... There were too many if-onlys to enumerate.

"When your son sold your jewelry, he had no idea what he was setting into motion."

Gagnon pressed his lips together.

"What did you do to him?"

"I found out where he pawned them." Gagnon walked toward her. When he crouched in front of her, she ducked her head, avoiding his gaze. Afraid of what he'd do.

He gripped her chin with his thumb and forefinger, lifting it until she met his eyes. "Go ahead and ask."

She swallowed hard. "Is he...is he still alive?"

He let her go. "I'm not a monster, Miss Wright."

Wasn't he, though? Asher was dead. Gagnon had just confessed his intention to kill Lois Whitmore. He'd threatened Souza's brother's life—a teenager.

How did Gagnon define *monster,* because in her dictionary, his picture would suffice for an illustration of the word.

"I told his mother to send him to rehab. My son, who's always balked at the idea, must've realized he ought to do as I say. He's in a facility now, one far away from Philadelphia. Maybe, by the time I see him again, my anger will have dissipated." He shrugged. "Maybe not. And yes, I recognize that, like everyone else in the world, I have that one vulnerability. As long as my enemies never discover his existence, I should be safe."

"Souza was there, in the jewelry store with you, so—"

"I'll take care of Souza." He stood and brushed his hands off on his pants.

Meaning, he'd kill him. Just like he'd kill her, when he knew he had what he needed.

The thought of sharing a grave with that creepy man had her stomach roiling.

Since that was the case, she figured she might as well get all her questions answered. "What else was in the box? The one in the safe?"

He shrugged. "As much as I love technology, I know how an electronic file can be breached or wiped out. An SD card can be crushed. So I have paper copies of all the information I've uncovered, as well as all the physical proof—like The Crimson Duchess—of everything I've learned."

He'd thought of everything.

The weight of it—Asher's death, her own impending murder, the knowledge that her selfish need for recognition had caused all of this—felt as heavy as a lead blanket. She closed her eyes, and her memory conjured the image of Asher outside the restaurant, the way he'd looked at her with such fierce protectiveness, such affection. He'd died trying to keep her safe, and whether she managed to survive or not, there was nothing she could do to change that.

CHAPTER TWENTY-TWO

No cars had passed on this lonely stretch of road. He kicked himself now for sticking to back roads. They'd have been safer on the interstate.

Where was Bartlett? Even if he was in Boston, he could've called the police, at least sent someone to check on him.

Patience, he told himself.

As if that would help.

When he heard an engine approaching, he kept to the shadows, afraid it might be more of Gagnon's men.

Three vehicles came into view. Asher pushed himself up from where he'd been sitting against a tree trunk and praying. His makeshift bandage pulled tight against his shoulder, the stinging pain a constant reminder of his failure.

A sedan, a pickup truck, and a familiar black SUV parked along the shoulder, their headlights sweeping across him as he hobbled into view.

His chest loosened for the first time since he'd woken up in the gorge. Bartlett and Alyssa had gotten his message.

The sedan's doors opened first, and a tall blonde stepped

out of the passenger side. This had to be Alyssa, though he hadn't seen Cici's older sister since high school.

Another man emerged from the driver's seat. Short blond hair, his bulk unmistakable even in the dim light. Was this the fiancé Cici'd told him about?

Asher recognized Grant Wright, one of the first protection agents, who'd arrived in a pickup with New Hampshire plates.

Bartlett exited the SUV.

"How are you already here?" Asher directed the question to all of them, glancing at his watch. It'd only been forty-five minutes since he'd texted.

Alyssa reached him first. "I tracked your phone when we talked earlier, figured your ETA. When you didn't show up in Shadow Cove, I knew something was wrong. I tried calling you, but—"

"So she called me," Grant cut in. "I contacted Bartlett. We were already moving when your text came through. Called Michael. He was out of town, but he's flying in tonight. Gavin is staying with Evelyn, but he's offered to get whatever we need."

Michael and Gavin were Cici's cousin and father, both willing to run to her rescue.

"We met up in Millerville," Bartlett gave Asher a once-over. "I shouldn't have sent you out on your own."

The barb stung, but Asher had no defense. Obviously, he hadn't handled the solo job well.

He touched his wound instinctively, feeling sticky blood that had seeped through his makeshift bandage.

"We need to deal with that." Alyssa's friend had gone back to the car for something. Now he approached, holding a black canvas case. He nodded to the wound. "What happened?"

"It's nothing—"

"It's something." The man's tone brooked no argument. "You're bleeding through your shirt."

"Once we find Cici—"

"You'll be unconscious by then." The guy nodded to the sedan. "Come where there's a little light."

Asher figured arguing would only cost precious time. He followed the man and leaned against the sedan, Bartlett, Alyssa, and Grant following.

"I'm Callan Templeton, by the way." Alyssa's fiancé helped Asher shift the sweatshirt out of the way so he could remove the T-shirt-turned-bandage. "I have zero medical education, but I do have a kid who gets hurt a lot, if that makes you feel any better."

"Doesn't," he muttered.

Callan laughed. "Wise man." He seemed to know what he was doing as he dabbed stinging antiseptic on the wound. "Gunshot wounds get infected, so..."

Asher fought to hide the pain.

"Gunshot? What happened?" Grant demanded. "How did they find you?"

"No idea." Asher gave them the condensed version—the ambush, the crash, waking up to find Cici gone. And then the guys who came back to search. Each word felt like swallowing glass, but he forced himself to stay clinical, professional. These people needed facts, and his guilt would only cloud the issue. "I put the phone in the pickup." He looked at Alyssa, who was standing beside Callan. "Hopefully, you—"

"I got it," she said. "The truck stopped at a paper mill. It's been stationary since then." She held up her phone, showing a map with a red dot. "Industrial area on the outskirts of Millerville."

Thank God his idea had worked. "That's where they have her." Every second they spent talking was another second Cici remained in Gagnon's hands. He itched to get moving.

Easy," Callan murmured, pressing a fresh bandage against

his shoulder. "The wound's too wide for stitches. Hopefully, we can stem the bleeding." He secured the dressing with tape, his movements quick and efficient. "You're going to be hurting, but you won't bleed out."

Asher adjusted his sweatshirt, ready to be done talking about his near-death experience.

"Got two guys there, Whiteman and Yartym." Bartlett glanced at his phone. "They're getting into position."

Asher pushed away from the sedan, testing his range of motion. The pain was manageable. "Ideas?"

Grant stepped into view, his dark eyes calculating. "Looks like it's surrounded by a chain-link fence. Hopefully, they'll see that as protection. If they're smart, they'll have lookouts posted."

"The thugs who came back here were no brain surgeons," Asher said. "But they're survivors. Souza seems calculating, and Gagnon's managed to stay one step ahead of us for days. Don't underestimate them." Like he had, and paid the price.

Rather, Cici was paying it now.

Alyssa's jaw tightened. "How many are we talking about?"

"I only know about those four. They thought I was dead, but when they came back, they realized my body wasn't here. Even these guys are smart enough to recognize that dead bodies don't just up and walk away."

"So they know you're alive." Bartlett's expression darkened. "They'll be expecting us."

"Maybe. But unless they found the phone in the truck, they don't know that I know where they are." Asher flexed his fingers, testing his grip strength.

"What'd they come back for?" Grant asked.

"Looking for something. It has to be in the bag Cici took from the jewelry store."

"The necklace," Alyssa guessed. "What else—?"

"She had the necklace on her." He explained about the

zipper pouch she'd bought. If not for the thugs having returned, he'd assumed Cici would be dead as soon as they found the jewels.

Maybe it was only desperation that kept his hope thrumming now.

He tamped down that thought. "They were looking for something else, something small, by the way they scoured the ground. Something that has Gagnon scared enough to risk everything."

Alyssa's golden eyes were sharp. "What kind of something?"

"No clue. But whatever it is, they're willing to kill for it." The weight of those words settled over the group like a shroud.

"Where is it? The bag. Did they find it, or—?"

"I hid it." He described where he'd stashed it, and Alyssa jogged into the woods, Callan following.

Bartlett's phone buzzed. He answered. "Talk to me." His expression grew grimmer as he listened. "Copy that. Hold position."

He ended the call and faced the group. "My men witnessed a van arrive. Eight guys got out, geared up. There were already two vehicles there, so we're looking at ten or more."

"Twelve." Asher refused to bow under the weight of what they were facing. "Gagnon, Falcone, and...Pretty Boy." He couldn't recall the guy's name. "Two came back looking for me. We have to assume Souza stayed with Gagnon and Cici. If eight more showed up, then—"

"Twelve." Bartlett nodded once. "Okay. The mill's got three buildings—main factory, office complex, and a smaller outbuilding. Four of the new guys went into the factory. The rest fanned out to surveil the perimeter."

"Six against twelve," Grant said. "I've faced worse odds."

"Seven." Alyssa's response emerged from the forest a moment before she did, Callan at her side. "I'm going to help."

Callan said, "Sweetheart—"

"Don't *sweetheart* me." She snapped, then turned to Bartlett. "She's my sister."

"Don't freak, cuz," Grant said. "You can provide overwatch."

Callan swiveled on him. "She'll stay where it's safe."

"I absolutely will not!"

Grant looked between the two of them and smirked. "Yeah, good luck with that, man."

Alyssa and Callen engaged in a useless staring contest.

"We need her," Asher said. "She's smart and competent, and we need all the help we can get."

Alyssa stepped close to her fiancé and rested a hand on his arm. "Callan, you have a sister. What would you do to protect Hannah?"

Callan looked away, obviously wanting to argue the point.

Alyssa dug into Cici's purse, pulled out the velvet bag, and scattered the contents on the roof of the car.

Grant drew Asher's attention back. "Tell us everything you know about these guys."

"Gagnon's the mastermind. Mid-sixties. He's made his fortune by digging up dirt on bad guys and then blackmailing them with it."

"The others?" Bartlett asked, checking his sidearm.

"If I had to guess, I'd say Souza's next in charge after Gagnon, but these guys don't have history." He glanced at Alyssa, expecting her to explain how the muscle came from two different operations in two different cities.

She was too busy picking through the contents of the velvet bag, Callan holding a flashlight so she could see.

Asher explained quickly their theory that Gagnon had used leverage against the leaders of organized crime operations in New York and Boston. "They aren't friends with Gagnon, and they aren't friends with each other. The two who came back here bickered the whole time they searched."

"Good, good," Grant said. "Disorganized, not a team."

"That's true for the guys we've dealt with," Asher said, "but this new crew—"

"According to Yartym, they worked together as a team," Bartlett said. "Seamless. Mercenaries, maybe."

Which meant they were well-trained, probably former military.

"What about Souza?" Bartlett asked. "What's your take on him?"

"Bald, built like a brick wall, determined and competent. No idea if he was acquainted with Gagnon before this all began. Gagnon's ostensibly a business owner in Philly. Souza's with a gang in New York."

"I got something." Alyssa held up the locket Cici had shown him the night before, the black one she claimed was silver.

"What about it?" Grant moved closer.

She shook it, eliciting the tiniest rattling sound, then opened it up.

"Whoa," Callan said, peering over her shoulder.

"What is it?" Grant asked.

Asher stepped closer and saw what they were looking at—an SD card.

Her eyes widened. "Power down all your phones. Now."

Bartlett said, "We can't. We need—"

"We need them not to know we found it!" She looked at Asher. "My guess is it's got some kind of tracking device, a locator."

A tracker, in that tiny locket? That explained how Gagnon and his men kept catching up with them. It wasn't a mole in Forbes's operation.

They'd been carrying it with them all along.

While everyone powered their phones down, Alyssa opened the passenger door and came out with a laptop. She powered it up and slid the SD card inside. "Let's see what we've got."

Asher forced his gaze away. It didn't matter what was on that card. It didn't matter what Gagnon was trying to find. All that mattered was saving Cici's life.

He met Bartlett's eyes. "Let's make a plan."

CHAPTER TWENTY-THREE

The heavy clank of boots on metal stairs announced the men's return before Cici saw them.

Souza appeared first in the doorway, his expression grim. Behind him, Mendez and Falcone shuffled like schoolboys caught skipping class, their earlier bravado replaced by something that looked suspiciously like fear.

Gagnon must've seen what she did because he pushed off the desk. "Well?"

The silence stretched, coiling around the room.

"We searched everywhere," Falcone finally said, his Boston accent heavy. "The bike was totaled, thrown all over the rocks. We went through every piece."

"And?" Gagnon's voice remained dangerously calm.

Mendez shifted his weight, still avoiding eye contact. "It wasn't there."

"What do you mean, it wasn't there?" Gagnon seemed to be daring the man to say it again.

"The bag." Falcone spread his hands. "We looked everywhere. Under the bike, in the water, scattered through the rocks. Nothing."

Before Gagnon could respond, more footsteps echoed outside, and then four more men filed in. They were trim and powerful, clad in black, from their jackets to their boots, and each carried a veritable arsenal of weapons.

Cici's blood turned cold. These weren't untrained street thugs. These men moved with the same controlled precision she'd seen in Grant and her father. They moved with a military bearing. Trained. Disciplined.

Lethal.

Her heart hammered against her ribs as she studied their faces—hard lines, cold eyes. Were these professional killers? Or some kind of commando team? Whoever they were, they certainly weren't the low-budget goons she'd grown accustomed to.

"Gentlemen." Gagnon's demeanor shifted, his confidence visibly swelling.

A man with graying temples and a scar bisecting his left eyebrow stepped forward, clearly the leader. "Situation?"

Gagnon glanced toward Mendez and Falcone. "We require protection. It's imperative that our guest remains with us." His gaze flicked to Cici.

The leader's gaze swept the room, lingering on Cici for a moment before returning to Gagnon. "Enemies?"

"She has people who are trained and lethal."

Who did he fear would show up? Dad, maybe Grant and Michael. Oh, and Callan. He was former CIA, so surely Dad would get him involved.

Of course, GBPA had been hired to protect her. They'd be coming as well.

The question was, did any of them know where she was?

"And?" the scarred soldier asked.

"Something of mine has gone missing, and these men haven't been able to find it." He glared at Falcone and Mendez, who'd backed into the corner nearest her and watched the scene silently.

"Timeline?"

"The longer this drags on, the more exposure I face. Meaning, the sooner I get my property back, the better for everyone involved, your boss included. Get it for me tonight, and there'll be a six-figure bonus in it for you." His gaze traveled among the newcomers. "For *each* of you,"

The man's broken eyebrow twitched. "What kind of security are you offering?"

Gagnon waved the words away as irrelevant. "If you give me an account—your account, not your boss's—I'll transfer half now. It'll be our secret."

The commando leader pulled a small notepad from one of his many pockets, bent over the table, and wrote something down. Then, he slid the paper toward Gagnon. "I trust you to get it done. Tell us what we're dealing with."

The leader and his men focused on Gagnon, who opened a laptop on his desk. They leaned in, studying what she assumed was a map.

They were effectively shutting Souza and the other two out, a fact that couldn't be lost on them.

They were so engaged in their conversation that, if she weren't tied up and surrounded by hulking killers, she'd make a run for it. She was surprised Souza, Falcone, and Mendez didn't take the opportunity.

But they couldn't, could they? Gagnon held leverage over all of them—threats against loved ones, debts to bosses, secrets that could destroy lives. He'd trapped them as surely as he'd trapped her.

The leader studied whatever Gagnon showed him. "Site's been searched?"

"Thoroughly." Gagnon's jaw tightened. "They say my property wasn't there."

"Someone took it." The leader glared at Falcone and Mendez. "Or it was never there to begin with."

It had been there, though. The velvet bag had been in her purse, beneath the motorcycle's seat. How had they not found it?

It didn't make sense.

When Gagnon and the soldier bent over his phone again, Mendez and Falcone started whispering, though by the little she picked up, they weren't sharing juicy secrets. They were arguing.

Mendez got in Falcone's face. "Do it, and I'll kill you myself."

She turned back to Gagnon and the other soldiers, who paid no attention.

Souza was watching through narrowed eyes.

A thump sounded, and Falcone stumbled back, crashing into the file cabinet she was propped against.

She ducked.

He fell, bumping her shoulder before scrambling away.

And then Mendez was on top of him, punching, pounding.

Souza and one of the other men yanked them apart.

Mendez could barely stay upright, his face bloodied and bruised.

"Tell him!" Falcone shouted. "Tell him or I will."

"The bodyguard." Mendez's voice was garbled. He wiped blood that dripped from his nose, gaze flicking from Falcone to Gagnon. "His body wasn't at the crash site."

The temperature in the room seemed to drop ten degrees.

Cici's heart pounded. Asher's body hadn't been there, which meant...

Asher was alive?

"What did you say?" Gagnon's tone lowered to that terrifying whisper.

"He looked dead," Mendez stammered, his mangled face paling. "I mean, I wasn't sure, but I figured after I tossed him over the edge..." He stopped, realizing he was digging his grave deeper with every word.

The man who'd hoisted Mendez up let him go and moved away. Souza and Falcone did the same, leaving Mendez on his own, only inches from Cici.

She curled herself into a ball, covering her head with her arms as if she could protect herself.

The gunshot was deafeningly loud in the confined space.

Cici screamed.

Mendez collapsed beside her, blood pooling beneath his still form. Her ears rang, and she pressed herself against the filing cabinet so hard the metal handles dug into her spine.

"Clean that up." Gagnon's voice was eerily calm.

When nobody moved, she dared to peek.

Falcone stood frozen, eyes wide, staring at the man's body.

"Now," Gagnon snapped.

Falcone's skin had taken on a green pallor, and she feared he'd vomit, but he bent and grabbed Mendez beneath the arms and dragged him toward the door, the man's blood leaving a dark smear across the concrete floor.

The scarred leader watched, then turned his attention to Gagnon, apparently unbothered by the execution he'd just witnessed. "If the bodyguard's alive—"

"Then he's coming." Gagnon checked his phone screen, then blew out a breath. "Still no sign of the locator." His gaze flicked to Cici. He smoothed his tie, regaining his composure with disturbing ease.

"You think he'll be able to track her down?"

"He's proved irritatingly competent," Gagnon said.

"We'll be ready." The leader turned to one of his cohorts. "Warn the men to be on the lookout."

"Yes, sir." The soldier stepped out the door, tapping his ear before talking into some sort of communication device.

Asher might be alive, but the hope that had soared at the prospect now crashed in pieces. Because if he was, then Gagnon was right—he'd come for her. But he'd have no idea what he was walking into.

CHAPTER TWENTY-FOUR

"Yartym's reporting a gunshot at the factory."

Asher's gaze snapped to Bartlett, whose expression was grim.

"It's not Cici," Asher snapped. "Gagnon won't kill her as long as he thinks he can use her."

Praying he was right, Asher put the gunshot out of his mind and returned his focus to the satellite image on the laptop screen, which looked like a blueprint for a nightmare.

Alyssa had found and disabled the tracking software loaded onto the SD card, so they'd powered up their phones again. Now, her laptop was connected to the internet—hotspot, he figured, but he didn't care how she'd done it before she'd wandered off to make a phone call.

The paper mill complex sprawled across the screen in grainy detail—three main buildings connected by covered walkways, surrounded by a chain-link fence, not to mention a summer's worth of growth—trees, bushes, weeds—where anyone could hide.

Cici was in the middle of that, surrounded by monsters. He couldn't think of a better setup for a horror movie.

He inhaled and exhaled, focusing his thoughts. *Work the problem. Don't think about all the things that could go wrong.*

"Main factory building." He tapped the largest structure with his index finger. "That's where the mercenaries went. It's got the most cover, multiple exits, and"—he tapped the exterior fire-escape staircases, which led from the roof, down to the second floor, then to the ground—"two floors. If this is like other factories I've seen, then the top floor probably looks down over the first, giving them the high ground. If I were holding a hostage, that's where I'd set up shop."

Grant had found photos of the paper mill from when it was still operational. His gaze bounced between his cell phone and the satellite image. "There're windows on the second floor." He turned to Bartlett. "Your guys see any lights on?"

Bartlett asked the question of his team on his cell phone. He shook his head. "No lights. Some of the windows look like they've been blocked."

"We have to assume they're watching," Grant said. "The covered walkways are a double-edged sword. They can move between buildings without being spotted from above, but so can we."

Callan's focus was on Alyssa, who paced a few feet away, still talking on the phone. He seemed to have to force his gaze back to the laptop. "We'll need to get inside the fence without alerting them we're there. Do they have guards outside it?"

Bartlett fielded that. "At least four, and my guys' view is limited."

Callan's gaze bounced back to Alyssa, who was coming toward them. "Well?"

"Michael and Dad are both working on getting us real-time satellite imagery. One of them will get it done."

Two more were working on getting them help, added to those who'd come when he'd called.

Asher felt something shift inside him. The familiar weight of responsibility hadn't lifted from his shoulders, but it didn't feel like it was crushing him anymore. He didn't have to do this by himself. He met each team member's eyes before focusing on Grant. He was a legend at GBPA. Some claimed that he'd attacked a boatload of killers, taken them all out, and rescued two hostages. Even if the stories were exaggerated, this guy knew what he was doing. "What's our best approach?"

"Simultaneous breach from multiple points." Grant's finger traced paths on the old satellite image. "We go in quiet, take out their sentries. Even if we're discovered, their attention will be divided. They'll be forced to respond on several fronts."

Bartlett stepped closer to the laptop. "My men are positioned here and here." He pointed to two spots on opposite sides of the property, outside the fence. "They're in high spots. They can provide cover."

"What about Cici?" Alyssa's pitch rose with worry. "As soon as they know we're there, Gagnon could cut his losses."

"He won't kill her." Callan wrapped his arm around Alyssa, giving her a little squeeze. "Not if he thinks there's any chance we have the SD card. It has names, dates, financial records—enough to bring down half the criminal organizations on the East Coast."

"But he doesn't know we have it," Bartlett pointed out.

"Doesn't matter." Asher tried to keep fear out of his voice, hoping his assessment of Gagnon was accurate. "Leverage is this guy's forte. He'll keep Cici alive as long as he believes he can use her life to trade—for the SD card, for his own freedom, probably for both."

Asher prayed he was right.

Callan nodded. "If it comes to dialog, we make him think we're willing to trade."

"Except we're not," Grant said flatly. "The moment he gets that card back, Cici becomes expendable."

Asher's jaw clenched, rage and fear threatening to cloud his judgment, but he forced them down. Think. Plan. Execute. There was no room for anything else. "Too many variables. Maybe they see us coming before we can get close. They regroup, surround her, and then we can't get to her. It'll be a shootout. Maybe we win—"

"We'll win," Grant said.

"But at what cost? We're good, but we're outgunned, and those guys who just showed up." His gaze bounced to Bartlett. "Pros, right?"

"Bearing and equipment of soldiers."

Grant said, "But we have the element—"

"Wait." Asher silenced him. "Just let me..." An idea started taking shape. "What if we draw his attention elsewhere?"

Bartlett raised an eyebrow. "Explain."

"He's got twelve men, most of them professionals." He nodded at Grant. "Our advantage is that they don't know we're coming. But think it through. He didn't bring in trained killers to search for an SD card. They're here because he expects trouble. His whole shtick depends on information. He must know who Cici is, who her family is. Meaning he knows somebody's going to come after him." Asher's mind raced through possibilities. "We have to throw him off. Create a diversion."

"That's what we're talking about doing, right?" Alyssa looked from Asher to Callan to Grant. "Two teams, each breaching at a different spot?"

Eyes on Asher, Grant gave the tiniest *go-on* nod.

"It won't be enough. They might separate to take us on, but that would leave plenty of them to protect her. They have the cover of buildings. Windows and doors. We'll be exposed."

"What are you suggesting?" Callan asked.

"I act as bait." As he spoke the words, the idea solidified in his mind. This was the answer, the only option. "I walk up to the front gate, hands visible, and demand a trade. The SD card for Cici."

"Absolutely not." Bartlett's voice rose in the night air. "That's suicide."

"They'll think I'm alone." He didn't rise to the challenge, just kept his cadence even, his voice low. "They'll think I'm the only threat, and—"

"That's because it's insane," Bartlett snapped.

"It's a risk." Asher focused on Grant, who waited, silently, giving Asher room to work out all the details.

"Gagnon's spent his entire life out of the line of fire," Asher said. "He's not going to change that pattern tonight. No, he'll send men out. I won't have the SD card on me. I'll convince them that...that if anything happens to me, it goes public."

"Your own dead-man's switch." Alyssa was nodding. "I can give you enough information to sound credible."

That would be helpful, since he didn't have the slightest idea how to make something like that work. "I'll insist on seeing Cici."

"There's no way they'll bring her out."

Even in the darkness, it was impossible to miss the growing flush on Bartlett's face. He was truly angry about this, all of it. But why? Did he think Asher was so incompetent that he couldn't come up with a plan? Or was there something else going on here?

He'd have to think about that later, when all this was over. Assuming he was still breathing. "Maybe they bring me in—"

"And then we have two people to rescue," Bartlett said.

"Cici's the goal." Asher kept his voice level. "Cici's life is what matters. If I can help from inside, then I will."

"Every life matters," Bartlett said.

"Agreed, and I'd rather not die today. But I will. For her."

The words seemed to float above the group, and a tiny part of Asher wished he hadn't said them, not because they weren't true, and not because he was embarrassed or ashamed of how he felt. Just because the last thing they needed was a distraction.

Everybody was staring at him.

He ignored the rest and focused on Grant, who seemed the least distractible.

Grant prompted with "While you're playing bait—"

"The rest of you breach from the rear. Get to her." Asher looked at each of them. "By the time Gagnon realizes what's going on, God willing, you guys will have saved her."

"But what about you?" Alyssa asked. "If something happens to you... Does Cici feel the same...? Is this thing between you—?"

"It doesn't matter," he said. "Saving her life. That's what matters."

Alyssa's eyes filled with tears, which was exactly the last thing he needed.

He met her gaze steadily. "I'm scrappy. I'll figure it out."

"'Scrappy' is not a plan," Callan said. "It's a death wish."

"You have a better idea?" His voice rose, and he didn't care. "Because I'm all ears. Please, tell me a better way to guarantee Cici is saved."

The silence stretched between them. Asher could see the calculations running behind Grant's eyes, the weighing of odds and outcomes.

"He's right," Grant finally said, his matter-of-fact tone cutting through the tension. "It's our best shot."

"No." Bartlett's shout was loud enough that it reverberated off the trees.

"Listen." Grant held up a hand. "Gagnon's got the high ground, superior numbers, and defensive positions. A straight assault gets people killed. But if we can draw their attention to the front while we hit from behind..." He nodded slowly. "It could work." His focus shifted to Asher. "But unless you have a death wish, we're going to switch it up."

He definitely *didn't* have a death wish. "Let's hear it."

"You're not walking up to the front gate. You're going to get in touch with him." Grant turned to Alyssa. "Can you get a number for Gagnon?"

"On it." She slid the laptop closer and bent over it.

"You call him. You tell him where you are. Maybe do something to prove it, but stay out of the line of sight. That way, if they want to find you, they have to send men."

"Drawing them away," Bartlett said.

"Exactly."

Asher asked, "Where will I be?"

Grant lifted his phone screen and tapped on the forest that surrounded the road leading to the front gate. "In here somewhere. We'll find a good spot to hide you. It's the most logical place for you to approach."

"They'll see my hiding as a way to protect myself, a way to start the conversation without acting like a sacrificial lamb."

"Exactly. While they're trying to find you—and you're making all sorts of threats about the SD card, which they may or may not buy—"

"You guys will move."

Alyssa's phone buzzed. She glanced at the screen, then looked up. "Michael says they can reposition a satellite, but it'll take a couple of hours to get into place."

"That'll be too late," Asher said. "We'll have to go without it."

Bartlett said, "We should wait—"

"No." Grant looked at his old friend and former employer. "We don't need it."

"Those aren't your people in there." Bartlett pointed to Asher. "He's not your people. You're not the one who has to tell his family that you got him killed."

Oh.

Bartlett didn't think he was incompetent. He thought he was valuable.

For all his talk in the last two days about the bottom line, what mattered most was the care of the people he protected and the people he employed.

Asher didn't hate his employer's priorities. But they didn't align with his own. Rather than argue, he decided it wasn't his place to jump into the conflict between the two men, but he trusted Grant. Bartlett hardly ever left the office anymore. His job was to coordinate the protection agents.

Grant, on the other hand, had field experience, and lots of it. He squared off with Bartlett. "You have to trust me."

The two men stared at each other while the rest of them waited.

Finally, Bartlett's gaze flicked to Asher. He blinked. "Right. Okay. Just…"

"I get it, man. I know." Grant's gaze shifted to Asher, then to Callan. "Let's nail down the details."

They figured out the timeline and assigned roles. Finally, they were ready.

Asher'd been involved in a lot of dangerous operations in his life, but none had ever had the stakes this one did, not for him, anyway. Because the woman he loved—and yeah, he was calling it that—was in danger. If he screwed this up, then…then she might not walk out of this alive.

That was an outcome he wasn't willing to live with.

CHAPTER TWENTY-FIVE

Cici barely dared to move, the silence in the office so complete that every shift felt magnified, drawing attention to her presence.

She'd scooched as far from Mendez's blood as the zip ties would allow, but the metallic scent clung to the stale air. The crimson pool had spread wide, forcing her to draw her knees up to keep it from seeping into her jeans.

Falcone had disappeared with most of the commandos twenty minutes before. She'd caught the relief in his eyes when the scarred leader had barked orders at him—anything, she assumed, to escape Gagnon's suffocating presence and the blood-stained office where Mendez had died.

What would it feel like to know your actions had led to someone else's murder? Falcone could've kept his mouth shut about not being able to locate Asher's body. He hadn't, and now a man was dead. It was possible he didn't care at all or was more worried about what Gagnon would do to him for keeping the information quiet for so long.

The more time that crawled by in oppressive quiet, the more Cici dared to hope. If Asher really was alive—and these guys seemed convinced—it was possible he was too injured to mount a rescue operation on his own. He'd been barely conscious before the men had gotten to them, then thrown over a cliff. She prayed he wasn't too hurt, just enough that he wouldn't come charging in alone like some action movie hero. Surely, he'd get help, call the authorities, let someone else—

"Status report." Gagnon's voice cut through her desperate thoughts as he spoke into the comm device the commando leader had left him. The response came in the form of clipped words that told her there was nothing going on, nothing to report.

Souza hadn't moved from his position near the door, hadn't spoken a word since Mendez's execution. But his dark eyes barely left her, boring into her with an intensity that made her skin crawl, as if she were personally responsible for every complication in his miserable life.

Gagnon's cell phone vibrated against the metal desk, the sound sharp and intrusive. He glanced at the screen, squinting as he read something there. Then he looked up, first at Souza, then at Cici, and she caught a flicker of something that might have been satisfaction.

"Interesting," he murmured, setting the phone down and drumming his fingers against its surface. "It seems your bodyguard is more resourceful than I gave him credit for."

Cici's heart lurched. "What do you mean?"

"No idea how, but he's made contact."

"We had your number." The lie slid from her lips before she'd fully formulated it. The last thing she wanted was for Gagnon to believe Asher had help.

But how else could he have gotten Gagnon's cell number? *Please, Lord, let him not be working alone.*

Even as she breathed the prayer, she realized Alyssa

could've gotten the number for him. That didn't mean there was anyone out there with him. He could still be alone.

Gagnon's smile was as cold as winter. "Seems he wants to negotiate."

Asher? Surely not. Surely he didn't think he could just talk her out of this. He'd only get himself killed.

Gagnon tapped on his phone. "He has me curious." He picked up the comm unit. "Get in here. I want you to hear this."

Three minutes later, the scarred commando leader stepped into the room. Unlike everyone else who'd come up the stairs, his approach had been stealthy and silent. "What's going on?"

"There's an enemy out there, and he's close."

"Copy." The leader turned away and spoke, presumably to men listening through the little earpieces she'd seen in their ears. He listened, then said, "And?" Another long pause, and then, "Check it out. Don't be seen." He focused on Gagnon. "We have movement on the north side, near the gate."

Gagnon shot Cici a cruel smile. "I'll get him talking. You close in."

No. What could Asher be thinking, trying to negotiate with a psychopath?

Lord, protect him.

Minutes passed, and then the comm unit on the desk cracked. "We're in position."

"Got it." Gagnon lifted his cell phone. "Let's just find out what your little bodyguard friend has to say, shall we?"

He dialed and must've put the phone on speaker because she heard ringing.

"I have what you're looking for." Asher's voice carried through the phone, clear as day. He sounded...normal. Not weak, not hurt, just confident and in control, as he always sounded.

He'd told her he'd choose her over all the women in the

world. Apparently, he was willing to prove that by dying...with her. Because he couldn't think Gagnon was going to let either one of them walk away.

It was impossible.

Gagnon's focus was on the phone, but Souza had moved toward Cici, his cold eyes broadcasting a warning. *Keep your mouth shut.*

Or what? He'd kill her? That was already the plan.

She wasn't about to let them take down Asher too.

She met Souza's eyes. And then she shouted, "Asher, run! They know where you—"

Souza's kick was swift, straight to her ribs. Her breath whooshed out, replaced by pain, sharp and hot.

The second blow came to her head. The office pulsated, the world around her muffled, shrinking to darkness.

She ducked, curled, and prayed...for relief. Mostly, for Asher.

She desperately wanted him to survive this.

CHAPTER TWENTY-SIX

The sound that followed Cici's warning—a sharp, sickening thump—ignited every protective instinct Asher possessed.

"Leave her alone." The words tore from his throat. Another muffled cry of pain reached him, and he squeezed his eyes closed. "I swear, if you hurt her—"

"Easy, Asher. Easy." Grant's voice cut through his earpiece, steady and commanding. "Remember, you're desperate. You're scared. Play your part."

Asher forced himself to breathe, to channel the rage burning through his veins into something useful. The emotion was genuine, threatening to consume him. "Please don't hurt her." His voice cracked with the weight of it. "Please."

The thought that she'd risked pain to warn him, that, as terrified as she must be, she'd tried to protect him, made his chest tighten with something that went far deeper than strategy or duty.

"Much better." Gagnon's voice carried a note of satisfaction, as if he were conducting an orchestra and enjoying the music.

"Now that we understand each other, perhaps we can discuss terms. What exactly do you think you have to bargain with?"

Asher pushed down the image of Cici crumpled and hurt. "I have what you're looking for."

"Do you now?" There was amusement in Gagnon's tone. "And what exactly would that be?"

"An SD card."

Asher counted twelve seconds that followed his pronouncement.

"Interesting." His tone was cooler now, more calculating. Far less amused. "And how exactly did you find it?"

"I was there when your guys came back looking for it." Asher kept his voice steady, injecting just enough smugness to sound believable. "Had a front row seat to their little treasure hunt. Amazing how much you can learn when idiots think you're dead."

Through his earpiece, he heard Grant's quiet "Good" and the barely audible sounds of his team moving into position.

"You were listening," Gagnon said.

Another GBPA agent, Whiteman, spoke in Asher's ear. "Two men closing in on your location."

He was well hidden behind an old oak tree. The ditch where he crouched was protected by bushes all around. Even if they managed to track him, he'd see them long before they saw him.

"I heard every word," he said to Gagnon, his gaze roaming the darkness, thankful for the night-vision goggles Bartlett had brought with the arsenal he'd distributed out of the back of his SUV. Asher picked out the first enemy, coming from the west, the direction of the road.

He continued speaking, his voice steady. "Including the part where they admitted they couldn't find it." Asher shifted.

Where was the second man? "I dropped a little present in their truck too—a cell phone with GPS. Led me right to your front door."

"You're alone?"

"Cici's got people, and I've got people, and they're all on their way." He let that hang in the air, still searching...

Got him.

The second man had circled and was closing in from behind.

Asher had gotten close enough to the front gate to let himself be seen. So far, the plan was working.

He needed to finish the conversation and move before they got close enough to hear. He had about two minutes.

"Thing is," he said, keeping his voice low, "I don't care about taking you into custody or bringing down your organization. I don't give a rip if you keep doing whatever it is you've been doing. I'm not here to make you pay. All I want is Cici. But if you and I can't come to terms now, well, our people will be here soon, and then it'll be too late."

"Why not just let them do their work?" Gagnon asked. "Maybe they could take us all out."

"We could kill every one of you, no problem. But she could be hurt, and I'm not willing to risk that. Do you want to deal, or take your chances? Because if you wait until every law enforcement agent in New England converges, I won't be able to control what happens to you—or this SD card. Your window's closing."

The men moving in still didn't show any sign they'd seen him, but he needed to shut this down. To take these two enemies out.

"Think it through," he said. "You have five minutes."

He ended the call and shoved the cell into his jeans pocket.

Through the night-vision goggles, he watched the men converge from opposite directions on his general location, their movements deliberate but uncertain. Both wore night-vision goggles and carried handguns.

The first man, compact and wiry, gestured in the direction where Asher hid. His partner, taller with broader shoulders, shook his head and pointed east. As the first man neared, Asher could hear his whispered words.

"I'm gonna swing south," the wiry one said.

The other guy must've answered because he snapped, "I don't see him yet."

Asher smiled grimly. *I'm about six feet below your eye line.*

He eased his knife from its sheath, the matte black blade catching no light in the darkness. Two targets, two different approaches needed. The wiry one should go down easily—he moved like someone who relied more on speed than strength. The bigger guy would be a problem if Asher didn't drop him fast.

The wiry man stepped closer to the oak, weapon drawn, scanning the forest.

His partner moved in the opposite direction, creating distance between them. Smart, but not smart enough.

Asher waited until Wiry was directly above his position, then exploded out of the ditch. His hand clamped over the man's mouth as the knife found its mark between his ribs, angled upward toward the heart. The man's body went rigid, then limp, and Asher lowered him silently to the ground.

He took the man's earpiece and listened.

"Marco?" The voice carried a note of concern. "You got something?"

Asher whispered, "Yeah," hoping the commando wouldn't realize the voice hadn't come from his partner.

"Coming." Sure enough, the larger guy started moving toward him.

Asher crouched behind the oak, controlling his breathing. His shoulder throbbed, his knee ached, but adrenaline kept the pain manageable. He had maybe ten seconds before the partner realized Marco wasn't there.

"Hold up. Patrol," Grant said in Asher's ear.

Hold up? They needed to move in. Asher could only divert for so long.

The larger man's footsteps crunched through the underbrush, moving toward the oak. "Marco, status."

Asher heard the words both through the enemy's comms and through the forest. He gripped the knife, sticky with blood. This one would be harder—bigger, maybe more experienced, considering the way he moved silently on the bracken.

Asher was creeping out from behind his tree when the commando spun, raising his weapon.

Asher dove, tackling him around the waist and driving him backward into a cluster of saplings.

The man's handgun discharged into the canopy above them.

They hit the ground hard, the commando's breath whooshing out. Asher drove his elbow into the man's solar plexus, then brought the knife up. The blade caught him in the throat, and he went still, his eyes staring sightlessly at the night sky.

Asher rolled off the body, chest heaving. The gunshot would signal where he was. He needed to move.

He shoved the enemies' comm units into his pocket, speaking into his team's. "Two down. Shot fired."

"We heard." Grant's deadpan reply might've made Asher smile under other circumstances. "We're moving now. Stay low and don't get caught."

Asher was already moving, needing to be far from this place before anyone reached him.

He ran deeper into the forest, making all sorts of noise on his way. *Follow my breadcrumbs, boys.*

His phone buzzed—Gagnon calling back.

He kept moving, silently now, and ducked behind a bush twenty feet from a fallen tree, hoping the enemy would look there first. He pulled out his phone and answered. "I bet you hoped I wouldn't pick up."

The question was met with a long beat of silence. "The men?"

"Won't be reporting in."

"You just signed your death certificate."

"You'd better hope not."

"You have no cards. Every second you evade capture is another moment of torture for your little girlfriend."

Cici screamed, punctuating the point.

"You will protect Cici, or I will end you." He let fury resonate with the words. "With a push of a button. And if your goons happen to get to me first, you'd better start running."

Speaking of goons, he spotted a couple moving through the woods, far enough away that he wasn't worried he'd be heard. Not yet, anyway.

Gagnon said, "What are you talking about?"

"If I don't check in, my dead-man's switch activates. Every name, every transaction, every dirty secret of every dirtbag you've collected goes public."

"You're bluffing. How could you possibly have—?"

"It's amazing what you can do with AI these days. Just had to upload the information to the cloud and type up an email, addressed to law enforcement and, for good measure, every newspaper I could think of. *Times*, *Herald*, *Globe*. Even added the *Inquirer* out of Philly. Wouldn't want your friends at the club to miss the news."

Guys like him always had a club, didn't they?

"It's scheduled to send in half an hour. Unless I stop it, that is." Asher let that simmer, then said, "Are you ready to make a deal?"

CHAPTER TWENTY-SEVEN

"Here's what's going to happen." Gagnon's words carried the smooth confidence of a man who'd orchestrated a thousand betrayals. He met Cici's eyes as he spoke to Asher on the phone. "You're going to come to me. Alone. No backup, no law enforcement, no clever little schemes."

Cici wished she could hear Asher's response, but Gagnon hadn't put this call on speaker. Whatever Asher said made Gagnon's mouth curve into that cold smile she loathed.

"Insurance?" Gagnon chuckled, the sound less amused than evil. "You want to play games with dead-man's switches? Understand this: the moment I suspect law enforcement is involved, the moment I see so much as a suspicious shadow, she dies."

Cici pressed herself against the filing cabinet, her zip-tied hands numb behind her back, wishing she could disappear.

He was quiet, listening. Then said, "Ruin me? Maybe." Gagnon's tone was conversational. "But she'll still be dead. And I could, as you suggested, run. You saw the contents of that SD card. Do I seem like a man who hasn't considered—and planned for—every contingency?"

Tightness around his eyes and a barely perceptible stiffening of his shoulders told her there was more going on than what he said.

He listened, then sighed. "One moment." He tapped the phone screen. Must've been the mute button, because he spoke to Souza. "He wants to talk to her."

"We can prove she's alive without a conversation." His flicker of eagerness had her stomach turning.

Souza took pleasure in hurting her. He'd proved that with every kick, every pinch, every slap—timed so Asher would hear.

"We've provoked him enough," Gagnon said.

Souza's lips slipped into a frown. "She'll give him information."

"You'll have to think of a way to keep her quiet."

Souza stared at her, and as much as she wanted to cower, she forced herself to hold his eye contact.

Despite the ribs that blazed with pain. Despite the way her cheek burned and her head throbbed, she didn't back down.

Crouching in front of her, Souza yanked off her shoes and socks, then pulled a knife from a sheath where it'd been tucked beneath his sweatshirt. He positioned the blade across her big toe. "It won't kill her." His evil grin returned. "But it'll definitely stop her from running."

Gagnon didn't bother lowering to her level, just looked down at her. "Do not try to give your bodyguard any information. Tell him you're fine and we're treating you well."

"So you want me to lie?"

"I want you to keep your toe."

As much as she was desperate to tell Asher where she was, how many men were here, and how she was guarded, in this, she and Gagnon agreed.

She was pretty attached to her toes. And Souza wouldn't hesitate to make good on his promise. "Fine."

Gagnon tapped the phone, then lowered it toward her.

"Asher?"

"Cici, thank God. Are you all right?"

She flicked her gaze to her captor, refusing to look at Souza and his well-placed knife. "Mr. Gagnon is as gracious a host as you'd guess."

He narrowed his eyes, not liking her answer.

"I'm going to get you out of there," Asher said. "I promise."

"Be careful. These people—"

"That's enough." Gagnon swiveled, taking the phone with him. "As you can hear, she's alive and well. I'll tell my men to stand down. You have five minutes to get to the gate. Bring the SD card with you."

Souza backed away but didn't return his knife to its sheath. Probably hoping he'd get the chance to use it.

She shifted to watch Gagnon.

"You must think I'm an idiot." He hadn't taken the phone off speaker, so Asher's answer rang through the room. "The card is in a safe place. You'll get it when Cici is too."

"Don't make me hurt her again." Gagnon tapped on his phone and read. What was he doing? Checking his texts?

"If you do," Asher said, "I'll send one of the files on the SD card to the FBI. Just one. We'll start with Maxwell Pierce's."

Souza's gaze snapped to Gagnon.

"Pierce's fall from grace will be complete and public," Asher said, "in light of all his community activism. I suspect he'll take Souza down with him."

The guard's eyebrows hiked, obviously surprised Asher knew his name.

His cheeks flushed, his eyes narrowing. If *deadly threat* had a face, Souza wore it.

Gagnon waved Souza down, but by the degrees Souza relaxed—somewhere around zero—he wasn't buying Gagnon's casual reassurance.

"It'll definitely be a hitch in the road for the Fourth Hood." Asher's tone was matter-of-fact. "Though I'm sure some other gang will step in to continue their work. Who knows, Wendall? Maybe you'll survive."

"If you release a single iota of what's on that SD card—"

"Keep your hands off Cici, then, and we won't have a problem. Tell your men to stand down. I don't want to have to take out any more. When I get to the gate, I expect Cici to be safe and ready to move. And be *able* to move."

"You expect me to just hand her over without getting the SD card?"

"I'll give you the card."

Gagnon glared at the phone. "But of course you've copied all the information off it."

"What do you think, Wendall? You're the king of leverage. What would you do?"

Gagnon should be nervous. He should be shaking in his boots. But he wasn't. He was angry, obviously, because this hadn't gone as planned.

But he wasn't defeated. He was calculating.

Here was a man who'd thrived for decades with money collected from bribing dangerous, powerful people. He'd said he had contingency plans. Cici guessed he was using one even now.

"Your problem," Asher said through the phone, "is that you think you've got all the power, but the truth is, you aren't holding any cards at all."

"You may be right. I look forward to speaking with you face-to-face." Gagnon ended the call, dropped his phone on the desk, and smiled that terrible smile.

Cici's stomach dropped through the concrete floor. He was up to something, and Asher was about to find out what.

CHAPTER TWENTY-EIGHT

Asher was still crouched behind the tree, watching for Gagnon's men.

Not only had they not found him, he saw no movement anywhere. As if they'd given up, or Gagnon had called them back.

Even if the man did expect him to march right up to the gate, they'd be there, wouldn't they? Watching? They should be.

Asher held the enemy's comm unit to his ear, desperate to learn what they were doing. He'd heard nothing but low static until a voice cracked over it.

"Status of the second team?" Gagnon barked.

A second team? How many more men had Gagnon called in? When? And why?

"Surveying the perimeter," a man answered, "then moving in."

Another voice cut through the transmission. "Switch channels. We might be compromised."

The static cut off, leaving silence.

Heart pounding, Asher tapped his own comm, understanding now why Gagnon's men weren't looking for him. Gagnon must've thought that, if Asher didn't march up to the front gate as promised, this second team would find him.

"Grant, we've got a problem."

"Go," Grant said.

"There's a second team. They're closing in from the perimeter."

"What? Where?" That was Callan, and he sounded furious. "Alyssa, report."

She'd been providing regular reports with information she got from the drone she flew overhead, another gadget Bartlett had pulled from his trunk.

Seconds ticked by, but she didn't answer.

"Alyssa!"

Grant said, "Don't jump to—"

"I told you it wasn't safe!" Callan's voice exploded through the channel, drowning out the rest of Grant's response. The raw panic in his tone made Asher's stomach drop.

In trying to save Cici, had he put her sister in harm's way?

"Check on her," Grant said. "Alyssa's probably finding cover and keeping quiet. Stay out of sight. They don't know we know they're coming. Keep it that way."

The comm went quiet for a heartbeat before Grant's voice came back, steady and controlled. "Asher, with you in possession of the SD card, what do you think Gagnon's play is, bringing more men?"

"He's lost a couple," Bartlett said.

Asher had taken out two, getting their numbers closer to even.

"There was that gunshot earlier," Bartlett said. "Whiteman reported it. So maybe they're down three."

"Best case scenario, that leaves nine," Grant said. "Maybe he thinks he can capture you? Torture you until you give it up?"

"No reason to capture me. I just agreed to go to him."

"But he didn't know you'd do that."

True.

Asher hadn't stopped scanning the forest, but there was no movement anywhere.

His mind raced through possibilities. Did they plan to torture him? Maybe Gagnon thought he could break Asher.

Or maybe he planned to torture *Cici* and force Asher to give up the SD card to protect her.

That scenario made Asher's blood run cold. He didn't bother asking himself what he'd do. He could think of no solution that would get them out of that situation alive.

Not without Grant and company. Thank God Asher wasn't alone.

But even if Gagnon did try torture, did he really think he could get the information before the dead-man's switch activated? Not that there *was* a dead-man's switch, but Gagnon didn't know that. He believed he still had a shot to keep his secrets from going public.

Or did he?

The pieces clicked into place. That "contingency plan" remark Asher had dismissed as bluster... Was that exactly what was happening now?

He considered every angle, and the longer he thought about it, the more his gut told him he'd stumbled on the answer.

"He's flipping the board." The truth tasted like poison in Asher's mouth. "He's not trying to get the SD card back. He's spilling gasoline on his operation and lighting a match on his way out."

Nobody replied to that, not Grant or Bartlett or the other team members who listened in. Not Callan, still looking for Alyssa.

"Think about it." Asher's pulse hammered as the implications crystallized. "Gagnon's whole operation depends on information and leverage. But I have the SD card now. If the information on it releases, he's finished. Prison's his best option, but even there, his enemies could get to him. I told him I uploaded it…"

Meaning, Asher had pushed Gagnon to this. Asher had *caused* this.

If he couldn't save Cici, he'd live with the implications of all his mistakes for the rest of his life.

"What are you saying?" Grant's voice was tight.

"He's planning to escape. But first, he's going to clean house. Take out Souza—whose boss will be fingered when that information goes public. Same might be true for these commandos. Who knows that they're not on loan from some criminal organization." Asher's throat went dry. "And he'll take out Cici just for spite. Me too, if he can get his hands on me."

Gagnon wasn't negotiating. He was buying time. He was going scorched earth. "He's going to kill her."

"Then why the second team?" Bartlett asked, bringing the question back where they'd begun.

"To make sure he takes out anyone who tries to stop him. You heard me. I told him I had people en route—my people and Cici's. He's expecting an army to come against him. This second team is here to make sure they don't get to him before he escapes. Are you two in position?"

"Inside the fence," Grant said. "It's your move."

If he walked up to the front gate, he'd be shot. He started working his way toward the chain-link fence. "We've got to get her. Now."

Bartlett said, "Without Callan—"

"We're out of time." Asher scanned for enemies as he jogged closer to the factory grounds. "Tell me where to go in."

Grant said, "Get right back to you."

One way or another, Asher was getting inside that factory. No more games.

He had to rescue Cici before it was too late.

CHAPTER TWENTY-NINE

Cici would rather be locked in a cage with a nest of snakes than precede Souza into the cramped storage room. On Gagnon's command, he'd manhandled her out of the office, his fat fingers digging into her arm. They'd walked along the catwalk overlooking the factory floor. On the way, they passed a meeting room and a break room. She'd glimpsed sofas and chairs, even a little refrigerator. Why would Gagnon set up shop in the office when he could've been in a more comfortable room?

Men's voices carried from below. They were making a plan, but she didn't hear enough to know what they were discussing.

She stared into the cramped storage space, too frightened to move.

Souza shoved her forward.

She stumbled against a metal shelving unit straight ahead, got her footing, and spun, terrified of turning her back on her captor.

He filled the doorway, his bulk blocking her only escape.

"He wants you hidden while they clean up your boyfriend's mess." His voice carried casual cruelty.

"How thoughtful of him to be concerned about my well-being." Behind her back, Cici stretched her freed hands. Souza had cut the zip ties to move her, and her fingers were still tingling as the blood circulated again. The last thing she wanted to do was draw attention to them, to have them bound again.

Souza stepped into the room, absorbing all the oxygen, and closed the door, then crossed toward her until he was close enough that she could smell his sour breath, see the way his eyes skimmed over her.

"You know what I think?" He leaned nearer, and she backed against the shelving. "I think Gagnon's soft. All this negotiating, all this careful planning." He reached out to tug a strand of her hair, and she jerked away. "Me? I would've put a bullet in your head the second we grabbed you." He tipped his head back and forth. "Except...I do like to play with my food."

His fingers grazed her cheek, and her skin crawled.

She forced herself to remain still, every instinct screaming at her to recoil from his touch. Instead, she lifted her chin and met his eyes with as much defiance as she could muster.

"You know what your problem is?" Souza's hand slid down her arm and gripped her wrist. With his other hand, he brought her free wrist close, then held them tight in one meaty fist. "You think you're better than people like me. Rich girl, daddy's little princess, probably never had to fight for nothin'."

"You don't know anything about me." She tried to pull away, but his fingers were like steel bands.

"I know enough."

"You tell yourself these lies to justify the horrible things you do."

His other hand moved to her throat, not squeezing but resting there like a promise. "You're scared." He spoke as if he hadn't heard her. "I can smell it on you."

"As well I should be." She hated how her voice wavered. "What I don't understand is why you're not."

Souza's hand stilled against her neck, his eyes narrowing. "I got nothing to fear."

"Gagnon told me himself that you're a liability, and we both know how much he hates liabilities."

Souza's face darkened, his hands dropping as he stepped away. "Like I'm gonna believe you. You don't know—"

"Don't I?" Cici gazed around, going for calm, as if her heart weren't hammering in her chest. She scanned the floor, then the shelves that lined the room, searching for anything that could serve as a weapon.

"When you were out looking for Falcone and Mendez—"

"How d'you know their names? How do you know me?"

"Traffic cams." She shrugged like it was no big deal. "Your face was picked up outside the police station in Philly—yours and Gagnon's, of course. And then again near the airfield in Massachusetts. Once those images were isolated, we were able to identify—"

"Who's we?"

"Do you have any idea who I am?"

Confusion looked a lot like rage on Souza's face. Cici needed to tread very carefully.

"My father was a spy with the CIA. Now he's a defense contractor." She let that information settle. "My cousin is a spy. My sister worked for the NSA, and her fiancé was a spy. Another cousin of mine is retired Special Forces. Oh, and the person who owns those rubies Gagnon was showing off earlier? He's a billionaire with virtually unlimited resources." She shook her head, going for surprised and disappointed. "Gagnon knows all that. Funny that he didn't choose to share the information with you."

Souza said nothing.

Keep him talking. Keep him wrong-footed. Anything to keep his hands off her—and sow seeds of doubt.

"Anyway," she continued, "when you were off looking for Mendez and Falcone, I asked Gagnon about his son. You remember, he mentioned him to Mr. D at the jewelry store?"

Souza nodded, listening. Processing.

"He told me..." Her gaze landed on a mug filled with pens. And a letter opener.

She focused on Souza again. "Gagnon said nobody knows about his son, that if word got out, his enemies could use him as leverage. Mr. D knew, and he's dead. I heard Gagnon mention his son in the store, and..." She made a face, trying to communicate that her having overheard was the reason Gagnon had pursued her. "You know what his plan is for me. Think about this, though. *You* know about his son." She worked for a compassionate expression. "There's a reason you're in here with me while other people fight the fight. You really think he believes Falcone is more capable out there than you would be?"

Souza's eyes narrowed. He might've been uneducated, but he wasn't stupid.

"Falcone's no Harvard student," she said, "but the fact that he doesn't know anything is working in his favor. Obviously, you're a thousand times more competent than Falcone. Anybody can hold a gun on a defenseless woman. Gagnon has you in here because you know too much. When he comes to kill me, you think he'll go to any lengths to protect you?" She let that simmer, half-expecting Souza to respond. But he didn't.

He was thinking. She was getting through to him.

"It's a shame," she said after a few moments. "Obviously, your little brother needs you, but..."

"Leave my brother outta this." Venom spilled out with the words, but she heard genuine fear in them.

"*I* didn't bring him into it. You can thank Gagnon for that. I just wonder who's going to be there for Alfonzo when he gets out of prison."

"I'll be there. Gagnon's not gonna... If he wanted me dead, then I'd be dead."

"You will be when he's done using you. If I were you..." She shrugged. "Not that you want my advice."

"What?"

"I'd escape while I still had the chance."

He swallowed, staring past her, hopefully thinking about what she'd said? Hopefully, planning his escape. Maybe, maybe...

A sharp crack echoed from somewhere outside. Gunfire?

Souza's head snapped toward the door, his hand moving to the comm unit in his ear. "What's going on?"

She couldn't hear an answer. Maybe he didn't get one because he scowled and turned his back on her, facing the exit.

She snatched the letter opener and concealed it behind her back, tucking it into the waistband of her jeans.

She prayed Souza would leave. That he'd heed her advice and take off. She'd started the conversation to plant doubt, but the more she'd talked, the more convinced she was that she was right. If Souza stayed, he'd be killed right along with her.

But that didn't mean he'd listen. And if he didn't...

She felt the cold metal pressed against her back and prayed that, if it came down to it, she'd have the courage to use it.

CHAPTER THIRTY

When gunfire erupted, the acidic taste of fear coated Asher's mouth.

He pressed himself between the chain-link fence and an overgrown bush. Through his earpiece, the staccato reports painted a grim picture. The second group of mercenaries had found his team.

He readied his Glock.

"Taking heavy fire on the east perimeter." Whiteman's voice crackled through the static. "I'm pinned down behind a transformer station."

"Copy that," Grant said. "Yartym?"

"Four on this side. I'm circling to get behind them."

"Copy." Grant's response was clipped, professional. "Bartlett and I are in position behind the main factory. Callan, status?"

A pause stretched too long, then Callan's voice, barely a whisper. "Four—no, five armed men closing from the north. I'm taking cover." After a breath, he demanded, "Alyssa, report." His desperation bled through his controlled tone.

Silence.

"Alyssa!" Callan's whisper was vehement.

Then—three deliberate taps through the comm system. A pause. Three more taps.

"Switch channels," Grant ordered. "Now."

Asher did, his stomach knotting. Those taps could mean Alyssa was alive and hiding. Or they could mean an enemy had gotten ahold of her comm unit and was trying to throw them off.

Either way, Asher needed to trust Alyssa to Callan. His job was to save Cici.

He scaled the fence in one fluid motion, ignoring the fire that shot through his wounded shoulder. His boots hit the gravel with barely a whisper.

"Inside the fence," he said into his comm. "Going in."

"Negative." Grant spoke with authority, as if Asher answered to him. "Hold position until—"

"She's out of time." But, though it went against his every instinct, he didn't move. He'd tried to go it alone, and where had that landed him?

Right here, with the woman he loved in the hands of a psychopath.

"Trust me, Rhodes." Grant's tone was mostly commanding, but Asher heard the undertone of understanding. "We need to get the power off. Bartlett, you—"

Taps interrupted again. *Tap tap tap.* Pause. *Tap tap tap.*

They'd switched channels.

He barely knew Alyssa, but she was Cici's sister, and from what he'd seen, cool under pressure. She wouldn't have enemies on the team's backup channel.

Meaning those taps were her. Meaning...

"Alyssa." Callan sounded almost breathless. "Is that you?"

Tap tap tap.

Callan muttered, "Thank God."

"Can you cut the power?" Grant asked. "Three taps, yes. Two taps, no."

Tap tap tap.

"Okay, on my mark," Grant said. "Yartym, provide cover. Rhodes, the office building is right in front of you. Get low and move around to the opposite side. Take the covered walkway. You'll meet a guard."

Asher wanted to sprint straight for the factory on the far side of the property, but Grant was right. Better to move stealthily. The closer they could get before they were seen, the better.

He followed Grant's order, trying not to think about what Gagnon would do when he knew he was trapped.

Hold Cici hostage? Use her as a shield?

Kill her out of spite?

Please, God. Do Your thing. Keep her safe.

He circled the office building, catching sight of a guard clad in all black, weapon at the ready. This was no dial-a-thug. He looked formidable.

Asher tracked the guard's focus as he scanned the overgrown landscaping between this building and the factory. When his gaze drifted in the opposite direction, Asher moved in silently.

The guard heard him coming, but he wasn't fast enough.

Asher tackled him before he could get a shot off. His knife found its mark just below the commando's bulletproof vest, digging into soft flesh.

The guy went down fighting, though he was easy to subdue. Asher kept his hand on the guy's mouth to keep him from calling out, tempted to finish him off. But he got a look at the guy's face. His eyes were wide with fear.

He looked like a farm kid from Iowa or something. Not an enemy, just a hired gun who had no idea who he was being paid to protect.

Asher lifted him just enough, then whacked his head against the cement.

By the time Iowa woke up—if he didn't bleed to death—this would be over.

Asher reached the back door—heavy steel being held open a crack, thanks to a brick wedged between it and the jamb. Whispering into the comm, he said, "Here."

"Hold."

Asher did, counting seconds. Ten passed before Grant said, "Alyssa. Cut power."

"Three seconds. Two. One." She answered with zero drama, as if she'd been there all along.

He hoped he lived long enough to hear her story.

There hadn't been any lights on outside, so there was no indication she'd done it, but Grant said, "Rhodes, move. Meet you inside."

Asher eased the open wider, the sound barely a whisper.

Lifting his night-vision goggles, he stepped into a cavernous space lit by emergency lighting that bathed everything in a bloody glow. The room was filled with all manner of machinery.

No enemies in sight.

The smell hit him. Oil, rust, and something stomach-turning —the metallic scent of fresh blood.

A body lay a few feet away, crumpled and spent.

Cici!

But it wasn't her. This was a man, shot in the head. Second glance told Asher it was Pretty Boy. Mendez.

Back at the accident site, he'd been terrified when he'd discovered Asher's body wasn't there. Seemed he'd had good reason to fear.

Why come back here? What kind of power did Gagnon hold over these people?

Asher slipped past him, his weapon drawn. The factory floor stretched before him. Overhead, a catwalk ran the perimeter of the building, disappearing into shadows.

Though he saw nobody, he sensed he wasn't alone.

Using the massive machinery as cover, Asher crept deeper into the factory.

A door opened on the far side. Asher ducked behind a rusted conveyor belt, raising his weapon.

Grant entered, moving with practiced silence, followed by Bartlett.

Asher caught Grant's eyes across the industrial wasteland, and Grant lifted a finger and signaled upward, then took aim.

A catwalk above was metal grating, so Asher could see the man who stood there. Grant had him in his sights.

One upstairs. Maybe one or more down here, though he hadn't seen them yet.

Another man materialized on the catwalk to his left, rifle trained on Grant.

Asher had no choice.

He fired, the shot echoing through the cavernous space like thunder.

The guard pitched forward, caught on the railing, but his weapon clattered to the factory floor thirty feet below.

Grant took out the other guard.

Asher had expected chaos to erupt. He expected more guards to come out of hiding, to start shooting. But they didn't.

It was weird.

"Cover me." Asher moved toward the exposed staircase. Somewhere up there, Cici was waiting.

He just prayed he wasn't too late.

CHAPTER THIRTY-ONE

Cici had always found something mesmerizing about the way big cats moved at the zoo—all coiled power and lethal grace, pacing their enclosures with predatory patience. Now, pressed against the cold metal shelving in the cramped storage room, she watched Souza prowl with that same deadly restlessness, and the comparison made her stomach clench with dread.

She was the prey here, and they both knew it.

The overhead lights had gone out a few seconds before. Only the red *Exit* sign illuminated the crypt-sized space.

The distant gunfire that had erupted minutes earlier seemed to have awakened something feral in Souza.

He moved from wall to wall, testing the door handle occasionally as if it might suddenly lock from the outside. Every few seconds, his dark eyes would snap to her.

She'd tried reasoning with him when the first shots rang out, suggesting he could still run, still escape whatever trap was closing around them.

Hoping he'd leave her to fend for herself.

For a moment, she'd seen him waver, seen the flicker of self-preservation war with whatever hold Gagnon had over him. But then more gunfire had cracked through the night, closer this time, and his expression had hardened.

The letter opener pressing against her spine felt pathetically inadequate now. She'd been so proud of herself for palming it, so certain she'd find the perfect opportunity to use it. But one stab of a letter opener wasn't going to bring this beast down. More likely, it'd just make him angrier than he already was.

Leave it to Cici to bring a letter opener and conversational skills to a gunfight.

Another gunshot, so close this time that the metal shelving vibrated. Male voices echoed from the other side of the door, urgent and commanding. Not the controlled whispers of Gagnon's mercenaries, but something different. Something that made her heart leap with desperate hope.

"What's goin' on?" Souza froze and pressed his ear to his earpiece, listening. Whatever he heard—or didn't hear—made his jaw clench. "This was not the plan." The way he muttered told her he wasn't speaking to her or to anyone else. He was thinking, calculating.

Cici forced herself to remain still against the shelving, though every muscle in her body screamed at her to move, to run, to do something other than wait for him to decide her fate.

"It's time to cut your losses," she said. "Get out of here before they come to finish you off." She was surprised by how steady her voice sounded.

It was a risk, encouraging him to run. He could decide to kill her first, his own loose-end operation.

When he didn't argue, she pressed her point. "All you've done is follow terrible orders from a terrible man. You haven't done anything irrevocable. You didn't shoot Mendez, that was—"

"Shut up." Souza whipped around, his eyes blazing.

"I'm just saying..." Now, her voice wobbled. "Asher's trained. And based on the gunfight out there, he brought backup—"

"I said shut up!" He crossed the small space in two strides and slapped her cheek with enough force to snap her head sideways.

Stars burst across her vision, but she didn't cry out.

He backed away, spoke into his comm unit. "Gagnon, what's going on?"

Souza stared past her. She couldn't tell if he was hearing an answer or not. After a moment, he grabbed her arm. "I'm done waiting."

"Where are we—?"

"You don't ask questions. You do as I say."

He dragged her across the small space, then yanked the door open and pushed her in front of him onto the catwalk.

CHAPTER THIRTY-TWO

Asher was making his way up the stairs when a sound had him pausing. A door opening. A man's voice, issuing a command.

Asher aimed his weapon toward the noise.

Fifty feet ahead and twenty feet above, Cici stumbled onto the catwalk.

A man's arm wrapped around her neck, the barrel of a pistol pressed against her temple.

Nausea and rage crawled up Asher's throat.

Her eyes found his through the hellish red light—wide with terror but alive. So alive.

Asher lifted a finger to his lips. *Shhh.*

The man holding her kept his back against the wall, Cici in front of him, inching toward the corner. Because of that, he didn't see Asher. Too much of a coward to peek around his human shield.

Maybe not a coward. Just smart. If Asher got his sights on whoever that was, the guy would be dead.

"Grant." Asher's whisper into the comm was barely audible.

"I see her. Focus. We're not alone in here."

A shadow moved to Asher's left, just past a huge machine on the factory floor. A commando trying to flank him.

Asher watched the spot where the enemy was sure to emerge. When he did, Asher fired.

The man went down.

A door opened below, then boots thumped on the concrete.

"Move," Grant said. "We'll cover you." A gunshot punctuated his point.

Cici and her captor had continued moving along the catwalk and disappeared. At least he knew which way to go.

Hold on, sweetheart. I'm coming.

CHAPTER THIRTY-THREE

When Cici had caught sight of Asher, her hope had soared like an eagle on an updraft. Of course he'd come for her. And based on the gunfire inside and out, he'd brought an army.

Maybe a stray bullet had hit her metaphorical bird because once she lost sight of him, that hope had been reduced to a few bloody feathers.

As they'd maneuvered along the catwalk, they'd had to step over the body of one of the commandos. Another one slumped over the railing.

The blood and death... It was more than she could handle. More than she'd ever wanted to know about war.

Now they were outside the office where Gagnon waited.

Souza stood with his back to the door, keeping her between him and danger.

A gunshot rang out on the floor below, followed by a thump. Someone was down. Asher?

Please, no.

From inside, Gagnon's voice carried. "Now. I need that bird

now!" He was shouting, though Cici heard no response. "If I go down..." His voice lowered, becoming incoherent.

Souza's arm around her neck tightened, and dizziness overcame her. She fought against it, managing to shift enough to increase the blood flow to her brain.

Souza pushed her toward the catwalk railing, then shifted to the side.

He fired at the doorknob.

The lock mechanism exploded in a shower of sparks and twisted metal.

Souza kicked the door open and shoved Cici inside ahead of him, his weapon raised and ready.

Gagnon stood in the center of the office, his phone pressed to his ear, his face flushed. The room was bathed in red light from a glowing *Exit* sign.

He stopped mid-sentence when he saw them, his eyes going wide before narrowing to slits. "Why are you here?" The question was directed at Souza like an accusation. "I told you to stay put."

Souza raised his gun, aiming at Gagnon. He kicked the door closed behind him and, with his free hand, pushed Cici away.

She stumbled against the cold metal filing cabinet where she'd been held before, her legs unsteady from the adrenaline coursing through her system. The crimson emergency lighting cast everything in a hellish glow.

"What's your play here?" Souza's voice carried deadly calm. He didn't lower his weapon.

Gagnon moved behind his desk, where a laptop bag stood upright, ready for him to grab on his way out.

The cabinet that had previously blocked the exterior door had been pushed aside, confirming Cici's suspicion that he'd been working on an escape plan. That exterior door was the reason he'd set up in this office instead of the more comfortable break room. But how did he think he was going to get away? Asher had men outside. They would surely stop him from getting to a vehicle.

She remembered what he'd been saying when Souza and Cici had been outside the door. Something about a bird.

A helicopter?

"I'm glad you're here," Gagnon's tone shifted to something approaching relief. "I was just about to call you. As soon as it's clear, we're going to move."

He was lying. Cici could hear it in the too-smooth cadence of his words, see it in the way his gaze darted toward his escape route. She thought Souza knew it, too, based on the way his grip tightened on his weapon.

"What was the plan? Leave us here, hope I got killed in the crossfire?" Souza's voice rose dangerously. "No." His head shook, but his gun was steady. "No, you don't leave anything to chance. You planned to kill us, or have one of your mercenaries do it. Right?"

"Don't be ridiculous," Gagnon snapped. "It's us against them. You'd better figure out who your real enemy is, and fast."

"My real enemy?" Souza's laugh was bitter. "You threatened my brother. You've been planning to dispose of me since this started."

"Your brother will be fine as long as you—"

"As long as I what? Die for you?" Souza took a step forward, his weapon never wavering.

Outside the building, the gunfight raged on, but only silence came from the factory below. Asher was out there, somewhere. She prayed he was still alive.

Gagnon's eyes flicked toward the door, then back to Souza. "We don't have time for this."

"Then you better start talking."

"There's a helicopter coming. We need to be ready to move."

Souza tipped his head toward Cici. "Her, too?"

Gagnon barely gave her a glance. "She's our ticket out of here. The only leverage we have left."

Cici couldn't let herself be taken. She braced herself, preparing to fight.

CHAPTER THIRTY-FOUR

Asher calculated each step on the metal catwalk, silent, his weapon raised as he cleared room after empty room. No enemies, so far.

Grant and Bartlett had taken out the few commandos assigned to the factory floor. They were down there now, holding off anybody who tried to get inside.

The firefight continued outside, but based on what he was hearing through the comms, Callan, Yartym, and Whiteman were observing the carnage from afar.

Gagnon's second team had arrived, and they were taking out the first team, along with all the men Gagnon had brought with him.

Was there a third team coming to take out the second? Maybe Gagnon thought he could control these new guys. Or they couldn't ID him.

Yeah, that was probably it.

The guy didn't leave loose ends.

Like Cici.

Dust motes danced in the crimson emergency lighting, and

the scent of death permeated everything. A trail of blood led him toward a door at the end of a corridor.

Through it, he heard two men arguing.

Cici had to be in there.

Asher pressed himself against the wall, straining to make out the words. One voice carried the cultured menace he recognized as Gagnon. The other was rougher. Souza, most likely.

Something about a bird? And then...

"She's our ticket out of here." That smooth voice belonged to Gagnon. "The only leverage we have left."

He was talking about Cici.

Asher itched to bang through that door, to fire off two shots and take both enemies down. Except Cici was in there.

A gunshot rang from below. Another answered. "Got him," Bartlett said.

"Second team is moving toward the factory," Whiteman said. "Should I pursue?"

"Negative. Hold your position. They won't get inside."

Alyssa's voice cut through, urgent and clipped. "Dad got the satellite repositioned. Helicopter approaching. Two miles out."

Asher's blood turned to ice. A helicopter meant escape. It meant Gagnon could disappear—and he'd take Cici with him.

"How much time?" Callan's voice was tight with tension.

"Two minutes," she said, "maybe less."

"Contact that pilot," Grant barked. "Tell him if he gets close, we'll shoot him out of the sky."

"With what?" The skepticism in Bartlett's voice was palpable. "The closest thing we have to a bazooka is bubble gum."

"They don't know what we have," Grant said.

The commandos outside weren't just cleaning up Gagnon's mess. They would provide clearance. Asher wanted to say as much but feared he'd be heard through the door.

He was trying to figure out how to get in and protect Cici when Alyssa's voice rang through comms.

"It's a military copter." Gone was her dispassionate tone. The words rang with fear. "Pilot refuses to back down. Says if we engage, so will he."

A beat of silence, and then Bartlett said, "I'm not shooting at military."

"Same," Whiteman said. "Sorry, but I'm not going to prison for this."

Prison? Asher didn't care about prison. He cared about rescuing the woman he loved, no matter what it took.

But he was rendered silent, too close to the enemy to risk speaking.

"Anyone have eyes on the fire escape?" Grant asked.

"Not close enough," Callan said. "Moving that direction. There're enemies—"

His words were cut off by gunfire.

Asher felt the helicopter hovering overhead. It would land at any second. He couldn't count on Callan getting into position in time.

If he wanted to save Cici, it was up to him.

CHAPTER THIRTY-FIVE

The helicopter's roar was deafening.
Cici kept her eyes trained on the men in front of her.

The aircraft must've settled on the roof above them, its rotors whipping the air, shaking the very bones of the building. Dust fell from the ceiling tiles.

"Told you it was coming." Gagnon's eyes gleamed with triumph as he moved toward the exterior door. "Time to go. Bring her."

Souza reached for Cici's arm, his fingers closing around her wrist like a vise.

A gunshot exploded in the confined space.

Souza's eyes went wide, his grip loosening as he looked down at the crimson stain spreading across his chest. He took one stumbling step backward, then collapsed onto the concrete like a discarded marionette.

Cici screamed, the sound torn from her throat.

Gagnon aimed the smoking pistol at her, the motion casual, as if he'd just swatted a particularly bothersome fly. "One less loose end to worry about."

Before she could get her bearings, before she could think, he lunged toward her and gripped her upper arm. He was yanking her away from the filing cabinet and toward the exterior door when the interior door exploded inward with a crash that rivaled the copter's roar.

Asher filled the doorway, his weapon aimed toward Gagnon. His eyes blazed with fury, taking in Souza's still form and Cici, who blocked Gagnon, in one sweeping glance.

"Let her go."

She felt Gagnon shift, hiding behind her and the cabinet that had blocked the door. The cold barrel of his gun pressed against her temple. "Drop your weapon," he shouted, "or she dies here."

"And then I shoot you in the head."

"Maybe. But she'll still be dead." Gagnon's breath was hot against her ear. "You let us go, and I promise to keep her alive. Once I'm safe, I'll release her."

That was a lie, and everyone in the room knew it.

Asher's expression shifted to something she couldn't name. Love, maybe. And desperation.

"Your choice, bodyguard."

Though the helicopter's rotors still spun, the sound of them seemed muted, as if the world slowed to watch what would happen.

Please, God. Let this work.

She pulled the letter opener from her waistband, gripped it in her fist, and lifted it the smallest degree.

Asher's gaze flicked to it.

She plunged it into Gagnon's thigh.

He pitched forward, loosening his grip.

She dove out of the way.

Asher pulled the trigger.

And Gagnon went down.

CHAPTER THIRTY-SIX

"Gagnon's down." Asher's report brought responses in his ears, but he ignored them, trusting the team to handle whoever and whatever else needed handling.

He crossed the room in three swift strides, his weapon still trained on Gagnon's motionless form, half-hidden behind a metal cabinet that stuck oddly into the room. The door leading to the fire escape was behind that. Blood pooled beneath the man's head, his pale eyes staring sightlessly upward. The threat was over, but Asher's pulse hammered like he was still in the middle of the fight. He kicked the enemy's gun away per years of combat training. Not that he'd ever seen a corpse squeeze a trigger.

Cici huddled on the floor, trapped between the body and the wall. The blade that'd saved her life was still clutched in her trembling fist. Not a blade, he saw in the hellish light. A letter opener.

He didn't want to think about the carnage she'd witnessed.

But she was breathing. She was alive.

"Cici." He crouched beside her and, before she did something she didn't mean to do, took the makeshift weapon out of her hand.

She blinked at him, her beautiful eyes wide with shock. "Is he... Is it...?"

"It's over, sweetheart." At least it was for them. Grant and Bartlett held the building. He and Cici were safe in here.

Asher tossed the letter opener aside and holstered his weapon, wanting to pull her into his arms, to hold her until the terror faded from both their memories. But in the hours since he'd seen her, she'd endured more than most would in their entire lives. He needed to move slowly, to be gentle with her.

"Are you hurt?" His voice came out rougher than he intended, filled with too many emotions to name.

"Yeah, I'm..." She started to nod, then winced. "I think..." Her gaze flicked to Gagnon. "I just want... Can you, please...?" She reached for him. "Help?"

He was dying to do just that. He stood and pulled her up, then swept her into his arms. His shoulder screamed, but he gritted his teeth through the wave of pain.

She sucked in between her teeth, color draining from her face.

"I'm sorry." Her pain hurt him more than his own. "I'm sorry. I can put you down."

"No, please." She gripped his sweatshirt. "Don't. I don't want to..."

"Okay, sweetheart. I got you. You're okay. I got you."

She tucked her head against his chest. She didn't cry, just held onto him like he was her safe place.

Thank You, Father. Thank You.

He focused on the steady rhythm of her breathing, the warmth of her body pressed against his.

She needed peace. She needed to be away from this space and the two lifeless bodies. He carried her out of the office and down the hall to a break room he'd found when he was clearing this floor. He kicked the door open. Inside, he lowered himself to a sofa, keeping Cici securely on his lap.

She needed medical help. Now that the trauma was past, she was in shock. There were no blankets. Nothing to do but hold her close, to share his body heat until someone came.

They sat there in silence, holding onto each other.

The lights came on in the factory outside the door, giving just enough light for him to see her properly. A bruise darkened her cheek, and her clothes were spattered with blood. Bright red splotches from just now, brown splotches from a different violent event

"I'm sorry." His voice was rough with emotion. "I'm so sorry I let this happen. I should have—"

"Stop." Cici lifted her head. Her hand found his cheek, her touch gentle, if shaky. "Don't apologize to me. You came for me. You saved my life."

He closed his eyes, leaning into her palm. "You saved yourself. That move with the letter opener—"

"I told you I could help." Her voice carried a tremor, but her smile was radiant.

This beautiful woman amazed him. "I never doubted you."

There were no more gunshots coming from outside or below. The helicopter's rotors began to wind down, the deafening roar gradually fading to a mechanical whine. Shouts and footsteps echoed across the factory floor, but they seemed distant, muffled by the bubble of quiet that had settled around Cici and him.

"Status report," Grant's voice crackled through Asher's earpiece. "Rhodes, you got Cici?"

"I got her. She's..." He paused through a wave of emotion. "She's safe."

"Thank God," Alyssa said.

"Mercenaries are surrendering," Bartlett said. "Law enforcement's here."

"Copy that," he said into his comm, then removed his earpiece. The team could handle the cleanup. Right now, all that mattered was the woman in his arms.

Cici tilted her head back to look at him. "Who are you talking to?"

"The team." At her raised eyebrows, he remembered that she didn't know what'd happened outside the factory since she'd been taken. He gave her a quick rundown on everyone who'd come and all they'd done to get her back.

Her eyes were wide. "Alyssa's out there?"

"And safe. She's the one who cut the power and got the layout of this place. She worked with your dad to get satellite coverage."

Her eyes widened. "Dad. He must be furious with me."

Furious? "Why would he be? You haven't done anything wrong."

"I mean... I'm sure I did. I just don't know what."

"Nobody's angry with you, sweetheart." If Gavin Wright blamed anybody for this, it would be Asher. "Your father just wants you safe, like the rest of us. Thanks to him, we knew the helicopter was coming." He studied her face in the dim lighting, cataloging each bruise, each sign of what she'd endured. "Tell me what hurts."

She closed her eyes, maybe taking inventory. "My ribs. My head." Her fingers skimmed over the darkening bruise on her cheek. "But I'm alive. We're both alive."

Against all odds, despite his failures and mistakes, they'd survived.

"I thought I'd lost you." The admission scraped his throat raw. "When I woke up in that ravine and you were gone—"

"I thought you were dead." Her voice broke on the last

word. "They threw you over that cliff, and I was so sure..." She pressed her face against his neck. "I couldn't bear it, the thought that you died because of me, because of my need to prove myself."

"Hey." He cupped her face gently, forcing her to meet his eyes. "Don't do that. You did something heroic, something amazing."

"Something stupid." But a slight smile crossed her lips. "But you came for me anyway."

"I told you I'd choose you." The words came easier now, without the fear of rejection—and the weight of imminent death —hanging over him. "I meant it, Cici. I know it's crazy, but..." He forced his lips to shut, not giving voice to the admission that wanted to escape.

She inched closer, holding his eye contact. "I love you, Asher."

Fireworks that rivaled the craziness of the past few hours exploded in his chest. This woman he'd secretly longed for since he was a high school student somehow loved him back.

He could hardly fathom it.

He pressed a gentle kiss to her lips, afraid he might hurt her. Afraid whatever this was would splinter and crumble. But knowing the truth, deep inside. "I love you."

Who knew how she'd feel when this was all over? His feelings, though, weren't fresh or new. He'd been fighting them since he was eighteen years old, or trying to anyway.

He didn't want to fight them anymore. He'd walked away from her once, smarting from her casual rejection. He'd found her, then almost lost her.

He didn't know what it was going to look like or how they'd make it work, but he'd figure it out. No way was he letting Cici go again.

CHAPTER THIRTY-SEVEN

The travel pouch sitting on Cici's childhood dresser looked so ordinary now, like a prop from someone else's nightmare.

Cici stared at it from her bed, the afternoon light streaming through the tall windows of her parents' house doing nothing to chase away the shadows that seemed to cling to the innocent-looking bag. The velvet pouch, the cheap locket, and the SD card were all in the hands of the authorities now, but she'd taken the jewelry, strapping it around her waist before she'd left the factory the night before.

She'd nearly died because of it. She hadn't been willing to let it out of her sight. Fortunately, she'd thought to retrieve the little pouch and the priceless jewels before law enforcement had swarmed the place.

When she'd first heard the second helicopter approaching the paper mill the night before, the sound had sent ice through her veins—too reminiscent of Gagnon's escape plan. But then Grant had appeared in the factory break room, his relaxed expression cutting through her panic. He'd squeezed her hand in that quiet way of his and told them Forbes had sent the helicopter for her and Asher.

A helicopter? Why hadn't Asher or Bartlett or Forbes thought of that before all this craziness? She and Asher could've met it at the fast-food restaurant the night before, or even at the little cabin in Nutfield where they'd spent the night.

Of course, considering they had carried a locator, even a helicopter wouldn't have saved them from Gagnon.

The hospital had been a blur of X-rays and questions—both from doctors and from cops—while the tests confirmed what she'd already known. Bruised ribs, a minor concussion, nothing that wouldn't heal.

Asher had been treated for his shoulder wound and other injuries inflicted from the terrible fall. He'd been in the room next to hers, and she'd found comfort in hearing his voice through the thin wall.

When they were released, her parents had been there, insisting she go home with them. She didn't argue, figuring she'd sleep better in her childhood bed surrounded by family and security than she would alone in her apartment.

She'd been right about sleeping better. She'd conked out and slept fourteen hours straight, only waking when the afternoon sun had grown too bright to ignore.

Now, voices drifted in from the living room below—familiar cadences that spoke of family and safety. She could hear her mother's gentle tone, punctuated by Brooklynn's laugh. The normalcy of it felt surreal after everything that had happened.

She wanted to talk to Asher, to find out how he was—and where he was. They'd been surrounded by her family and his team at the hospital the night before, barely getting more than a *we'll talk tomorrow* in beneath all the chatter. She would call him, but she had no cell phone, and neither did he. More than that, as weird as it seemed, she didn't even know his phone number.

She'd see him today even if she had to track him down.

Though she'd showered the night before, she did again, washing her hair and scouring her skin. Mr. D, Mendez, Souza, Gagnon. All had been murdered in front of her eyes. Though she'd despised three out of four of them, they were human beings, created in God's image and loved by Him. Their deaths had been brutal, motivated by greed and lust for power.

If only the memories would wash out like the shampoo that circled the drain.

While she'd slept, someone had left a pile of clothes on her bureau. She slipped on a pair of jeans and a bright purple T-shirt that had to belong to Brooklynn. At least it wasn't adorned with pansies. Small favors.

She brushed her hair, careful of the bumps on her head. The bruise on her cheek had darkened. She figured it would get worse before it got better. Her lips were swollen. She had bags under her eyes despite all the sleep. She looked horrid.

But she was alive. The bruises would fade, and maybe she'd be stronger for what she'd endured.

She crossed to the window, gazed out at the Atlantic, at the surf crashing against the rocks below the house. *Thank You, Father.* The words were a paltry offering after everything He'd done to save her and Asher. But they were all she had.

She put on an old pair of slippers she found in her closet and headed toward the voices.

Halfway down the stairs, she paused to take in the scene in the living room. Alyssa sat curled in the corner of the sofa, her laptop on her knees, Callan beside her, his arm draped protectively around her shoulders.

Forbes occupied the wide leather armchair, looking uncharacteristically rumpled in jeans and a polo shirt. Brooklynn had squeezed in beside him. Both of them propped their feet on the ottoman.

Mom stepped in from the kitchen, carrying a tray that held cheese, crackers, and what smelled like her famous chocolate chip cookies.

The normalcy of it made Cici's throat tighten with emotion.

From Dad's office came the sound of raised voices. Unfortunately, that was also normal. She could make out his distinctive bark, though not the words.

After Mom set the tray on the coffee table, she hurried down the hall to close the office door, muffling the shouts.

On her way back, she caught sight of Cici on the staircase. "Oh! You're awake. How are you feeling, love?"

"Better." Cici took the last few steps down and accepted the gentle hug her mother offered. "What's going on with Dad?"

"Oh, he's just—"

"Processing." Alyssa crossed toward her. "You look like you got hit by a truck."

"You always know just what to say." Cici infused her tone with affection. Her sister had put herself in harm's way the night before. Cici'd heard the story, how a second team of mercenaries had shown up, how Alyssa had seen them coming through the drone feed.

Because apparently, they'd had drones, which was crazy enough.

Alyssa had managed to climb a tree, just high enough to be out of sight. And then she'd been stuck there until the commandos had searched all the vehicles and the forest surrounding them.

From the tree, she'd continued her surveillance of the property and even managed to cut the lights. All in an effort to save Cici's life.

"Thank God you're okay." Brooklynn's voice was filled with

emotion as she approached. "When Forbes told me what happened…"

In the foyer around the corner, the front door opened, and Cici's heart skipped as a familiar voice carried through the house. Asher's low rumble, followed by other voices she didn't recognize.

A moment later, one of Dad's security guards—she didn't know this one's name—escorted four people into the room. Cici didn't recognize the woman or one of the men.

Her cousin Grant nodded in her direction as he slid a suitcase near the steps. *Her* suitcase.

"It was in the backseat of one of the cars at the factory last night," he explained. "I convinced them it wasn't evidence."

"Thank you." Her things were back, not burned in the barn fire like she'd thought, though her soft-sided bag definitely carried the scent of smoke. She didn't care about anything inside that bag, not nearly as much as she cared about Asher.

It was him she'd longed for.

He stopped a few feet away, staring at her.

She squeezed between Mom and Brooklynn, her heart hammering against her ribs. The sling supporting his left arm reminded her of how close she'd come to losing him, but his eyes were warm and alive and focused entirely on her.

"How's the shoulder?" she asked, stopping just close enough to catch the familiar scent of his cologne.

"Better." His voice was rough, and she caught the way his gaze swept over her face. "You?"

"Better." She wanted to touch him, to reassure herself he was real and safe, but the roomful of people watching made her hesitate.

Before she could decide, Dad strode into the room, his face flushed with anger. When he saw her standing with Asher, his expression darkened further.

"So this is what happened?" Fury dripped from the words. "You got distracted from your mission and nearly got my daughter killed?"

Dad's anger always raised the same reaction in Cici—fear and shame, the certainty that she'd done something terrible, something to deserve such awful wrath. Even though it was directed at Asher, her heart thumped, knowing Dad would turn it on her if she dared make a sound.

But Asher didn't deserve it. Asher, who'd nearly died trying to save her life, deserved nothing but respect and gratitude. She swallowed her fear and gripped Dad's arm. "Don't, please. Asher did everything he could."

Dad shook her off and stepped closer to Asher. He was a few inches shorter and a couple of decades older, but he wore power like a crown. Not many men stood up to him.

Asher straightened, lifting his chin. He didn't take a step back. He didn't even flinch.

She was overwhelmed with pride for this man she loved.

"You were hired to protect her." Dad poked Asher in the chest.

He looked down at Dad's hand, then back at her father. The look held just enough threat that another man might've stepped back.

But not Gavin Wright.

"Dad, stop it."

He glanced at her as if he'd just noticed she was there.

"That's enough." The authoritative voice belonged to the older man Cici didn't recognize. He stepped closer, his bearing military-straight despite his silver hair. "Mr. Wright, if you have a problem with my agent's performance, take it up with me. You will not berate my agent. You owe nothing but gratitude to the man who saved your daughter's life."

Dad shifted his fury. "Who are you?"

He stepped forward and held out his hand. "Clarence Bartlett, head of GBPA."

Dad didn't shake his offered hand.

Bartlett dropped his arm. "I understand you're upset. Any father would be. But after Asher was shot and thrown over a cliff, he managed to figure out what Gagnon was after, track him back to that paper plant, and get our team there. What he needed was backup. The fact that he didn't have it is on me. I should have assigned more men."

Dad's expression was unreadable, and the tension in his shoulders didn't lessen a bit.

"*I* underestimated the danger," Bartlett continued. "The only reason your daughter is standing here is because of Asher Rhodes."

Dad's gaze flicked to Asher, eyes narrowing like he wasn't convinced. Then, he caught sight of Grant, who'd moved closer, maybe preparing to step in if necessary. Dad shifted to face him. "What about you?" His voice rose again. "She's your cousin. You're supposed to be a pro—"

"Uncle Gavin." Grant actually smiled. "I don't work for GBPA anymore, remember? I was home with my *newborn* when I found out Cici was in trouble. I was there *because* she's my cousin."

Dad had no answer to that. He was furious, but he couldn't figure out where to unleash his fury.

Cici tensed, knowing she was next. To get it over with, she squeezed his arm. "Dad, it was my fault. I'm the one who—"

"What are you talking about?" His words were sharp. "You witnessed a murder. None of this is your fault."

"I took the bag, which started this whole thing. I was trying to..." What? What had she been trying to do? Save a necklace?

It felt so foolish and inconsequential now.

Her father focused on her for a long moment. He blinked,

then wrapped her in a hug. "My precious girl. How do you feel? Are you all right?"

Whoa.

What?

He was squeezing hard enough that her ribs complained, but she didn't tell him that.

He'd called her *precious*.

"Come on. Why are you standing here? You should be sitting. You need to rest." He ushered her into the living room, causing all her family to make way, then settled her on the sofa. "Do you need anything?"

"I'm okay."

"You've slept all day. You must be thirsty."

She was, now that he mentioned it. "Water, I guess."

He started to move, but Mom said, "I'll get it. Everyone, find a seat. I'll be right back."

"Thank you, darling." Dad plopped down beside Cici and took her hand.

She was so confused.

Where was the yelling? Where was the anger? He'd directed them elsewhere. Was she to be spared?

Was he really not angry with her?

Did he really not blame her?

Sitting in the love seat, Alyssa met her eyes and shrugged one shoulder. At least she wasn't the only one to notice Dad's bizarre behavior.

Whatever was going through his head, if it meant avoiding his wrath, she'd take it.

CHAPTER THIRTY-EIGHT

Asher had seen wealth before, but this was ridiculous.

The Wright family estate sprawled along the Maine coastline like something out of a magazine—all weathered shingles and soaring windows that faced the rocky Atlantic coast. Luxury whispered from every corner, from the marble floors to the artwork that probably cost more than he'd make in a decade. Cici had told him that her mother came from money, and this place reeked of generational wealth.

He'd known the Wrights were rich, but this...this was stratospheric.

Gavin Wright's accusation still rang in Asher's ears.

The words had hit like physical blows. Asher had been assigned to keep Cici safe, and she'd ended up zip-tied in a warehouse, bruised and terrorized, while he'd been unconscious at the bottom of a ravine.

Bartlett's defense had been swift and professional, but it hadn't erased the sting of truth from Gavin's words.

Bartlett had been at the hotel that morning and insisted on meeting Asher before they came over here. Asher'd half expected to get fired.

But Bartlett had apologized, even going so far as to ask his forgiveness.

"We've lost a few long-standing clients," he explained. "I've been too focused on the bottom line. When Cici was taken, when you were offering to get yourself killed to save her, I remembered what really mattered. It wasn't whether or not we could give bonuses this year, or even if we could keep the lights on. My job is to make sure that the agents who trust me to have their backs stay just as safe as the clients."

"I should've asked for help," Asher said.

"Not your job to ask for it," Bartlett growled. "It's my job to do what's right, whether you like it or not."

Asher was still coming to terms with all of that. What he knew was that he wasn't perfect, but he'd done his best. And God had protected him and Cici despite all his mess-ups.

Now, as Asher stood in the cavernous living room taking in the opulent surroundings, he felt a little more of the weight dissolve away. Cici's father was only worried about his daughter, evidenced now by the way he sat beside her, awkwardly holding her hand.

Cici needed that. She needed to know her dad would do anything for her.

The knowledge didn't keep Asher from wishing he could squeeze himself in there.

Mrs. Wright returned with a tray filled with glasses of ice water. She carried the tray to Cici, who took a glass, then moved on to Asher, looking up at him with clear blue eyes that shimmered with tears.

He took a glass. "Thank you, ma'am."

"Thank you, Asher. For Cici." She sniffled, then shifted to the woman beside him. "I'm Evelyn Wright. Would you like some water?"

"Thanks."

She took a glass, then Mrs. Wright set the tray on the coffee table and focused on Grant. "Would you introduce our guests, please?"

"Yes, ma'am. You met Asher last night." He nodded to Bartlett. "My former boss, Clarence Bartlett."

She shook his hand. "Pleasure to meet you. Thank you for your part in bringing Cici home."

Despite his wisdom and experience, Bartlett seemed a little flummoxed. Maybe it was Cici's mother's graciousness. Maybe it was her stunning beauty. Whatever the cause, Bartlett stammered, "Uh, sure. Of course."

"And this is Detective Harris of the Philadelphia PD," Grant said.

Mrs. Wright nodded to the woman who seemed even more out of place than Asher. She wore a business suit that looked two sizes too small and had graying brown hair and no makeup, not to mention the deer-in-the-headlights shock that probably came from being ushered into a house that dripped money like rainwater.

"Ma'am," Harris managed.

"Grab a seat." Mom directed them into the living room.

Callan and Forbes dragged chairs in from the dining room, making a circle around the coffee table.

Asher took the one directly across from Cici. If he couldn't hold her hand, then at least he could look at her, even if her bruises reminded him of his failure.

Detective Harris remained standing. She pulled a small notepad and pen from her bag. "I was tasked to investigate Anthony Delvecchio's murder, along with the fire and, we assumed, a theft, considering all the valuables in a jewelry store." Her gaze found Cici. "Surveillance videos confirm your story, Miss Wright. Wendall Gagnon and Gustavo Souza entered the store, then were seen running from the back a few minutes later, chasing you."

"That's a relief," Cici said, though Asher doubted she'd been worried about the fact that she'd been a suspect.

"Gagnon and Souza are both dead," Harris said. "The SD card's been sent to the FBI."

No one asked what that was about. They'd all heard the story by now, at least the important parts.

Harris flipped the page in her notebook. "Talked to an agent at the Bureau this morning. They're working with my department, searching Gagnon's house. They've called in somebody to open that safe he mentioned to you, Miss Wright. They're already watching the people he'd been blackmailing. Maxwell Pierce is in custody—caught trying to run when he heard what happened."

Asher felt a grim satisfaction at that news. One less predator on the streets.

"How did he hear?" Gavin asked

"We assume from a guy named Falcone. He was apprehended last night, the only one who survived of the original team. The leader of what you called"—this time, she nodded to Asher—"the second team confirmed that they'd been commanded to kill everyone at the compound except Gagnon himself. He claims they were told everyone on the premises were criminals. He claims they thought they were working for law enforcement." By the twist of her lips, she wasn't buying it.

Asher wasn't, either. Good guys didn't kill everyone in sight. That wasn't how operations were meant to go, especially on US soil.

"They're all in custody up in Augusta." Harris smiled grimly. "I'm glad it's not my jurisdiction."

Bartlett cleared his throat. "One of the names on the SD card belongs to a general. Whatever Gagnon was blackmailing him with, it was enough to get him to send that military helicopter to rescue him last night."

"Right," Harris said. "He's been arrested by MPs and is being held pending investigation."

"Is Mr. D's niece safe?" Cici asked.

"She is. She took our advice and left town. She's been staying with a family member in Florida. I notified her of Gagnon's death this morning." Harris flipped another page in her notebook. "I assume more arrests will come once all the evidence is cataloged. You'll need to reach out to the Bureau for updates. All to say, that SD card's going to bring down a lot of criminals." She looked at Cici. "Credit where credit's due, ma'am."

Cici waved off the praise, color rising in her cheeks. "I wasn't trying to bring down criminals. I was trying to give Forbes back his family's property."

Forbes smiled at her from across the room. "Funny how that happens."

"Oh, and by the way"—Cici focused on him—"Gagnon admitted to me that he'd been at your house the night of the murders. He said Leo Taggart and Lois Stratton were in the room when your parents died, that Leo pulled the trigger—but Lois was just as involved—and that he'd been blackmailing them for years."

Forbes leaned forward, his expression intense. "Did he name any other names from that night?"

Cici shook her head. "Sorry, no. Just those two."

Forbes was quiet for a moment, then sighed. "Maybe it's time to let the rest go. The main players were thieves and smugglers. The worst of them have paid for their crimes one way or another."

"Speaking of paying..." Cici excused herself and headed upstairs, moving slowly. She held one hand against her ribs, and

Asher's stomach turned as if he were the one experiencing her pain.

The group made small talk and munched from a tray of snacks resting on the coffee table until Cici returned. She carried the small travel pack she'd bought at the sporting goods store what felt like a lifetime ago and handed it to Forbes.

He set it on his lap and opened it, then reverently lifted out the necklace that had started this whole nightmare. The Crimson Duchess caught the afternoon light, its diamonds and rubies gleaming like captured fire.

Forbes's eyes looked watery when he gripped Cici's hand. "You can't know what this means to me."

Brooklynn scooted closer, gazing at the jewelry with wonder before looking at Forbes with such love that Asher felt something twist in his chest.

Cici's voice grew thick with emotion. "I wanted to do something that mattered."

"You did." Forbes's voice was rough. "This matters to me. Not because it's valuable, but because it was my mom's."

Asher felt a swell of pride wash over him for this incredible woman he loved. He'd tried to convince himself she was shallow, that she was still that girl who'd casually humiliated him back in high school. But she was so much more than that. She felt things deeply and wanted to change the world in her own beautiful way.

The bruises on her face would heal, but the courage she'd shown—stabbing Gagnon with a letter opener, warning Asher even when it meant taking a beating—that was who she really was. Strong. Selfless. Breathtaking.

He had no idea how they were going to make this work. Her father still looked at him like he was something stuck to the bottom of his shoe. The wealth surrounding them felt like an ocean between their worlds.

But he loved her. And miracle of miracles, she loved him back.

Maybe that could be enough.

Detective Harris cleared her throat. "I think that covers everything from my end. There'll be more questions and statements, but that can wait until you're both feeling better."

"Thank you, detective." Gavin stood and scooted around the coffee table. "I'll get someone to escort you out."

As she gathered her things, Asher caught Cici's eye across the circle. She was watching him with an expression he couldn't quite read—something soft and questioning.

"While you're doing that," she said, her voice cutting through the polite murmur of conversation, "I need some air. Would you mind walking with me?"

The question was directed at Asher, and he was already standing before she finished speaking. "Of course."

"You need to rest." Her father had frozen halfway across the room, his words coming out on a growl.

"I'm not going far, Dad." Cici didn't wait for him to argue, just squeezed his hand and walked deeper into the house.

Asher followed, and they made their way past artwork and expensive furniture, family photos and perfectly placed books, toward a set of French doors that opened onto a stone terrace. The crisp salt air hit him, along with the sound of crashing waves against the rocks below.

Cici moved to the railing, wrapping her arms around herself as she gazed out at the ocean. The bruise on her cheek looked darker in the natural light, and Asher had to fight the urge to reach out and touch it.

"You've been quiet," she said without looking at him.

"Just taking it all in." He gestured toward the house behind them. "This place is incredible."

"Intimidating, you mean." She turned to face him, her eyes searching his face. "Right?"

He shrugged. "A little."

"Asher." She stepped closer, close enough that he could smell her unique scent. "This doesn't change anything between us. The house, the money, my father's attitude—none of it matters."

"Doesn't it?" The words came out rougher than he'd intended. "Your father made it pretty clear what he thinks of me. And honestly, can you blame him? I'm a bodyguard who let his daughter get kidnapped."

"You're the man who saved his daughter's life." Her voice carried a fierce edge. "And if my father can't see that, then that's his problem, not yours."

Asher wanted to believe her, but the gulf between their worlds felt as vast as the ocean stretching before them. "Cici, look around. This is your reality. Private helicopters, estates on the coast, and artwork worth more than most people's houses. I live in a one-bedroom apartment above a deli."

"So what?" She rested her hand on his chest. "Do you think I care about any of that?"

"You should." The admission tasted bitter. "You deserve someone who can give you everything you're used to."

"I deserve someone who loves me." Her eyes flashed with something between hurt and anger. "Unless this was all just... adrenaline or something. Unless you didn't mean—"

"I meant every word."

"Okay then. What I deserve, Asher, is someone who sees me for who I am, not what my bank account looks like. Someone who would throw himself off a cliff to save me."

"I didn't throw myself. I got tossed."

Despite everything, she laughed. "There's that humor I fell in love with."

The words were a balm, soothing all his fear. She'd said it before, in the break room at the paper mill, but hearing it now, in the clear light of day with no danger pressing down on them, made it real in a way that stole his breath.

"I love you too." The admission came more easily now. "But that doesn't solve the problems we're going to face."

"Like?"

"Like the fact that your father probably has a background check on me sitting on his desk right now."

"You have something to hide?" Her eyebrows hiked, her question carrying a certainty that she knew the answer and wasn't worried.

"No, but also, the fact that I earn in a year what you probably spend on shoes."

"First of all, don't be ridiculous. All my extra money goes to jewelry."

That brought a smile, even if her casual words didn't change anything. Shoes, jewelry, whatever. He couldn't afford it.

"Second, I told you, I make my own way. My parents have money, but they don't support me or my sisters. I know what it means to struggle to pay the rent."

Right. But if Cici's income fell short, she had a safety net, and that was a huge difference between them.

Except, maybe not that huge.

"Third," Cici said, "my father's opinion isn't going to dictate my life. Not anymore."

"You sure about that?" Because he got the impression her dad's opinion meant everything to her.

"I'm twenty-eight years old, and I've been trying to earn his approval my entire life. Trying to be the perfect daughter, make the perfect choices, to prove that I'm worth something." She looked out at the ocean. "You know what I realized when I was tied up in that warehouse?" Her gaze found his again. "Life's too short to live it for other people's expectations."

"But your father's opinion *does* matter."

"Maybe, but how much? Enough that it affects how I live?" She shook her head, then winced, reminding him of all her wounds he couldn't see. She continued as if the pain were irrelevant. "I've spent so much time trying to prove I matter that I forgot to actually live the life God gave me. To choose what I want instead of what I think will make other people happy." She touched his face, her thumb tracing his jawline. "I want you, Asher. I want us. Everything else is just details we'll figure out."

The conviction in her voice, the certainty in her touch...

And why was he arguing with her? She was everything he wanted. If she wanted him, too, then what kind of an idiot would he be to talk her out of that?

He pressed his palms to her cheeks. "I love you, Cici Wright. And I'm going to fight for you, even if it means taking on that scary dad of yours."

She laughed, but he didn't miss how her eyes sparkled with tears.

She wrapped her arms around him, and he returned her embrace, careful, so careful, not to hurt her.

This precious, incredibly breakable woman he loved.

CHAPTER THIRTY-NINE

The Wright family estate felt like heaven this Labor Day afternoon, with four generations sprawled across the expansive deck overlooking the Atlantic.

Cici shifted in her deck chair, watching Callan's eight-year-old daughter, Peri, holding Grant's eight-week-old baby while Summer, Grant's wife, hovered nervously nearby.

Cici's grandparents reclined in a nearby seating area, chatting with Mrs. Ballentine, Forbes's grandmother, who'd been adopted into the family along with Forbes.

Mom and Aunt Peggy were bustling around, refilling drinks and pushing appetizers. Dad and his brother, Uncle Roger, were playing horseshoes in the yard.

The late summer sun painted everything in golden hues, the overlapping conversations creating a symphony of belonging that made Cici's heart overflow with gratitude.

Delaney was missing, her absence the only pall on the gathering.

Two weeks had passed since the horrifying incident that had changed Cici's life. Her bruises had faded, though her ribs still ached. She was eager to feel normal again, if not to get back to work.

"Aunt Cici, look!" Peri held up the tiny baby like a trophy. "She smiled at me!"

"That's probably gas," Callan called from where he flipped burgers at the grill.

"Daddy! That's not nice!"

Cici grinned, catching Asher's eye on the far side of the little seating area. Also there were Michael, his wife, Leila, and the youngest Wright brother, Derrick. His wife—Leila's twin—had just stepped away.

The sight of Asher fitting so naturally into her family's chaos made something warm unfurl in her chest.

At a break in their conversation, she said, "Michael, I never properly thanked you for everything you did. With Gagnon and..."

"Don't mention it." He waved her off with a flick of his wrist. "Uncle Gavin beat me to the punch. His contacts are much higher level than mine are."

The mention of Cici's father made her stomach flutter with a familiar mix of anxiety and confusion. Since the incident, Dad had been...different. Gentler. More attentive. He'd called her every day, checking on her healing, asking about her business, actually listening to her answers. It was...bizarre.

She excused herself and made her way inside, finding Alyssa and Brooklynn in the kitchen. Brooklynn had a flair for making a charcuterie board a work of art.

Alyssa, ever the practical one, kept her from going crazy. "You don't have to turn the pepperonis into flowers." Her eye roll hinted at her exasperation. "It just makes people feel guilty for eating them."

"But it's so much prettier—"

"What's going on with Dad?" Cici interrupted.

Both sisters looked up, and she caught the meaningful glance they exchanged.

"Right?" Alyssa said, unscrewing a jar of olives. "I wondered if he was doing it to you too."

"What, exactly?" Cici managed to shimmy onto a stool on the opposite side of the counter, ignoring the twinge in her ribs.

"He's been..." Brooklynn wagged her head. "Nice?" She said the word as if it tasted foreign. "Like, genuinely nice. Not his usual 'I'm-being-civil-because-your-mother-is-watching' nice."

"He apologized to me." Alyssa looked behind as if someone might overhear a terrible secret. "After everything that happened with Ghazi and Peri."

Earlier in the summer, Alyssa had been kidnapped by a terrorist. Well, Peri'd been kidnapped. Alyssa had allowed herself to be taken so she could save the little girl. No wonder Callan was head-over-heels.

"He apologized?" Cici clarified. "Dad?"

"Yeah. And told me he was proud of me." Alyssa shook her head in wonder. "I was still in shock after all the...well, you know, and I honestly thought I was hallucinating."

"He's been the same way with me," Brooklynn added, leaning against the counter, giving up on her pepperoni flowers. "Ever since the fire, it's like he's trying to...I don't know, make up for something. He told me my picture—the sunrise one?"

She asked the question as if they might have forgotten the gorgeous photograph that'd won her a coveted prize. As if they didn't all have a copy hanging in their homes.

Cici tapped her nose. "I think I know which one you mean."

Alyssa laughed, and Brooklynn said, "Shut up." But her cheeks were turning pink. "I'm just saying, he told me it was beautiful, that he was... yeah, like you said." She flicked a glance at Alyssa. "Proud of me."

Alyssa set a handful of cheese slices on the wooden board. "I think...I think he's finally figured out that he's been a terrible father."

The blunt assessment hung in the air between them.

Brooklynn fixed the cheese, arranging it just so. "He wasn't...terrible."

Alyssa's eyebrows hiked. Cici just stared at her.

Brooklynn laughed first, and Alyssa and Cici joined in.

"Well, it's weird," Cici said.

"But nice," Alyssa said. "I mean, maybe you didn't need it, but I did."

"Hmm." Brooklynn returned her focus to the charcuterie. "Maybe a little."

Cici had needed it. She'd craved her father's love all her life. Apparently, all it took was a little near-death experience to—

"Girls." Mom poked her head into the kitchen. "Hurry up with that. Forbes has some kind of grand announcement."

Cici and Alyssa both looked at Brooklynn, who was careful not to meet either of their eyes as she grabbed the charcuterie and followed Mom toward the deck.

Cici and Alyssa followed. "You think he's going to propose?" Alyssa whispered.

"Ooh, I hope so!"

"They've been together for like...five minutes."

The engagement ring on her big sister's hand glinted in the light. "Right. While you and Callan waited the respectable, what, month? Two months?"

"Whatever." But she was grinning as they stepped onto the patio.

"There she is!" Forbes called. Brooklynn crossed the deck and stood beside him, beaming as if she knew exactly what this was about. So, probably not a proposal.

Brooklynn was looking right at Cici. Come to think of it, so was everyone else

"Uh..."

Asher slipped up beside her and took her hand, whispering, "Any idea what's going on?"

Before she could answer, Forbes drew everyone's attention. "First, thank you, Gavin and Evelyn, for inviting Gran and me today. And to the rest of you. You've welcomed us into your family, making us feel like we belong."

"You do belong," Evelyn called. "You're one of us now."

"God help you," Derrick added, earning some chuckles.

Forbes grinned. "Cici, Asher, could you two come up here?"

She looked at Asher, whose face had paled the slightest bit. She had a sudden flashback to high school. He might've been the smartest kid in their class, but he'd always fumbled through presentations, blushing and umm-ing his way through his speeches.

She couldn't help the giggle that escaped as she hooked her arm in his and urged him forward.

When they got to the edge of the deck where Forbes stood, he addressed the crowd again. "I know you've all heard the story, so I won't tell it again. Suffice it to say..." He focused on her and Asher, "I can't thank you two enough for what you did. Not only did you return a family heirloom, but your actions also brought one more person to justice for my parents' murders. Thank you."

Cici gripped Asher's arm, unsure what to say. *It was a pleasure?* Yeah, that'd be a bald-faced lie.

Anytime?

More like, never again.

Fortunately, Forbes didn't expect her to speak. He reached into his jacket and pulled out two envelopes. "A gift, a token of my gratitude and that of my grandmother for your heroism. What you did means more than you'll ever know."

Cici took the one he handed to her. A brief glance inside told her it was a check. She held it out toward him. "Forbes, I can't accept this. You're practically my brother."

"I like the sound of that." But he didn't take the check. "As your *practical* brother, I should tell you that it would be rude to reject it."

That was true for gifts, but this was something else.

Asher had opened his envelope and pulled out the check. He was staring at it, his face pale. "I-I can't take this."

"Yes, you can. And you will." Forbes spoke like a man accustomed to getting what he wanted. "I know your dreams, Asher. This is enough to make them happen."

Over the past few weeks, Forbes and Asher had struck up a friendship. She had no idea what the billionaire and the former trailer-park kid had in common. She loved that it didn't matter at all where either one of them was from. They were both good men, and they liked each other.

"I don't think..." Asher stammered. "It doesn't feel right."

"It wouldn't feel right to Grandmother and me not to do this." Forbes lowered his voice, speaking just loudly enough for Asher to hear. And Cici, if she eavesdropped, which she did. "That necklace is worth a lot more than the check in your envelope, and Cici's life is priceless."

Cici peeked at the check in her envelope. Oh, my. Her dream of her own jewelry store could come true too.

Asher said, "I get that, but—"

"Just take it." Forbes chuckled, raising his voice again. "Sheesh, I've never had so much trouble giving money away."

The crowd laughed, all except her father, who watched, arms crossed, from across the deck. His enigmatic expression had her heart dropping. Something was up.

He stalked forward and stopped at Asher's side. "I'd like a word."

Asher's shoulders went rigid, and Cici caught the way his jaw tightened. He looked like a man about to face a firing squad.

"Dad? Is this necessary, right now?"

"It'll only take a minute." His tone was measured, but she could see the steel beneath it as he spoke to Asher. "Please."

Funny how, even when he asked nicely, it sounded like a command.

The conversations around them gradually died as everyone sensed the shift in atmosphere. Even little Peri stopped chattering about the baby, her wide eyes darting among the adults.

Asher handed the envelope to Cici, his movements careful and controlled. She wanted to grab his arm, to tell her father to leave him alone, but Asher's expression stopped her.

He didn't want her help. He could handle himself.

"Of course." His voice was steady and professional. The same tone he'd used when he was her bodyguard, and the formality of it made her chest ache.

They walked toward the far end of the deck and around the corner, out of sight.

"What do you think that's about?" Brooklynn appeared beside her, concern creasing her features.

"Nothing good." Cici's voice came out small. She'd seen that look on her father's face before—the careful neutrality that preceded his most devastating conversations. "He's probably going to tell Asher to stay away from me."

"He wouldn't do that," Alyssa said, joining them, but her tone lacked conviction.

Mom stepped between Cici and where her dad and the man she loved had just disappeared. "My goodness, sweet girl. You look like you're awaiting a jury's verdict."

"Do you know what's going on?"

"I don't, but I do trust your father."

Well, sure, because Dad adored Mom. He'd do anything for her. And he'd do anything for Cici, up to and including threatening the man she loved if he thought he wasn't good enough for her.

Before her thoughts could spin further, Asher and Dad appeared at the corner again.

The two men walked back toward the group, and Cici held her breath as she searched their faces for clues. Her father's expression was unreadable, but Asher looked like someone had just told him the sky was green—and the clouds were marshmallows.

Mom stepped away, drawing Dad toward her, and Asher approached Cici and grabbed her hand.

That felt like a good sign.

"Walk with me?" he whispered, already moving away.

"Sure."

He said nothing while they meandered through the crowd to the steps that led down to the yard, then across to the stone wall that separated the grass from the rocky shore. Once there, he turned to face her. And smiled.

"What? What did he say?"

"He wrote me a letter of recommendation. Said he could get me a job in DC. Anywhere I wanted."

Dad was trying to get rid of Asher, and Asher looked ready to take the bait.

He was still smiling, a knife to her chest. "I thought he was trying to bribe me to leave you, but then... He offered a second choice. A job."

Cici blinked, certain she'd misheard. "He what?"

"I know, it's..." His voice carried a note of wonder, as if he couldn't quite believe it himself. "He's developing a security division for Wright Industries. Short-term contracts, working with law enforcement and intelligence services. He wants me on the team. Said the guy he hired to head it up is temporary, that if I proved myself competent, I could take over."

"But..." She struggled to process this information. "I thought he didn't approve—"

"So did I." Asher's laugh was shaky. "I was ready for him to tell me I wasn't good enough for you. Which I'm not."

"Asher—"

"That I should disappear from your life, which I absolutely won't, not as long as you want me around."

Cici was reeling from information overload.

"Instead, he..." Asher shook his head, running his free hand through his hair. "I guess he's been checking up on me. Talked to my SEAL team leader, to Bartlett, and even to Grant, who barely knows me. He wanted to get their take, and I guess it was okay. He insists I finish my degree but said I could do that part-time while I work."

There had to be a catch. "Where exactly is this job?"

"Here. I mean, there'll be training, of course, but since it's his company, he can have that anywhere, so why not Maine?" Asher searched her face. "He said the offer stands whether or not you and I...whether we stay together. But—"

"He's giving you a chance?" It seemed too good to be true.

"More than that." Asher's voice dropped to barely above a whisper. "He's giving us his blessing. I mean, he also threatened to have me killed if I step out of line, so there's that." Even though she had no doubt Dad had said that, Asher was grinning. Either he wasn't afraid of her father, or he didn't plan to step out of line.

Tears pricked her eyes. After years of trying to earn her father's approval, he was finally offering it—not just to her, but to the man she loved.

"But what about your condo in Boston? I know you had your heart set…"

Asher laughed, the sound rich and warm in the salt air. "You think I'd rather live in some sterile condo in a city I hate than be wherever you are?"

"But it was your dream—"

"No, Cici." He stepped closer, cupping her face gently. "That wasn't a dream. It was just my way of insulating myself against…I don't know. Poverty, I guess. Risk." His thumb traced her cheek. "But you know what I realized when I thought I'd lost you? To live is to risk. Security is an illusion."

The tears she'd been holding back spilled over. "What's your dream, then?"

"You." The word was simple, absolute. "A life with you. Maybe a little house by the water where we can hear the waves at night. Maybe kids who can run around on the beach, play in the waves." His smile was soft, tender. "Growing old together, holding hands on the porch while we watch the sunrise."

"Asher…" Her voice broke on his name.

"I know it's fast, and I know you still have your job, and we have a lot to work out." His eyes creased at the corners, as if he worried he'd pushed too hard. "You barely live here."

"I will, though, if you're here. I like what I do, but I can appraise jewelry in Maine. I traveled because I liked it, I wanted to. And I wanted my business to be…more. To seem important. Now…I just want to be here, with my family. With you."

His grin returned. "Okay, then."

"And about all the rest of that. All the forever stuff?"

His grin faded. "I shouldn't have—"

"Yes. Yes to all of it. The house, the kids, growing old together. Yes to forever." She rose on her tiptoes and threw her arms around him. "I love you, Asher Rhodes. I choose you."

The End.

I hope you enjoyed Asher and Cici's story. If you'd like to read what happened next for them, download the bonus epilogue.

Curious about what happened to Delaney Wright? Find out in *Fighting for You,* book 9 in the Wright Heroes of Maine series. It releases January, 2026. Turn the page for more information.

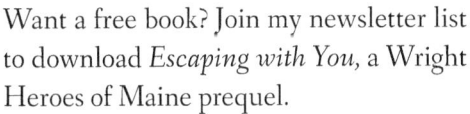

Want a free book? Join my newsletter list to download *Escaping with You,* a Wright Heroes of Maine prequel.

Now, turn the page for more about *Fighting for You.*

She's running from her past. He's protecting his future. Together, they must fight for what matters most.

Delaney Wright has always believed the best of everyone—even when she shouldn't. After her ex-boyfriend's shocking betrayal, Delaney flees Shadow Cove, determined to rebuild her shattered confidence. She lands a nanny position in Virginia, caring for precious four-year-old Charlotte. Her new employer is everything she should avoid—wealthy, worldly, and far too handsome for Delaney's peace of mind. But this job is not the haven it seems.

Everett Aylett is desperate to hang onto his family's legacy, despite a stalker who's getting bolder every day. When his brother abandons his daughter, Everett takes in Charlotte, hiring a live-in nanny to give his niece stability. Though Delaney is young and attractive—the worst combination for a man trying to avoid scandal—her gentle touch breaks through Charlotte's grief. But Everett needs more than just a nanny to secure his niece's future. He must complete a business merger amidst compounding danger. Someone is determined to sabotage the deal...no matter what it takes.

When threats close in on all sides, Everett and Delaney must join forces to protect the little girl they both love. Trusting each other might be the only way to save Charlotte—and themselves.

A heart-pounding suspense and a swoon-worthy romance as Everett and Delaney discover that some battles can only be won with the right person at your side.

ALSO BY ROBIN PATCHEN

The Wright Heroes of Maine

Running to You

Rescuing You

Finding You

Sheltering You

Protecting You

Capturing You

Defending You

Fighting for You

The Coventry Saga

Vanished in the Darkness

Redemption for Ransom

Betrayal of Genius

Traces of Virtue

Touch of Innocence

Inheritance of Secrets

Lineage of Corruption

Wreathed in Disgrace

Courage in the Shadows

Vengeance in the Mist

A Mountain Too Steep

The Nutfield Saga

Convenient Lies

Twisted Lies

Generous Lies

Innocent Lies

Beautiful Lies

Legacy Rejected

Legacy Restored

Legacy Reclaimed

Legacy Redeemed

Sleigh Bells & Stalkers

One Christmas Night

Amanda Series

Chasing Amanda

Finding Amanda

ABOUT ROBIN PATCHEN

Robin Patchen is a *USA Today* bestselling and award-winning author of Christian romantic suspense. She grew up in a small town in New Hampshire, the setting of her Coventry Saga books, and then headed to Boston to earn a journalism degree. After college, working in marketing and public relations, she discovered how much she loathed the nine-to-five ball and chain. She started writing her first novel while she homeschooled her three children. The novel was dreadful, but her passion for storytelling didn't wane. Thankfully, as her children grew, so did her skill. Now that her kids are adults, she has more time to play with the lives of fictional heroes and heroines, wreaking havoc and working magic to give her characters happy endings. When she's not writing, she's editing or reading, proving that most of her life revolves around the twenty-six letters of the alphabet.